Down on
CYPRUS AVENUE

Previous Titles

Detective Inspector Christy Kennedy Mysteries:
I Love The Sound of Breaking Glass
Last Boat To Camden Town
Fountain of Sorrow
The Ballad of Sean & Wilko
The Hissing of the Silent Lonely Room
I've Heard The Banshee Sing
The Justice Factory
Sweetwater
The Beautiful Sound of Silence
A Pleasure to do Death With You

Inspector Starrett Mysteries:
The Dust of Death
Family Life

Other Fiction:
First of The True Believers
The Last Dance
The Prince Of Heaven's Eyes (A Novella)
The Lonesome Heart is Angry

Factual:
Playing Live
The Best Beatles Book Ever

www.paulcharlesbook.com

Down on
CYPRUS AVENUE

by Paul Charles

Dufour Editions

First published in the United States of America, 2015
by Dufour Editions Inc., Chester Springs, Pennsylvania 19425

© Paul Charles, 2015

This is a work of fiction. Except for public figures, all characters
in this story are fictional, and any resemblance to anyone else
living or dead is purely coincidental.

ISBN 978-0-8023-1358-4

2 4 6 8 10 9 7 5 3

Jacket photos by David Torrans
Map: © OpenStreetMap contributors
openstreetmap.org

Library of Congress Cataloging-in-Publication Data

Charles, Paul, 1949-
  Down on Cyprus Avenue / by Paul Charles.
    pages ; cm
  ISBN 978-0-8023-1358-4 (hardcover) -- ISBN 0-8023-1358-2 (hardcover)
  1. Detectives--Ireland--Belfast--Fiction. 2. Murder--Investigation--Fiction.
  I. Title.

PR6053.H372145D69 2014
823'.914--dc23

                                                              2014029288

Printed and bound in the United States of America

ACKNOWLEDGEMENTS

My first trip to Belfast would have been when I was about six years old. My dad took me down on the bus. I'd never been in a city before and I just loved the buzz and the unique aromas of the city. Coming from a small rural village I couldn't believe the actual volume of the noise around and about the streets in Belfast. In my home town, Magherafelt, if someone sneezed up the town it was news in the following week's edition of *The Mid Ulster Mail*, and, most likely on the front page at that.

My memories of that precious trip to Belfast are of streets crammed with exotic cars; lorries packed so high you felt they might actually topple over; my first ever sighting of double decker busses; busy, hyper or chilled people, mostly laughing and joking, and, the hustle and bustle of Woolworths, crammed so full you could hardly move through it. The shop assistants appeared so sophisticated with such chic make-up they looked like movie stars. But packed though Woolworths was, my dad worked his way around the super-shop diligently buying hardware: hinges; brackets; hooks; nails; thingamabobs and cuttermegigs, lots of cuttermegigs. Things, that on paper he'd no need for, but then over the course of the next few years bit by bit, item by item, they'd all get used up. He used them in a manner that was always vital to making pieces of furniture and suchlike, which had such a positive impact on our lives that we wondered how we'd ever done without them. In a way I suppose that's where I picked up the habit of hoarding; yes, hoarding things like: words, character-sketches, accents, traits and sayings. You just never know when they're going to come in handy, do you?

The memories of that day, both of my introduction to the tangible excitement of Belfast and of being there with my father, have stuck with me so far though my life, and very vividly at that.

My next memories of Belfast are of me visiting the city in my teenage years seeking bookings for my first band, the Blues by Five. So thanks are also due and offered to Vince, Paddy, Miles, Ian & Terence. Thanks also to Taste, The Interns, Cheese, The Gentry and The Method, because it was on my next pilgrimages down to Belfast to see and hear the above groups at The Maritime Club, Sammy Huston's Jazz Club, Betty Staffs, and Clarks Dance Studio, that was my first introduction to that side of Belfast. Sadly I never got to witness a live performance by Them. Later again came The Pound, The Ulster Hall, Fruupp and EMS at Queen's Student's Union. I also need to mention in these dispatches: Colin McCelland, Good Vibrations, Chris Moore, Tim Nicholson, Jim Aiken, Cityweek, Thursday Magazine, K 46024, Radio Ulster, The Belfast Telegraph, Ivan Martin, UTV, GIM and the legendary Eddie McIlwaine.

While starting work on this new adventure two men, Gary Mills and David Torrans, were tireless in introducing me to, and showing me around, their Belfast. I'm forever in their debt. I'm also indebted to Claudia who held down the fort at No Alibis while her old man accompanied me around town. Big thanks to City Hall and The Custom House for showing me what these amazing buildings are like on the inside.

Also big thanks to Christopher May for not only giving a home to McCusker, but also for taking the time out to let me introduce him to Belfast, particularly McCusker's patch; to my editor Duncan May for keeping me on McCusker's patch, and to Larisa and Brad at Dufour Editions for their continued support and energy.

To Catherine for being Catherine.

And once again big, big thanks to the man who introduced me to Belfast in the first place all those years ago, my father, Andrew.

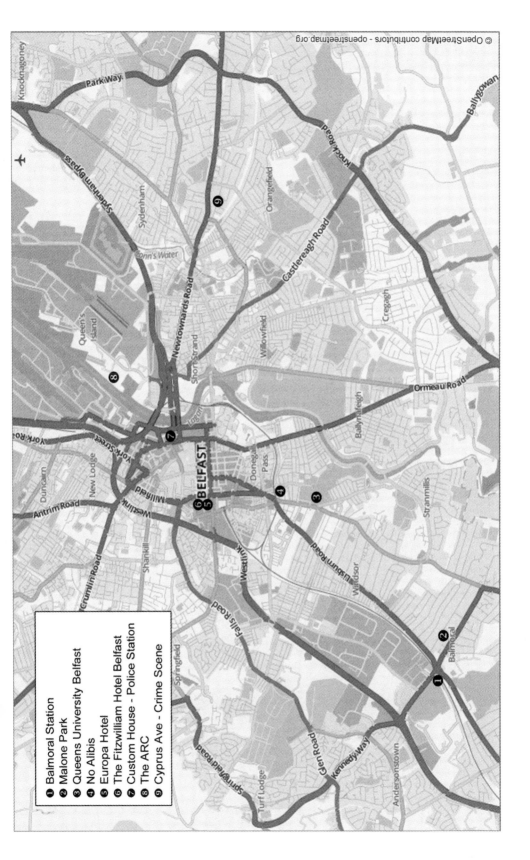

© OpenStreetMap contributors - openstreetmap.org

1. Balmoral Station
2. Malone Park
3. Queens University Belfast
4. No Alibis
5. Europa Hotel
6. The Fitzwilliam Hotel Belfast
7. Custom House - Police Station
8. The ARC
9. Cyprus Ave - Crime Scene

CHAPTER ONE

If he leaned back in his captain's chair at a perilous forty-five degrees – that is to say, at the nosy-angle tilt – McCusker could just about hear half of Detective Inspector Lily O'Carroll's conversation.

"Okay, Mrs O'Neill, let's take this slowly," O'Carroll said, sounding a little short on patience. "When was the last time you saw both your sons – Ryan and…you didn't tell me the name of your second son?"

McCusker found himself scribbling the name Ryan O'Neill on his note pad.

"Sorry, okay, I think I get it. Ryan is in fact your second son and your firstborn son is Lawrence?" O'Carroll was nodding positively to herself as she too committed something to paper. "Right. You saw them last on Wednesday. Well, as that is over forty-eight hours you can come down to the station and fill out a missing person's report."

McCusker counted twenty-three loud clicks on the office clock high above them before O'Carroll spoke again.

"Sorry, I couldn't hear you there, you were very quiet. Could you repeat that for me?" she said, as she scrunched up her eyebrows. Although he barely knew O'Carroll, McCusker could tell from her eyes that her brain was clicking into its over-active gear. "Good Mrs O'Neill, I got you that time. In that case, would you like *me* to come and visit *you*?"

Detective Inspector Lily O'Carroll stood up and, in a complicated and elaborate, not to mention potentially dangerous, manoeuvre, swung the jacket of her black pin-striped trouser suit over her head and on top of her dark blue polo-neck jumper.

McCusker clicked audibly as she swished past him.

She stopped in her tracks.

"Okay McCusker, obviously you're bored. Do you want to tag along?"

"Answer me this first," he replied, in his gentle Ulster tones. "What did she say to make you agree to visit her?"

"She said her husband wouldn't let her leave the house," O'Carroll replied as she exited the office with the air of a fisherman confident that the worm just cast would be sufficient for the catch.

CHAPTER TWO

O'Carroll drove McCusker down the busy, boutique-lined Lisburn Road to the exclusive Malone Park in near silence. With the sun shining it would have been easy to think they were entering Beverly Hills. Towards the end of a driveway, which McCusker was convinced was leading all the way to heaven, they eventually arrived at a Georgian mansion updated with two modern symmetrical add-ons.

Before they had a chance to discover a knocker or a doorbell, the large oak door quietly and slowly opened to reveal a much younger woman than McCusker had been expecting.

"Mrs O'Neill, Mrs Polly O'Neill?" O'Carroll asked, as she and McCusker flashed their warrant cards.

"Yes...do please come in," the soberly dressed woman almost pleaded in a whisper. "Please go as softly as you can. We'll go straight through to the kitchen."

Mrs O'Neill looked too slim for her own good and her classicly sculptured features were stress-beaten with years of worry. Her greying brown hair was pulled back in a spinster's bun. She managed, however, to retain her dignity with a perfectly upright gait in her country Barbour outfit.

"Tea?" she began, as she showed them through to an outrageously large but dated oak wood kitchen.

"Water will be grand," O'Carroll replied, on both of their behalf. They sat at a more casual table in a conservatory alcove to the rear of the kitchen, close to the large French doors leading to the garden.

"Tap is fine," McCusker offered, with a smile.

Mrs O'Neill looked at McCusker like he'd just admitted he didn't use toilet roll and went to pull out two small chilled bottles of Perrier from a fridge she literally had to walk into. She unscrewed the bottle caps 95 per cent, the way a mother does for her children, before handing them over with glasses to the two employees of the Police Service of Northern Ireland.

"So Ryan and Lawrence…" O'Carroll offered, pouring the water into her glass and drawing out her notebook with such little fuss McCusker didn't even notice her doing it.

"Yes," Mrs O'Neill grimaced.

"Is your husband in the house?" O'Carroll asked.

Mrs O'Neill nodded, "Yes."

"Why would he not allow you to leave the house?" McCusker asked.

"He thinks I'm stupid for worrying about them. He says they're fine. But they've always come to see me every day, every day of their lives, since leaving home."

"So they don't live here?" O'Carroll asked, looking like she'd prefer to ask all her own questions.

"Goodness no, they have their own place up in Saint Anne's Square in the city centre."

"How are you so sure they are missing?" O'Carroll continued, as she noted down the address.

"I've been to their apartment yesterday and on Wednesday and I've been ringing them non-stop on all their numbers."

"What ages are they?" O'Carroll continued on her fact-finding mission.

"Ryan is twenty-six and Lawrence is twenty-eight – just."

"And what do they do for a living?" McCusker enquired, his semi-conversational approach somewhat slowing down proceedings, a fact he wasn't unhappy about.

"Ryan and Lawrence have this big internet project they are working on. I don't really know what that means to be honest, but they're always talking about it."

"Do you know if it's up and running or are they still developing it?" O'Carroll cut in.

"Oh, I wouldn't know, but my husband knows all about it."

"What does your husband do?" O'Carroll asked.

"O'Electronics."

"Right, O'Electronics – the big place on the corner of Bedford Street and Donegall Square South, over the Nationwide Building Society," O'Carroll said, writing down the name. "What does he do for them?"

"Oh, he owns them," Polly O'Neill replied, betraying more contempt than pride.

O'Carroll shot McCusker a knowing glance, her interest now piqued. Was she impressed by the father's status or the fact that his obvious wealth would make them a more likely target for a kidnapping?

"Do Ryan or Lawrence have girlfriends?" O'Carroll asked, before quickly adding, "or partners?"

"They've lots of friends, both male and female, but Ryan is always saying women won't figure in their life plan for another two or three years."

"Could you give me the names and details of some of their friends please?" O'Carroll asked.

Polly O'Neill walked very regally over to a cupboard, removed an expensive-looking leather-bound address book, flicked through a few pages and said, "Pat Tepper, he's a friend, he's also their solicitor. He works for his father's firm, Tepper, Bryson, & Torance. Pat's a good man, sensible and a good influence on my boys."

"Anyone else?" O'Carroll continued, now openly impatient.

"Susanna Holmes, she lives three doors down from here. She and the boys have known each other since childhood and are still good friends." Polly replied, before reading out Susanna's details. She flicked on quickly through the book and beat O'Carroll to her next question, "and of course there's Tim Black, her boyfriend; the four of them went to Queen's together."

"There's no chance the four of them just popped over to Greece for a wee break?" McCusker asked, trying to lighten the mood. He wanted O'Neill to relax a little, to get her comfortable so she would really talk to them.

"No! Ryan would still ring me, no matter where he was in the world," O'Neill said, and then added as a clear afterthought, "and of course Lawrence does…"

At that precise moment Polly O'Neill froze as the kitchen door was roughly opened. A wee man with a big belly waddled in. He wore dark blue trousers, low on his waist (to catch the slimmer part of his torso, McCusker reckoned) and supported by bright red braces over a light blue shirt, with the top button undone and a Queen's University tie loosened a few inches from the collar. His large feet were bare and he looked like he was searching for his six colleagues and Snow White.

"Who?" he barked.

"This is my husband James," Polly explained to the police officers and then continued to her husband. "This is Detective Inspector O'Carroll and McCusker."

"And they are here…why?" he snapped.

"They're going to help find Ryan and Lawrence."

"Silly, silly woman. They're off having fun somewhere. When I was their age…" James O'Neill grunted, he obviously thought better of what he was about to say. "For heaven's sake woman, stop smothering them."

He focused on McCusker at this point. McCusker thought O'Neill's head was much too big for the rest of his body. Perhaps his well-groomed, bushy grey hair added to the illusion.

"I don't know you. Who are you?" he asked, addressing McCusker as a school teacher might.

"As your wife already mentioned, I'm McCusker from PSNI and your wife is clearly very concerned about your sons. I'd like to ask you a few questions."

"Would you indeed. Who's your super?"

"Superintendent Larkin," O'Carroll offered, trying to be helpful.

"Is he now? Well, it so happens I know Niall very well – on a few committees with him and so forth."

"Yes," McCusker replied, "that's all very well but I think it would be more helpful if we could get some more information on your sons."

"Well, actually I think you'd be even more helpful if you'd just scoot off and leave the boys alone, or I'll get Superintendent Niall Larkin on the blower and see if I can't get both of you back on the beat again."

"But James…" his wife pleaded.

"Shush woman," he barked. "Now, if you'd kindly leave my home."

"Mrs O'Neill, unless you tell us otherwise we'll treat the report of your missing sons seriously," O'Carroll said in a rush.

James O'Neill's naturally red face advanced to scarlet. "Out!" he screamed as he stretched both his arms wide and quite literally herded O'Carroll and McCusker out of the kitchen of his grand house.

Polly O'Neill nodded her head to both members of the Ulster police force as they left the house.

"I'll take that as a yes, Mrs O'Neill," McCusker offered, as the man of the house slammed the front door, which kissed the heels of the detective's well polished black leather shoes. He continued, addressing the closed door, "Obviously sir we have to advise you that the PSNI pledges to protect all life and property and to uphold the peace, so we are within out rights to continue our investigation into your sons' whereabouts."

CHAPTER THREE

O'Carroll knocked over a couple of the red and white cones while parking her car illegally on Exchange Street West, just behind St Anne's Cathedral. The numerous dints and scratches about her metallic yellow Renault Mégane testified that this wasn't the first such mishap.

They walked past the Potted Hen Bistro into the small Saint Anne's Square to be greeted by a bronze sculpture – a nude who looked like she was about to leap from an imaginary high diving board in the general direction of the detectives. The entire left-hand side of the Regency-styled square was taken up with the new arts theatre complex, the MAC. The three remaining sides were faced with seven-storey buildings, residential apartments with retail units in the bottom two floors. A few of these units were yet to be occupied. McCusker liked the feel of the square and for a split second he regretted not spending more time sourcing his own accommodation on his recent move down to the city.

As luck would have it, someone was exiting the ground floor communal door as O'Carroll and McCusker approached. If he wasn't mistaken, the beautiful young thing who, thanks to O'Carroll's warrant card, happily let them in was a TV celebrity – her success due entirely to her looks and bubbly personality. She even flashed McCusker one of her famous on-screen smiles, which resulted in him walking straight into the door. If he wasn't mistaken, O'Carroll had assisted the door in its closing speed.

O'Carroll buzzed the top floor bell while McCusker simultaneously knocked loudly on the door. They could hear the chiming from somewhere deep in the apartment but no other sound. O'Carroll searched in vain for a key – under the doormat, under a long-dead plant pot, along the top edge of the door frame – while McCusker simply turned the large brass door handle. The door opened noisily into a large empty hallway.

"You seemed to know it wasn't locked," she said, searching her pockets.

"It would be my bet the boys didn't work for or pay for this flat, so they wouldn't care about it."

"The mother did confirm she wanted us to search for her children?" O'Carroll asked, as she handed her colleague a pair of clear gloves.

"Correct," McCusker replied, and they both gloved-up.

"Okay, at this stage all I want to do is to be sure Ryan and Lawrence are not in the apartment," O'Carroll cautioned McCusker. "Then I want to turn it over to the CSI team."

"It's your football; I'm happy to play by your rules," McCusker confirmed. "Split up and search or stay together?"

"Stay together."

The apartment was untidy but not dirty. The aromas of scented candles still lingered. The almost uncomfortably-sized apartment looked more like a shared student accommodation than a home. It was sparsely furnished – no photos, no art – with several Kate Moss posters absentmindedly peppered about the walls. The main room (and certainly the biggest in the apartment) was jam-packed with computers, desks, printers, shelves full of files, the biggest collection of telephone directories McCusker had ever seen, and some expensive looking paper and envelopes marked with the letterhead 'Larry's List.'

Two rudimentary signs, written in red felt-tip pen on foolscap paper and pinned to each door, confirmed the occupants of the two main bedrooms: 'Ryan's Crib' and 'Larry's Crib.' The rooms, both with micro en suite bathrooms, were in much better condition and far tidier than the rest of the apartment. Certainly they showed evidence of a woman's touch – perhaps the mother's – McCusker thought.

Back in the hallway O'Carroll wrote NSOL (No Sign of Life) in her notebook, along with the time, and closed the door behind them. Before they had a chance to get back in the car, her mobile started ringing. Suddenly an unmarked car with blue light flashing sped up the narrow Exchange Street West towards them. Two uniformed officers and a plainclothes man hopped out of the car. The latter screeched at them in an ear-piercing whine.

"On the ground! On the ground, on the fucking ground now!"

"Come on…" O'Carroll protested, her mobile still ringing.

"Shut yer bake and on the fucking ground now!" the plain clothes officer shrieked, as his gun barrel, aping a wagging finger, preached to her while the uniformed officers clearly hung back.

"Cage, stop this shite, you know it's me."

"Just because I know you, doesn't mean you're not a bent copper. I got a tip-off that a burglary was in progress at this apartment block and here you are."

O'Carroll sneered, "McCusker: meet Detective Inspector Jarvis Cage."

McCusker wasn't clear if he should also get on the ground or shake this man's hand.

Cage's attention didn't waver from O'Carroll. "On the ground, now!" DI Cage ordered.

"Cage…"

"Oh please, please just give me the excuse to charge you with resisting arrest!"

She reluctantly dropped to her knees and half-heartedly stretched full length, face down.

"Okay spread them," Cage ordered as he stood behind her and kicked her feet wide apart. He turned to face McCusker and winked at him.

McCusker walked over to O'Carroll, bordered on one side by Saint Anne's Square and the tidy rear regal entrance of the Cathedral to the right, and bent down to take the phone, "I better answer this just in case it's important." He searched about for a while before finding the answer button. "Oh, yes, here we are. Hello this is Detective Inspector O'Carroll's phone. Oh, sorry for keeping you so long Superintendent."

He held his hand up to Cage signalling him to wait a moment. The two uniformed officers grew increasingly embarrassed.

"Ah yes sir, we were working on that case when an unmarked car nearly ran us over and then this madman pulls a gun on us and orders DI O'Carroll on the ground."

McCusker reached down and helped O'Carroll back up on her feet while he concentrated on the phone.

"No sir, he didn't flash his warrant card, still hasn't in fact," McCusker said into the phone as Cage sheepishly re-holstered his gun muttering that the safety catch was still on. "Yes he was accompanied by two uniformed officers but they didn't get involved, I think they felt it was inappropriate behaviour."

McCusker made a fuss of helping O'Carroll up and brushing the dirt and dust from her suit, holding everyone's undivided attention as he did so.

"Well sir, she's a bit shook up and her nice wee pinstripe suit is in a bit of a mess," McCusker stopped talking and returned to listening mode, eventually pronouncing, "I'd say a ton will cover it, you know, getting the suit dry cleaned and all that...Okay, that seems fair, hang on a minute..."

"What?" the gangly balding DI Cage asked.

"He says you should give O'Carroll £100, immediately and in cash, so she can have her suit cleaned and he wants you to apologise to her and he wants me to listen and make sure the apology seems sincere, something to do with a soft-shoe investigation into police conduct," McCusker offered in an 'I wouldn't like to be you if you don't' tone.

Five minutes later O'Carroll and McCusker were driving back towards the police station when she said, "I don't know whether I liked the apology or the money most. So, am I meant to split the £100 with you?"

"I don't know..." McCusker said, "the wee Indian man trying to sell you double glazing didn't specify."

CHAPTER FOUR

The sun was all but set before they reached the station house, which was located in the Custom House just off the Donegall Quay, in the recently redeveloped Custom House Square. Superintendent Niall Larkin and his team had moved into the right wing of the iconic palazzo-influenced building three years ago – about a century and a half after the original duty collectors set up shop. Larkin and his gang's flit was meant to be a temporary measure while they awaited the building of a brand new station house in the Waterfront development area. Then two things happened: a budget couldn't be agreed on and in the meantime they lost the site to a hotel, so it looked like the Custom House would remain their base for the foreseeable future. McCusker was extremely pleased about this as he loved the Charles Lanyon-designed building, which made his exile from Portrush up on the north coast just that wee bit more bearable.

"Do you want to leave this until tomorrow?" O'Carroll asked, as they walked up the sixteen steps, passing through a coded security gate in the high railing fence before taking a right, then up another twelve steps and through the varnished semicircular crowned door and into their part of the building.

"*You* clearly don't…" McCusker replied, as they entered the echo-crazy reception. His reply was interrupted not by his words coming back at him but by the stellar Station Duty Sergeant, Matt Devine. Devine, like a lot of the PSNI Station Duty Sergeants, ran his police station, the Custom House, as though it were a ship. The role carried the nicknamed, Skipper. A nickname, it has to be said, Devine was rather proud of.

"Right youse two, the super wants to see you both, as in immediately!" the skipper announced, his South Derry accent bouncing around the reception walls. "I've been ordered to report your arrival to wee Sheila the minute you arrive."

Wee Sheila, as in Mrs Sheila Lawson, a secretary who knew how to keep a secret and had been keeping Superintendent Larkin's secrets for fourteen years now, welcomed them with a "you're in for it," nod, but she seemed happy to allow McCusker to charm a cup of coffee and a few of Larkin's prized Jaffa Cakes out of her.

"So," Larkin began expansively, before either McCusker or O'Carroll had a chance to settle into the comfortable seats in his plush office. "What have you pair been up to?" The super was smallish, solid, and moustachioed, with friendly brown eyes and short wavy brown hair. Dressed in his black three-piece suit - but he always seemed to be minus the jacket - he looked like he'd just walked into the office to start his day. McCusker was convinced he had a drawer full of clean, white, starched shirts, and he changed them at least three times a day. Larkin troubled McCusker; from the very first time he'd laid eyes on him in his interview, he was convinced he knew him from somewhere, but he couldn't place the guy and it continued to bother him.

"Well I received a call..." O'Carroll began.

"I bet you did, and now I'm paying the price."

"Sorry about that, but Mrs O'Neill seems genuinely concerned about her two sons, Ryan and Lawrence."

"She's officially reported them missing?" Larkin asked.

"Yes," O'Carroll confirmed. "She hasn't heard from either of them for over two days now and before Wednesday she says they were in contact at least once a day."

"James claims they're most likely off somewhere sowing their wild oats," Larkin said, looking at his watch.

"Yeah, and his wife seems very scared of annoying him," O'Carroll offered tentatively. "He threw us out of the house even though she'd invited us in."

Larkin turned his attention to the detective. "You're being unusually quiet McCusker...what do you think of this?"

"I think..." McCusker started, then appeared to opt to choose his words carefully, "I'm...*we're* inclined to favour the mother's concerns in this affair." He appeared proud to have gotten to the end of his sentence without stepping in the smelly stuff.

"And what about Mr O'Neill himself?" Larkin pushed.

"I think he's a first class, self-important buffoon," McCusker offered.

O'Carroll looked as though her heart had sunk right through the floor. But she needn't have worried.

"I'm so happy I've found someone who agrees with me about the pompous eejit. My wife has often said that if Cavehill got Napoleon's nose then James O'Neill was left with his arse."

Both O'Carroll and McCusker knew Mrs Larkin was much too polite a woman to entertain such a thought, let alone broadcast it. Equally they knew the superintendent famously liked to quote his wife as the author of thoughts he preferred not to attribute to himself.

"So what is his story?" McCusker asked, relaxing somewhat.

"Family money, made during the Industrial Revolution. James O'Neill himself was in the right place at the right time to take advantage of Raymond O'Sullivan's floundering and under-financed business. O'Neill bought a controlling interest in exchange for a large injection of development money. O'Sullivan suffered a boardroom coup, stage-managed by O'Neill, and was left with no company and no money. He committed suicide."

"Oh my goodness," O'Carroll exclaimed.

"It gets worse," Larkin continued immediately, looking at his watch again. "O'Sullivan's wife took up with O'Neill. Some say the affair had started before O'Sullivan took his life. Some also say he could have put up with losing his money and his business…but not with losing his wife and two sons."

"Surely we're not talking about Polly, Ryan, and Lawrence here?" McCusker asked, hoping he was jumping the gun on this occasion.

"Sadly, yes," Larkin replied.

"So Ryan and Lawrence are not even James O'Neill's sons?" O'Carroll asked.

"No, they're not," Larkin replied, checking his watch again. "Look, I've got another appointment just about to start, but I'm with you two on this one. I'd also be inclined to follow the mother's instincts. What were you planning to do next?"

"Try to track their movements from their mobile phones. And we've got three names: Pat Tepper…"

"I know his father – good solicitor," Larkin said, and then appeared to be annoyed at himself for prolonging the proceedings unnecessarily.

"He looks after Ryan and Lawrence's business," O'Carroll continued, completely ignoring her superior, "something to do with the internet – we think the company is called Larry's List. Then there are two old friends of the boys, Susanna Holmes and Tim Black."

"Are you going to see them now or leave it until tomorrow morning?" Larkin asked as he stood up, "I can't approve overtime on anything at the moment."

"Actually we were going to try and interview them all this evening."

"Right answer Detective."

At which point there was a knock on the door and, like a ghost, Mrs Lawson's blue rinse appeared to announce, "Superintendent, your barber is here."

CHAPTER FIVE

As luck would have it, when O'Carroll rang Susanna Holmes' mobile it was in fact answered by Tim Black. He and girlfriend Susanna were both up at Café Conor on Stranmillis Road. The restaurant was just opposite the Ulster Museum. McCusker knew the spot as he infrequently sampled their amazing Big Breakfast, while his eyes feasted on Shawcross' trademark massive soulful canvases.

It turned out Susanna shared Mrs O'Neill's concern over the boys while Tim, although not quite as blasé as their father, James, didn't seem to think there was a problem.

"Tell me the last time the boys weren't around for two whole days, Tim?" Susanna asked her boyfriend once he'd made his point. They were seated in a comfortable corner of the restaurant with one end of a bench table to themselves and were enjoying the pre-dinner rush.

McCusker ordered a tea, but before it arrived, he couldn't resist the temptation of one of Café Conor's special generously sized scones. O'Carroll, who claimed she was meeting her sister later for dinner, settled for a pick-me-up coffee, one of three she would use for gear changes over the following thirty minutes.

McCusker wasn't really a coffee man, but he was always amused by how much fuss some people made over the ingredients and equipment, and yet it was still mostly undrinkable. Café Conor did an ok coffee, but they didn't seem to create such a level of fuss making it.

"Well, I can't speak for yourself, Suse, but I've certainly gone a lot longer than that without hearing from them," her boyfriend replied implying a bit of history over the subject.

"Okay detectives, cards on the table time," Susanna said. "I should probably advise you at this stage that Ryan and I used to go out with each other."

"Right," O'Carroll said, as she scribbled in her notebook. "Look, would you be more comfortable if we interviewed you separately?"

"Nah, it's fine," Tim joked, "it was a long time ago. They were childhood sweethearts."

"It was a long time ago, but it hasn't been forgotten," she replied, evening up the score a little.

"Okay," McCusker interrupted, not exactly happy with the way this was going and sensing it wasn't as cosy as they tried to make it appear. "Susanna, when was the last time you saw either Ryan or Lawrence?"

"I saw both of them together," she replied. "They usually hang out together. I mean, they would try very hard to do things separately, just so they..." and here she paused, using a finger from each hand to create air-quotation marks, "weren't always together."

"But they would always end up together," Tim added.

"They weren't twins?" O'Carroll asked.

"No," McCusker replied, "there was about a year to a year and a half between them."

"Of course," O'Carroll said, remembering their earlier conversation with the mother. "Sorry, I interrupted you...when did you see them last?"

"It was last Saturday. I bumped into them in Pure Gym, just the other side of the Square from their apartment. They liked to keep in shape," Susanna said. "Look, all joking aside, we were all good friends; we liked to hang out together and we'd do that at least twice a week."

"And you Tim?" O'Carroll asked.

"Friday night, we were all up here for a late dinner after a Nick Lowe concert at The Limelight."

"And the brothers seemed...?"

"Fine to us," Tim interjected before O'Carroll had finished her question.

"No problems?"

"No," Susanna replied, "I mean we all have things that niggle us in life, but pretty much we try to get on with it, don't we?"

"How do they get on with their parents?"

"They were both very close to and protective of their mother, especially Ryan," Susanna offered.

"The father?"

"Well, he was hard work for all of us," Susanna admitted.

"But at least he wasn't our father," Tim added.

"He's a fabulously successful businessman," Susanna stated, once again using her fingers as quotation marks.

"And he behaved like a fabulously successful businessman," Tim finished.

"What do you know about the brothers' business?" McCusker asked.

"It was a totally brilliant idea," she gushed. "Do you know anything about it?"

"Just the name – Larry's List?"

"Yes," Tim said, sounding very impressed. "I mean, for as long as I can remember, any time we needed to know anything about…"

"…anything," Susanna added.

"Yes, absolutely anything at all," Tim continued, "all we needed to do was to go and ask Larry and if he didn't know already, he'd find it out PDQ.

"So we were all messing around on the internet, trying to develop a Facebook, YouTube, Amazon, anything – our own Google really. Susanna and I fell by the wayside, but Larry and Ryan kept going. At the same time, Larry was building up a database of his own information – contacts, places he'd go to, stores he'd order from – and then one day Ryan said 'It's here, we've had it all the time. We should just try and find a way to charge people to use your list.' You know what we're talking about – restaurants, shops, chemists, cinemas, best antique stores, best holidays, best place to meet girls…" Tim said.

"And boys," Susanna added seamlessly. "And they spent all their spare time building Larry's database into a website."

"They had taken it as far as they possibly could, without calling on development money," Tim added.

"Why not go to their dad?" O'Carroll asked.

"He'd made it clear to them that he'd pay them only if they worked for him, and he promised them the opportunity to work their way up through the company, but outside of that he wouldn't give them a single penny."

"They became desperate and borrowed £20,000 a few months ago from a loan shark. They were due to pay it back and Ryan had told me the £20,000 had now escalated to £50,000."

"But I thought you said they had no worries?" O'Carroll said.

"Well, Ryan didn't seem worried about it," Susanna said. "He felt they were a matter of days away from a major breakthrough with the site. He was confident that when they launched it properly on the internet, the cash would just roll in, then they could sell the site to Google or Amazon, or someone similar, for multi-millions and retire."

"But Larry had no real interest in money. He'd no interest in retiring," Tim added.

"Did Ryan or Lawrence mention anything about this at the gym?" O'Carroll asked.

"Nah. They were both excited by Ryan's latest idea of trying to get golfer Rory McIlroy on board as an ambassador for Larry's List, which would bring worldwide publicity."

"We asked their mother about their friends. She mentioned only you two and Pat, their solicitor," O'Carroll said. "But surely two young guys would have more friends than that?"

"Not really. They'd always been enough for each other. They were really completely happy in each other's company."

"Tell me this," McCusker started, his mind obviously elsewhere. "Surely they could just have gone to their mother for the development money?"

Susanna and Tim looked at each other and shook their heads in synchronised sympathy.

"She didn't have a penny of her own money," Tim said.

"Ryan told me that his mam went to their dad and asked for the development money and he just laughed at her, saying he wasn't going to waste his hard-earned money on a silly internet company."

CHAPTER SIX

McCusker and O'Carroll left Café Conor just before 8 p.m. McCusker volunteered to interview Pat Tepper alone, but O'Carroll wanted to be there as well. However, she'd arranged to pick up her sister, Grace, from her apartment in the Titanic Quarter at eight. She decided to ring Tepper, who was on standby for their interview, and have him meet them in the bar of the Fitzwilliam Hotel at quarter past instead. That way they could pick up Grace en route, have her wait at the Europa Hotel Bar, and collect her after the Tepper interview, whereupon the sisters could go to their dinner, leaving McCusker to walk home.

But Grace wasn't ready when O'Carroll ran up to collect her. She'd have to make her way to the Europa herself, leaving O'Carroll and McCusker to head off for their rendezvous with Pat Tepper.

O'Carroll had just finished tut-tutting about families and the effort they required even just to mark time, when a casually dressed young man walked up to them and introduced himself as Pat Tepper.

"How did you know it was us?" O'Carroll asked.

"Well. Neither of you are interested in each other, you know in a romantic manner, so I concluded you were either work colleagues or you've been married for a few years. Since neither of you are wearing wedding rings, although one of you used to wear one," the well-spoken Tepper addressed McCusker directly, "I knew you must be McCusker and O'Carroll."

"Very good," O'Carroll replied, "maybe you should be working for us."

"Well it was a lot easier than that actually," Tepper confessed. "Look around…there are no other mixed couples in the bar."

McCusker went off to get three pints of Guinness while O'Carroll confessed, "You know that really was very good – I've known Mc-Cusker - mind you, only a few months - but I never realised he'd been married."

McCusker found himself wondering about O'Carroll as he returned with two of the three pints. What was her story? Why had she and he no interest in each other? She and the younger Pat Tepper seemed to be getting on great in his absence though. Yes, there was a bit of an age gap, but the solicitor seemed mature and...and...they looked like they were connecting.

"So," O'Carroll offered semi-officially when McCusker returned with his drink, "when did you last see Ryan and Lawrence O'Neill?"

Pat Tepper sighed with pleasure, enjoying his first taste of the dark brew before he answered, "That would have been Monday afternoon; we had a meeting in my office."

"And you haven't heard from them since?"

"I spoke to Ryan on the phone on Tuesday morning. I should explain the dynamics of the brothers. Larry was the ideas man; he was preoccupied about getting Larry's List up and running and dealing with all the logistical and technical problems that entailed. Ryan was the business head. He'd seen how all these other internet success stories seemed to end up with the principals fighting in the courts."

"Like Facebook?" O'Carroll suggested.

"Like Facebook," Tepper agreed. "And even Apple ended up in the courts for years over borrowing the name of The Beatles' company. Anyway, Ryan was totally convinced that their idea was going to work and he wanted their paper trail to be 100 per cent watertight and legitimate."

"Are you aware that he took out a loan?" O'Carroll continued, revealing that she had been pondering Susannah and Tim's earlier revelation.

"You see," Tepper started and then stopped, perhaps considering how much he should disclose. "Well, just in case anything has happened to the boys, I should tell you all I know. Ryan could easily have raised the money he needed if he'd been prepared to give a percentage of the company in return. Heck, even I could have found him a couple of substantial investors, but he really wasn't interested in giving away a share of their idea. He was happy when Susanna and Tim fell by the wayside, because, although they had put a lot of energy in, Ryan said he never really felt they were part of it."

"Who put in the £20,000?" McCusker asked.

"The honest to goodness answer is: I don't know. Ryan swore to me it was just a loan shark, nothing political, you know, just an ODC."

"How long had he the loan?" O'Carroll asked.

"A couple of months."

"Well, £15,000 a month interest for a £20,000 loan doesn't sound like the work of an ordinary decent criminal, aka ODC, to me?" McCusker offered, as he took his inaugural sip of his favourite brew.

"What can I tell you? Times are tough out there in all walks of life."

"And his parents really wouldn't give them any money?" O'Carroll asked.

"Well, his mum siphoned off as much of the house-keeping money as she could, but her husband just wasn't interested in helping."

"So when you spoke to Ryan on Tuesday, which was the day before he disappeared, had you any idea where he was?" O'Carroll asked.

"No, sorry," Tepper said. "But surely you guys can trace his movements by doing a triangulation on his mobile?"

"Yep, we're already onto that," O'Carroll said. "So we know of yourself, Susanna Holmes, and Tim Black, but no one else. Was there anyone else who the boys were in regular contact with?"

"They weren't really friends with anyone else."

"There must be some girlfriends?" McCusker said.

"Not since Ryan and Susanna split up."

"How long ago was that?"

"Oh a good few years – they've remained good friends though," Tepper said, appearing deep in thought. "I've never been able to work out if Susanna would have taken Ryan back or he her, but I can tell you they really get on great together. Tim Black, in one of his more uncharitable and drunken moments, had suggested that Susanna was just idling time with him as she waited for Ryan to come into his father's money."

"Really?" McCusker asked. When he thought back on the pair that seemed to make sense – there hadn't really been enough of a natural fire between Susanna and Tim, even with their party-trick of completing each other's sentences, to suggest they'd end up together.

"I tell you that, not because I wish to gossip, but because there just might be a wee grain of truth to it."

"And Lawrence?" O'Carroll continued.

"He's obsessed with this project. I mean he was always going to be obsessed with something; better Larry's List than drugs, drink, or a woman."

"What do you think has happened to them?" McCusker asked, throwing out the only curve ball he had up his sleeve.

"Well, obviously I've been thinking about this and they've either disappeared until they can get some money and get the loan shark off their backs or they've just nipped away for a few days. Ryan was always saying that Larry worked too hard, but he kept himself pretty busy too."

"They wouldn't have done anything silly like…"

"Commit suicide?" Tepper asked and answered his own question. "No way. They were too happy in each other's company and much too ambitious by far."

"Kidnapped?" McCusker asked.

"Well, James O'Neill would seem like an ideal target."

"If the family were so rich why are the boys so ambitious?" McCusker asked.

"Oh, that's an easy one," Tepper said, pausing briefly for another sip, "they wanted to make enough money so their mother didn't have to depend on their father."

***

"He'd be a nice man for some girl," O'Carroll said, as she and McCusker took the Great Victoria Street exit of the Fitzwilliam Hotel en route to the Europa, and in the process walked past the ugliest extension to one of the city's most beautiful buildings, the Grand Opera House.

"Yeah, I could tell youse were getting on well. Did you exchange numbers?"

"No, not for me you oaf, I'm already spoken for – for my sister, Grace."

***

Luckily for McCusker he didn't get to see Grace O'Carroll that evening. He declined her sister's invitation to join them for a drink in the Europa, choosing instead to cross the street and enjoy another Guinness in the Crown Bar, the renowned destination. In fact, he happened to bump into someone he knew from his last station house up in Portrush. McCusker stretched his pint out to his former colleague's three and left him as he was about to tackle a fourth. Given the choice, he'd have much preferred to sip on his Guinness alone, enjoy the vibey, unique pub, and consider the missing O'Neill brothers.

Two brothers from an extremely wealthy family disappear without a trace but no sign of a demand for a ransom. The mother is worried, the father is not. Could the father possibly be dealing with kidnappers himself? Does he really not care about their well-being? Could the brothers simply be keeping out of the way of a loan shark, as their solicitor would have it? Could they be off doing some secretive research for the website? Might they just be being extremely discreet, having shot off somewhere for a dirty weekend? Where would they go? Dublin? Paris? London? Bangor? Or maybe even Portrush or somewhere up in the wilds of Donegal. They'd be very hard to track down up there, McCusker thought. Portrush would also seem to be the best-suited location due to their lack of funds.

He hadn't really had a chance to discuss the next step with O'Carroll – should they place photos in the press or send them to the local news? Or would that endanger the boys? The photos they had sourced (surprisingly enough on the internet) were already on the radar as an official alert, along with the boys' names. It still wasn't really a case – and it wasn't even his case – but there wasn't a lot of action around the Custom House at the moment, so he was happy with anything that distracted him from his thoughts about Portrush. By the time he reached his first-floor flat on University Square Mews, he was happy to be further distracted by the bliss that is sleep.

CHAPTER SEVEN

It seemed but a matter of minutes later when he was offended by a third distraction; this time the sound of the Big Ben chimes of his doorbell. As he stumbled out of bed he was shocked to discover sun-tinted daylight streaming into his living room. He checked his watch – barely 7.30 a.m. Where had the night gone? He wasn't allowed to dwell on this thought too long because on and on Big Ben chimed. The mini (make that micro) screen on his door buzzer clearly showed DI Lily O'Carroll standing in the porch outside the front door of the three-storey house. She was hopping from foot to foot while holding two cups of something. He prayed it was a wake-me-up coffee as he buzzed her in.

He used the time it took her to walk up the stairs to pull on a pair of trousers and yesterday's shirt, which he was still buttoning up when she knocked on his door.

"Rise and shine country boy!" she sang, as she breezed past him into the tiny hallway of his flat. She came to a quick halt at the door to his living room. "McCusker, colour me impressed! I was expecting a student hovel. Never in a million years would I have pegged you as house proud."

McCusker enjoyed the sin of pride for but a moment. He had spent an earlier weekend cleaning, decorating, and furnishing the two bedrooms, bathroom, kitchen, and living room of his flat. He couldn't stand dives, dirty or untidy houses or flats, and even in his student days he had avoided domestic chaos like the bubonic plague. At £485 a month to rent it was a bit more than he'd planned to spend, but, in his line of work, he felt it necessary to have a sanctuary to return to at the end of each day. On top of which, thanks to his early retirement money courtesy of the Lord Patten scheme, he could afford to throw a few extra cushions around his living space.

Actually the Patten windfall allowed McCusker to be able to stretch way beyond the few extra cushions.

As a bi-product of the 1994 Peace Process and by way of the Good Friday Agreement of 10th April 1998, Chris Patten (as he was then known) was invited in 1999 to lead a commission to make recommendations to Westminster on policing in Northern Ireland. His basic brief was pretty much along the lines of: if the police force were to serve the community then its members had to be from the community. Included in the 175 recommendations the Lord (as he became) Patten Commission made, was one where the RUC (the Royal Ulster Constabulary as it was originally known) should change its name to The Northern Ireland Police Service. Shortly thereafter this was revised to The Police Service of Northern Ireland, (PSNI) no doubt in order to avoid the NIPS acronym.

Along with the name change it was decided that the police force should be completely reorganised with the emphasis on human rights. Patten's commission recommended that the new police force should be, 'broadly reflective of the population of Northern Ireland.' The PSNI were instructed that, 'an equal pool of Catholics and Protestants should be drawn from the pool of qualified candidates.'

In order to achieve this fair balance of staff the PSNI had to lose a lot of members from their ranks over the following decade, and so the Patten Commission offered - in recommendation number 106 - handsome packages of pensions and payments to those willing to accept voluntary retirement. McCusker pondered the option for years and eventually decided to bite their hand off with a plan to retire to the good life, mostly focused around, but rarely on, the golf course.

It wasn't exactly that he was tired, or even tired of police work, no, far from it in fact. He still loved, with a passion, the mystery of the puzzle of the crimes. It was more that, just before accepting the voluntary retirement , McCusker had started to accept he'd reached the stage, with his seniority, where he'd become a desk-bound pen-pusher, rather than a case solver. So perhaps it was not so much a case of him not knowing what he wanted to do, but more a case of him knowing what he really didn't want to do.

McCusker realised that at Custom House he had fallen on his feet in that he was no longer an official member of the PSNI. He was but a hired hand; a hand hired to do what he absolutely lived to do, solve crimes. Not only that, but he was set apart from all the PSNI career politics and, as O'Carroll frequently reminded him, 'you're only here because Patten paid you handsomely to retire, but you got bored, so now you're back and even better paid than you were when you were a member of the RUC.'

And of course also in the new mix of his life there was Detective Inspector Lily O'Carroll. The jury was still out on whether she was on the plus or minus side of his new life, although he accepted he already had a fair idea how he'd vote.

"On the other hand," he heard her say, handing him his coffee and drawing him out of his daily moment of gratitude to Lord Patten, "maybe you should take a look in the mirror before you greet anyone at the front door again."

McCusker strode, early-morning speed, into his bathroom and did in fact look in the mirror. Not a pretty sight he would agree; his dishevelled straw-like copper-coloured hair refused to bid the orchestration of his fingers, even when dampened. He was solid rather than overweight (which he felt was always just around the corner), not tall, not small, awkward and shy, but he wasn't quite the fool – even with his shirt buttons done up out of sync – he sometimes liked people to think he was.

"Give me ten minutes for a quick shower," he shouted back to his colleague.

"For the sake of hygiene I can give you three. We're in a hurry McCusker."

"Why?" he asked as he turned on his shower.

"Someone just delivered a pint of blood and a disposable camera to O'Neill's doorstep."

Seven minutes later a freshly showered and dressed – like he was off on a date – McCusker was speeding in the direction of the Custom House. Actually, O'Carroll was doing all the speeding and McCusker was trying desperately hard not to spill any of his hardly touched coffee over his fresh set of clothes.

The fact that McCusker was shocked about the pint of blood seemed to permit O'Carroll to be equally shocked, having initially appeared a bit flippant about it. They discussed whether or not a whole pint of blood would be deemed a big loss to the human body.

"Well if they were like me, when I gave my pint, a three-minute rest, a cup of tea and a wee digestive bickey was all it took to get me back on my feet again," McCusker admitted.

O'Carroll wondered if the captors had taken half a pint from each of them.

"There would be no need," McCusker offered. "Once they started with one they'd have drawn the whole pint."

"So we're looking for someone with medical experience?"

"Or someone who watches a lot of *E.R.* or *Grey's Anatomy*," McCusker replied.

"Or *House*," O'Carroll added, "now there's a man..."

Station duty sergeant Matt Devine raced out to meet them with, as prearranged by O'Carroll, a report and a set of photo prints.

"We don't think it's real blood," he said, as he exchanged said items for McCusker's coffee. "It's effing cold!" he could be heard shouting as they screeched off in the direction of Lisburn Road en route to Malone Park.

"I wonder, did the skipper mean the suspected blood or the coffee?" McCusker laughed, as he started to check the photos. "Four shots, two with each of the boys holding a copy of yesterday's *Belfast Telegraph*."

"Any bruises?" O'Carroll asked, eyes glued to the road.

"No, they seem to look okay, considering."

"How are they dressed?"

"Black hoodie sweats."

"Are they restrained?" O'Carroll asked.

"Yep, plastic cuffs," McCusker confirmed. "Tell me this: Was there a ransom note delivered with the blood and photos?"

"Nope."

"Who discovered them and where?"

"Their mother found them on the doorstep at 6 a.m. this morning. She rang the station immediately – Matt Devine woke me up."

"Lucky me," McCusker offered, still studying the photographs.

"Oh don't worry, I'd say after your cold coffee trick this morning, you'll be on the early morning and later night roster for a few weeks at least," she sneered.

"Surely the milk wouldn't have been delivered by 6 a.m.?" Mc-Cusker said, as much to himself as her.

"Your point?"

"Why would Mrs O'Neill have gone out to collect the milk so early?"

"Oh, McCusker, people like the O'Neills do not have their milk delivered in bottles and left on the front doorstep. We're talking about Malone Park for heaven's sake. And even if they did, they'd have people who would go out and collect the milk from the steps for them. No, she said she always gets up early and the first thing she does is take her dog out for a walk. And here we are," O'Carroll said, as she semi-carefully parked her car in the O'Neill's drive.

"Does her husband know?"

"No, she said he sleeps in on Saturdays, on top of which she didn't want him stopping her giving the blood and camera to us."

"It's a prank," were the first words out of James O'Neill's large mouth. "Look, you've already admitted that the blood is fake, flat rasberryade, no doubt. Come on, please couldn't someone be a little bit more inventive than that? I mean, at least pig's blood would have got us all going."

"And the photos?" his wife asked.

"Shows they're fans of the *Belfast Telegraph*. This is all kindergarten stuff, compared to what we used to get up to in Rag Week."

At which point his wife ran from the very formal sitting room in tears.

O'Carroll gave chase.

"Oh let her wallow," was O'Neill's only remark as he turned his back on the detectives.

"I should advise you that we're treating this matter seriously sir," McCusker said and, before laughing-boy O'Neill could retort, he continued, "and just so that you're aware, Superintendent Larkin has also been apprised of the situation."

"Makes no difference to me if it's two or three bobbies I put back on the beat," he boasted. "Perhaps you should further apprise Niall that at the next Council meeting at the City Hall I intend to mention that tax payer's good money is being wasted by the PSNI on foolhardy investigations."

"Please look at the photos again sir, you can see clearly that they are both being restrained?" McCusker persisted.

"Where did the photos come from? Surely there is a computer trail – who took them? Who developed them, etc., etc.? I thought absolutely everything could be traced these days?" O'Neill asked, seeming to backtrack a little.

"Actually, they were very clever with the photos. The captors..." McCusker said and paused – he felt it was important to get the word "captors" into James O'Neill's consciousness, "...the captors used a disposable camera, thereby avoiding the usual trail."

"Were there any fingerprints on the actual camera?" O'Neill continued.

"Just one set, sir," McCusker replied

"Well there you go, there's your lead."

"I'd bet we'll find nothing but your wife's prints on the camera, sir. They're not going to be clever enough to use a disposable camera and then not wear gloves when they're using it," McCusker surmised.

Just then O'Carroll returned to the room, she walked confidently up to James O'Neill.

"I believe you're going to get a call very shortly demanding a ransom," she said, her voice steady and calm. "What I'd like to do is to set up our specialist team in here so that when the call comes we can assist you."

"What I'd like you to do is to remember you are trespassing on my property and I'd like you out of here immediately. If there is a situation to deal with, and I'm still not convinced that there is, I can assure you my people will deal with it. If I see you lurking around embarrassing me in front of my neighbours I'll be on to your super quicker than a rat up a drainpipe." Now McCusker came to think about it, O'Neill had a few things in common with the murinae family other than the ability to nip up a drainpipe quickly.

As McCusker and O'Carroll drove back to the Custom House with their collective tail between their legs McCusker broke the silence: "Well it's worthwhile remembering that even though Jesus could walk on water he still couldn't avoid getting his feet wet."

"Meaning?"

"Meaning that even though laughing-boy O'Neill thinks he's the great 'I am,' he still has to go to the toilet and he still has to clean his own arse."

"Oh McCusker, you've just ruined my lunch. T.M.I."

"T.M.I?"

"Too much information," she replied, and then after another minute of silence as they drove up Waring Street, she added, "There's something that doesn't quite fit here."

"You mean with Laughing Boy?"

"Yeah. You just don't alienate the police if there is the slightest chance your two boys have been kidnapped."

"His wife's two boys," McCusker offered, feeling compelled to correct her.

"Even so, she's still his wife. There's bound to be some kind of paternal instinct there, don't you think?"

"So what are you thinking? He stages the kidnapping to raise the money? Is his business in trouble?" McCusker asked, writing something down in his notebook.

"O'Electronics? Surely not – one of the biggest success stories in the province."

"Well, just pick up the *Irish Times* and you'll see lots of supposedly blue chip companies having to be bailed out by NAMA," McCusker said, feeling very comfortable with this line of thought. "Would the sons be insured?"

O'Carroll suddenly went ghost white.

"What?" McCusker asked; she was frightening him now.

"I was just asking myself would they be worth more dead or alive."

CHAPTER EIGHT

The remainder of the Saturday was spent following up various leads. As predicted, Polly O'Neill's prints were the only ones found on the disposable camera and the milk bottle, which, as predicted by James O'Neill, had in fact been filled with flat raspberryade.

The last sighting of Ryan and Lawrence O'Neill had been on the Monday afternoon at the meeting with the solicitor Pat Tepper. Their regular eateries seemed to be Café Conor and Deanes at Queen's, but the last time they'd been seen there was on the Saturday. They didn't have a favourite pub or club. They apparently regularly used BAGEL: a bagel, coffee bar, soup and sandwich joint on Donegall Street, a very short walk from their Saint Anne's Square apartment, but they hadn't been in there for over a week, which, on consideration, appeared to surprise the staff a little. They preferred DVDs to going to the cinema. Ryan read a lot, mostly magazines, newspapers, and non-fiction books, while Lawrence apparently lived by the computer screen. Their local corner shop was Sandy Ford Food and the owners checked their memories and their security camera tapes (which were subsequently confiscated by PSNI), both agreeing that the boys had last been seen on Saturday, only this time in the morning – 7.57 a.m. to be exact. Their purchases, always paid for separately, were a copy of the *Daily Telegraph*, an *Autosport* magazine, milk, eggs, beans, wheaten bread, and Alpen for Ryan, and Jacob's Mikado biscuits, several bars of chocolate, and a tin of pears for Lawrence. There were no reported sightings at The George Best or International airports, or at the docks of either Belfast or Stranraer.

Their mother confirmed that both were keen on Formula One motor racing but would only occasionally visit the races in person and, as far as she knew, then only to Silverstone in England and Spa in

Belgium. She further claimed they both supported "Jason Button," who in fact turned out to be Jenson Button, whom DI O'Carroll voiced more than a passing interest in. The brothers didn't bother with football, rugby, or cricket; both had been keen long-distance runners through school and university. As far as she knew they both jogged regularly. "Lawrence's only exercise and exposure to fresh air," she claimed.

"Really, the perfect couple to kidnap," McCusker claimed, as he and DI O'Carroll exited the Custom House at 7.30 p.m.

"I suppose," O'Carroll replied, appearing distracted. "So what are you up to tonight?"

"If I hadn't been working today I was going to pop back up to the Port to take care of a few bits and pieces."

"So what is it you need to do up there?" O'Carroll inquired. "Okay, let's see now," McCusker started, knowing that she was just trying to find out more about him and his previous life. "Well for one, I'd visit 55° North, the restaurant with the best burger and the best view in the North.

"Two, I'd walk around Barry's Arcade to get energised once again by the buzz and the sheer wall of noise.

"Three, I'd go for a walk on the beach," McCusker continued, omitting the fact that walking on the East Strand beach up at the Port was one of his favourite things to do.

Sometimes he'd have to walk at 120° to the horizontal to counter the force of the wind, which frequently was of such a force he'd be scared of being blown over flat on his back. At the very least the power of the wind would suffice to quite literally blow all the cobwebs from his brain. He found his walks to be totally invigorating, delightfully indulgent, especially in the morning when the East Strand beach was completely empty. Even if his work dictated another time of the day, the noise of the waves trying in vain to wear down the sands would wash away all the sounds of his fellow beach-walkers.

"Pretty self-indulgent so far," O'Carroll observed, but looked like she was trying really hard not to come off as too judgemental.

"Okay," McCusker replied, realising she was not going to stop with her probing until he gave something away. Either that or she was looking for an excuse to swap some of her personal information with him. "Where was I?"

"You got up to item number three but, as far as I'm concerned there's been none so far worth troubling yourself with a drive up to Portrush over," she continued.

"Well there you go, garages," McCusker offered.

"Where did you get the garage from?" she asked, appearing to be amused by his thought process.

"Well, simple really, I talked about driving up to the Port, a drive implied a car and a car implied a garage, and then that garage implied another garage, so, don't you see, really I should have said garages."

"Garages?"

"I better explain," McCusker offered.

"That'll be helpful," she replied and added as an afterthought, "hopefully."

"I've got most of my previous life packed away in boxes. My friend Matt McCann, who is a bit of a hoarder himself, has all my boxes neatly lined up in his garage. I'm feeling a bit guilty because I know for a fact that I'm never ever going to open those boxes again, let alone examine the contents. So the reality is that all the boxes are on a one-stop to the new Recycling Centre on Causeway Street."

"Would they be similar boxes to the one you have in the hallway cupboard in your flat?" she asked, appearing to have regretted leading him into this line of conversation.

"Yeah, only that box contains all my parent's stuff, so I do want to keep that one safe."

"What's in it?" she asked, appearing intrigued again.

"You know what, it's so long since I looked that I don't rightly know," McCusker admitted.

"And you're never tempted to just look?"

"Never," he said with such a degree of finality O'Carroll knew she shouldn't try to dig any deeper into that one. But dig she did.

"So it would be stuff from your school days?"

"No, it would be stuff that my parents felt a need to keep," he admitted.

"What do you remember from your childhood McCusker?"

"Well there's a funny thing," he started with a sad smile, "none of my childhood memories are my own, all the ones I have are ones my mother would have told me."

"Weird, just weird," she said, looking like she was still intrigued and itching to dig further. "So that's four, dump your boxes, what else would you need to do up at the Port?"

"Okay at the same time as I'm relieving Matt of my boxes in his garage, I'd solve another problem: namely what to do with my golf clubs. I've decided to give them to Matt as a thank you for helping me out when…ah…," he muttered for a bit before finishing with, "and for storing some of my stuff for me."

Either O'Carroll had just missed the gift of an opening into his private life or she felt she didn't want to put him through the pain again, either way she let him away with nothing more than, "You better think carefully about that McCusker."

"And why's that?" McCusker asked.

"Well wee Rory dumped his trusted clubs and look how long it's taking him to get his game back up to scratch again."

Meanwhile McCusker was wondering if he really needed to nip up to the Port. He realised that people, such as himself for instance, wanted to have somewhere else they could simply go. Somewhere 'else' they'd have that would suggest to people around them, O'Carroll for instance, that there was somewhere else they needed to be to conduct some business or other. Thereby he would be suggesting that his spartan Belfast existence was not all that was going on in his life. He knew that people needed a bit of a mystery in their lives, and equally he knew that people, such as O'Carroll for instance, needed others in their lives, like him, to have their own mysteries going on. It was vitally important for both parties that neither party be just an open book. But, truth be told, there just wasn't anything else major going on in McCusker's life. O'Carroll had once muttered about him being a good man in a world of few good men. McCusker took her words not as much as a compliment but more as a reflection on the other men in her life. McCusker felt he knew better about himself, and was more aware of what he considered the biggest failure in his personal life. That very same failure was also one of the reasons why he really wasn't in a hurry to visit Portrush. He found it a lot easier not to think of his failure when he wasn't in Portrush.

"Come on McCusker, what else do you have to do when you're up there?" O'Carroll quizzed. "Is there a woman you're not telling me about?"

McCusker just laughed and then said, quietly, "Ah that would be a no to that one. Tell you what though, just before I left I sold my car to a garage."

"The other garage?" O'Carroll guessed.

"Yes indeed, the other garage," McCusker confirmed.

"Okay, and this car you sold," she probed, "how does that fit into your visit?"

"I've still got a grand to pick up on it."

"O-kay!" O'Carroll said triumphantly, as if she'd discovered the real reason at last. "Now that's the first valid reason you've given me for going up to the Port."

"Not to mention the rainbows."

"Sorry?"

"You're a bit short on rainbows down here in Belfast; we had great rainbows up in Portrush. I'd like to see a rainbow again."

"Sure it's still early, it wouldn't take you long to get up to Portrush would it?"

"About an hour and a half, but I prefer to travel when it's not too dark. The journey passes much quicker when you can enjoy the sights," McCusker replied.

"Sights like rainbows?" she said through a genuine smile.

"Sights like rainbows," he nodded, "and yourself? What are you up to tonight?"

O'Carroll stopped and looked at McCusker. He, as a recently separated man in a strange city, knew that look; it was the look of pity. A look he hated.

"I'm out with my fella. Sorry McCusker, we'd invite you along but we're taking my sister out on a blind date with someone my fella went to University with. A fivesome wouldn't really work, you know?"

"So it's serious, you and this man of yours?" McCusker asked, totally ignoring her awkward moment.

"I hope so," she said, slightly hesitantly and starting to walk again, this time at more of a stroll and in a slightly different direction. She continued talking about her relatively new boyfriend and McCusker followed her lead. A few minutes later they arrived at McHugh's Bar & Restaurant. "A pint of Guinness again?"

"Aye, go on then."

The Saturday night crowd were obviously still at their preening-in-front-of-the-mirror stage, so he found them a place to sit easily enough.

McCusker looked around the room, pausing on a few of the faces before eventually returning to O'Carroll resting on the bar. He'd never really studied her carefully before; well, he didn't with colleagues. She had brown hair worn securely clasped up and out of her way, was slim, about 5' 8" in her black comfortable Converse trainers. She hid her femininity well in her masculine pinstripe suits – today's was dark blue – and polo-neck cashmere jumpers – today's was red – but her femininity was there, maybe not screaming, but most definitely whispering to get out.

Three minutes later she walked over and placed their two proud pints on the table between them.

"Jeez that was great! But that's me bluttered for the night drink-wise. Aye, but after today I needed it," she said, contentedly after her first sip. "Can I give you a tip McCusker?"

"Go on," McCusker said, thinking that bluttered was a great word – descriptive but not rude.

"It's only the first time you catch a woman's eye that you can smile."

"Sorry?" he said, stopping short of his first sip.

"I was watching you from the bar and that woman over there, the good looking one with the blonde French bob hairstyle?"

"Yes?" McCusker said, now intrigued where this was going.

"Well, it was fine to smile at her the first time your eyes met, but you must not be seen to be smiling if she should ever look back."

"Right," he said, a smile creeping across his face. Part of him felt that he should be annoyed, but it was overshadowed by his gratitude for the advice. "Any other tips?" he said, only half in jest.

"Yeah, and this is important – even if you're not looking for a woman, put a bit of fake tan on the band of white skin on your wedding ring finger. The type of girls you may someday wish to meet will just think you're an auld married man who's out on the prowl and they'll totally ignore you, thinking you've just taken the ring off for the night."

"Right...and the other type of girls?"

"Believe you me, you don't want to know about them at all."

"Why?" he asked.

"You're a total innocent McCusker," she said, smiling gently at him, a side of her he'd never seen before. "They'll eat you up and spit you out!"

"Perhaps not the best choice of words?" he said, as he tore into his Guinness.

"You're only saying that because I said you were an innocent," she countered, the gentleness disappearing quicker than it had arrived. "What happened with you and your ex?"

"You mean you don't know?" McCusker asked, thinking the whole station house would know about his situation.

"I just heard that because of the recession you were no longer a Robert. That you'd accepted the retirement package but because of the recession had to un-retire and came back as a Yellow Pack."

"A Yellow Pack?" McCusker quizzed, clearly amused by her turn of phrase.

"Yeah, you know in Tesco supermarkets they do cheaper versions on all the big household brands and all these cheaper versions are in Yellow packaging, so, that's what we call the agency cops," she replied not showing the slightest embarrassment. "Anyway I only became aware of your marital status when Pat Tepper pointed out your missing wedding ring."

"Okay, okay, long story short. I wasn't a great husband. My wife was a golfing widow. I'd been planning my retirement for ages, building up my nest egg with a few properties and banking on the bonus the Lord Patten Reform was offering for early voluntary retirement. All the properties were in my wife's name to minimise our tax liabilities. My wife obviously felt that I was going to be on the golf course even more in retirement than when I was working. So, quite literally, as I was processing my retirement she was liquidating all my, sorry, make that all of our, assets. Obviously our properties weren't worth what they would have been a few years ago but, at that, they were still worth a hell of a lot more than what we bought them for. She arose, took up the bank balance and walked."

"Did youse have a big fight?"

"No never. She left no note, no letter; there was no screaming, no fighting, and no solicitors. If it wasn't for the empty space on her side of the bed I'd be forgiven for thinking I'd never even been married. She'd even sold the house we were living in and rented it back for a few months from the new owner, without telling me. The only thing she didn't take was my pension and my not-so-wee Lord Patten nest egg."

"But not enough to live on for the rest of your life?" she said, as though she'd considered the option herself.

"Well that's the £64,000 question isn't it – how long are we going to live and do we have enough money to see us through to the end of our lives?" McCusker said, with the weariness of a man who looked like he'd toiled over the equation on a mental calculator for many a long hour.

"Where is she now?"

"I really don't know," he admitted.

"You *really* don't know?"

"Well she has a sister who lives somewhere in America and they were always tight."

"Where in America?" she asked.

"I haven't a clue."

"McCusker?"

"I haven't!"

"But don't you want your money? Or at least half of it?"

"You know, I'm not even sure that what she did was illegal, and I've only myself to blame. We married young, very young and…"

"Did you love her?" she asked.

"I've come to realise that I didn't."

"Never?"

"I don't believe so."

"Did you ever cheat on her?"

"No, never," he said, without a moment's hesitation.

"So you've only ever been with one woman?"

"Well, there's been the odd donkey."

"It would have to have been very odd to let a culchie like you near it," she laughed. "I'll take that as a no then."

"Just because I'm from Portrush doesn't mean than I'm a culchie."

"Did she cheat on you?"

"The donkey or the wife."

She just glared at him.

"I don't believe so," he eventually admitted.

"Jeez!" she sighed. "I think I'm going to need another Guinness after that."

McCusker rose quicker than a homesick angel and walked over to the bar, purposely avoiding eye contact with the woman with the blonde hair, snow-white skin, and Ferrari-red lips.

Five minutes later he made his way back through the busier, noisier bar with two white tops.

"So you obviously wanted to get out of Portrush?" she continued, as though there'd been no break in their conversation.

"No," he admitted, eyeing his Guinness intently, "I'd have preferred to stay there but my replacement had already started. I thought about it long and hard and decided this: being a policeman is the only thing I can do. I enjoy being a policeman, I really do. My super up in Portrush, who is a good mate, rang around a few of his mates and Superintendent Larkin recommended Grafton, a recruitment agency just across the square from the Custom House, and within a week they'd found me a position on the detective side in the Custom House."

"So you're not a detective inspector?" she said, matter of fact.

"Just plain McCusker, thanks."

They both drank in silence for a few moments before McCusker ventured, "Have you ever been married, Inspector O'Carroll?"

"Lily's good when we're off duty, and no I haven't. Been close a few times," she offered through a regretful laugh, "but as you well know, having a life and being a member of PSNI just don't go together."

"But you are hopeful about the new man?" McCusker asked, noting that most of the Belfast police officers tend to pronounce the name of their force as "PS-Nigh".

"Well, I've discovered to my cost that single people rarely connect with single people who are looking for people – so they are mostly attracted to people already in relationships."

"You don't mean he's married?"

"No of course not!" she half laughed. "I can't believe I'm telling you all of this – it's just that he…well, let's just say there seems to be someone else waiting in the wings who he seems to be having a hard time getting rid of."

As they were leaving McHugh's she said that, as she was running a bit late, she would return to the bar, visit the ladies and freshen up before going straight out on her date. McCusker offered to wait with her.

"No, I'll be fine," she said rubbing his arm affectionately, "you scoot off now, I'll be fine. Toodaloo."

CHAPTER NINE

Sunday morning, same thing happened as Saturday morning; O'Carroll picked McCusker up at his flat early with an announcement on his door buzzer: "There's been a ransom note."

Belfast on a Sunday morning is one of the quietest cities in the world. McCusker based this thought on his time in Derry, Portrush, and his infrequent golfing trips to various exotic locations in the warmer parts of Europe. Most cities seemed to be quieter on Sunday mornings but Belfast positively languished in it. It was like a ghost town. As they drove past the stately Queen's University Lanyon building, McCusker would not have been surprised to have been confronted by balls of tumbleweed rolling down University Road.

"So, talk to me about golf McCusker – after all those years you must soon be ready to take on Rory McIlroy," O'Carroll started, as she sped through the streets.

"Actually, when Anna Stringer left, I realised I didn't even like it," he replied. McCusker didn't really mind having such conversations over a quiet drink in the evening, but he much preferred to talk about, and consider, current cases during the day.

"Who's Anna Stringer?"

"She was my wife."

"That's a weird way to address your wife.?"

McCusker ignored her – he didn't want to get into it now. "So what's the story with Polly O'Neill this morning?" McCusker asked, not even attempting to find a subtle way to change the conversation.

"Right, so..." O'Carroll replied, appearing equally happy to move the conversation back to their work, "as she was preparing for her early morning walk she found a foolscap sheet of paper had been dropped through her letterbox."

"Handwritten?"

"In your dreams McCusker!" she laughed. "Cut and paste from newspapers and magazines."

"And the gist?"

"The gist was something like: 'We have your boys in separate locations. Prepare £999,950 for Monday delivery – to be advised. Do not involve police. We will kill.' End of message."

"Fifty quid short of a million...that's strange, isn't it. Any more photos?"

"No photos, just the short and sweet message," O'Carroll replied. "I was going to check kidnapping insurance policies to see if the system is easier if the ransom is under a million pounds."

"Fair point, and you'd have to think a distinct possibility. What about the father – what's his take on the new development?"

"Polly said he wasn't up yet and she didn't want to wake him because he won't allow her to involve us."

"Well, Ryan and Lawrence's lives are clearly in danger. The super will allow us to investigate," McCusker said, as they pulled into Malone Park. "The kidnappers are clever. They're not getting involved in any direct discussions or negotiations and by stating the boys are in separate locations they are insinuating that if we find one, the other will be killed."

"Do you think there is any chance that they are monitoring this house?" O'Carroll said, suddenly becoming very self-conscious.

"Good point," McCusker said, straining his neck in every direction possible. "Just pull in to the side of the road. You wait here."

Even for a policeman, if you imagine there are men hiding in trees, then you most certainly twitch at every rustle of every leaf in every bush. If you imagine men with binoculars to be lying on rooftops, then every rook shadow and squawk cannot fail to provoke a double-take.

McCusker walked up the entire length of Malone Park and down the other side, and after he was convinced no one was overtly monitoring O'Neill's house he directed O'Carroll into the driveway through the perfectly manicured lawn. Once again Mrs O'Neill beat them to the punch by opening the door before they'd a chance to ring the bell.

She presented the ransom note to O'Carroll, who was already gloved up. McCusker would have bet a month's pension on the fact they'd find no fingerprints or other incriminating evidence on or about the page.

"I can't let you keep it," Polly O'Neill whispered, "even with this he'll still be saying I'm stupid, to anyone who will listen."

"What time did you discover it?" McCusker asked.

"6.20 this morning."

"What time did you go to bed?" McCusker continued.

"About half past midnight."

No wonder you're so thin and stressed, McCusker thought as he said, "And the note wasn't here then?"

"Definitely not," she replied, looking like she desperately wanted to be able to help the police. "I'd a quick look before I double-bolted the door on my way up to bed and it most certainly wasn't here then."

If they had been allowed, the detectives would have taken the note back to the Custom House and within six hours the independent forensics department would have identified which publications the cut-out letters had come from, the make of the paper and possible points of purchase, and the type of glue used to secure the lettering to the page.

McCusker had to admit to himself that the final line of the note, "We Will Kill," was much more dramatic and threatening on the page than when O'Carroll had recalled the words to him.

They heard movements upstairs. Polly reacted like a deer alerted by the snapping of a distant twig in a forest. Her head nearly managed a complete 360 degrees in two quick movements. She speedily tore the note from O'Carroll's grasp, hopped back into the hallway, and closed the door in one beautiful unchoreographed movement.

"So what can we do?" O'Carroll asked when they were back in her feisty Mégane.

"We can continue our investigation," McCusker started, and retreated to thought for a few moments. "Or we put the house under twenty-four-hour surveillance, whether we embarrass Mr O'Neill in front of his neighbours or not, knowing that at some point either James or Polly is going to take the million – minus fifty – quid to the drop point and they'll hopefully lead us to the kidnappers."

"You're sure there's more than one?"

"Yep. They say 'we' in the note and one person is never going to be able to kidnap two young men in their prime."

"Do you think any one of them would be suitable for my sister Grace?"

"Lily!" McCusker laughed.

"Just kidding," O'Carroll said sheepishly, "well only half kidding. And I did say you could call me Lily, but only when we're off duty."

"Noted," McCusker replied officially. "And I'm assuming you were referring to the O'Neill brothers and not the kidnappers for your sister," he said, picking up the original thread.

"McCusker! You're just as bad as me!" O'Carroll said taking a half-hearted punch at him with her left arm. "Mind you, the kidnappers are definitely going to be a lot richer than the O'Neills."

McCusker hadn't a reply to that one, choosing instead to spend the remainder of the journey back to the Lagan-side Custom House in silence.

Once again Station Duty Sergeant Matt Devine greeted them at the door with a message to report immediately to Superintendent Larkin.

"What's he doing in on a Sunday morning?" O'Carroll asked, as they climbed the large ornate staircase.

"I'm figuring we're just about to find out."

CHAPTER TEN

"The body of an American has been found down on Cyprus Avenue," Superintendent Niall Larkin announced as they entered his office.

Before they'd a chance to digest the news Larkin, who was clearly dressed for the golf course continued. "O'Carroll, you're the lead on the Brothers O'Neill kidnapping, so I'm going to keep you on that with DI Jarvis Cage. McCusker you're on…"

"Ah, come on sir, not DI Richard Head, please!" O'Carroll pleaded.

"There is no other way I can cut it and shake it at this time Detective Inspector; clear up the kidnapping quickly and we'll have another chat about it."

O'Carroll clearly knew when not to push her luck, and complied with a bordering-on-unnoticeable curtsy, hands clasped dutifully behind her back.

"Okay here's the thing," Larkin continued, addressing McCusker, "we have no Senior Investigating Officers available so I am going to be the SIO on record on this case McCusker; you'll be my point man. Please for heaven's sake just remember that as you are agency staff you really will have no official jurisdiction so always ensure you have Detective Sergeant Willie John Barr - or whomever I nominate - by your side to make sure your searches, questioning, and arrests are by the book. Apart from that just go about your work the way you normally do. Barr is waiting for you in your office, McCusker. He'll get you up to speed and take you down to the scene. The CSI team are already in situ. Thanks," Larkin concluded by way of dismissing him.

McCusker left O'Carroll bringing Larkin up to speed with the recent developments on the Brothers O'Neill kidnapping, as the super seemed to have christened the case.

Mrs Sheila Lawson, her famous fresh brewed coffee and Jaffa Cakes were nowhere in sight.

CHAPTER ELEVEN

As McCusker was driven down Cyprus Avenue, by the aforementioned DS WJ Barr, he wondered what had happened on this leafy upmarket street that would have troubled a teenage Van Morrison so.

Barr, a much more considerate driver than O'Carroll, carefully parked the unmarked car alongside three yellow-and-blue-chequerboard police patrol cars, one Land Rover, an ambulance, and one large Scene of Crime portable wagon.

They remained in the car for a few minutes while the DS briefed McCusker on what he knew.

At exactly 8.40 a.m. a Miss Julia Whitlock made a 999 call. As a recording of the telephone conversation, courtesy of Police Control at Castlereagh, would later prove, Miss Whitlock was in a hysterical and distraught state. She had apparently, as was her usual Sunday morning habit, gone to collect her brother, Adam.

When she'd arrived that morning she discovered her brother's front door was already open. She noticed it hadn't been forced. She claimed she knew she shouldn't have entered the house but something stronger pulled her, in spite of herself. She thought her brother might have been in danger and she was helpless in trying to resist being there for him, whatever that entailed. She was relieved to find the living room, bathroom, main bedroom, spare bedroom, and makeshift of-fice-cum-gym were all empty, although she did note that her brother's bedroom had been slept in. She claimed her brother was good at look-ing after himself, as in being able to make his own bed every day and keep the house relatively tidy.

She sat down in the living room, relieved that nothing untoward appeared to have happened. She admitted to herself that she had feared the worst. Perhaps her brother had been burgled and he had probably gone off to report the incident to the police. Her heart was still pounding and she was surprised by how much the whole incident had exhausted her, so she went to her brother's kitchen to help herself to a strong, heavily sugared cup of tea to fight off the effects of the shock to her system.

Julia Whitlock's legs completely buckled under her and she collapsed into his splattered blood when she saw her brother, Adam Whitlock's, sad remains.

Still panicking – fiercely because her brother's blood was all over her – she called the police on her mobile. When two uniformed constables arrived to secure the scene she had been screaming so loudly her throat was raw and her voice was totally shot. She filled them in as best she could and was then sedated by members of the ambulance crew who had just turned up.

Barr then checked his notebook.

The deceased was a thirty-three-year-old American, living in Belfast since his university days and working at Mason, Burr & Co., one of the oldest firms of solicitors in the city. His sister claimed she would pick him up every Sunday morning to drive to the Queen's University Sports Complex in the Botanic Gardens. Rain or shine, they would do a little light training, have a fruit juice, stroll along the Lagan side on the Stranmillis Embankment, have a coffee, collect their Sunday newspapers, and finally she'd drop him back home again by 11.30 a.m., at the latest, whereupon they'd both go about their own business for the remainder of the day.

That was as much as Barr knew. He and McCusker exited the car and simultaneously crunched their way up the gravel drive to the grand red-bricked, Edwardian, detached house, down on Cyprus Avenue.

McCusker disliked the new casual dress code (or lack of it) of modern day detectives. He liked detectives to be smartly turned out, mainly for two important reasons that were lurking in his subconscious. Firstly, their salary was paid by the general public, therefore it seemed only fitting that they would be properly turned out while serving the same public. Secondly, in today's society it was easier to pick out suited, shirted, and tied people in crowds. However, equally he accepted that there were exceptions to every rule and some detective inspectors and even superintendents thrived on scruffing up in order to blend in better with their foe. DS WJ Barr was not one of those detectives. He was just under five foot, ten inches, slim, in good shape with neatly side-parted brown hair and very well turned out in his white chinos, black blazer, blue shirt and his one token to a laid-back approach: his red Manchester United tie.

McCusker accepted that these thoughts about the collective dress sense of the PSNI served only to delay his first examination of the corpse. He also knew, having been through this seventeen times before, that when he eventually set eyes on the victim for the first time, his tongue would be tied every time he tried to speak.

Nonetheless he was forced to try when he came upon the remains of Adam Whitlock in the deceased's kitchen. "Oh my Go…." McCusker could not remember a time when "remains" more aptly described a corpse.

Thanks to DS Barr, McCusker was already dressed head to toe in a blue translucent suit with only the skin of his face uncovered. He had to take a step backward and steady himself on the back of one of the six matching white farmhouse-style chairs positioned around a large, rectangular pine table. He was tempted to sit down for a moment or two but was aware he was being discreetly observed by other members of the Custom House CSI team.

One of these was the pathologist Anthony Robertson, a Scot, who was quietly going about his work. McCusker focused on Robertson's examination as a way of escaping the undeniable pull of the corpse.

The pathologist had already sealed the victim's hands in plastic bags to protect the potential evidence the perfectly manicured fingernails might be hiding. He was focusing on the corpse's head, which was slumped away from McCusker. It appeared that someone had made an attempt at severing it completely.

Robertson's progress distracted him just long enough for his delaying tactic to be effective and the shock of the scene started to ebb away. It was at this point that McCusker felt strong enough to address the corpse as the primary source of evidence, rather than a victim. He clicked into gear; his motive to find who did this to Adam Whitlock and prevent it from happening to anyone else.

Whitlock's matching royal blue sweats, trainer bottoms and shoeless white socks were totally drenched in blood. It was hard to tell the original colour of his blood-matted hair, which looked like it had been spiked by a cricketer's barber.

McCusker knelt down beside the corpse on his hunkers. Through the mass of cuts, welts, and blood McCusker thought he could make out a face; thought he got a glimpse of the man the corpse had once been.

When he looked into the eyes of a stranger, McCusker often wondered whether it was possible to deduce the physical battles their body had been through, just by reading their face. Did that person smoke, eat bad food, drink too much – would these indulgences manifest themselves physically? He always found it funny that unhealthy people compensated with a bit of yoghurt or honey in their diet, like this would somehow balance out their junk food diet. What could the lines on a face tell you? What could an observer detect from the purity in the whites of the eyes? Would it be possible to tell how much time the stranger had left? He sighed loudly and accepted that no matter how much of this was possible, nobody could ever have accurately predicted Adam Whitlock's demise; what had he done in his life that had resulted in his body being destroyed in such a gruesome way?

On first glance the only distinguishing feature on the corpse was that his fair, sun-deprived skin looked like it had never once been subjected to a shaving blade.

Before McCusker stood up again he silently muttered the two questions he always found himself asking the corpse: "Who did you love? What were your dreams?"

At a suitable break in the proceedings Barr introduced McCusker to Robertson.

"Bloody frenzied attack," Robertson started off in his broad dialect. "It's impossible to say which, if any, of these slashes killed him."

"Surely it must have been more than one of them?" McCusker offered, thankful to be back on solid ground again.

"Well on first examination all of the cuts look somewhat superficial," Robertson said. He sounded like Billy Connolly on a half dose of Valium. The only characteristic missing from the comedian's repertoire was the frequent "Aye."

"Hatchet?" McCusker guessed, if only from the amount of spilt blood.

"Nah, much smaller, I'm pretty sure it was more like a knife," Robertson assessed, "and I'd have to say we're looking at the work of someone who didn't know what they were doing with the weapon, whatever it was."

"Male or female?" McCusker asked, happy to have met a pathologist who seemed happy to entertain thoughts this early.

"I'll be able to take a better stab, oops sorry…I meant…I will be able to take a better *guess* at that when I get him on the slab, that'll be first thing in the morning."

McCusker kept looking at Robertson.

"At least you have the decency not to ask me the question in your eyes, but I will, at the very least, hazard a guess for you, if you'd don't hold me to it?" Robertson responded.

"But of course," McCusker agreed.

"Okay, if you work in the midnight to 3 a.m. window, I don't think you'll be far wrong."

Barr duly noted this down in his notebook.

"Aye," Robertson said, when he noticed Barr's diligence, "and could you also laddie note down there in your wee book that I said I didn't want to be held to it."

"I already had, sir," Barr confirmed, as he hit a full stop somewhere on his page as if to emphasise the fact.

***

The house wasn't as large as it appeared from the outside. The décor was too modern, the colour selection too bland, the lighting trying too hard to be hip and cool. The overall result was much too disrespectful to the integrity of the house for McCusker's taste. It was clean and tidy though.

The fingerprint girl reported she was finding several good examples at the scene. There were no traces of blood outside of the kitchen. There had not appeared to be a robbery. There were no broken windows. The CSI team couldn't find a safe, a stash of cash, or any drugs or pills.

The house down on Cyprus Avenue could have been anyone's house really. Well, anyone who could afford the £500,000 to £600,000 it would take to secure a house in that area, that was.

As Robertson supervised the removal of the body, McCusker and Barr quickly examined the living room with its hi-tech entertainment centre, antique drinks cabinet, three large comfortable and expensive-looking matching leather chairs, and quite a few pieces of modern art, both sculptures and paintings.

Next stop for McCusker and Barr was Adam Whitlock's bedroom and en suite bathroom. They discovered nothing untoward there either. The only medication was Strepsils (several packets) and Aconite dispensers (a few) in the medicine chest above the bathroom sink, along with his wet-shave gear, toothpaste, toothbrushes (two, one unused) and some Armani body spray. His largish wardrobe housed clean shirts, mostly white with a few blue; expensive looking jeans and trousers; one silvery blue two-piece suit; several jackets; one leather jacket; drawers with fresh underclothes and socks; and maybe half a dozen loud ties.

"Let's hope there are more pickings in the office-cum-gym," McCusker muttered, as Barr led him in that direction.

The office was obviously where Adam Whitlock spent the majority of his time. The gym section was nothing more than a bench with weights, a rowing machine and a cycling machine, all tidily placed in the far corner of the room, next to a large window overlooking his back garden.

By contrast his desk was placed just behind the stripped pine door (the only such door in the house) into the room closest to the top of the stairs. The desk was tidy with a Dell computer set up in the centre, a printer to the left, and a radio (tuned to Radio Ulster); a pen and pencil pot and a notepad to the right. The drawers contained files, blank paper and designer stationary. Each of the three non-window walls were decorated with photos: on the wall to the left of the entrance door hung a large Getty print of Paul Newman, cigarette at the draw. Next wall to the right had a large eye-catching colour photograph of Belfast's city lights, then the window wall, and then on the fourth wall a group of three identically sized and framed photos. The central one showed Whitlock posing for the camera with a distinctive-looking woman Barr confirmed as Whitlock's sister, Julia. The photo to the right was another of Julia by herself, wearing the same outfit, and the third showed Whitlock solo. All three photos looked like they were from the same session. Underneath them was a large bookcase neatly packed with paperback editions of airport thrillers and crime fiction titles.

To McCusker's eye this room – the whole house in fact – looked more like an expensive hotel set-up, rather than a home. He left Barr to give the drawers a thorough check and supervise the CSI team packing away the computer for closer examination. He went off in search of a basement and found a den space, with a gigantic television screen and, quite literally, thousands of DVDs.

He wandered out into the overgrown back garden as darkness fell. He hadn't admitted it to even himself but he secretly hoped that he would discover a garden shed that would contain all the clues he needed on the victim's life.

His hungry stomach groaned. Where had the day gone? DS Barr wandered across to him.

"Apparently Julia Whitlock is still too heavily sedated to be interviewed. Tomorrow morning would be best, the doctor reckons."

"Other family members?" McCusker asked.

"None here in the city," the DS reported. "Father, Wesley, and brother, Jaime, are booked on a flight out of Boston this afternoon their time and will be here in the morning."

"The mother?"

"She died several years ago."

"Okay, in the meantime let's get back to the Custom House and see what we can dig up on Adam Whitlock. Let's also see what the team can pull from the computer. And you know what," McCusker ordered, as what sounded like an afterthought but wasn't, "let's get every constable we can muster out knocking on all the doors on a thorough house-to-house around here. Someone must have seen or heard something."

His biggest fear was they were about to enter the hurry-up-and-wait phase of the investigation just a wee bit too quick for comfort.

CHAPTER TWELVE

As McCusker entered the Custom House just after 6 p.m. he met O'Carroll in the reception area. She hadn't turned up any additional information on the Brothers O'Neill case. By now they'd reviewed as much CCTV footage as their eyes could manage and there hadn't been a single sighting anywhere in the city.

McCusker brought her up to speed on his case and they discussed when she was going to take her days in lieu off. As a DI, O'Carroll wasn't entitled to overtime, but rather time off for each official hour she worked over and above. McCusker was happy to work all the hours God sent him. As a member of Grafton Agency staff he got overtime for everything over thirty-seven and a half hours each week. It wasn't just that the agency took a third of his income – he didn't bill anywhere near the hours he worked. No, mostly he was happy for the complete distraction his work brought, due entirely to the sad fact that he did not have a life outside of it.

McCusker, like a lot of men, went into denial when his wife up and left him. His other truth was his acceptance that at least some, if not the majority, of the fault was his. He knew he wasn't a particularly good husband. He'd also recently admitted to himself that he wasn't in love with his wife and accepted that he never had been. His real love, the one and only love of his life, was his love for the art of detection. Pure and simple, he loved the art of solving the puzzle of the crime. He conceded that the addiction for his fix came not from catching and incarcerating criminals, or even ensuring that the innocent went free, no, not at all in fact. It really was all about the solving of the puzzle. His study of why humans might wish to harm one another was undertaken only as being a useful aid in his endeavours to seek the solution of the crime.

He was prepared to put up with anything as long as he put himself in a position to be able to follow his passion. Yes, even to the extent that he was prepared to return to student style accommodation in an area of Belfast densely populated by students. In point of fact he neither minded his apartment nor its location. Students were always going somewhere, doing something or conversing with each other as though their lives depended on it. Their collective energy was truly infectious. And now here he was barely a month after leaving Portrush, and a couple of months on from losing his wife, and he was in the middle of a case he could really get his teeth into. McCusker would never admit, even to himself, to taking actual enjoyment from his cases (as in taking enjoyment from other people's misfortune), but it was something he just *had* to do, and enjoyment was never really a consideration. McCusker was more than satisfied to block everything else in his life out in order to best serve, and hopefully solve, the case.

O'Carroll hoped her case might be wrapped up by the following weekend mainly because she was hoping to head down to Dublin on Thursday night with her sister, for a long weekend. "A better class of men down there, McCusker," she claimed.

"In your dreams," McCusker teased, as he silently assumed her date the previous evening mustn't have gone well.

"Aye, well it looks like my dreams might be the only place I get to meet Mr Right," she said, studying McCusker. "So...what age are you?"

"Sorry?" McCusker responded in disbelief.

"No, no, you fool, not for me – I was thinking of introducing you to me sister, but on second thoughts you're right, best not. Mañana, McCusker."

"Hopefully," he replied, as they both walked off in opposite directions.

As McCusker started to wonder what O'Carroll's sister looked like – and he'd have to admit that the signs were not great if O'Carroll had to work so hard to fix her up – he suddenly flashed back to the remains of Adam Whitlock. That was more than enough to remove all invasive thoughts from his mind.

Chapter Thirteen

"I was very, very close to Adam," Julia Whitlock volunteered the following morning. "I had a brother who died at birth and so when my next brother, Adam, was born I kept asking my mum 'How old does Adam need to be before we are sure he's not going to die?' I was only four or five at the time but I remember willing with all of my might that Adam would not die the way my other brother had. I suppose maybe that fear has never gone away; I'd just buried it in my subconscious."

"I'm really sorry to put you through this now," McCusker offered, visibly moved with her information.

"Excuse me," she replied, "I need to take a break; I'll be back shortly."

Actually, she didn't look that upset to McCusker.

They were in Julia's flat, the top floor, right-hand, corner apartment in the number twelve block of The Arc, which was situated in the dramatic Abercorn Basin in the Titanic Quarter of the city. Spring was just around the corner and the sun lit up the waterfront area spectacularly. It was easy to see why so many people had committed to properties in this development. Sadly, by the time the triad of twelve-storey apartment blocks had been completed, the original investors' enthusiasm was tempered by the 2009 recession, and some buyers turned to the courts in an attempt to avoid their former agreements. Not so for Miss Whitlock – her father had bought her the apartment and he was, according to DS Barr's internet research, "recession proof."

McCusker spent the beginning of the first day of the new week and the first real day of the investigation basking in the glory of the views from Julia's lounge windows (noting that both the lounge and the windows were very large) and appreciating how the landscape was free from the eyesore electricity-generating windmills now generously peppered around the island of Ireland.

McCusker was surprised at just how much pleasure he got from being in Belfast. Until his recent separation from his wife he'd considered himself, at fifty-one years of age, a committed Portrush man, and he thought he'd see out his years there. Belfast had always left him cold and as the majority of his infrequent trips to the city concerned various aspects of his police business, he was always happy to get back on the M2 in the direction of Derry and Portrush as quickly as possible. But now that he was living there, in admittedly a more relaxed era in his life – a single man with a lot of time to kill – he was happy to get to know Belfast, slowly, cautiously; maybe even a little similar to how it is getting to know a new friend.

Belfast was buzzing again. The drab decades worth of engrained dour greyness had given way to loud modern splashes of colour all around the city centre. It was as if David Hockey and Neil Shawcross had challenged each other to a colour infused duel around the streets and buildings of the city. Even the high streets' apparent preference for the uniform, trade-mark branding of shops and store frontages, which had a tendency to make all city centres look the same, was okay…for now. Later, when troubles and recessions were but a distant, though not forgotten, memory, Belfast's uniqueness and originality would rise again and surely put an end to the superstore's world domination plan.

The same shops and stores plus the hotels, pubs, clubs, and concert venues were heaving with people again. The people who currently couldn't afford any of those fine establishments were content simply to take to the streets for their entertainment, happiness, and joy. The welcoming smiles and hospitality offered to strangers, such as McCusker himself, were as genuine as they were grand. And this was all from a city that had been in real danger of becoming a ghost town in the not too distant past. McCusker took note of this fact and was heartened by it.

It was as if Belfast too, like McCusker, was single again and maybe even feeling a wee bit frisky. McCusker found that he was involuntarily giving Belfast's legendary beautiful women the second and sometimes even third glance, something he couldn't remember doing since late school or college days.

McCusker reckoned that he and Belfast had both reached a good time in their life cycle. They were both starting over, and both were happy in doing so. He was thrilled to be getting to know the city; getting to know it in this era.

McCusker then remembered what he'd committed himself to when he'd left Portrush. He'd promised himself that he would forget the past, ignore the future, and get lost in the present. Looking down over Belfast from Julia's spectacular flat he hoped he'd make as good a stab at it as Belfast seemed to be doing.

From the kitchen end of the lounge McCusker could hear Julia Whitlock return.

"Would you like tea or coffee?" she called out to him, perhaps as a signal that she was back.

"Coffee would be great."

He got up from his ringside seat of one of the greatest views on earth. On the left, the Black Mountains rose gently, just over the arena of the Odyssey Complex. To the right, the water, boats and banks of the Lagan faded into Cave Hill, with Belfast Castle cosily set into the trees just below Napoleon's Nose, which was framed by the right-hand side of Julia Whitlock's spectacular vista. Lower down to his right was the silvery, angular, Titanic Exhibition Centre, the new eye-catching six-storey building. McCusker reminded himself that Quasimodo could also have been considered eye-catching. He thought that if there was a local filmmaker who could do justice to these sights say, for instance, the way Woody Allen had managed to capture the magic of Manhattan, then tourists from all over the world really would flock back to the city in their thousands. He reluctantly turned his back on the window and wandered back towards her.

"I'm sorry about that Inspector," she started.

"McCusker will do," he offered remembering the agency rule of always making it clear he was void of rank. "I'm what is known as an agency man."

"What, like freelance?"

"Kind of," McCusker said, unsure of where he was going with this.

"Oh my goodness, you mean like the Pinkertons?" she gasped.

"Something like that," McCusker offered, thinking that Grafton Recruitment's thirty-odd years in business didn't quite match up to the Pinkertons' recent 150th anniversary.

"Oh, that's absolutely fabulous! I'd no idea you did that over here."

"It's become more popular recently with all the early retirement offered at the time of the Patten Report," McCusker offered, thinking that Julia Whitlock was visibly relaxing a little.

"I'm sorry about earlier there, it's just I had spent the morning preparing myself for a more formal type of interview and then you...well, you looked and sounded like you really were sorry that we need to do this now and I felt myself welling up again. But look, here's the thing: I've talked to my father about this and I know it's vitally important to you that you get as much information as quickly as possible in order that we find the terrible people who did this to poor Adam, so I've got myself psyched up and ready for this."

"Can I help at all?"

"An Ulsterman making coffee? I don't think so!" she laughed. "You should go back over there and enjoy my expensive view a bit more. I'll bring some proper American coffee over in a minute or two," she said, betraying the fact that she still had a little more psyching up to do.

She joined McCusker by the movie-screen window and poured coffee for them both. The smell alone was enough to ensure he would be alert for at least the next twelve hours.

"Would you like one of these cakes?" she offered. "I just love them. The man in the shop downstairs sells them; they're rock cakes or something, I believe."

"Paris buns," McCusker offered, as his first gulp of coffee had his eyeballs explore the entire 360 degrees of his sockets.

"Sorry, so they're French are they? I thought they were local."

"You're 100 per cent correct, they are from Ulster. They're called Paris buns because they're vaguely, supposedly, in the shape of the Eiffel Tower," McCusker explained, mentally setting up his first question.

"Of course," she smiled, studying the cake closely. "How quaint."

McCusker figured Julia Whitlock was in her mid-thirties. She was not beautiful in a classic way, but there was something about her that McCusker found attractive. He wondered if perhaps it was her physical confidence. Today, as a mark of respect to her brother, she was wearing a classy sober black dress with a black woollen cardigan. Her make-up didn't exactly enhance her features as much as have her look like she was wearing make-up. Her long, thick, dark brown hair looked like it benefited from having recently been blow-dried.

"How long have you and your brother lived in Belfast?"

"Let's see now..." she began slicing off a quarter of her Paris bun, "Adam, encouraged by our father who'd also spent some time in the city, moved here when he was eighteen; that would have been in 1999. I was a late bloomer; I arrived in 2001 when I was twenty-five. He finished at Queen's in 2005 and flew home to Boston for the rest of that year and all of 2006. Then he returned here to Belfast again early in 2007 to start his job with Mason, Burr & Co. I finished at Queen's in 2007 and started work with the City Hall information department the same year."

At the end of her answer she started nibbling on her Paris bun, using a napkin to catch the crumbs.

McCusker had, by this stage, already devoured a quarter of his bun. He felt he desperately needed something to soak up the triple-A strong coffee in order to save his insides for another day. He jotted the dates in his notebook and appeared to consider them before saying: "So what did youse both study?"

"Adam always wanted to be a lawyer like our father so he'd already decided on the law course. That's why he came to Belfast; he and my father did their research and discovered that an old and respected colleague from my father's time in Belfast was in charge of the course at Queen's. I, on the other hand, only really came to Belfast because Adam was here. I did Social Studies and Media. I was quite lucky, getting a job so quickly at the City Hall. They had their refurb planned and they wanted to have a new team in place when they re-opened to the public last year."

"Do you know much about what Adam does?"

"He wasn't allowed to discuss his work," she replied.

"Where is Mason, Burr & Co. located?" McCusker asked, and then finished off the last of the fresh bun.

"It's that old bank building on Royal Avenue."

"Do you know who he reports to?" McCusker asked, his fountain pen at the ready.

"He heads his own department, Inspector," she said proudly.

"Sorry...just plain McCusker," he corrected her again.

She shot him a quizzical glance, looking slightly confused, but didn't voice the question in her eyes, even managing to force a smile.

"Adam's apartment didn't look very lived in," McCusker began awkwardly.

"You're trying to ask me if he was dating?" she offered, playfully and helping him out.

There were times in their conversation when it was clear that she had...forgotten would be too strong a word, maybe more like it had slipped her mind...that her brother had died. Since her brother's death was a very recent event, McCusker knew that she hadn't come to terms with it yet. Equally he knew that, in fits and starts, the horrific circumstances of his death would creep into her consciousness until there'd be nothing left but the sense of loss. It would totally overwhelm her life from then on for a time and perhaps, partially at least, forever.

"Well, yes?" he answered.

"Adam is..." she started and then McCusker noticed the powerful effect of one of his predicted gunks hitting her. This one was clearly massive and smashed straight bang into her like a full speed train "...sorry, sorry, Adam *was*...preoccupied with his work. He trained a bit, he worked a lot and we hung out together for the rest of the time."

"So, no girlfriends or...partners?"

"No girlfriends or boyfriends, McCusker," she said, pronouncing his name without his title like she was trying it out for the first time.

"And yourself?"

"Currently no boyfriends," she admitted easily. "Nor girlfriends."

"Okay."

She studied McCusker like she was trying really hard to ascertain his thoughts.

"Sorry," she offered, "I don't mean that we'd both forsaken boys and girls because we had each other. Of course I went out on dates and Adam sometimes took colleagues, or friends of colleagues, or friends visiting from America, out to dinner, but neither of us was in what you would call a serious relationship."

Again, she appeared to sense McCusker's uneasiness. He felt she was too physically confident, without even a hint of flirting with him, for her not to be a veteran in the troubled fields of romance.

"Now I will admit to you," she began, looking like she hoped to clear up this matter, "that if Adam wa...hadn't been around and I hadn't been around in his life so much then perhaps we would have been forced to try, shall we say, more diligently in the dating stakes."

That seemed to do it for McCusker, so she moved on. "When my dad bought this apartment for me Adam loved it and he preferred to spend time over here rather than at his own house. You know, what can I tell you – we were brother and sister, we were close, we…we enjoyed each other's company and were 100 per cent content in each other's company."

The words registered effectively with McCusker – he found it interesting that the last person to have made that claim was Susanna Homes in reference to her friends, the missing brothers O'Neill.

"So, tell me something about these dinner dates, these visiting friends of his, and yours?" McCusker asked.

"Okay, I suppose one of his closest friends would have been Ross Wallace, another ex-Queen's student from the same year as Adam. He works for Ulsterbus…" she paused for the effect of someone setting up an often used punchline "…no, not as a driver, but as an important part of their management team."

"Anyone else?" McCusker pushed.

"Adam also got on well with Angela Robinson – they were also at Queen's together - and Craig Husbands. We'd regularly have dinner together and the answers to your next two questions are: no, Angela is married and no, Craig is not my type, but our dinners together were always entertaining."

"Are you aware of anyone, anyone at all, who would have a grudge against Adam, you know, maybe as a result of some dealings which went wrong?"

Julia Whitlock looked like she was trawling through the memory banks of her brain. But on closer examination McCusker reckoned she looked like she could be considering whether or not to tell him something she'd rested upon.

"Well it…nothing really…I mean…"

"It's okay Julia – why don't you tell me and let me be the judge on whether it's important or not? Like your father advised you, this part of the process is vitally important," McCusker offered, feeling she needed a little encouragement.

"Okay. Well, back home in America our father had a house on Martha's Vineyard, just outside of Vineyard Haven on the way up to the library," she said as if McCusker would know either Martha's Vineyard, Vineyard Haven, or the road to the library in Vineyard Haven.

"When we were younger we used to summer there as a family. That would have been my mother, who's been dead now just over ten years; my father; Adam and our younger brother Jaime. As we got a bit older we felt we were a too old to hang out with our parents in the summer and so eventually we were allowed to go there by ourselves with some friends. In 1998 we went there – Adam, Jaime, and I and five other friends, there were three girls and five boys and…"

Julia Whitlock paused, as though recalling something from her past was too much for her in her present state.

McCusker didn't push her; he topped up her coffee cup to fill the space between them in her vast apartment.

"Goodness, I'd forgotten all about this, or maybe even pushed it out of my mind," she admitted, taking a large breath. "Okay, this is for Adam, get on with it Julia," she chastised herself before continuing. "One night we all went to Carly Simon's Hot Tin Roof, a club out by the airport. It's now known as Outerland. John Hiatt was playing and Adam's mate, Bing Scott, was a big fan of Hiatt. Bing's sister, Cindy, was younger than the rest of us but she hung out with us, a) because she was Bing's sister and b) because she had the hots for Adam."

Julia took another sip of her coffee and a few more crumbs from her Paris bun.

"So Hiatt plays. Bing is disappointed that Hiatt didn't have his band with him, but anyway we all sang along with him when he performed 'Have A Little Faith In Me' – a totally beautiful song. Eventually, it's time to go home. Somehow Cindy's had a bit too much to drink and is still totally flying when we get back to the house. We all go out into the garden, it's a really beautiful garden that goes right down to the water's edge. Bing goes to make a pot of coffee, mainly for his sister, who's over on the swing under the tree. She'd been calling Adam over to push her. Adam felt she was trying to get him under the cloak of the low lying branches for something other than pushing her on the swing, and so he pretended to ignore her."

Julia paused once again for another large intake of air.

"So Cindy keeps shouting for Adam but starts herself off on the swing, you know, leaning forward at one end of the arc and then back as far as possible at the other. Then we heard this loud dull thud. I swear to you McCusker, I'll never get that sound out of my mind for as long as I live. What can I tell you? It sounded positively fatal to all of us the moment we heard it. We all rushed over to her and she'd obviously been leaning so far back in the swing she'd fallen off and banged her head on the ground. Now if only there'd been earth below the swing, she might have gotten away with it. But some of the roots were exposed and that's what we all felt she must have come into contact with. She was a goner. Immediately! The freaky thing was that in a matter of half a minute her life was over. Finished! She didn't even have time to cry out in pain."

"Did Bing blame Adam?" McCusker felt compelled to ask.

"Not as much as Adam blamed himself."

"But it wasn't his fault," McCusker felt equally compelled to say.

"I know, and we all told him that, but Adam felt that if only he'd gone over to the swing he could easily have handled her childish, amorous advances. More importantly he'd have been able to control her drunken swinging."

"Was there an inquest?"

"Accidental death."

"How did Bing and Adam get on after that?" McCusker asked.

"Ah, Bing kept trying to keep the friendship alive but Adam was the one who let it slip away."

"Does Bing still live Stateside?"

"Yes, he qualified as a lawyer and stayed in Boston, is now happily married with a boy and a girl. The little girl is called Cindy."

"My next question might sound strange or even inappropriate to you but before I ask it I'll explain *why* I'm asking it," McCusker said in a quieter voice. "With an investigation, the important thing is to rule people out, as much as looking for suspects; the more people we rule out, the fewer suspects we have."

"It's okay," she said, helping McCusker out. "My father told me you would ask me what I was doing at the time of Adam's death. He also explained the thing about wanting to rule people out of the investigation, and he said that in a lot of cases the deceased will have been murdered by a family member or someone close to them. He advised me not to get worried when you asked these questions, as it is normal. So. Please tell me the time you need me to account for?"

"Between the hours of midnight Saturday night and 3 a.m. Sunday morning please?"

"Oh my, oh my, I didn't realise you'd have that worked out yet," she said welling up. "That's definitely the time? Poor Adam…"

"That's the time we believe he passed away," McCusker offered picking his way through a potential emotional minefield.

"But we both know he didn't just 'pass away', McCusker," she sobbed, now fighting for a breath which would allow her to get out what she needed to say. "That is the time he was brutally taken away from me. The time that my dear brother Adam was mur…"

That was as far as she got. She totally and uncontrollably broke down again, exactly as she had the previous morning.

McCusker waited with Julia Whitlock until her doctor turned up and sedated her again.

CHAPTER FOURTEEN

By the time McCusker returned to the Custom House it was just before noon. He was still happy to run on the Paris bun he'd enjoyed in Julia Whitlock's apartment and the porridge he'd made for himself before he left his flat at eight that morning.

O'Carroll was up and beyond high doh (as in doh-ray-me) in the detectives' office. Her chair and McCusker's to their respective desks virtually backed on to each other. In fact, their chairs were so close that her opening remark, on McCusker's third morning at the Custom House, was, "I wouldn't sit this close to you unless I knew you took a shower every morning."

Maybe that's why she hadn't spoken to him at all on McCusker's first or second day in the PSNI station; she was still checking him out.

"Oh God, am I happy you're back," she announced. "Polly O'Neill has just received another note from the kidnappers with details of the drop for the ransom." She passed a photocopy over to McCusker.

Ransom to be packed in sports holdall.

Left at Balmoral station today at 1.47, sharp.

Place in bushes, behind blue railings under

"Trains to" sign at entrance to Lisburn Platform no. 1

No tracking device. No police.

6 hours after successful collection

your sons will be released.

If this collection fails We Will Kill.

"A bit public a place for a drop, don't you think McCusker?"

"Or a very clever place," McCusker started, still studying the note. "There will be people around. The ransom collector can hide amongst the passengers until they are convinced there are no police about. Who's making the drop?"

"Polly O'Neill," O'Carroll said.

"Polly!?"

"I know, I know. The husband refused to do the drop. At first he even refused to pay the ransom. She threatened to leave him unless he paid up. He still refused. She then threatened him that she would tell everyone who would listen that they were having an affair while her first husband and O'Neill were still partners. But even with that she still had to threaten to produce evidence of his cheating her first husband out of his share of O'Electronics before O'Neill would pony up the ransom for the boys' release."

"Will a million quid fit in a holdall?"

"Apparently," she replied quickly and winked at McCusker before saying, "maybe the clever kidnappers had already calculated that the last fifty quid wouldn't fit in."

"And can Polly carry that amount of weight?" he continued, ignoring her attempt at humour.

"Okay, here's the thing; DI Cage is going to pretend to be a minicab driver and take her to Balmoral station, on the corner of Stockman's Lane and the Lisburn Road. He's wetting himself with excitement and he is down in the toilet at the moment 'getting into character'."

McCusker rolled his eyes.

"Meanwhile, you and I will be there 'as passengers', watching the proceedings to see if we can get a tail on the person the kidnappers get to collect the holdall."

"Is it even legal to be able to withdraw that kind of money these days?" McCusker offered as much to himself as to O'Carroll. "Surely the bank would have to file an SAR – a Serious Activity Report?"

"I've come to the conclusion that if you are the type of person who has those kinds of funds you are the kind of man who can put your hands on it, no matter what the laws of the land."

McCusker realised she was correct and spared no more time thinking about the SAR. He had his own case to get stuck into but he realised if O'Carroll solved her case, then there was a great chance she'd join him on the Adam Whitlock murder. But the Portrush detective also had to accept that there was a good chance, probably more like evens that Superintendent Larkin could assign DI Jarvis Cage instead.

"Okay, give me a few minutes...to get into *character*...and I'll be right with you."

She playfully punched him in the arm. McCusker noted that since their couple of drinks at McHugh's she'd become a lot friendlier with him. But she appeared self-conscious at her playful friendliness because she looked all around the busy office to make sure no one else had clocked it. Once she was confident it had gone unnoticed, she reverted to a harder tone. "Cut out the shit McCusker, let's get out of here."

"Let's put a car at both the station before and the station after Balmoral," McCusker said, as they waved off an in-character taxi driver, aka DI Jarvis Cage.

"Adelaide and Finaghy?" O'Carroll offered. "Why?"

"Because of the wording on the ransom note demanding they make the drop at the exact time," he replied as they climbed into her trusted, but bruised, Mégane. "They obviously plan to hop on the next train to make their escape."

"Good thinking Batman," she replied, buzzing away.

"What happens at Balmoral?"

"The King's Hall Showgrounds."

"Oh, I know it!" McCusker replied, happy to place it. "I went there in the summer of 1980 to see Van the Man, Mike Oldfield, Lindis-farne, and The Chieftains."

"Jeez, McCusker, if you ever get to meet my sister, please keep quiet about things like that. I'll bet you anything you want that you were wearing flares too?" she jibed. "How are we doing for time?"

"We're good, just gone 1 p.m.," McCusker said quickly, avoiding the flared trousers issue.

***

McCusker was a little uncomfortable in that he didn't know any-thing at all about the area. He'd been a teenager the last time he was there, for heaven's sake. As they drove up the Lisburn Road he had O'Carroll describe the Balmoral station and the surrounds as much as she could. He closed his eyes and had her repeat her information a second and then a third time. He then repeated it back to her and listened to her corrections.

He'd been on a few kidnaps up in Portrush. But none with anywhere near this hefty of a ransom. Of late, most kidnaps were 'tiger kidnaps', where an employee, usually the manager, of a bank or a building society, would receive a call from their home advising them that their families were being held captive, but they would be perfectly okay if said manager co-operated with the 'men' just about to visit him. McCusker didn't remember ever hearing of a kidnapping going wrong. But for some reason he was unable to take any comfort in this fact.

The Balmoral station was a Translink run enterprise on the Bangor to Newry line. The problem for McCusker was that most of the beautiful wee stations had recently enjoyed a makeover and they now all looked the same, and consequently boring. Balmoral was no exception, but quite possibly the station was about to experience the most exciting day in its 153-year history. And if everything went according to the PSNI plan then neither the station nor its staff would even be aware of what was going down.

McCusker had been expecting a small station, but not the absence of one entirely. Balmoral Halt (as it was actually referred to) turned out to be merely a platform departure and arrival facility. The kidnappers were really exposing themselves using this location for the drop-off and collection of the valuable holdall. The aforementioned entrance to platform number one was five yards down a sloping tarmac slip path, just opposite the pink art deco front of the historic King's Hall. Going straight on down the sloping tarmac path, there was a heavily graffitied, walled entrance to the right, and then straight was a sky blue tunnel, signposted "Trains to Belfast."

When O'Carroll and McCusker arrived it was 1.35 p.m. and there were a few people wandering around. McCusker clocked all of them. To his eyes no one looked suspicious. He checked again to see if any of them were acting a part; looking like they were, to quote DI Jarvis "in character."

"Nope," McCusker said to himself quietly. "No plonkers in sight."

He thought about Ryan and Lawrence. Could they possibly be aware that if everything went according to plan, this was the appointed time when their freedom might be won? Were they worried their father might not come up with the necessary funds? Were they together or had they been separated? Who suffered most when they were apart? O'Carroll reckoned that Ryan was the leader; did this mean Lawrence was the one having the more difficult time in captivity? Did either of them manage to get a good look at their captors and if they did, did they realise the serious implications of such a sighting?

O'Carroll and McCusker had agreed in advance to totally ignore each other. In a space as small as the entrance to platform number one, this was quite impossible to do. McCusker, in his dark blue suit, with uncombed hair, reading a crumpled copy of the *Belfast Telegraph* and giving off the air of someone who was totally happy in his own company, hoped he looked like a typical commuter. He strolled onto the platform where he had a perfect view of the selected drop point. O'Carroll, on the other hand, was slightly over-dressed and looked like she was either on her way to have her blow-dried hair blow dried one more time, or she was about to break the number one commuter rule and start up a conversation with one of her fellow passengers.

At exactly 1.45 p.m. Mrs Polly O'Neill walked down the slip path. Taking even the laws of gravity into consideration she was still making a very hard job of pulling a holdall attached by multi-coloured elasticised rope to a set of wheels and handle. She was sweating profusely but no one appeared to be paying any attention to her. McCusker's instinct, and what he would have done were it not for the current situation, would have been to go over to her and offer her assistance. His logic, always: if that was his mother, he'd hope someone would help her. He resisted, knowing Mrs O'Neill would most likely totally freak out and blow his cover if he did so.

The O'Neill's mother seemed to grow in confidence once she also established there were no unsavoury looking types in the vicinity. She trudged over to the designated area and, with a great deal of huffing and puffing, she eventually managed to get the holdall, minus the temporary wheels, into the bushes. O'Carroll shielded the manoeuvre as best she could by standing right behind her. McCusker suddenly realised that no one had given Mrs O'Neill instructions for what to do next. She hung around, appearing as though she was actually expecting someone to walk in with her two boys and take the holdall, hand the boys over to her, and leave the station. DI Jarvis Cage, as a Belfast City cab driver, came in and rescued her, leading her away.

Still McCusker could not see anyone who either looked suspicious or was eyeing up the holdall, now perfectly camouflaged in the broad-leaf bushes. McCusker shuddered at the thought of someone unconnected with the kidnappers spotting the pregnant holdall, fancying their chances and nabbing it. Hardly stealing?

McCusker heard the hissing of the 1.46 Lisburn-bound train coming down the track. O'Carroll, still avoiding eye contact with him, walked onto the platform.

The train was getting closer and closer, slowing down as it pulled into the station. Still no one appeared to be focusing on the bushes under the sign. McCusker could feel his heart beating faster and faster. It wasn't even as if they were going to try and apprehend the collector of the ransom. No, the deal was he and O'Carroll were there only to observe, to get a description of the person who collected the stash and pass the information on to the constable at the Adelaide Halt. He, depending on developments, could either board the train to keep eyes on the collector, or follow them by road if they alighted there.

The train pulled into the station, the doors wheezed open. Two elderly passengers got off and the doors hissed shut, but still no sign of activity around the bushes and still no movement.

Then a vision in black, from hoodie to toe, with a thick black beard, jogged down the slip path and made straight for the bushes behind the blue railings under the platform sign. He grabbed a handful of canvas of the holdall and yanked it out of the bushes in one confident energetic movement but, instead of heading in the direction of the train, he continued on down the slip path in the direction of the tunnel. The train had been an effective decoy. The collector had focused on the bag in the bushes, not bothering to scan the area for police. In fact, he didn't need to and the members of the PSNI all thought they knew where he was going next.

McCusker's first instinct was to pursue him but his second and more predominant was for the safety of the O'Neill boys so, figuring he was probably being watched, he stooped to untie and retie his shoelace, cautiously clocked the area and then, slowly at first, headed off down the tunnel in the same direction as the collector. By the time he reached the footpath down on Stockman's Lane – which was dangerously peppered with pigeon droppings – O'Carroll, some way or another, was already at the opposite side of the road in her dependable Mégane. Before McCusker had a chance to close the door and buckle up, she was in gear and speeding out of the underpass back up the Lisburn Road towards the city centre, signposted as being two and a half miles away to the north.

Within a few wordless seconds she and McCusker spotted the collector confidently jogging along the other side of the road past Paton Memorial Hall.

"What the fuck is that prat Cage doing?" she said, as they passed the hotchpotch of buildings better known as Kingsbridge Private Hospital on their side of the road.

"Shit, is that his cab?"

"Sadly," she shouted. "He's going to fuck this up."

Two cars ahead of them was DI Jarvis Cage, complete with his passenger Polly O'Neill in the back, barely five yards behind the collector and gaining on him all the time, although the collector was across the flow of traffic from the detective.

"Can you believe it? He looks like he is trying to apprehend the kidnapper!" O'Carroll hissed.

"He might just be the kidnapper's bag man out to collect the ransom," McCusker felt a need to add.

"Kidnapper or collector, either way it doesn't matter, Cage is going to fuck it up," she snapped at McCusker as if it were his fault.

Just then the collector took a sharp right off Lisburn Road into Malone Park. Cage looked like he'd just angled the car across the street in the direction of the collector, closed his eyes and put his foot down. Barely missing a bus, he followed the collector into Malone Park. A split second later he came to a very sudden halt with a loud metallic bang.

All McCusker and O'Carroll could do was to shake their head in disbelief and fear the worst, namely that Cage had ran over the collector.

Before O'Carroll had a chance to park the car properly McCusker was out of the metallic yellow Mégane and high-tailing it across the road in the direction of Cage. Mrs Polly O'Neill was very agitated, but otherwise fine apart from being slightly winded, having been strapped in. Without the luxury of his seat belt, Cage had gone head first into his airbag, which was now covered with rich tributaries of blood.

McCusker ran to the bonnet, expecting to find the collector in a poor way under the front of the car, only to discover that Cage hadn't run down the collector at all. No, in fact he'd driven into a series of eight steel bollards subtly positioned across the gated entrance to prevent vehicles from entering the park. At that same moment, he heard a scooter start up over to his right beside the single-storey, red-bricked Gate House which guarded the exclusive but lonely-looking park. McCusker turned just in time to see the collector, now wearing a white crash-helmet with a red flash, drive off into the distance, without even a backwards glance.

Cage's face was in a bad way but he was receiving not an ounce of sympathy from O'Carroll. She was attending to Polly O'Neill who was still screaming at Cage for endangering her sons' lives.

"'bout ye?" O'Carroll grunted to Cage through the driver's open window. When she saw that he'd live, she continued "Would you just look at yourself, Mucky Jarvis, Belfast's answer to Dirty Harry. Why don't you make *my* day and retire before the super sets you up with your next assignment: monitoring the sinkage cracks on the Custom House walls."

McCusker radioed the incident in, describing as best he could the black-bearded collector and the direction in which he'd sped off. The scooter's number plate had been concealed with mud, but no doubt the speedy two wheeler had been stolen anyhow. McCusker remained with Cage while they waited for an ambulance, while O'Carroll drove Mrs O'Neill back home, almost a million pounds the poorer and still no sign of her precious sons.

CHAPTER FIFTEEN

McCusker caught a taxi – a real taxi – back to the Custom House, arriving just in time to meet DS WJ Barr leaving to interview Angela Robinson, Adam Whitlock's QUB acquaintance and possible friend. Barr looked and acted decidedly disappointed when McCusker said he would accompany him on the interview.

Angela Robinson was waiting for Barr as they'd arranged in the reception of BBC Radio Ulster, which maybe accounted for Barr's disappointment. Angela was a producer and, introductions over, she secured the required passes and took them through to a suite of studios on the first floor. She offered them the choice of "bad coffee or worse coffee" – both of which they declined, taking instead a small cup of water from the cooler – before taking them through to a small empty studio. She closed the Venetian blinds on the internal window, affording them maximum privacy. They sat at the guest's arc table in the dimmed studio.

The BBC Radio Ulster producer seemed to have spent all her money and her attention on her hair, which was dark brown and worn with a fringe and down to a straight line just above her shoulders – a bit like Elizabeth Taylor in *Cleopatra*; in fact, a lot like Liz Taylor in *Cleopatra*, with not a single hair out of place. Even when she turned her head around quickly, as she was prone to do, her hair would umbrella out but then fall perfectly back a second after her head stopped. She had a boyish figure and wore no make-up, when a little would have helped to disguise her tiredness and strained features. Her work outfit comprised of a pink, short-sleeved, three-buttoned polo shirt with a BBC Radio Ulster crest and a shapeless, badly creased pair of either dark grey or black trousers – McCusker couldn't tell in the dim light of the studio.

Mrs Robinson seemed to have a preference for the younger DS WJ Barr. That was until she heard that McCusker had been stationed at Portrush for several years. She knew people up there and she reminisced about working at Barry's Amusements in holiday time to help fund her move to Belfast.

McCusker was distracted by all the microphones, decks, effects racks, computers, multi-coloured leads, lights and knobs – everything really that one person needed to broadcast a message or music to the province. Due to his junior's reticence, McCusker decided he'd start the proceedings. Barr was seated in the middle so McCusker spun around in his silent seat to face Angela Robinson.

"I believe you went to Queen's University with Adam Whitlock?" he said.

"Yes," she said as she looked up with that classic Princess Diana pose, head tilted to one side, both parties appearing to make eye contact by accident. "Detective Sergeant Barr told me the sad news. Have you any idea what happened?"

"We're still looking into it," Barr offered officially.

"So how long had you known him?" McCusker asked.

"Ah let's see," she began interlocking her fingers together and using them to hoist up her right knee, "probably a good six years or so now."

McCusker flashed her one of his "how did you meet?" looks. Surprisingly it seemed to work.

"You see, my future husband-to-be was friends with Adam's friend, Craig Husbands, and I seem to remember I was introduced to Adam and Craig around the same time I met Richard, my husband-to-be."

"And you've all been friends ever since?" McCusker asked.

"Well, not exactly. Adam went back to Boston after he won his PhD and he was there for a time; I think about a year. Richard and I got married in that time. When Adam came back and we all started to work – for some reason or other and I've never fully understood why to be honest – it was me who hung out with Craig. My husband…well, I've found that we seem to have his friends and my friends and, don't get me wrong, I believe that's quite a healthy situation."

"Did Adam and Richard have a falling out?" McCusker asked, as Barr continued to take notes.

"No," she sighed, "at university they all got on great; after university they just didn't seem very interested in each other's lives. This was

fine, because Adam, Craig, Julia, and I have a right old hoot some
nights and maybe as a fivesome, you know, and especially with a husband in the mix, the dynamics of the group can become unbalanced."

"Did Adam ever go over to your house for dinner or anything?"

"Nope, never – he's never ever been over at our house," she started
and stopped in her tracks, "I've just realised he's never going to do so
aga…"

Angela seemed to well up. Barr fussed around her for a bit trying
to comfort her.

"The advantage of not wearing make-up at work," she eventually
offered, "is that I can never spoil it."

"Okay," McCusker said, rubbing his hands to try and infuse some
energy into the interview. "Did Adam have any friends other than you
and Craig?"

"He must have had," she admitted, "but I really just knew him as
part of a foursome."

"Like you'd never see him by yourself, for a drink or something?"
McCusker asked.

"I don't think my husband would have been too happy with that,"
she said, trying to smile.

"That wasn't why Richard and Adam fell out, was it?" McCusker
pushed. "You know, over you?"

"They never fell out," she protested, "they just grew apart."

"What about you and Julia?"

"No, no Craig…as I said, it really was one of those American 'frat'
situations where it was always the four of us." She stopped and laughed
to herself. "I was just thinking we used to say, when we'd had a few and
we were on a particularly good evening, that we would do this, you
know have dinner together, the four of us, forever. That's not going to
happen again."

"Did he have a girlfriend?"

"He claimed not," she replied quickly.

"Does Craig have a girlfriend?"

"I think so," she replied, appearing to think before answering.

"Do you know much about Adam's work?"

"Bits, but I don't think it would be appropriate for me to talk about
it. Our chats were based on our friendship and not meant to go any
further…"

"But we will need to find out what he did," McCusker said.

"Then you're going to have to get that information from his work colleagues I'm afraid."

"How often would the four of your meet up?"

"Twice a month?"

"What were his hobbies?"

"He trained a bit, but not seriously. He went to the movies a lot, and I do mean a lot. I think he saw every new movie the first week of its release. No matter how busy he was he'd always make time for the movies. And if a film didn't make it as far as Belfast he'd wait for the DVD. He never mentioned football or sport or the likes. As I said, he trained or worked out a bit, I can never tell the difference. He was one of those people lucky enough not to consider their work a chore. He loved his work – *everything* else was a distraction."

"Music? Concerts?" McCusker pushed, since he was having a hard time getting some kind of sense of Adam Whitlock.

"He'd often say that music was like wallpaper to him. It was always there, but in the background. He never went to concerts; he felt there was too much focus on the lifestyle and not on the art."

"He and Julia seemed very close..." McCusker said, heading in another direction.

"They were brother and sister," Angela replied.

"Yes," McCusker conceded, sensing yet another dead end, "but even taking that into account, I didn't get the sense from her that it was a family obligation-type of relationship."

"Yep, I can see that," she offered. "Maybe though it was because they were really two exiles?"

"Possibly, but I don't think so," McCusker mused.

"Well Inspector..." she started.

"McCusker," he corrected.

"So you're not an inspector or a detective inspector?"

"No I'm an agency cop," McCusker offered, still concerned about how to deal with this issue and a little worried it might get in the way of things. "You were about to say something about Julia and Adam?"

"Oh yes. I was about to say that Adam was quite an extraordinary man, quite incredible really. Super intelligent and with all the downsides that produces. Julia, I feel, realised Adam's qualities and knew that the downside to it was he would, quite literally, have trouble tying his shoelaces."

"You mean she was happy to be there for him because he was someone special."

"I believe I do McCusker," she said, "I believe I do."

"What were you doing on Saturday past between the hours of midnight and 3 a.m.?" McCusker said, concluding that he had gathered as much as he would at this stage.

"I do believe I would have been with my husband at that time, sir," she said, flashing him another of Princess Diana's coy looks.

Chapter Sixteen

Just under two hours later at 6.40 p.m. as McCusker and O'Carroll, and later, her sister Grace, were about to leave for a drink at McHugh's to celebrate Monday's finish, a telephone call came in from the famous *Belfast Telegraph* columnist Eddie McIlwaine.

Eddie had just received a call from a person who claimed to know the whereabouts of Ryan and Larry O'Neill. The caller was female, or at least someone putting on a female voice. It sounded like it had been made from an outdoors phone box with very loud traffic in the background.

O'Carroll wrote down an address and advised the canny McIlwaine that she couldn't yet tell him what had happened to the O'Neill boys, but if he'd keep the information under wraps until she'd a chance to check out the location, she'd give him a proper exclusive on the full story. She politely resisted his persistent request to accompany them and finished her call with her telephone trademark "Toodaloo."

"Where are we going?" McCusker asked, as they headed back down the stairs.

"Tea Lane."

"Okay, where's Tea Lane?"

"Off Meeting Street, apparently."

"Where's Meeting Street?" McCusker continued, keen to add to his growing knowledge of Belfast.

"I haven't a clue," she admitted, "but if anyone knows it'll be the skipper, Matt Devine."

"Nope," Station Duty Sergeant Matt Devine admitted after some careful consideration, "new one to me." He continued as he drew out a few maps from his drawer and drew a blank on every one.

"Hang on a minute..." McCusker said, appearing to remember something, "someone is having fun with us."

"How so?" Devine asked.

"I have a feeling I've been there," McCusker said, trying to recall one of his numerous recce trips around the city. He liked nothing better than to spend his downtime exploring Belfast, and on every available opportunity he was off, some map or other in hand, embracing and exploring his new city. He thought he'd feel like he'd be "putting up" with Belfast because of his new circumstances and the need to make ends meet, when in actual fact he found himself to be very excited about his new workplace. Equally, it was an incredible time to be in Belfast now that it was in the throes of its long delayed rebirth. He felt that when the sun shone in Belfast there was no better a place to be. It was just that the sun had been losing the battle to the dark clouds for way, way too long.

The penny finally dropped for him and he said, "Just wait there a moment."

He dashed back upstairs to his desk and rummaged around in his drawer of prized maps and brochures for a while before he found what he was after. He returned to Devine and O'Carroll and threw down a UFTM pocket-sized map in front of them.

Matt Devine examined and unfolded it, smiling broadly as he smoothed it out. "Of course Ballycultra in the Folk Park – well remembered McCusker!" Devine said.

"What are youse two on about?" O'Carroll asked impatiently.

"It a replica of a typical Ulster town from about a hundred years ago, down at the Folk Museum on the Bangor road, out past the George Best Airport," McCusker offered, as the Station Duty Sergeant pointed to one side of a three-dimensional hand-drawn map and said: "Look there!"

On the extreme right hand side was Meeting Street, running parallel to the edge of the map and bordered on one side by the Presbyterian Meeting Church and by a tree-lined green on the other. Tea Lane lay alongside it.

"You're kidding me?" O'Carroll said.

"There's no other Tea Lane that I'm aware of," Devine volunteered.

"And as it's currently closed, what a perfect place to hide two kidnapped victims," McCusker offered to the empty space, which had until very recently been occupied by O'Carroll.

"Okay McCusker, let's go to your toy town, but let me warn you – on your head be it," she advised, cautioned, and then ordered, "Matt could you have an ambulance and another patrol car follow us out there as soon as possible, please."

Which is how twenty minutes later, accompanied by two Ulster Folk & Transport security men and a caretaker, they walked up a torch-lit Meeting Street in the Folk Park and turned left into Tea Lane. The street consisted of a sweet shop (O'Carroll reckoned the sweet shop was the prime reason McCusker remembered this spot) and six labourers' houses, which were built in the classic two-up, two-down, outdoor-toilet style. If McCusker hadn't known better he would have pegged these buildings as *really* having been built over a hundred years ago, and not within the last twenty years for the Folk Park. Unlike O'Carroll, mind, he'd had a chance to also examine them in the daylight.

The first two houses had been converted into public toilets. They tried the labourer's house nearest to the sweet shop. It was already locked and totally empty. The next wee house was also deserted, appearing as though the family had just been snatched from its midst by aliens leaving everything as it would have been last century.

They found Ryan O'Neill upstairs in the third house, sitting on the floor, his back against the far wall of the small bedroom. He was gagged with his hands bound with plastic cuffs behind his back – as were his feet. He looked a bit battered and bruised around his face and his hands.

"Have you got Larry? Is he okay?" were Ryan's first words once they'd managed to remove the gag from his mouth.

McCusker remembered that one of the ransom notes stated that the brothers were being held separately, and so he crossed his fingers and ran downstairs and into the last remaining house in the street.

Larry O'Neill was relatively more comfortable than his brother in that he'd been placed on a primitive bed. He was also bound with similar plastic cuffs, which had been secured to the bed frame, but he wasn't gagged, neither did he have any visible bruises. His small tuft of white hair was still intact.

"Is our mum okay?" He sat up, rubbed his wrists and unfolded and put on his trademark Buddy Holly glasses, which had been placed on a hard wooden chair beside the bed.

The brothers O'Neill seemed very well considering their ordeal – their clothes looked expensive, yuppie-ish, but extremely crinkled. Upon reuniting, they muttered a quick "are you OK?" but through their brotherly bond they seemed to already know the answer from a mere glance. Ryan immediately protested that his bruises were nothing, "Just a little misunderstanding with one of the kidnappers."

Both rooms had Coke cans, mineral water bottles, chocolate bar wrappings, empty crisp packets, lots of banana skins, orange peelings, apple cores, and a red fire bucket in the corner, the vile smell of which betrayed its contents, but apart from that nothing else to suggest two people had been detained there for five nights and six days.

The brothers took turns to complete each other's sentences. Late Wednesday afternoon they were returning home when a white transit van pulled up beside them. The side-door slid open, three men in balaclavas hopped out, stuck black hoods over their heads, bundled them in the van and drove off. Neither O'Neill brother saw their captors minus their balaclavas. They drove them straight to these houses; Ryan was greatly amused that they were being detained in fake houses in the Folk Park. The captors bothered them little except for delivering food – nothing but the likes of the remnants noted – and taking some photographs. At the end of his photo session Ryan tried to escape and, in fact, made it as far as the bottom of the stairs where his rough recapture resulted in his current state of bruising. They never heard their captors speak.

"Have you any idea who would do this?" O'Carroll asked, as Ryan concluded their take on the kidnap.

"Do what?" Lawrence asked. Ryan glanced at him.

"Kidnap you?" O'Carroll replied.

Lawrence looked at Ryan and then back at O'Carroll, "We were kidnapped?"

"Obviously," O'Carroll stated quickly as McCusker looked on.

"Kidnapped implies a ransom," Ryan ventured, as Lawrence continued to stare at him. O'Carroll didn't reply. "So, does that mean our mother's husband paid a ransom?"

"You were released," O'Carroll qualified what should have been her answer.

"How much was it?" Ryan asked, as his brother made eye contact with O'Carroll for the first time.

"I can't say," O'Carroll replied.

"But was it a lot?" Lawrence asked.

"Well, let's just say that it was enough," she said, and then Mc-Cusker thought he saw her looking directly at Lawrence, as if to think "enough for me to want to introduce you to my sister." He raised his eyebrows before O'Carroll moved swiftly on.

"Ryan, I understand you're being fleeced by a loan shark?"

Both the brothers seemed surprised with her statement.

"Well it's our own fault, but we hope to sort it all out shortly," Ryan said.

"No, that's not what I meant – borrowing is your own business," O'Carroll said, flashing her fingers through her hair to try and put a fallen strand back in place, "but when and if it gets to extortion then it does become our business. Who did you borrow from?"

"Do I have to tell you?" Ryan asked, a nervous-looking Lawrence sat beside him.

"No you don't," O'Carroll admitted.

"But," McCusker interrupted, "if he or they were behind you being kidnapped then there's nothing to say he or they won't try again. I think it would be better if you advised us who your loan shark is so that we can rule them out of our kidnapping investigation."

"I think I'd prefer it if we didn't, to be perfectly honest," Ryan said, and then added as an afterthought "On a different matter entirely, are there any television cameras or photographers outside?"

Ryan O'Neill had only been enjoying his new-found freedom for less than an hour and here he was, McCusker figured, already conjuring up a PR opportunity for the brothers' fledging internet company.

"No," O'Carroll advised a crestfallen Ryan, "but I can confidently predict this much: you're going to be on the front page first edition of tomorrow's *Belfast Telegraph*. Following that you'll have all of the media you want and more queuing up at your front door."

The detectives left the soon-to-be very famous brothers O'Neill for a quick check-up by the paramedics. O'Carroll instructed the other two constables to drive the brothers home after their examination.

**

"You'd seriously consider introducing Grace to one of them?" McCusker asked as they passed the George Best Airport on their right, on the way back into Belfast.

"Nah," she started. "I will admit though that the thought did briefly cross my mind."

"Why briefly?"

"Well I realised the brothers O'Neill are never going to get a penny from their father so I felt that was most definitely a lost cause."

"Okay, that figures."

"By the way, McCusker," she started up again, following a few moments deep in transparent thought, "how much did you say your Patten early retirement buy-out was?"

CHAPTER SEVENTEEN

"I've just realised – you're only picking me up so you can check if I've had anyone stay over," McCusker said, as he and O'Carroll drove out of his mews, coffeed up. It had been the third morning out of four she'd collected him from his apartment.

"Okay, three things I'll say to that," she replied, as she sped past the fine No Alibis Bookstore on the corner of Botanic Avenue and Mount Charles. "Firstly, the super wanted us to make you feel welcome; secondly, you never bring your car to Custom House, and thirdly, Mc-Cusker, if I'm to be your partner I need to hear chapter and verse about every woman you have in your room."

McCusker mulled over her words as BBC Radio 4's *Today* show played in the background. Then he suddenly broke his silence. "Partner? Does this mean that the super has also assigned you to the Adam Whitlock case?"

"Yes it does," she said, appearing happy enough with the development, "apart from which, and lucky for you, DI Mucky Jarvis Cage is out of action for a few days so the super didn't have much choice."

A few minutes later McCusker realised they were passing the No Alibis Bookstore for the second time in not quite as many minutes. "Sorry?" he said, pointing to the store.

"I wondered when the penny would drop," she joked. "I'm waiting directions."

"Sorry?"

"Look, you've been working on this case already so you're the lead detective…so lead and tell me where you want to go?"

"Right. So…" he replied, nodding and taking out his notebook, "I need to…we need to talk to Craig Husbands, who along with Angela Robinson was another of Adam and Julia's infrequent dinner partners. Craig and Angela, and Angela's husband Richard, were at Queen's together. And then I need to see Adam and Julia's father Wesley who it seems has been ringing me non-stop since he arrived at Aldergrove Airport."

"Please don't go old and fuddy duddy on me McCusker, we all tend to call it the International Airport now."

"Really?"

"Yes but only for about ten years."

"Good, that's okay then – for a moment there I was beginning to get worried I was out of date. Okay, let's head to…" McCusker said, cutting her off while looking at his watch, "Craig Husbands – it's 8. 55, he should be in work now."

Craig Husbands was the manager of the box office in the Grand Opera House, which was right across the road from the world famous Europa Hotel on Great Victoria Street. The Opera House, at least the original building – which opened in 1895 and cost less than a grand to build – was one of the most beautiful venues, not just in Ireland, but in the British Isles. Unfortunately the extension to the Grand Opera House, which was opened in 2006 and cost £10.5 million to build, was one of the ugliest buildings, not just in the British Isles but in all of Europe. Unfortunately for Craig Husbands he got to work in the not-so-grand wing…

For all of that Craig was quite a cheery chappie, particularly considering he'd just lost one of his friends. His black hair was cut quite short with dyed blonde highlights. He immediately stood out from his box office team in that he was the only one not wearing a GOH uniform, electing to don instead an expensive-looking grey shirt, darker grey well-pressed trousers and black laceless Campers.

Ever efficient, DS WJ Barr had notified Craig Husbands that McCusker would be calling. Barr's chores for the morning were to chase up the autopsy report, check how the forensic report on Adam's computer was coming along, push the limited team on the House to House enquiries, unearth a copy of Adam Whitlock's will and pacify the ever-persistent father, Wesley Whitlock III.

Husbands brought the two detectives up to the quieter (as in empty) second-floor bar. By way of trying to make conversation, McCusker asked how business was going.

"Well absolutely everyone is suffering due to the recession, but we've a safe wee musical in at the minute, *Dancing Shoes* – it's the George Best story told for tourists. It's doing great business for us and people love it."

Husbands certainly wasn't a Belfast native but McCusker couldn't pin down where he was from due to him heavily Ulsterising his accent.

"I could comp the two of you if you'd like," Husbands offered, and then made a call on a wall phone ordering a pot of coffee, a pot of tea and "some nibbles."

"Thanks, but I'm not a big one for the theatre," O'Carroll politely replied as Husbands lead them over to a table.

"I'm a bit tight on my free nights to be honest," McCusker said, hoping not to sound ungrateful, "but our Detective Sergeant, WJ Barr, is a big Man U supporter – I'm sure he'd love to go."

"Yeah, Willie John thought he would loike it so I've already comped him foive," Husbands replied, divulging the fact that perhaps the show wasn't doing as well as he'd claimed and betraying his Birmingham monotone roots.

When the tea, coffee, and nibbles arrived they got down to the business in hand: discussing the life (and death) of Adam Whitlock.

"You know," Husbands began expansively, "Adam found it hard to believe that I ended up in the entertainment business. He was always saying, 'Craig, with your brain I thought you'd have ended up in politics.' Can you imagine me in politics?"

"Well, you know," McCusker said, "someone has to."

"No, no!" Husbands protested. "That wasn't my point. You see he felt that both of us had turned out doing things that neither of us had planned."

"Really?" McCusker said, his ears and interest picking up several notches. "What had he planned to do?"

"Oh you know the same as the rest of us when we were at university: change the world. Didn't you ever want to change the world Inspector?"

"I'm not an inspector."

"But I am," O'Carroll cut in. "So what had youse planned to do to change this wee world of ours?"

McCusker was happy for her intrusion because, a) it kept the interview on track, and b) it meant he didn't have to go into the rigmarole of explaining that he wasn't a member of PSNI, but an agency policeman.

"Well, we were looking for this mystical thing which would change our lives and make the world better for everyone, and if we'd manage to invent or create some mystical thing, the world would be an even better place for us. I read somewhere that Steve Jobs once said 'Just look around you and all you will see are things that were made and invented by people not as intelligent as yourself.' Apparently he cited that as the genesis of his genius."

"I thought Adam had come over here to study law?" McCusker said, choosing to ignore Husbands' preferred track.

"Well he had of course..." Husbands agreed. "His father was an important lawyer in Boston. He'd spent a few years in Belfast and so he still had enough contacts to pull a few strings for Adam. To be fair to Adam though, he always wanted to go his own way and decided to come back here to Belfast rather than work with his father in Boston."

"Were you and Adam planning anything? A change of career?" McCusker asked, happy to continue with this approach for now.

"No, no, definitely not," Husbands started. "I find that living your life is fine but it's your lifestyle that causes all the problems. You get to a point where you realise that you're no longer a student any longer. You don't want to live with four other guys in a house. You don't want to live on beans on toast and takeaways while going from one drinking session to the next, while at the same time trying to ensure you keep up with your course. I like my comforts, my nice clothes, my cool pad, my car, trips abroad, all of that, and I don't want to slum it anymore and to change jobs. That's exactly what I'd have had to do if I'd taken Steve Job's advice and followed his path."

"Did Adam feel the same way?" McCusker asked.

"To a certain extent, yes, but at the end of the day his father's money was always going to give Adam and Julia a cushion if they needed it."

"If lifestyle hadn't come in to it, what would you have liked to do?" O'Carroll asked.

"Well, I can't pretend I didn't think about this because I have," he started looking around to check no one from the theatre staff was listening. "I'd love to produce my own shows and failing that I'd love to open my own boutique hotel."

"And what about Adam?"

"Sorry, I don't understand – did you mean what were Adam's dreams?"

"Yes," McCusker replied.

"Well, sadly for me he'd no interest in either the theatre or in hotels, no matter how exclusive they were going to be." Husbands laughed. "He really didn't have anything that drove him. He was like…directionless."

"Really?" O'Carroll said automatically.

"Yeah," Husbands replied, "you know, maybe we all just had too many dinners together and we had started to tread water without even realising it, but you know when you reach that point in a relationship where you think it's going to progress and that you're going to take it to the next level. You're not even sure what the next level may be or what if anything is waiting for you there, but then you get home and you sit down and you think, 'Well that was a…just such a big waste of time.' When we were all at uni together and were getting on great I thought…I suppose what I'm trying to say is you think this is all going to be so exciting being friends with these people and then you realise that the uni days were not just the start of the relationship, but the peak of it."

"Did you get on well with Julia?" O'Carroll asked.

"Do you mean did I get on well with her or do you mean did she and I have a scene?"

"Okay," Carroll asked, "I'll take your answer on both, please."

"We nearly had a scene – it was in the Queen's days and on one famous occasion when we were about to…you know…"

"It's okay," O'Carroll smiled warmly, "we don't need pictures."

"Well, she ran off, saying this is just too weird and muttering something about Adam. But having said that, and in answer to your second question, we have always got on great."

"And Angela Robinson?" McCusker asked.

"Good God no, she's too tight with Adam."

"I actually meant do youse get on okay…"

"Yeah, we do actually; she's always been great fun, a bit wild and likes a laugh. She's the one who keeps Adam's spirits up."

"Did Adam get down?" McCusker asked.

"Down might be too strong a word," Husbands replied, looking like he was searching for the correct word, "but maybe, as I mentioned earlier, he wasn't always driven."

"Was he happy in his work?" McCusker pushed the questions again in the hope that one would open the mystical door.

"Yes," he answered hesitantly, "in that it gave him a certain status and it gave him a certain lifestyle that he didn't need to go to his father to finance. But, he could do it in his sleep."

"Hobbies?" O'Carroll asked.

"All non-participating activities, apart from his trips to the gym with Julia of course. But he loved the movies and he'd go and sit in a darkened room all day long if he was allowed to and watch flickering images up on the screen. You know, maybe if he'd been into some action sport or driving fast cars, or hiking or mountain climbing or such like, maybe then he would have had a stronger motivation in his life."

"Did he make any enemies?" O'Carroll again.

"Not that I'm aware of, but I doubt he would have had any at work either; he just didn't care enough to upset people much, let alone enough to make them want to kill him."

"Well someone wanted to, Craig," McCusker said.

"Yes, I guess you're right," Husbands replied, slowing down in his tracks. The phone on the wall rang and he jumped to answer it, "Yes?"

He looked at McCusker and then at O'Carroll, his eyes fixing on her for the remainder of his conversation. "Yes," a pause then "they can't do that," another longer pause then, "they confirmed the booking," another short pause, "but I blocked all the seats for them and sold all the seats around them." Then a grimace followed by "I should be finished here soon. I'll be straight down but tell them we can't accept this."

"Look, we're nearly done," McCusker started, "we've just got one more question for you at this point. Could you please tell me what you were doing on Saturday night between the hours of midnight and 3 a.m. on Sunday morning?"

"I was here in this very bar until about 12.50 a.m. and then I went home."

"By yourself?" McCusker asked.

"Yes, by myself," Husbands replied directly to O'Carroll.

***

"Do you think he's gay?" McCusker asked, as they got back in the Mégane, which was badly parked on the Europa forecourt.

"Surely you're not saying that just because he wants to produce musicals and he wouldn't tell you who he went home with on Saturday night?"

"No," McCusker replied quickly, "but I am happy you also thought he went home with someone on Saturday..."

"Yes, he's keeping something from us," O'Carroll said, appearing deep in thought, "I say he's little camp, yes, but gay? Definitely not."

"Really? How can you be so sure?"

"Believe me, McCusker, a girl knows these things and he is a ladies' man. But that doesn't necessarily mean Mr Husbands is going to make a good husband. There was only one thing he wanted to do with me or that wee girl who brought in our coffee and you're clearly much too innocent for me to go into that kind of detail with you."

CHAPTER EIGHTEEN

M cCusker and O'Carroll were debating whether or not it was too early for a lunch pitstop. McCusker thought the time was good for "a wee bite on the hoof", O'Carroll thought he was crazy. Both were saved further debate when O'Carroll's mobile went off and the efficient DS Barr informed them that Wesley Whitlock III had once again rang the Custom House and was ever so keen "to hook up." McCusker gave Whitlock Senior ten extremely rare points for at least having the decency to avoid the easy route of ringing someone, who knew someone, who could get through to Superintendent Larkin and persuade him to order the meeting.

Wesley Whitlock, in residence at the Europa, was both happy and willing to treat the detectives to a late breakfast in his suite. "Would 11.30 a.m. be convenient?" A mere seven minutes later.

"The Europa do a great Ulster Fry..." McCusker offered to the mobile-bound O'Carroll, "tell Barr to advise Mr Whitlock that 11.30 would be *very* convenient."

As it turned out, 11.30 wasn't exactly convenient for Wesley Whitlock; upon their arrival at the Clinton Suite McCusker and O'Carroll were greeted by Kristin, one of Whitlock's two PAs (or secretaries). Her boss was running late, she said, but would arrive presently. In the meantime they could order whatever they liked from the breakfast menu. McCusker plumped for his full Ulster Fry with great enthusiasm while O'Carroll, tutting under her breath, went for the continental option – an OJ, coffee, and croissants.

The suite's lounge was very large and very comfortably furnished. Whitlock's PA's were Amazonian: Kristin, a clear-skinned, black-bespectacled, long-haired blonde, and Bobby, a dark-skinned equally long-haired brunette. McCusker was convinced their identical white silk blouses would start popping buttons at the next breath and their grey skirts were so tight he silently suspected they'd have great trouble slipping out of them. He hoped O'Carroll wasn't picking up on the direction his daydream was taking.

Wesley Whitlock III and the room service trolley arrived at the same time. Without even acknowledging McCusker and O'Carroll, Whitlock Senior lifted the plate domes to inspect the food.

"Ah, good Kristin – you told them how to prepare it," he said in a rich baritone voice and then addressed his visitors, "I much preferred it when they had the Whip and Saddle dining area in the lobby. They knew how to prepare an Ulster Fry without any directions but now with the Causerie it's all prepared buffet style – can't abide it."

"This is McCusker and Detective Inspector Lily O'Carroll," Bobby said by way of introductions.

"Ah yes," he said shaking McCusker's hand enthusiastically, "Grafton Recruitment's police officer, down from Portrush. I've heard all about you," he continued, switching his attention to O'Carroll, "and you too miss."

Wesley Whitlock III was an imposing man, probably 6'2", McCusker guessed. He wore a dark blue suit with a long overcoat of the same material and weight as a jacket. Bobby helped him to remove it, adding valet to her list of PA services in the process. He had a blue shirt with a white collar, a crimson Harvard University bow tie, and expensive-looking, gold, elasticised arm bracelets to ensure his cuffs remained the perfect length. His perfect snow-white teeth were too perfect, by about three decades, for his tanned features, longish snow-white hair and gold wire-rimmed glasses, which were strong enough to enlarge his big blue eyes. He was carrying a black rucksack which he flamboyantly swung off his shoulder in a well-practised movement, utilising both his right shoulder and hip. He quickly unzipped one of the pouches and extracted a white Apple iPad, which he proceeded to carry the way a fervent preacher carries a bible. He looked like a friendly old uncle, in the way Warren Buffett had perfected, yet he'd flash an occasional look that said, loud and clear, "mess with me and I'll crush you in a heartbeat." He pointed to the food, now proudly displayed on the large circular smoked glass table. "Come, come, won't you join me for breakfast?"

He sat down and pointed to a bottle on the trolley, nodding to Bobby: "Two fingers." He turned his attention and gaze back to Mc-Cusker and proceeded to explain. "I'm seventy-seven years old – I've touched John Harvard's shoe. I've a healthy appetite, I walk at least five miles a day and my only medicine is Jack Daniels. Will you join me?"

A simultaneous "no" came back from the detectives.

"Right answer guys," he stated very quickly, while caressing the forefinger of his right hand continuously over the screen of his iPad. "So, how are you getting on with your investigation into my son's death?"

"Well sir," McCusker began, noting that there was no interruption to drop the formalities, "we've just started to collect our information and we're very happy of this opportunity to get some background on your son. You see your daughter Julia is very upset..."

"Yes, yes," he replied, tearing into his breakfast with all the gusto of a young wolf. He held his fork in his right hand as if it were a pen and he frequently used both his hands, complete with cutlery, to punctuate his conversation. "If I'd been able to do anything it would have been to spare her being the one to have found him. Who would do such a thing to another human?"

"So you know the circumstances?" O'Carroll offered.

The American looked at her in shock and for a split second Mc-Cusker sensed that Whitlock's breakfast table was no place for a woman to speak.

"Well, yes miss, Superintendent James Larkin has been kind enough to keep me up to speed. I wanted..."

"Did you speak to your son often?" McCusker interrupted, as Bobby offered them all tea or coffee.

"At least once a day."

McCusker was distracted enough by Bobby's scent and proximity to miss Wesley Whitlock's reply.

"Sorry?" McCusker asked, shaking his head.

"Yes, at least once a day. You see, as well as being his father I was also his mentor," the old American offered by way of explanation.

"Were youse in business together?" McCusker asked, trying to get a fix on this, in the knowledge that he hadn't spoken to his own father for at least a couple of months now.

"Well here's the thing; I sent him over here to study and work so he'd get a broader worldwide experience for when he eventually came back to Boston to become a senior partner in the family firm. But I'd never factored in that he was going to fall in love with this place and want to settle here."

"So his move was permanent then?" O'Carroll asked and was rewarded with another of those 'you're only a wee girl, it's fine to dine with us but please keep quiet,' looks.

"No, no, not at all. He didn't have any roots over here, no serious girlfriends." Whitlock stopped talking, placed his cutlery alongside his half-finished breakfast and wiped the corners of his mouth with his napkin in a manner very elegant for a man his size. He then downed half of his Jack Daniels, shaking his head aggressively to shortcut the alcohol into his bloodstream. "Let's just say that Adam's sowing-his-wild-oats stage was taking a lot longer than he'd figured. I think if I'm being candid, what he really needed was the love of a great woman. You know, someone to start a family with, produce some heirs for me, and create a reason for all of the other smelly stuff we call life."

McCusker immediately thought of O'Carroll's sister Grace and he would have bet money the DI was sharing that thought at that exact moment.

"We have a saying up on the northwest coast, sir," McCusker started, "which is this: 'Why aren't the birds flying? The worms are all fat and juicy.'"

"I get your point, McCusker," Wesley replied, breaking into a gentler smile than the detective thought him capable of. "And you know, the answer to why the birds weren't flying could be that there were so many fat and juicy worms around they didn't need to bother; they could just glide down and pick and choose as often as they wanted."

"Meaning that Adam had too many women to pick from?" O'Carroll asked incredulously.

"No dear, the worms and the birds are just metaphors," Whitlock replied. "You see Adam, like the lazy birds, didn't need to worry where his next meal came from. It was all there, the family fortune waiting for him and so, like the birds, he'd no motivation. He lost his mother about ten years ago; that hit us all pretty hard, but particularly Adam."

"Were you and your son very close?" O'Carroll asked, risking further Whitlock wrath.

"Not really; I believe we were both duty-bound to each other. But equally I felt it was a phase he was going through and if we could just both hang in there and be civil to each other for the next few years we would reap the rewards in our relationship down the line. As I say, DI O'Carroll, all he needed was the love of a good woman."

"But you stood by him, speaking to him every day?" O'Carroll persisted.

"I'm afraid I'm a victim to my own impunity of character..." he offered, then suggested, "Why don't we all take our tea or coffee and move over to the comfy chairs?" He led the way, carrying his iPad and the remainder of his Jack Daniels.

No sooner had they done so when Bobby and Kristin reappeared from an adjoining room and in about 20 seconds flat had cleared away the dirty dishes onto a trolley and restored the table to its former flowered and magazined glory.

When the girls returned from whence they came, Whitlock continued in a quieter voice, "You know, talking about my wife, she would never ever forgive me for allowing this to happen. I need the both of you to know that if it's the last thing I do and if I need to spend my last cent doing so, I have...I *need* to find the person or persons who committed this ghastly crime and I need to ensure they receive their just punishment."

For the first time since they'd met, McCusker sensed this was Whitlock Senior suffering a weak moment, and it was probably as close as he would ever come to breaking down. "Were you aware of what his work entailed on a day-to-day basis?" he asked.

"You know, run-of-the-mill conveyance stuff," the American replied. "You've got to hand it to Adam – even in the middle of this recession he was still managing to keep his figures up to target in his department."

"Any difficult clients he would have reported to you?" McCusker continued, discreetly nodding at O'Carroll whom he hoped was picking up the signal to ask the next question.

"No sir."

"Julia told us about the Cindy Scott incident," O'Carroll started.

"Okay, you know about that...good."

"She thought that Cindy's brother Bing didn't hold Adam responsible for the death of his sister."

"And nor was he – the inquest returned an accidental death," Whitlock replied, immediately.

"I know that, sir..." O'Carroll said slowly, "I was just wondering if Bing saw it the same way."

"Yes, yes fine boy," Whitlock replied quickly. "I think he got over the incident a lot quicker than Adam did."

"Anyone else in Bing's family have an opinion on the verdict?" McCusker asked.

"You don't mean to say you think Cindy's death might be tied into the death of my son do you?" Whitlock said, as his finger furiously worked the iPad screen.

McCusker took a large intake of breath, "Well, sir, at this stage we're not in a position where we can rule anything or anyone out. Adam had few friends here, he didn't have any money problems, from what we can gather from his friends he didn't indulge in illegal drugs, on top of which there were no traces found on his premises. From what you say he seemed not to have made any enemies at work..."

"He wasn't politically active," Whitlock offered.

"It wasn't a robbery-based crime," McCusker continued. "The only thing we know...the only clue we have is that it was a violent attack. And it appeared well planned, in so far as the murderer didn't leave a single clue or piece of evidence at the scene."

"Could it have been something which went wrong? You know, where something got out of hand and went horribly wrong?"

"It's much too violent for that...can I be candid with you?" McCusker asked mid-sentence.

"Yes of course."

"We believe just one of the several blows to your son's body would have been enough to render him unconscious."

Whitlock grimaced in pain, his face turning the colour of a wind-burnt leaf and for the first time since the beginning of the interview he looked every single one of his seventy-seven years on this planet.

"Did, erm..." McCusker started hesitantly. "Did Adam ever discuss any of his girlfriends with you?"

"I seem to remember there was someone back home he was serious about, but I never got to meet her or find out anything about her."

McCusker made a note to ask Julia about this as he asked, "What about in Belfast?"

"Well there might have been something..."

"Anything can be of help at this stage," McCusker prompted.

"Well, on more than one occasion when we were on the phone together he'd say he had to cut it short because he was off to see someone. I'd ask him if he was meeting up with Julia for dinner and he'd say no. Either that or I'd be speaking to Julia a few minutes later and I'd ask her if she was seeing Adam on that particular evening and she'd say no."

"And did you ask Julia who Adam was meeting up with?" O'Carroll asked, appearing a bit happier now that she was no longer drawing the Whitlock glare.

"Well, sometimes discreetly. I didn't want either of them to think I was being nosey," Whitlock replied. He averted eye contact from both McCusker and O'Carroll before saying "I mean, I know my kids, I've got two healthy boys and one healthy girl; I can tell you that for a fact."

McCusker and O'Carroll looked confusedly at him.

"You know, my boys like girls and my girl likes boys."

"Right, right, of course," O'Carroll said, "and, ah, Julia had no idea who he was off to see on these particular evenings you're referring to?"

"None at all."

"When did you last speak to your son, sir?" McCusker asked.

"Saturday evening, about three in the afternoon."

"Boston time or Belfast time?" O'Carroll asked.

"Boston time, which with the time difference, would have been 8 p.m. Belfast time."

"Really?" McCusker said, a little thrown.

"Yes. I know it was three because I'd just got back from a lunch at my club."

"And how was he?" McCusker asked, feeling his heart start to beat a little faster and the pulse in his temples grow more noticeable.

"He sounded absolutely fine – good spirits, no hurry to get off the phone..."

"What did youse talk about?"

"You know, I was thinking about that on the flight over. My mind was racing away for the whole journey – I couldn't catch a blink of sleep. If I'd have known it was going to be my last conversation with my son I'd have listened closer to his every intonation, I'd have cherished his every word. Let's see now, we spoke about Julia, about my youngest son, about how he was getting on. I was asking Adam to look out for a job for Jaime, something in Belfast."

McCusker's interest piqued. "Was your other son planning to come over as well?" he asked.

"Look. In the interest of full disclosure...I'll tell you everything, even some of our dirty linen, in the hope that it might help you, but also in the hope you'll be discreet about it."

"Of course," O'Carroll replied.

Whitlock looked at McCusker who nodded positively.

"Alright...My youngest son...he fell into the company of a bad woman, in that she did drugs. In point of fact, she is a judge's daughter who has been cut off by her family entirely. I'm not quite sure, but I believe Jaime didn't indulge too much, but at the same time I think he was taking..."

"Are we talking about dope or coke?" O'Carroll asked.

"Coke – Jaime was doing coke and I think she was taking heroin and methadone," Whitlock admitted. "Anyway, I only found out about it when Jaime came back home one night a little worse for wear and eventually confessed to me he was on coke and Allison was on H and owed her dealer just over 30 grand."

"What did you do?" O'Carroll asked.

"I struck a deal with him. I said I would pay the $30,000 off for her and give her another $20,000 to draw on, but only if he would agree to my two conditions, the first being that she had to get on a programme immediately and the second that he had to give her up. I knew it was cruel love and I knew where it would end up. He agreed and I do believe he's sticking to his side of the bargain, but I thought if Adam could just find something for Jaime over here, even just for six months, he'd either get her out of his system altogether or he'd meet a beautiful Irish Colleen and fall helplessly in love."

McCusker suspected that, this time, Grace was not the first person to spring into O'Carroll's mind.

"Did Adam know about Jaime's problem?"

"Ah no," Whitlock Senior admitted, "I couldn't...I didn't want him judging his brother."

"Did Adam have any leads for Jaime in Belfast?"

"He said he was still trying to find something interesting, but he didn't really seem all that keen on Jaime coming over."

"Did Adam and Jaime get on well?" O'Carroll asked.

"Yes, very well – always have been close. But Adam started to watch out for Jaime a lot more after their mother died."

"So why do you think he wasn't keen for him to come to Belfast?" McCusker asked.

"I think he didn't want to have to put his brother up at his place. He knew that if he didn't, Julia would have to. I said I didn't mind getting him somewhere, or even putting him up in a hotel, but Adam said he couldn't do that to his brother either. He said Jaime would be terribly hurt if he came over to Belfast and couldn't crash with him, like he had done a few times while he'd been at Queen's. In the call on Saturday he'd said that now just wasn't a good time for Jaime to come over to Belfast, but that he would keep thinking about it and wouldn't stop looking for him."

"Did he elaborate on what he meant by, 'now is not a good time'?" McCusker offered sensing an angle.

"Never did," Whitlock replied straightening it out again.

"Was Jaime aware you were planning all this?" McCusker asked.

"No, but I was looking at other options as well."

"Anything else stick in your mind from your telephone conversation with Adam?"

"Not really."

"Would you say he was in a good mood?" McCusker asked.

"Oh yes," Whitlock replied without a moment's hesitation. "You know, my son always tried to have a new joke lined up for me every time we spoke on the phone. It was a bit of a ritual between us. No matter what kind of mood we were in we'd always make time for his joke. Julia used to tell me about the length Adam would go to, to collect these jokes – he had a backlog of them waiting by his telephone."

"Do you remember Saturday's joke?" O'Carroll asked.

"Yes I do, as it happens," Whitlock said breaking into a large friendly smile. "He delivered it just like it was part of our conversation, you understand. We were talking about Jaime's education. Adam said that he used to have a cross-eyed teacher, 'Really,' I said, falling for it, 'what was he like?' 'Oh,' he said, 'he was okay, except that he had trouble controlling his pupils'."

Whitlock looked at McCusker as he laughed, followed shortly by giggling from O'Carroll. He grimaced again for what seemed a long time. He looked very vulnerable.

"Now that was one of his better jokes," he offered in an attempt to lighten the mood. "So listen," he said as it became clear proceedings were winding down, "I've still got some good friends in this city – what say you if I get them organised and we all pool our resources into finding out who did this to poor Adam?"

"If you discover anything which could be helpful to us, we'd like to feel you'd share it with us immediately," McCusker said, in opposition to the vigilante approach.

"But of course," Wesley Whitlock III replied, appearing to receive the message loud and clear.

CHAPTER NINETEEN

As the two detectives exited the lobby of the world-famous hotel they noticed the banner headline on the freshly printed *Belfast Telegraph*.

KIDNAPPED BELFAST BROTHERS FREED!

The exclusive story accompanied by a post-release photograph, courtesy of Eddie McIlwaine, re-told the proceedings verbatim except for the fact that Eddie claimed a big part of solving the crime and discovering the location of the kidnapped brothers to himself. There was even a photo of the golfer Rory McIlroy on the front page, the caption stating that the boys hoped to secure him as ambassador for their Larry's List website. McCusker figured it was a win-win situation all round.

"Do you think James O'Neill will pony up the £50k Ryan owes the loan shark?" McCusker asked as they exited the hotel.

"Well, even if he doesn't, with this kind of coverage, I imagine they'll pull in a lot more than that from selling their story. No, I think the boys will be fine from here on in."

"And the kidnappers?"

"The super thinks it was one of the cleverest he'd ever witnessed. I mean, not a single clue," O'Carroll replied, unlocking her double-parked car, much to the relief of the Europa's finely dressed concierge.

"And?" McCusker continued, amused once again at her approach to parking.

"The super also thinks this gang did so well – secured a big ransom, without hurting the victims – that they'll be back again. And next time he's hoping the family involved will be more co-operative – and that we'll be ready for them," she said as they got in the car and buckled up. "Back to your case McCusker. Where to next?"

"Let's get back to the Custom House and take stock. We'll plan the rest of the day as well – you know we have to fit in a lunch some-where."

"McCusker..." she said, taking her eyes off the traffic. "You've only just sat up from your breakfast! Where *do* you put it all?"

***

No sooner had they climbed the stairs into their office in the right-hand wing of the Custom House then McCusker received a call from Anthony Robertson's pathology office. Robertson would be at the Royal Victoria Hospital, waiting to discuss Adam Whitlock's autopsy and to offer them a Preliminary Cause of Death form.

As they pulled into the recently refurbished, five-storey, Victorian red-bricked hospital on the Grosvenor Road, O'Carroll looked at Mc-Cusker and waited.

Feeling he'd no option but to oblige, he opened with "This build-ing was completed in 1905 and it can claim to have been the first build-ing in the world to house an air-conditioning system."

"I bet you could recite a whole list of things about this hospital," O'Carroll said, gently ribbing him.

"Nah," McCusker sighed, silently making the decision to leave the fact that Frank Pantridge, the godfather of emergency medicine, de-veloped the first portable defibrillator on these premises for another time. "That's about it," he shrugged.

Anthony Robertson, the top pocket of his white lab coat packed with pencils and pens, all of which seemed to have left their own dis-tinctive skid marks, greeted them both warmly in his crowded Dick-ensian office. He invited them to remove the piles of precariously stacked files from the two hard seats in front of his desk while he rum-maged through the piles on the desk, eventually recovering the file marked "Adam Whitlock."

"Okay," he started, breaking into one of his large, if-you're-ready-I'll-start, smiles. "Adam Whitlock's life ended within seconds of the pulmonary artery in his chest being severed by a sharp instrument.

However, there were eight other stab wounds, seven of which were delivered post-trauma."

"Do you think…" McCusker started.

"There's not much more to go, McCusker," Robertson said, interrupting the detective in his best slowed-down Billy Connelly accent, "you can ask all the questions you want when I've finished."

O'Carroll rolled her eyes while McCusker closed his.

"There was no evidence to suggest he would have had time to put up a fight. There were no cut marks on his hands or arms but there was a little bruising around his knuckles. There was a large circular bruising on his chest."

"Any ideas what would have caused the chest bruising?" McCusker asked.

"If I didn't know better I'd say he was hit full force by a football."

"A football?" O'Carroll repeated.

"That's what it looks like…by itself it wouldn't have done any more than wind him," Robertson offered. "Can I continue?" he said, without waiting for confirmation. "There were marks around his wrists and ankles, I'd say they were made by restraints, like a five–centimetre strap or belt, but they were at least a week old. There were no deposits under his fingernails. He had eaten a pizza and drank some red wine shortly before he died. An Americana from Pizza Express."

"Really – you can tell where he bought his pizza from the autopsy?" O'Carroll said.

"No, Detective Inspector," Robertson replied, looking like the cat who'd not who only got the milk, but had finally snared the juicy mouse as well. "I could detect that from the pizza box still lying on the kitchen table."

O'Carroll conceded gracefully as Robertson continued. "Physically Adam Whitlock was in good shape, obviously ran or worked out regularly, maybe drank too much wine, but then don't we all."

"Well even if he had been healthier, it still wouldn't have saved his life," O'Carroll added.

"Fair point, fair point," the pathologist conceded before returning to his notes. "He'd broken his left wrist, probably while he was in his teens, and that's about it. Questions?"

"Do you think the attacker knew what he was doing?" McCusker asked, returning to the question he'd wanted to ask earlier.

"Or did he get lucky?"

"Yes," McCusker agreed.

"Impossible for us to know…but…the first stab was 100 per cent spot on, executed with the finesse of a surgeon."

"Implying medical knowledge?" McCusker asked.

"Or access to the internet," O'Carroll added.

"Precisely," Robertson said, seeming happy it was no longer predominantly a monologue.

"But why would the attacker continue stabbing the victim?" O'Carroll asked. "Particularly if, as you say, Whitlock would have expired within seconds?"

"Okay, scenario one: Someone for some reason or other goes to Adam Whitlock's house with intent to do him harm – right so far?" Robertson surmised.

"Correct. We have to believe this was the case as there was no evidence of a robbery," McCusker agrees.

"If you want to murder someone and you've never done it before, you don't really know what ending someone's life entails. Maybe the murderer just wanted to make sure he was definitely ending Adam Whitlock's life," Robertson said.

"Or, he wanted to make a point?" McCusker offered.

"Or he wanted to make a point," Robertson agreed.

"But then, who to?" O'Carroll asked. "It's too late for the point to have any effect with the victim."

"Or the murderer was just so convulsed with rage he couldn't help himself," McCusker suggested.

"Or *she* couldn't help herself," O'Carroll said putting in her tuppence for women's rights.

"Or the murderer – male or female – was paid to hit Adam Whitlock?" McCusker offered.

"It's much too messy a method to murder with a knife for a professional hit…" Robertson said. "Too close, too much can go wrong and too big a chance of leaving your DNA behind."

"Maybe the assassin wanted to throw us off the scent?" O'Carroll said.

"And our murderer didn't leave a single part of DNA behind," McCusker said. "The knife…any ideas?"

"Large, twenty centimetres, sharp, smooth edges," Robertson replied, shutting the file.

"And the time of death?" McCusker asked.

"The time of death..." Robertson sighed, "I thought you'd never ask. Actually my guess at the scene of the crime was pretty good but perhaps it was closer to midnight than to 3 a.m. I'd work around the 1 a.m. window if I were you."

**

McCusker and O'Carroll rehashed their conversation with Robertson on the way back to the Custom House without managing any eureka moments.

"I'll tell you this for nothing," O'Carroll said as their chat petered out, "I want to die peacefully in my sleep."

"That's all very well and fine," McCusker replied, "the only problem I see is you'd need to wake up first to be able to take full advantage of that particular luxury."

There was a message waiting for them with Station Duty Sergeant Matt Devine when they arrived. Wesley Whitlock III had proved he also hadn't been idle since their meeting, visiting his son's former place of employment, Mason, Burr & Co., and discovering that his son had filed a will with the company. He invited McCusker and O'Carroll to the firm's offices, an old bank building on Royal Avenue, to discover the contents.

McCusker was quite surprised to see how comfortable Mr Whitlock was in the company's offices, with everyone seemingly knowing him and fussing and flapping over him.

The detectives were shown through to the oak-panelled conference room, which had been set up with tea, coffee, finger sandwiches, shortbread, and muffins. McCusker felt the muffins were perhaps a nod in the direction of their American friend, Whitlock Senior. Julia Whitlock was also present in the conference room, and she gave McCusker a nod of acknowledgement.

The last will and testament was opened and read by a Mr Kurt Wolf, one of the senior partners. He read it very quickly, his north German accent betraying no compassion for the family members present at the reading.

Adam Whitlock had willed all his property – a family house in his name in Boston and the house down on Cyprus Avenue – back to the

Whitlock family estate. He had no debts. All of his cash at the time of his death (£287,560) he willed to Julia. His vast collection of DVD movies and documentaries went to his friend Angela Robinson. All of his other worldly goods were to be sold and the proceeds donated to Dupaul, Ireland, a charity for the homeless.

Herr Wolf admitted there was one issue still to resolve: the tax liability due to the status of the work-permits involved.

"Make sure Julia fully receives what Adam bequeathed her. I'll handle all and any of the tax liabilities with you separately," Wesley announced, appearing disappointed in the results of the will. Julia made no comment either on her gift or her father's offer to pay the tax on it.

McCusker suspected that Wesley Whitlock's disappointment wasn't over the fact that he wasn't mentioned in the will, outside the family estate. Rather, it was common to find survivors expecting a revelation from beyond the grave at such a reading, something that would help them to make some sense of the death, or at the very least, offer them a suggestion as to the meaning of life. McCusker knew, as he'd already accepted, that death was a lonely construct, but to someone of Wesley Whitlock III's age it must be a continual preoccupation.

McCusker and O'Carroll noted Angela's inclusion in the will, but gave it no more attention until they discovered just how big his DVD collection was: 4928 of them, stacked floor to ceiling and filling an entire room. It wasn't quite the throwaway gesture they had first thought.

"Does this mean they were a lot closer than we figured?" O'Carroll asked when they were back in the Mégane and making their way back to the office.

"Not really," McCusker replied, as he considered the question. "They were probably just movie buffs."

"Most people are," she replied, "well, maybe not so much *buffs* as *fans* – I mean, most people I know love a great film. Grace claims she could happily watch movies all day long."

"Do you not think all she needs to do is get out of the house a bit more?"

"McCusker!"

"No, no, I mean, I'm just saying that if she was out there interacting a bit more, you know, she wouldn't have as much trouble finding herself a good man."

"McCusker!"

"No, really...I'm just saying!"

"Well just don't," she ordered. "Next you'll be saying the same thing about me!"

"No, no, not at all," he added, happy to shift tracks. "Sure you're out there all the time. And when you're not chasing men for yourself you're chasing men for her."

"I'm not so sure that was meant as a compliment McCusker," she said, appearing content to leave this subject behind. "Do we know if his sister Julia liked films?"

"She only brought them up in reference to her brother."

"Yeah, and besides, she's nothing to grumble about – she got £287,000, tax free, so I can't see her being very upset about not getting her brother's DVD collection."

They drove in silence for the remainder of the journey.

"What's next?" O'Carroll asked, as they ran past the anonymous speaker statue and up the steps of the Custom House.

"I think we need to have a chat with Mr Ulsterbus himself, Ross Wallace," McCusker replied, as they both nodded to the diligent Station Duty Sergeant.

"It all seems so slow," she said, as much to herself as to McCusker.

"Yeah, this part always is," he replied, as much for himself as her, "but it's vital we have all of the pieces of the puzzle before we endeavour to try and put them together." McCusker wasn't sure just how much O'Carroll had heard of that last bit as she'd made a beeline through the crammed busy office, straight to her desk.

CHAPTER TWENTY

B arr, obviously concerned that he'd no additional information for them, had used his initiative: not only had he interviewed Ross Wallace, but he'd also typed up a copy of the interview and had it waiting for McCusker and O'Carroll on their desks. The transcript in full read:

> Interviewed Mr Ross Wallace at his spacious and tidy Ulsterbus office in the Gt Victoria St Station behind the Europa Hall.
>
> Mr Wallace, born in Randlestown and now residing at Willowfield Street, Belfast, is thirty-one years of age, a former student of Queen's University and currently employed by Ulsterbus as their Director of Schedules.
>
> Mr Wallace met Mr Adam Whitlock (the deceased) while they were both studying at Queen's University. He reports that, although they never shared digs, they did become firm friends dating back from the first week they met in the student's union in September 1999. Unlike several other students, including Mr Richard Robinson and Mrs Angela Robinson – who would have been Miss Angela Booth at the time – Mr Wallace had remained friends with Mr Whitlock ever since.
>
> Mr Wallace said that Mr Whitlock was a solicitor who dealt mostly in conveyancing. Mr Wallace was not aware of anyone with a reason to murder Mr Whitlock. He felt he was well liked. He believed Mr Whitlock was romantically attached in

a long-term affair, but he never knew the identity of said female.

Mr Wallace and his wife, Samantha, were married in 2008. Mr Whitlock was his best man and his sister Julia also attended the wedding. Mr Wallace had his first baby, a boy, Tom, later in 2008 and a daughter in 2010. Mr Whitlock was Tom's godfather. Mr Wallace felt that Mr Whitlock was not a hands-on godfather and he had a sneaking suspicion that Mr Whitlock had forgotten all about being Tom's godfather. Mr Wallace found with the birth of his two children that he and his wife had less and less time for friends. Their weekly meet-ups gradually became monthly, and more recently every second month. He last met up with Mr Whitlock on Wednesday past. Mr Whitlock did not seem to Mr Wallace to be unduly worried about anything and was his usual self; not exactly happy-go-lucky but more subdued.

Mr Wallace had not spoken with Mr Whitlock since Wednesday last. Mr Wallace was at home on Saturday evening. His sister-in-law and her husband visited them for dinner. They left shortly after 1.00 a.m. on Sunday and Mr Wallace and his wife both retired to bed, without doing the dishes, at just after 1.30 a.m.

McCusker noted the two important points and filed the report neatly in his Whitlock file, while O'Carroll, after half reading it, allowed it to disappear into the mess that was her desk. She was clearly preoccupied with something and giving off a very strong do-not-disturb-me vibe. McCusker duly took note, heading off to find DS WJ Barr.

"Okay WJ; the Wallace interview was fine in as far as it went but I've got a few additional questions for you."

"Okay, fire away," the chirpy DS replied.

"What did Ross Wallace look like – how was he turned out?"

"He was wearing a clean white shirt, blue tie, no jacket, dark-blue suit trousers and brown leather shoes."

"Were his shoes well-polished or scruffy?" McCusker asked.

"Neither, he wore trainers," Barr offered and then added, "but they looked like they were well looked after."

"Was he overweight? How about his hair? Did he look like he cared about his appearance?"

"He was in good shape physically. I'd say 5' 11", 170 pounds, clean shaven, longish but clean, central-parted blonde-closing-on-brown hair."

"Good, good, well observed," McCusker said in praise, "but please put these points in your report."

"Okay."

"Look, you're going to have to humour me," McCusker started, quiet and gently. "I know it's probably more of a country police approach but everything you see and hear and sometimes even smell can be a clue. Tell me this: Did he appear happy in his work?"

"Very much so," Barr responded immediately. "Wallace volunteered that he'd fallen on his feet with Ulsterbus; he enjoyed the work and they paid well."

"Anyone that pays regularly in this climate, DS, pays well."

"You're not kidding, sir – my brother got laid off just last week."

"Any other opportunities for him to follow up on?"

"Well, he'd put a few bob aside and he's still positive, but our auld man says 'Get out there, get a job, any job'. He reckons it's better to have a job while looking for a better job than to have no job at all."

"Your father is not wrong WJ," McCusker replied, acknowledging the fact that the DS's father came from a generation of Ulstermen who felt shame at being unemployed. "Tell me this: Did your man Wallace think a lot before he answered or did he answer off the cuff?"

"All immediate answers."

"Thanks WJ, I've got a bit better an impression on him now," Mc-Cusker replied. "Maybe just a routine check with the in-laws about the Saturday dinner date and then take a constable with you to interview Adam's brother, Jaime. He's at the Europa in the next room to the father. I get the feeling we're still missing a lot on Adam. O'Carroll and I will interview his other friend, Richard Robinson – Angela's husband – and then we'll meet up back here at 3 p.m. to compare notes."

CHAPTER TWENTY-ONE

McCusker hated chippy people. He didn't know why he *did*, he just did, always had. Well, maybe *hate* would have been too strong a word; he tended not to waste time hating people or things, so he figured *didn't like* chippy people would be a more accurate phrase.

Richard Robinson immediately struck McCusker as such a type. In fact, he almost seemed to wear his chippiness as a badge of honour, to the extent that, if the makers of *Grumpy Old Men* were ever to do a follow-up programme, he could play a central character in 'Chippy Middle-aged Men.'

When he greeted McCusker and O'Carroll on the steps of his house on the once elegant Balmoral Avenue, he was wearing black Doc Martens, shapeless, grey-black, corduroy trousers and a two-button, long-sleeved polo shirt, in a slightly different shade of black to his trousers. He was thin but with a pot belly, with untidy, medium-length, brown hair and a five o'clock shadow. He had incredibly big hands with perfectly manicured nails.

As befitted his personal appearance, the Robinson house was very clean and not-a-speck-of-dust-anywhere tidy. He'd been expecting the police and had set up three places at a small basketwork table in his conservatory. He seemed keen to get down to business; he quickly poured three cups of coffee and invited the officers to help themselves to milk, sugar, and chocolate digestive biscuits. He opened his half used pink WH Smith's notebook, implying he was going to keep his own notes of the interview.

"What do you do?" McCusker asked, the house being deficient of clues.

"Actually, I write songs mate," Robinson replied quietly, his Aussie twang ringing through.

"Really," O'Carroll said, displaying her first bit of interest in the case for a few hours. "Would I know any of them?"

"No," the man in grey replied, in a tone that belied an acceptance that very few would.

"Right," O'Carroll said, appearing to drop back into her reticent mood.

"So have any of your songs been recorded?" McCusker asked, trying to get a bit of a conversation going.

"Just demos," Robinson replied, fidgeting as he rolled his pen around and around in the fingers of his right hand.

"So am…" McCusker started back up again.

"Look, I write lyrics for a few local musicians, and it's something I've just started to do again recently. I used to write a lot when we were all at Queen's. But you know what it's like; we all tend to relinquish our lofty creative ambitions in order to fulfil our more basic ones. You know, like being able to pay off the mortgage, for instance."

"Right," McCusker demured. "Okay…so what do you do to make money then?"

Robinson scribbled something down in his notebook before replying, "I, you know…well…I'm perfectly qualified as a house husband," he laughed nervously, noticing a look of quiet disdain from O'Carroll. "I was going into journalism. The plan was I would move to London and become a stringer for one of the Australian rags, but Angela's career started to take off here with the BBC and so I've found myself being the supportive partner and dabbling in various things: handiwork; designing websites; cutting lawns; carpentry; writing lines for greetings cards; a script doctor; writing obituaries – but I'll tell you that's an extremely closed shop. A few months ago Angela and I made a decision that I would give all of that up and concentrate on my lyrics and poetry."

O'Carroll discretely flashed McCusker a knowing look as if to say "Jeez –we've got one here", the first twinkle of the day visible in her eye. "So the BBC pays well then?" she asked.

"Not when you count the hours," Robinson claimed and laughed nervously as he had a habit of doing. "Sometimes she doesn't get back here until after midnight."

It was O'Carroll's turn to jot something down in her notebook.

"So you and Angela met at Queen's?" McCusker asked, trying to manoeuvre the conversation towards the subject of Adam Whitlock.

"Yes," Robinson replied drawing out the word with a large smile, "our student days; now they were the good old days. You know, I'd a lot of competition for Angela. There was certainly a lot of that feeling of 'you Aussie's over here, stealing our Sheilas'."

Robinson paused, appearing to drift off to a thought or maybe even to his student days in general. McCusker decided not to fill the space. O'Carroll immediately picked up on this.

"It's funny how things turn out," Robinson eventually said, with a half laugh, "I mean, at the time I thought winning Angela's hand...or should that have been heart...?" he paused to write a few words in his book. "Anyway, I thought that if I could just find a way to be with Angela then everything else would automatically fall into place for me...for us. Don't get me wrong, I'm still happy with her but really, if I'm being honest, we haven't moved on from then. Well, maybe if I wanted to be painfully honest, I haven't really moved on from then. I seem to have trouble getting my life into any kind of gear career-wise."

McCusker wondered for the first time if perhaps Robinson was on some kind of medication or maybe he'd smoked a bit of dope to get in the mood for the interview.

"It's the basic problem with the education system, isn't it?" Robinson suggested. "I mean, you do all you're told to do in your school life, you get to university, and even though you come out with a degree, you still find yourself..."

"Unemployable?" O'Carroll suggested, uncharitably.

Robinson wrote a single word in his book and flicked the pen successfully around his fingertips a few times. Maybe he should have added juggler to his list of failed careers, McCusker thought.

"So maybe it would help if I told you how we all met up?" Robinson offered, seeming as frustrated with the interview as McCusker was.

"That would be very helpful," O'Carroll chipped in.

"Well, when I arrived at Queen's Craig Husbands was one of the first people I met and became friends with. I don't remember how we hooked up, but Craig had always been very keen on going out and getting to know people. One of the people he befriended was Adam Whit-

lock and he, for some reason, succeeded me as Craig's new best friend.
I suppose even in those days an American still trumped an Australian."

"And then you met Angela?" McCusker suggested, hoping to avoid
a spat of chippiness.

"Actually, Adam was the first of us to spot Angela – he met her one
night in the union bar and then dragged Craig and myself along the
next night for moral support. I was immediately aware of Angela's
qualities, whereas people like Adam took advantage of her."

"How so?" O'Carroll asked. McCusker smiled to himself, seeing
her interest resume as soon as the dating game was mentioned.

"Well, let's just say that she's certainly a beautiful woman but she's
also a person."

"A person?" O'Carroll said, appearing confused.

"Yeah mate, you know," Robinson said, nodding furiously at
O'Carroll, "there's more to her than just the body."

"Oh, right," the detective inspector agreed.

"Did, ahm, Adam and Angela ever have a relationship?" Mc-
Cusker asked.

"You mean before we were married, don't you?" Robinson said, in
a nervous laugh.

"Yes, yes, of course."

"Well, you know, there was something between them, like a matey
kind of thing. We all shared a flat on Fitzwilliam Street at one point.
There was the four of us: Angela, Craig, Adam and myself. It seemed
the most natural thing to do; we were hanging out together all the time
and..." Robinson stopped dead, thought of something, wrote a bit in
his notebook and continued in a rush. "Of course, we all had our own
rooms. That's when we all became friends. Angela and Adam hung
out a lot together, claimed there was nothing going on...oh, they'd fool
around and laugh and joke a lot; I mean, we all did. A couple of years
passed and we moved into better accommodation and Craig met his
future wife and moved out. All the time Angela and I were becoming
closer and closer. Nothing sexual, you know, just good friends –when
'just good friends' isn't a regret."

O'Carroll noticeably shook her head from side to side.

"What, you think it's impossible for a boy and a girl to be just good
friends?" Robinson snarled, taking exception to O'Carroll's put-down.

"Oh, a boy and a girl being just good friends? That's certainly not impossible," O'Carroll said through an insincere smile. "But a man and a woman, well, that's another matter altogether."

"You were saying," McCusker said, trying to get back on track again, "that Craig moved out leaving you and Adam and…"

"…and Angela and myself," Robinson replied, also choosing to ignore O'Carroll. "Time passed. After our finals Adam returned to America. There was talk at one point of us all moving to Boston and, although Angela denies this now, I felt she was quite serious about the adventure, but, you know, I felt more at home here than I felt I'd ever feel in America. Adam packed up and left. I expected Angela to want to move out. Let's see now, we would have had a few romantic evenings at that point, or maybe just after; I find it hard to remember when all of these things happened in relation to each other. Anyway, Adam came back to Belfast to be best man at Craig's wedding – he's already had his first boy by the time he got married. Of course, he stayed with us. Angela, for the sake of appearances, moved back into her room for the week. Adam returned to the States. Then a friend of mine's father died and he returned to Scotland to run the estate – he said I could have this place if I'd take over the mortgage repayments, and I jumped at the chance. I invited Angela to move in with me to help with the mortgage and she said if we were going to do that we might as well get married."

O'Carroll looked sad, even a little envious.

"Fast-forward to today," Robinson continued, "we got married, Adam came over, and as Angela's father died when she was a kid, she asked Adam to give her away. He returned to Boston to live happily ever after. Angela secured a brilliant job at the BBC. Ross became Mr Ulsterbus. I started the first of my many jobs. Something happened in Boston, so Adam came back to Belfast and walked into an amazing highly paid job and he ends up…"

Robinson didn't finish his sentence.

"Your wife had dinner with Adam quite regularly?" McCusker said, noticing O'Carroll had jotted something down in her notebook.

"Well, you make it sound like a dinner date when in fact it wasn't just Angela and Adam – there was always Craig and Julia as well, the four of them. *Always* the four together."

"Yes, yes, of course," McCusker agreed, "but you never went?"

"No I didn't," Robinson admitted.

"Did you see a lot of Adam?" McCusker asked, setting up his next topic.

"You know, when you're a student, different things and people amuse you. When you grow older and you realise that the four of you going out and getting drunk and staying out half or all of the night isn't going to right the wrongs of the world you ...you kind of..."

"Grow up?" O'Carroll offered.

"Exactly," Robinson agreed. "Well, after I was married I realised I didn't really have a lot in common with Adam, apart from the fact that he was a very good and loyal friend to my wife. And you know that was okay because I also have some good friends who my wife isn't interested in. In fact, she can't stand some of the musicians I write lyrics for. And that's fine: it's very healthy to have separate lives. It keeps us interested in each other, doesn't it?"

"When was the last time you saw Adam Whitlock?" McCusker asked.

"Wow mate, now that is a hard one," Robinson gushed, his Aussie accent ringing through. "Adam, Craig, and Julia would have come here about two months ago to pick up Angela and take her to a BBC night in Downpatrick. They were too drunk to drive back so they stayed the night at the hotel. But it was one of those 'hello, goodbye' meetings."

"What were you doing between the hours of midnight on Saturday night to 3a.m. on Sunday morning?" McCusker asked.

Robinson looked at both detectives, wrote something in his book and said, "Now let's see, Saturday...Saturday...oh yes, 57 Joe – one of the acts I write for – was doing a gig in the Errigle Inn and ah...it would have been a late one, I would have got back here somewhere between 2.30 and 3 a.m."

"And how were they?" McCusker felt compelled to ask.

"Well, here's the thing: the point of a confessional song is that it is certainly much more successful when the singer-songwriter has a profile worthy of embarrassment. For example, should Jackson Browne, Paul Simon, Leonard Cohen or Joni Mitchell confess that they too have been unlucky in the game of love, well, then that's certainly going to grab our attention, but if 57 Joe tells you about his unlucky and unsuccessful adventures in love..."

"Who's 57 Joe?" O'Carroll asked.

"Exactly – my point entirely."

***

"Well, at last we have a suspect," O'Carroll said, as they pulled away from Robinson's house, leaving the Australian standing in his open doorway.

"Or maybe even two," McCusker offered, clicking his seatbelt, not as much following the rules as in preparation for O'Carroll's unique straight-line style of driving, particularly at roundabouts.

"Who, you mean Angela as well as Richard Robinson?" O'Carroll asked, checking her watch.

"We don't yet know which one of them gave us the false alibi, but it won't take us long to find out," McCusker said, as the five o'clock news came on Radio Ulster. "But great to see you're thinking about the case again O'Carroll – I thought I'd lost you there."

"Sorry McCusker. Look, here's the thing; I've got a date with a new man tonight and, well, I'll come clean and admit to you that a common complaint I get from men is the fact that I always seem distracted. Of course, my mind is usually on my current case, so what I've been trying to do since lunchtime is clear my head, free it up from the facts and theories that are rushing around so that I can give him my full attention."

"Right, okay, I think that make sense."

"I have a good feeling about this fella, McCusker."

"How so?"

"I just have – he's nice, clean, well groomed, well turned out, good manners, doesn't turn into an octopus the minute he stops the car."

"You seem to know him well," McCusker said, trying to recall if she'd mentioned him before. "How many times have you been out together?"

"Well, tonight is our first proper date…"

"But you just said he doesn't try and maul you in the car?"

"He dropped me home in a cab."

"Surely no one but an idiot would try it on for the first time with a taxi driver clocking every move in his rear-view mirror?"

"You'd be surprised McCusker," she said, adding, "you'd be surprised; but he really is nice. Wish me well."

"Oh I do."

"And then if he works out, all I'll need to do is find a fella for our Grace."

McCusker grimaced in silence.

"What?" O'Carroll asked, in annoyance. "What's that look you're pulling on me?"

"It's just," McCusker started, trying really hard not to burst her bubble. "Look Lily…"

"Ah you used 'Lily' – I'm not going to like this, am I?"

"No, look, it's fine – you go and have a fine night, off you go."

"Oh no, don't do that to me!" she protested loudly. "Don't patronise me! Say what you were going to say – you're my partner and if you don't tell me the truth, who will?"

"Well look, all I was going to say…" he hesitated again. "But before I do say anything I should qualify it by saying that I haven't exactly got the best track record in the romantic stakes. I've been out with one woman, married her, didn't love her, ignored her so much she left town with all our assets, don't you know."

McCusker paused for thought; that was a very brief, not to mention strange, summary of a woman he was married to for nearly twenty-five years. But then Anna Stringer had been a strange woman. He wondered if strange men attracted strange women. Or maybe, if he was prepared to look at the situation from her point of view, did strange women attract strange men. He couldn't remember ever feeling a *need* to find a woman. If anything he'd tried to give them a wide berth. He'd been hurt beyond his imagination as a teenager when his first attempt at a relationship with a girl had crashed in flames around his ankles. Jet-black-haired Angela Hutchinson had been a great teenage friend. A friend whose sultry stunning looks had launched a thousand of Mc-Cusker's daydreams. She was one of those girls who didn't have to utter a single world because she gave off the air of someone who was always preoccupied with not only seeking her own pleasure but with sharing it with others. Angela and McCusker had been barely seven weeks away from becoming more than just good friends. However, her mother had apparently been reading Angela's diary, and was aware of just how special a present her daughter was going to offer up to McCusker on the day of her eighteenth birthday. She quite literally nabbed Angela from McCusker's greedy (but amateur) paws, and deposited her in Wimbledon, in faraway London town. Apparently over in London town there was a better chance that the eligible boys might be of the same religion as Angela. And even if they weren't, none of the nosey neighbours would ever notice. Sadly Angela, after all her mother's trouble, and maybe even because of all the trouble her mother had gone to great pains over, had been deflowered by a SW19 cad, and Angela boasted as much when she and McCusker next bumped into each other by accident in Portrush, their home town. At that point Angela had given up on the London boys and was back home looking for a father for her one-year-old daughter, and she seemed to be enjoying immensely the process of auditions, deductions, and eliminations. McCusker kept his broken heart hidden, feigning career priorities as his excuse. But the truth was he'd never forgiven her for not saving herself and delivering her maiden self, wrapped in birthday ribbons, and not much else, as promised. He wouldn't even have worried if the present she'd originally offered had been, one, or two, or, heck, *even* three, years late, just as long as it was delivered…well…intact as it were. He accepted now, but not then, that he'd been guilty of some double standards.

There had never been a similar physical attraction between him and Anna Stringer. As McCusker thought this he was overcome by sadness at the fact of how true it was, and if he hadn't been considering Angela and Anna Stringer in the same thought, he'd never have realised it. He also still had great difficulty trying to work out how he went from a grilling style first date with Anna Stringer, to marriage in ten short months. And all of that without even the threat, or even a hint, of the patter of tiny feet. This patter of tiny feet excluded, of course, the patter of the tiny feet of her cat (one interchangeable cat replacing the other when they got to be too old and lethargic). *The* cat had always been Anna Stringer's last line of defence when it came to McCusker's amorous overtures. The cat in the lap meant no chasing the butterfly and the cat was always, but always, in the lap.

Anna Stringer looked like she permanently felt sorry for herself. On the troublesome first date McCusker felt like he was being interviewed for a post in the civil service. Their one sided conversation was peppered with, "Your eyes look too hungry for me." Or, "If you think

I'd be interest in any of that auld carry on, you've got another thing coming." Then the big, big downer, "I wouldn't be interested in being intensely in love with anyone. My Ma says all that does is give you a migraine." McCusker felt that Anna Stringer had been taking great pleasure in failing him on all points and would take even greater pleasure in reporting as much to her 'Ma'. But then didn't she only go and concluded the interview by saying, "Oh go on, you can kiss me now if you want to." And it hadn't exactly been a request! It hadn't been a request at all in fact. McCusker felt that their relationship would have been entirely different if only she'd said, in conclusion of that first disastrous date, "I've been dying to kiss you all night," and then risked her migraine by trying to tickle his tonsils.

At least then they might, just might, have stood a chance.

McCusker still couldn't really understand why he and Anna Stringer had married ten months later, a month after his twenty-seventh birthday. He did accept though that as you get older, and this applied to both men and women, you started to consider partners you would never have considered earlier in your life.

"Get on with it McCusker, what were you going to say?" O'Carroll asked, drawing him out of his trip down memory lane.

"Well, it does seem to me that the only time you are not thinking about finding a man for yourself is when you are thinking about finding a man for Grace."

"You say that as if it's a bad thing!" she replied in amusement. "Listen, I've got news for you McCusker: that's all anyone normal thinks about. You know, careers, ambitions, promotions, bigger bank balances, nice clothes, pampering – I'm talking about the whole shebang that preoccupies all of us, and it's all leading to setting us up for the most important part of our lives. In fact, I would go as far as to say that the only reason we're put on this earth is to find a fella, or in your case, McCusker – in case you're still confused – a woman."

"But it can't be?"

"A woman?" she snapped. "Now I am surprised."

"No you eejit, I meant it can't be the reason we've all been put on this earth."

"Think about it McCusker, and I have thought about it a lot and nothing else makes sense."

"And even if that is true, do you really need to go chasing it so aggressively, would it not be better to just let someone come into your life more naturally?" McCusker offered, showing perhaps that he'd also thought about this subject a lot as well, "and in the meantime there are other things we can enjoy?"

"Really? Like what, for instance?" she asked, in clear disbelief.

"Like your work, like movies, like books, like walking around Belfast," McCusker said, warming to his own answer. "You…you realise what an absolutely amazing city this is? Don't you see – just to walk around slowly, soaking everything up, all these spectacular buildings, and enjoying those experiences."

She rolled her eyes.

"So my point would be," McCusker continued unperturbed, "it's better to enjoy all the pleasures that are already plentiful in our lives and then…well, surely there is a much better chance of finding true love if you let things happen more naturally?"

"Oh Holy Mary, Mother of God! McCusker, I don't believe it – not only are you an innocent but you're also a romantic!"

McCusker exhaled loudly.

"Okay McCusker," she began patiently, "let me put my case. You have two people out there living this life. One, as in myself, grabs every opportunity to meet someone and because of that will no doubt, a) have a much better level of experience to call on, and b) a much greater number of partners to pick from than the man, such as yourself, who married the first girl he slept with and was so interested in walking around looking at buildings that he didn't notice his life go by or his marriage slip out of the door. So, my question to you would have to be: who of the two is better equipped for the most important part of our lives? QED and toodableedin'loo."

CHAPTER TWENTY-TWO

Thirteen hours later on Wednesday morning they met up again on the steps of the Custom House.

"Hi O'Carroll – how did last night go?"

"He's a through-other culchie – a cad, a dinosaur in sheep's clothing, a drunk! He'd horrible breath, BO, massive hands, didn't even bother to shave. He's hair implants, he wore odd socks, his shirt looked like he'd fished it out of the dirty linen basket just before he came out and his shoes were scuffed and his trousers wrinkled. I'll tell you this for nothing, McCusker, if I never see another man again it will be too soon. To top it all I had far too much to drink so if you're very good to me McCusker and don't shout at me again until the hammer in my head runs out of steam – I'll let you take me out at lunchtime and show me some of these..." she took her first pause and then whispered, using her fingers to signify quotation marks "'beautiful buildings' of yours around this wonderful city of ours. Now...how are we getting on with this case of yours?"

"Well, funny you should ask but I visited the Errigle Inn up on the corner of Ormeau Road and Jameson Street last night on the off chance," McCusker started, keeping his voice to a level that her eyebrows seemed comfortable with.

"Okay," O'Carroll whispered, "now you've got my total undivided attention and I swear to you I'm going to allow nothing into my head today apart from the facts of this case."

"Okay Lily," McCusker continued happily. "As I say, after a bite of supper at Deanes I went to the Errigle Inn yesterday evening. The entertainment establishment was friendly and cheerful. There was a great wee girl called Isobel Anderson performing when I was there. The venue was quite packed."

"McCusker can we, ah…"

"Sorry, okay," he said smiling happily at the fact that she was interacting again. "I just wanted to see if 57 Joe had performed there on
Saturday and then pick up their contact details so that I could check
out Richard Robinson's alibi."

"And?"

"And not only were 57 Joe playing there on Saturday, but the manager and one of the members of the band, the drummer, were down
last night as well."

"And?" O'Carroll said. "I feel I would be enjoying much more success if I was using a syringe and a stone."

"They think Richard is a Rodney – according to the drummer that's
the new word for plonker – and they think that his lyrics are crap,
'laboured' was the word they used. They told me they've never used
any of Robinson's lyrics, nor will they ever, they claim. They also said
that Robinson had boasted that if 57 Joe do one of his songs, his wife
could get them on Radio Ulster."

"And they still didn't?"

"They still didn't," McCusker said, raising his eyebrows.

"But was he down at the Errigle on Saturday?"

"That's the only bit of bad news…" McCusker admitted. "They say
they certainly didn't see him on Saturday night but the place was so
packed there was a fair chance he could have been in the building and
they'd just not seen him."

***

"Why are you in such a rush to get to the Europa, and why do we
have to walk?" O'Carroll asked, as she followed McCusker, who'd insisted on walking to the hotel, which in the seventies and eighties had
had the cheapest heating bill of any hotel in the UK.

"You tell me?" McCusker teased.

"Which?"

"Both?" he insisted as they hit Donegall Square.

"McCusker, please, my head…you promised you'd go easy on me
this morning."

"Okay. Well, if I'm not very much mistaken, breakfast at the Europa
finishes at 10.30 and you know Belfast, particularly the city centre – it's

really very small, so when you factor in the traffic and parking it's just as quick to walk."

O'Carroll still struggled to keep up with him.

"Besides, it's a truly beautiful morning and this fresh air will blow the cobwebs out of your head."

"So would a blast from a double barrel shotgun, but I'm not going to try that route either," she moaned. "McCusker, please…at least slow down to a rate humans can keep up with."

Barr had arranged to do the interview with Whitlock Junior but he'd got caught up on another part of the case and had to shy off, so McCusker was happy to step in for his Detective Sergeant. Unfortunately for McCusker the only thing Jaime Whitlock was offering was the Europa's complimentary coffee and a cellophane-wrapped Danish pastry. He claimed his room wasn't anywhere near as grand as his father's, insisting that they conduct the interview in the Europa's spacious, busy, and windy lobby.

McCusker secured them three comfortable seats by the fireplace as Jaime produced a sighting of his room key in exchange for the meagre breakfast.

O'Carroll poured herself a large cup of strong-smelling coffee, took a swig, produced her notebook and appeared as though she might settle into an eyes-open nap.

"How is the investigation progressing?" Jaime asked, getting down to business.

Whitlock Junior – the deceased's younger brother – had a preppie image in his chinos, blue shirt, Red Sox jacket, brown and white leather brogues, and Harvard scarf. He was clean cut, with short well-tended hair and had the demeanour of a wannabe Wesley Whitlock III.

"At this stage it's all about amassing information; we really can't get enough of it," McCusker replied, happy to ignore his coffee after his first sip. "So the more information you can give us now, the more helpful you'll be to us."

"Shoot."

"Okay," McCusker started, deciding to bite the bullet and go straight for it. "We now know quite a bit about Adam's background, but there are two areas I'd love your help on. Firstly, the Cindy Scott incident and then…look, Jaime, I'm really not looking to dig the dirt on Adam but I really need to find out what was going on in his life.

From what we can gather, he'd no enemies, no problems at work, he wasn't romantically involved with anyone, and he wasn't involved in anything shady. From all the info we've gathered, he really was a model citizen."

"And your point would be that model citizens aren't brutally murdered?" Jaime asked.

"Well in a word, no," McCusker replied, admiring his apparent no-nonsense approach. "Unless of course it's mistaken identity."

"But you don't believe it's that, do you?"

"Most definitely not," McCusker agreed. "Can I be blunt with you?"

"Absolutely," the American confirmed immediately.

"Okay. Your brother was killed by the first knife wound..." McCusker said, his gentle Ulster accent making it sound less solemn than it actually was. "Whoever murdered your brother wanted to make a statement and continued to stab him viciously and repeatedly."

"Which kind of rules out mistaken identity?"

"Most likely," McCusker agreed. "I suppose a clever lawyer could argue the opposite if they needed to, but I'm thinking the person who murdered your brother felt he needed to and wanted to make a statement."

"A statement to those of us left behind?"

"That's what I'm thinking," he admitted, as O'Carroll, having now caught her first breath, looked mighty impressed at him. "Otherwise, why bother?"

"He could have also been making a statement to himself," O'Carroll suggested.

"Or herself?" Jaime Whitlock added.

O'Carroll shrugged as if to suggest a woman would or could not have carried out this murder. McCusker was inclined to agree.

"Okay," Whitlock said, "let's think about it. My father and I agree that Bing Scott was long over his sister's death and that he'd never held Adam responsible in the first place, but if we need to be out there looking for suspects, you'd have to say that none of us really ever know what goes on in another person's head."

"When was the last time you spoke to Bing?" McCusker asked.

"I would have bumped into him a month or so back. He was always friendly, always asking after Adam and Julia."

"So he would have known they were both in Belfast?" O'Carroll asked.

"Most definitely."

"Would he have travelled to Europe in his line of work?" McCusker asked.

"I don't believe so, but I can ask my father's firm in Boston to check it out," Jaime offered, as he pulled a notepad out of an inside pocket and made a note.

McCusker made a mental note to also have Bing Scott checked out by the FBI or the CIA, he was never sure which– anyway, that was a task for Superintendent Larkin.

"Was there any chance at all that Adam might have been carrying on with Cindy?" McCusker asked, sheepishly.

"No, not a chance, not a chance in the world," Jaime claimed. "Adam was never really interested in girls, particularly girly girls. I don't mean he was interested in boys, but he'd only date girls who were either mature or pretended to be mature. So no, and whereas he most certainly wouldn't have been rude to Cindy, neither would he have led her on. I was too young for that group as well, but I believe she was infatuated with my brother and it was quite simply a terrible, terrible accident."

"Okay, we'll regroup on Mr Scott," McCusker said. "Anything else?"

Jaime stared McCusker straight in the eye.

"What?" McCusker eventually felt compelled to say.

"Well...it's probably nothing and I do hate to stir up a hornet's nest but..."

"But?" McCusker coaxed.

"Well, I often told Adam that he should stop messing around with Angela."

"Define 'messing around'?" O'Carroll said, finally blowing the end of her hangover away.

"You know, I honestly never really knew what was going on between the two of them; they went way back. Adam claims to have known her from before she met her husband, claimed they were just great friends. But they were close, very close and when I stayed with Adam once in Belfast, Angela spent the night."

"Just to get this clear...would this have been before or after she married Richard?" McCusker asked slowly.

"Oh most definitely afterward," Jaime said. "Mind you, he said nothing happened – they were friends, she'd just drank too much and couldn't drive home. He claimed she slept on the sofa, but I was jet-lagged out of my brains and got up a few times during the night to get a drink of Coke and I can tell you she most definitely wasn't on the sofa when I went through the lounge."

O'Carroll scribbled furiously in her book.

"Look, it's most likely nothing," Jaime Whitlock said, a wee bit self-consciously. "I had words with him and told him it didn't really matter what actually did or didn't happen; no, I told him it would be more important to his well-being what the husband *imagined* might have happened. But Adam wasn't in the slightest bit concerned about it."

"Okay," McCusker asked, thinking there had, thanks to Jaime's honesty, just been a bit of a breakthrough on the case. "Anything else you can think of?"

"There's really not," Whitlock Junior said. "I really wish I could help you more, if only to get my father off of this. He's thinking about nothing else at the moment and...listen McCusker, I will admit to you he's got some of his mates from way back in the day running around like chickens with their heads cut off trying to solve this. The sooner you guys break this case, the sooner I can get him home and allow him to start his grieving. I mean, I know he doesn't look it, but he is a very old man and I fear what this will do to him."

***

Five minutes later McCusker and O'Carroll were waiting for the pedestrian lights just outside the door of the Europa to change, so that they could cross the road to the Crown Bar side of Great Victoria Street. "We're not far from the Beeb – do you fancy nipping around and having a wee chat with Angela Robinson?" McCusker asked.

"Count me in," O'Carroll replied, but quickly revealed her mind was elsewhere. "This Cindy Scott thing...I'm not so sure her brother Bing would get over her death that easy."

They cut through Amelia Street, left into Brunswick Street past Belfast Metropolitan College aka 'the College of Knowledge,' and then took a quick right into James Street, an area well developed since it's early days as a hooker haven.

"You think Bing could hold Adam Whitlock responsible for his sister's death?"

"It wouldn't be too big a leap of the imagination to land on that particular leaf."

"But surely to go from there to murdering him for revenge *would* be too big a leap?"

"Perhaps, perhaps not," O'Carroll replied, as they crossed Bedford Street at the Franklin Street junction, to the front steps of the historic Ulster Hall, the spiritual home of guitarist Rory Gallagher. "It really depends on the mental state of Bing Scott."

"Okay then, let me ask you this: if say you lived in the States and you thought someone was responsible for the death of your sister, would you want the state to execute your sister's murderer?"

"No," she replied, totally surprising McCusker.

Then after a short pause she continued, "I wouldn't want the state to do it – I'd want to flick the switch myself and put the a-hole out of his misery."

CHAPTER TWENTY-THREE

"We started out on Bushmills and soon hit the harder stuff," was Angela Robinson's opening line when they eventually got to see her. McCusker had quickly confronted her with the fact that they knew she was having an affair with Adam Whitlock.

They'd been shown through to her small office on the third floor of Broadcasting House because she was, another producer noted, "on air for another seventeen minutes, then I take over."

In the intervening seventeen minutes – which had then dropped to fifteen and a half minutes, according to the large, loud, ticking clock over the door facing her desk – DI Lily O'Carroll had negotiated her way through Angela's Blackberry to discover, with some degree of excitement and pride, that the producer did not have her husband registered in her speed-dial list; equally telling was the fact that Adam Whitlock was included in her most used list of telephone numbers.

"We'd started out on Bushmills..." she reiterated, staring straight into McCusker's eyes and looking close to tears herself. "We made out the first night we met. We were in the student's union bar and of course I'm talking American standards here where making out is heavy petting and nothing more."

She searched around in the bottom drawer of her desk until she produced a small bottle of Bushmills whiskey and three small plastic cups she'd nicked from the stash by the water cooler in the communal area. She poured herself a stiff one, which she gulped down before bothering to pour one each for McCusker and O'Carroll and another one for herself. With her second one she toasted: "To Adam, I miss you and may you forgive me for what I'm about to tell a pair of coppers."

McCusker raised his cup to Angela and then to his mouth, barely letting the fine brew kiss his lips. He knew it was unacceptable to be drinking with a witness, but he felt that if at least Angela thought they were joining her in a drink she might be more inclined to talk freely. With a case as light on leads as this one, he needed someone talking freely. O'Carroll also seemed to sense this and followed his lead, although she appeared to take a generous gulp.

"We got on great from the first time we met. Our common bond was our love of movies and we agreed it was much better to fail while going for the big things in life than to succeed in domestic bliss. Perhaps that was our downfall."

"I made it clear to Adam that I wasn't interested in anything other than 'making out.' And he was fine with that. He felt there was something noble about waiting for someone special; someone so special you'd be happy to spend the rest of your life with them rather that shagging the first person you meet at university. He was also helped by the fact that he wasn't a doctor – I can't abide doctors. Adam was a clean-cut kid and he'd been to college too. We became great friends though, more a Butch Cassidy and the Sundance Kid than a Bonnie and Clyde. Just in case you are wondering, I was the Sundance Kid by the way."

"After a few months we were still into our heavy petting and he never hassled me to go further. I'd met Richard and Craig by that stage we'd all go to the union together, and then Adam and me would stagger home to the shoebox the four of us shared – separate rooms, of course, as far as the rest of our flatmates were concerned. I remember this time – it would have been mid-term because most students had disappeared home. Adam and I had stayed in Belfast because he hadn't wanted to go back to Boston. I stayed over in his room one night, again we were just kissing. Adam never pushed the issue with me, he was a good guy. That's why we grew to be such great friends. He was such a gentle guy and he'd no hidden agendas; everything was out on the table for all to see."

"One of the things he put out there – on the table as it were – totally flummoxed me at the beginning. He admitted that he felt that sexually speaking he was very inexperienced and he wanted to do something about it. He'd obviously thought through the subject beforehand in a very academic manner. He pointed out that we were both clean, both very hygienic in fact, and that we could both use each other to gain our sexual experience without compromising my virginal state, as it were. He felt that we could both teach each other how to pleasure the other in every way possible, although he stated he was only interested in wholesome pleasures, nothing perverted. You know, that admission of his was probably the single fact that encouraged me to allow myself to embark on our sexual adventure."

"Like friends with benefits?" O'Carroll, who seemed just as intrigued as McCusker by the admission, suggested.

"Well yes, I suppose," Angela said, "although today I believe that phrase usually means friends who can bonk each other's brains out without any emotional commitment while they continue to seek and date prospective life partners. Our benefits were to pleasure each other, where we both felt, I believe, that pleasuring each other wasn't second best.

"I can't believe I'm talking to you about this," she said nervously as she took another large swig of Bushmills and topped up her own cup again. "But I think it's important you know exactly the basis of my relationship with Adam."

McCusker noticed that not once in the conversation so far had the BBC producer spared O'Carroll more than a passing glance.

"Okay, this is the difficult bit for me, but here goes…off into the blue wild yonder," she said, taking yet another gulp from her cup. "Soon we were stealing away at every single opportunity to continue our education in the art of pleasuring a partner. Oh my God! Now here I have to tell you that it became very, very clear that Adam was thinking about our new subject quite a bit, I mean a lot more than I was. I was enjoying it of course, as much if not more than he was, but I was thinking about it, about the pleasuring, whereas he, like a true academic, was preoccupied with the theory of the subject. He felt mystery, romance, creativeness, thoughtfulness, and care were the main ingredients required for the final pleasure. Adam liked to play-act, where we would do things we'd done before but add variations and pretend like it was our first time. Some of those adventures were just truly unbelievable.

"But it wasn't always him leading the way. Sometimes as we lay blissfully exhausted in each other's arms he'd say 'Okay Booth – that's my maiden name by the way – next time you come up with the fantasy.' And next time he'd be the willing participant in *my* soft porn script."

"None of your friends ever knew you were enjoying this kind of a relationship?" O'Carroll asked.

O'Carroll's use of the word "enjoying" seemed to make Angela take note of her because, for the first time, she looked at her, the respect obvious in her eyes. "No, no one had a clue," she said. "Not even to this day."

"Adam's brother, Jaime, guessed," McCusker admitted, laying some cards of his own on the table.

"Oh ri-ight," Robinson said, visibly betraying that the penny had dropped. "That's how you knew...the sleepover. I told Adam it was a bad idea and that Jaime hadn't fallen for me being drunk and sleeping on the sofa. Mind you," she continued, looking wistful, "from my memory of a relationship with lots of highs, that night was a particularly amazing and unforgettable one. Maybe the danger of being discovered by his brother lying a few feet away added the extra element."

"But that night occurred, if I'm not very much mistaken, after you and Richard were already married," McCusker offered.

"Yes, right, of course, so you'd be the detective then," she said, the fresh swig of whiskey following the previous, which was now clear in her eyes. "I was getting to that. And now, as we say in radio land ...back to the music, actually back 'to face the music' might be more apt in my case. Adam and me, how should I put this...were thoroughly enjoying ourselves – lots of adventures, but he insisted we avoid making it a regular habit, claiming it would be much more exciting and consequently rewarding if we didn't know when, where or even if it would happen again. I think, but equally I wouldn't swear to it, but I think Adam was the first of us to get a proper partner. She called herself XL Rose, a rock chick from Bellaghy; more Mama Cass than Cher, but I think she amused him as much as anything else.

"Then he shocked me when he told me that just because he was seeing someone else, he didn't think it was necessary for us to stop our 'adventures,' which was a blessing for me because I can't describe to you how absolutely exquisite our wee explorations had become. He explained that our friendship was healthy, if somewhat occasionally erotic, but never emotional. Then I started dating a boy. I'll tell you a story. By this point we – Adam, Craig, Richard, and I – had all moved into a new flat together up on Fitzwilliam Road – and Richard was always hitting on me. I mean, he was never obvious about it; he always behaved in that uncharming kind of way of dating. You know, Inspector," she paused as she looked only at DI O'Carroll. "Where a man who you can't avoid, though your instincts tells you that you should give them a wide berth – a very wide berth – continuously finds something to talk to you about and they talk and talk and after time they get a wee bit over familiar with you – never enough to drive you away, mind you – and before you know it you wake up one morning and you find you're sharing a pillow with them. Richard was one such man, and he'd made a unilateral decision to attach his person to my wagon. I figured if I had a 'boyfriend,' Richard would leave me alone. So I dated Rune Lem, a sweet Norwegian boy, and at the same time Adam and I continued our adventures.

"Adam changed girlfriends a lot, after XL Rose was Sam, then…oh I forget now. I, on the other hand, changed boyfriends once, well…maybe twice at the most. I initially liked the second one a lot but he became a pain and eventually he started to scunder me a bit….more about him later. Now sometimes Adam and I wouldn't see each other for an adventure for months but that's what always made it very exciting!"

"And during all of this time you and Adam never…never made love?" O'Carroll asked.

"We never, ever made love," she replied flatly.

"Did you never, you know…feel like you'd like to try it with him, even just once?"

"You see Inspector, I know exactly where you are coming from on this. Undoubtedly you feel that our adventures were always second class to the main event. But all I can tell you is that some of the experiences I had with Adam in our play-acting, our experimental sessions, were the best I ever experienced in my life to this day. If they could make a drug that made me feel like that again I know for sure I'd be a junkie."

O'Carroll shook her head slowly, not in disbelief, McCusker figured, but out of amazement. He hoped that O'Carroll wouldn't want to try something similar with him and then he wondered immediately why that thought had even entered his mind.

"Time passed, Adam moved back to Boston, and I woke up one morning and, yes, you've guessed it, I was indeed sharing a pillow with Richard. I still don't know to this day how he pulled it off. I'd always viewed him as someone with one foot in the grave, the other on a banana skin. The only thing I will say is that the contrast between Adam and Richard was incredible in that Richard never, ever even pretended to be interested in my pleasure: wham, bam and (not even) thank you ma'am.

"In my defence, I will say that it is my belief that should Adam have remained in Belfast, then Richard and I would never ever have hooked up, let alone get married. Adam, believe it or not, even came over for the wedding. He stood in for my dad, who died when I was seven, and gave me away," Angela said dropping to a whisper. She looked through her glass door to see if anyone was outside. Happy to see they were alone, she took another swig of Bushmills and said, "He was entitled to give me away – I was his to give. He turned up at the stag do the night before the wedding, but since he'd never really got on with Richard, he left after half an hour and was waiting for me back at the hotel when I got back from my own hen do.

"Now, before I tell you what happened that night I need to give you a bit of background. First, I hadn't seen Adam for nearly a year; second, I was on the verge of not going through with the wedding; third, Richard is, well…he loves to go to bed…but just to sleep, and finally, your honour – and you too missy – I will admit to having had a lot to drink. I wasn't plastered but I was flying, and so when I got back to the hotel and saw Adam in the bar I sat with him for a while. I asked him to give me fifteen minutes for good decorum before following me up to the room.

"We didn't discuss the rights or wrongs, we just fell into our play-acting routine, one I'd come up with, where this bride-to-be is having doubts about her husband, and so meets an ex for one last night of passion. The ex says no, but my role was to seduce him using one of our favourite routines. The secret to the success of this one was his strength to resist me and my ability, without being slutty or gross, to tempt him.

"Anyway, I'll leave the rest of the details to your imagination but because I felt it was our last time, I begged and begged him for full intercourse. He refused and I got upset, saying my wedding was a farce and that I couldn't possibly go through with it."

"Sorry, forgive me for interrupting you," McCusker said to Angela who by now was visibly tipsy. "I will admit that I'm a wee bit confused now, was that last part about you and Adam not having full intercourse and you not wanting to go through with the wedding...was that real or was that also play-acting?"

"No, that bit was real, Inspector," she replied sweetly.

This was most definitely not one of those occasions to stop and correct the girl on his job title. "Right," he said.

"So Adam talked me down," Angela said, and then went a wee bit solemn. "He said he'd a special surprise for the wedding. I assumed he meant he'd got me something special for us as a wedding present. The next day, Richard and I were married. He was completely oblivious to everything. A few hours after the reception had started I was quite merry. I bumped into Adam. He appeared to be quite drunk as well, which was very unusual for him. I asked him about his surprise. He said the day was yet young. He'd a room at the same hotel as the reception, the Culloden out at Bangor. Richard never knew this but Adam paid for the entire reception. His logic was that he had the money, I didn't, and, as he was standing in for my dad, he had to pay for it, with it being a father's responsibility. A few hours later Adam passed out and Richard and I saw Craig and Ross carry him out, his feet trailing along the floor. I assumed they were taking him up to his room to sleep it off.

"A few hours later I go to my room to change from my wedding dress and into my going-away trouser suit, you know, just before the bride and groom's grand exit.

"I'm no sooner in the room when Adam, sober as a judge – he'd been play-acting again – creeps up behind me and says something about kidnapping the bride. In the little scenario he'd cooked up he didn't want to overpower me, but he wanted me to beg for it. Again I will admit I didn't for one second stop and think, 'I'm married now, I can't be fooling around any more with him.' No, I also slipped into my role and then...well...long story short, we had full intercourse for the first time."

McCusker and O'Carroll continued to stare, dumbstruck.

"What? What's up? You weren't expecting me to go into all the gory details, were you? You were, you pair of pervs you!"

McCusker was happy she hadn't gone into the details – it would have been way too embarrassing and he'd have to face O'Carroll on the walk back to the Customer House. How much of the gory details would the girls have gone into without him there? On second thoughts, perhaps Angela Robinson thought her only confidante at the interview was BM – as in Bushmills.

"But you told us you and Adam had never made love?" O'Carroll said, appearing very disappointed that the two of them hadn't been able to stick to their agreement.

"And that's true," Angela replied, "we never ever made love – we frequently had sex."

"So you had full sex from then onwards?" O'Carroll asked, ending the awkward silence.

"Sometime, not all of the time," she replied in a sing-song style that referenced Bob Dylan for the third time in the interview. "Look, it's difficult for me to say this when he's not around to defend himself, but I began to realise that me getting married was just another part of his play-acting game. It was an elaborate part, but a part nonetheless. I soon got over any wee hang-ups I was feeling over that and pretty soon we were acting like I'd never got married, you know. Hey, and you know what? At no point could I have stopped, even if I'd wanted to."

"But you were married..." McCusker said, in sheer disbelief, unable to contain the words.

"Look Inspector," she started.

"He's not an inspector, he's freelance," O'Carroll interrupted, obviously feeling all the juicy bits were over.

"Well how am I meant to address him?"

"McCusker will do," the freelance detective said.

"Okay *McCusker*, as I was about to say, I wasn't the one who was short-changing the other in my marriage. My husband never came to that particular well...shit, mixed metaphors abound – let's just say I always fulfilled my marital obligations, always. On top of which, I was the bread-winner in the family: I cooked the food as well as paying for it. I paid the mortgage. I never rubbed his nose in it. Adam and I were very discreet, so discreet we used to call ourselves the 'silent lovers'."

"But why stay with Richard?" McCusker continued, showing that he was still trying to come to terms with this.

"Two reasons mainly, and both of them equally important," she said, draining the remainder of the Bushmills direct from the bottle. "Firstly, please don't forget that there was never ever going to be a conventional orthodox relationship between myself and Adam. He did not want me in that way; he didn't want me ensconced as his wife. He much preferred to spend time dreaming up what he was going to do to me or what I was going to do to him, or what we were going to do to each other. Perhaps he didn't feel like he could do that kind of thing with a wife. I'll tell you this: our fire of passion was still burning as brightly and as feverishly as it ever had been; it never waned. I was madly, passionately in lust with him. Secondly, Richard genuinely cares about me. He will look after me when I need looking after. He will never be the one to leave me, never! That's always been the way and now that Adam is no longer alive do you realise just how comforting that is?"

McCusker shook his head in disbelief slowly and sadly from side to side.

"Oh, get over it McCusker, some women are lucky enough to be able to find lust, friendship, excitement, entertainment, knowledge, companionship, and caring all in the one man. Me, I'm resigned to having to recruit seven separate men just so I can tick all of those boxes."

"I need you to think very carefully about this Angela; is there any chance at all Richard had a clue as to what was going on between you and Adam?" McCusker asked.

"Not at all, not a chance."

"You know you said that you paid the mortgage and put the bread on the table – did Adam ever help you in this area, you know, with finance?" McCusker suggested, his question prompted by Angela's admission that the American had paid for her wedding reception.

She looked shocked at McCusker's question and the brief time it took her to regroup was answer enough to betray the truth.

Before she'd even a chance to put her thoughts into words, McCusker pushed on: "Okay, did he give you cheques, cash, make payments on your behalf?" It became clear that Angela Robinson had become more preoccupied with his untouched glass of Bushmills, and he quickly realised the interview was pretty much over.

He and O'Carroll helped Robinson vacate her office and found her a cab coming up Bedford Street. She offered to drop them off somewhere but McCusker voted for a bit of air. O'Carroll agreed, and so they made arrangements to meet again in the morning. She promised to text Angela the same information "just in case."

***

"It seems to me," McCusker started, as they passed the Ulster Hall again – only this time going in the opposite direction – and proving that his mind was miles away, "that love and sex are two completely different things and the mistake most of us make is thinking they are connected."

"Grace once said something like that," O'Carroll offered, not shooting McCusker down in flames the way he thought she would. "But were you referring to Angela Robinson?"

"Perhaps," he agreed, "although I think her problem might not be about the connection, or lack of the same, between love and sex but more that she thinks love doesn't exist at all, don't you see?"

CHAPTER TWENTY-FOUR

"How do you feel today?" Superintendent Larkin asked McCusker the following morning, just before the briefing started.

"If I felt any better I'd be twins," McCusker replied.

"More power to your elbow, Mr McCusker," Larkin said and then, ending the civilities, "Right, where are we on this case?"

Suddenly a flash of inspiration hit McCusker: that's where he knew the superintendent from and it was maybe why he smiled at his boss a wee bit too much! The famous statue of the anonymous speaker on the steps of the Custom House: he was the exact same build, same moustache, similar hair, same waistcoat, same height…McCusker questioned where fact ended and fiction began; had Larkin always naturally resembled the statue or had he modelled himself, perhaps even unconsciously, on the figure he passed by every day to work?

"Okay," McCusker started, realising everyone was waiting for him to answer the super's question. "On the suspect list we have…" McCusker wrote with a white marker on a very large Perspex board. He recited the names as he wrote them: "Bing Scott – whose sister Cindy had an accident and died while trying to flirt with Adam Whitlock. Craig Husbands – university friend who couldn't get Whitlock to invest in his project. Angela Robinson – was having a long-term affair with Whitlock behind her husband's back. Perhaps Whitlock wanted to break it off. Richard Robinson – Angela claimed her husband didn't know about her affair with Adam, but if her husband *had* discovered it, he'd have a pretty good motive. Also either he or his wife's alibi is suspect, maybe even both. The sister, Julia Whitlock…"

"Surely not?" Larkin interrupted.

"Am I grasping at straws? Most definitely," McCusker admitted, "but at the same time did she and her brother have a strange relationship ...and again, you have to say: most certainly. Did she benefit from her brother's death? So far as we can gather she's the one who benefited the most, to the tune of £287,000 in fact."

"Any others?" Larkin continued.

McCusker was about to admit that there were not when he caught DS Barr's eye, who appeared to want to inject but wanted McCusker's approval before doing so.

"You have something DS Barr?" McCusker responded.

"I've been trying to find as many of Adam Whitlock's old Queen's University mates as possible. Just this morning, in fact, I had an email back from one lead in the USA: a Professor Bob Ceverto from Berkeley University. He was in the same year as Mr Whitlock. He said Adam, Craig Husbands, Ross Wallace, and Angela were thick as thieves; they'd no time for anyone else. He claimed that Samantha, a girl he used to date, dropped him for Ross Wallace. A year or so later Samantha and Ross had a shotgun wedding and a few months later Tom was born. The professor and quite a few of his circle were convinced that Ross wasn't, in fact, the father but that Adam Whitlock was."

"That ties in with what Angela Robinson told us..." O'Carroll said. "She said Adam Whitlock had a girlfriend called Sam."

"Well done DS Barr," McCusker said, as he wrote the names Ross Wallace and Samantha Wallace on the suspect list. "Great initiative."

They all stared at the list for a few moments. McCusker read the names out aloud again:

Bing Scott
Craig Husbands
Angela Robinson
Richard Robinson
Julia Whitlock
Ross Wallace
Samantha Wallace
POPU

"Who's POPU?" DI Cage asked.

"Person or persons unknown," Larkin replied, deadpan. "It's really unbelievable," he continued still looking in shock. "I always knew that if you scratched the surface of anyone's life it's incredible what you find underneath, but these students really do take the biscuit. I mean un-be-liev-able."

"Of course, we can't rule out a CWM," Cage offered, still a bit red-cheeked from the POPU exchange and still badly bruised from his RTA. When no one bit his bait he continued, "Yes, CWM – it's a relatively new phenomenon but it's becoming more and more common these days, where people commit crime without having any motives to do so. Crime without motive – CWM. I was on a conference recently about this very topic and the conclusions are quite disturbing."

"Jeez, sure, that's a great one for you Detective Inspector Cage," O'Carroll said. "You're now going to be able to report a 100 per cent success rate with the rest of your cases: crimes without motive equals CWT."

"CWT?" Cage inquired, biting her bait.

"Chastisement without trial," O'Carroll replied quickly, hitting her imaginary cymbal.

"All joking aside," Larkin said, ending the scattered laughter, "it *is* a very significant development when people, sometimes not even criminals, are literally beating up victims and damaging private and public property for no other reason than they think they can get away with it – either that or they get a major buzz from doing so. The next step down this particular path is unthinkable."

"Anything turn up on the house to house enquiries on Cyprus Avenue?" McCusker asked hopefully.

"Not a lot," DS Barr replied. "I left all the reports on DI O'Carroll's desk."

O'Carroll flashed Barr what McCusker imagined was a 'thanks a fecking million' glare.

"Okay, time is passing," McCusker said, noting that Superintendent Larkin was starting to look a little bored, either that or he had his personal barber awaiting him, hungry scissors eagerly snapping away furiously mid-air in anticipation. "DS Barr, you continue with your initiative with Whitlock's fellow students please. DI Cage, could you carry out a full check on Richard Robinson's background please? I bet there'll be quite a few treasures there. He wasn't beyond compromising his wife's position at the BBC; he's idle, so he's had a lot of time to sit around with nothing whatsoever to do but stew over what Whitlock was doing with his wife, with an equal amount of time to plot his revenge. The state Adam Whitlock was found in testifies to the fact that someone positively hated the victim. This would have to put Richard Robinson and Ross Wallace top of our list. DI O'Carroll and I will do a similar check on Mr Wallace and have a chat with his wife and with Angela Robinson."

"And if someone would like to give me a floor brush I'm sure..." O'Carroll started, interrupting McCusker, only to be interrupted in turn by the super.

"O'Carroll! We've heard the end of that line before and we don't need to hear it again."

"Sorry, sir."

CHAPTER TWENTY-FIVE

So that was Thursday off and started. Just a week ago Adam Whitlock was still alive, enjoying his life to the full, but, McCusker thought, doing something – or having *done* something – that had pissed someone off big time.

This morning's briefing hadn't gone bad really, with his and O'Carroll's info on Angela Robinson, courtesy of Jaime Whitlock, and DS WJ Barr's info on Ross Wallace, thanks to Professor Bob Ceverto. He hadn't made as much progress as he'd have liked to at this point, but at the same time he'd learnt that investigations are best not rushed, mainly because jumping to conclusions might not only result in the wrong person being punished, but equally allow a guilty person to go free, thereby possibly jeopardising another life.

When McCusker had been stationed in Portrush, there had been a case where the wife of a local doctor had told anyone who'd listen, including McCusker, that that her husband was abusing her and was going to kill her. Basically she had two main problems getting people to consider her accusations. One, there were no marks or bruises about her person. Two, her husband was a local mover and shaker, very well connected to both politicians and senior RUC personnel - including some of McCusker's superiors. The doctor in question was also a prominent member of the local tennis club and what he lacked in skill on the courts he more than made up for with his wheeling and dealings in the club house afterwards.

A few months after the initial allegations the doctor discovered his wife in his study at his desk, lifelessly slumped by the keyboard of his computer. The doctor claimed he searched his wife's body for vital signs. On discovering no such signs of life he rang 999 for the RUC, as they were then known, and an ambulance. He further claimed he immediately left the study as he'd found it to await the police.

Detective Inspector, as he then was, McCusker was the first on the scene. He arrived at the doctor's house fourteen minutes after the doctor made the 999 call. He discovered the computer screen above her head was gently pulsing away, displaying what appeared to be her unfinished suicide note. The detective noted an overturned, half-emptied, box of sleeping pills just to the right of her head and three inches to the right of that was a Waterford Crystal tumbler, full of whiskey. At least he guessed that the smokey brown liquid was whiskey, helped in his guess work by the opened, but still quite full, bottle of Bushmills standing guard just to the rear of the glass.

As he was examining the scene the computer went into, 'sleep' mode with the Windows logo acting as screen saver, indiscriminately floating all about the monitor.

McCusker found himself being unable to move his eyes away from the pills, the glass, and the bottle of whiskey. He really wanted to continue his initial examination of the scene, but his eyes just wouldn't heed his wish. He knew there was a reason and he knew to heed the call of his natural instincts. He was glad he did. Following a few moments of collecting his thoughts, he realised that anyone desperate enough to want to hasten their exit from this planet would, most likely, want to ensure success by taking each and every one of the pills available. If the whiskey was as untouched as it appeared to be, then he wondered how she had been able to physically swallow the number of pills the evidence was leading him to believe she had. Surely she'd have needed a lot more than a few drops of whiskey to get them down. Yet her glass looked barely touched. And while he thought on about it, again assuming anyone was intent on such an exit route, then McCusker was convinced the victim in question would want, maybe even need, the remains of the glass, if not most of the entire bottle of Bushmills, to ensure the transition to the other side, as it were, was, at the very least, a blurred one.

The Portrush detective also noted, with interest, that the doctor's tipple of choice was in fact a gin and tonic, two of which he helped himself to in McCusker's company, just to, 'steady my nerves.'

"You said you haven't touched anything in here since you discovered your wife?" McCusker inquired, as he went about his work.

"No, not a single thing," the doctor confirmed, "Sure that's what all the cops on the TV shows advise you to do."

"Right," McCusker replied, thinking it just didn't add up.

Well actually, as he later admitted to his senior, it all did add up, added up in fact to what looked like a staged suicide to McCusker's eyes.

He put on a pair of blue opaque evidence gloves and went over to the well-stocked drinks cupboard, drawing a knowing, "Yes indeed, needs must, help yourself to a stiff one" from the doctor.

McCusker hoaked around in the mahogany drinks cupboard for a few seconds until he found what he was looking for. There were clearly no other bottles of Bushmills Whiskey in the cupboard, but he did find a similar sized, and shaped, brandy bottle. He poured the remains of the brandy into another of the Waterford glasses. The liquid nearly reached the brim of the glass. This drew a look of respect, coupled with a certain degree of admiration from the doctor. Next McCusker filled the empty brandy bottle - up to not quite the top - with water from a tap in the silver sink in the drinks cupboard. He also filled yet another Waterford glass with water and brought both over to the death-desk with the already cold corpse. He measured the glass of water to the glass of whiskey and took a few sips from the glass of water, until, to the naked eye at least, they both appeared to contain the same amount of liquid. He then repeated this comparison process, only this time between the Bushmills bottle and the brandy bottle containing water. Again he helped himself to a few swigs of water from the brandy bottle to ensure they were, as near as dammit, equal. Okay, he thought, now for the important bit.

With the doctor's undivided attention he carefully poured the water from the Waterford glass into the water in the brandy bottle. When he concluded this exercise it was clear to both himself, and the doctor, that the brandy bottle was filled to the brim. The inference being that the doctor's dead wife had not touched a single drop of whiskey in her so called efforts to commit suicide. The whiskey bottle, which had grated with McCusker's eyes on his initial examination of the scene, had clearly been a plant, and not a very good one at that. It had been a small thing but enough to ensure McCusker's brain clinked into his considering other possibilities gear.

Next he leant over the victim, gingerly hit a few of the keys on the keyboard and navigated his way into the control panel of the computer.

He discovered that the computer was programmed to revert to 'sleep' mode following ten minutes of inactivity. The doctor had clearly not left his study as he'd found it to await the arrival of the police, as he'd claimed. Clearly, at the appropriate moment – most likely when Mc-Cusker had rang the doorbell – the doctor had hit a key on the computer keyboard to 'awaken' his computer screen again, so that the incriminating attempt at a suicide note would be clearly visible.

McCusker took the doctor into custody immediately, considering him to be a serious flight risk. The doctor didn't deny, nor admit, the charge. He just shot McCusker a smug, 'do you really think you are going to get me on this?' glare. Sadly for the doctor the autopsy proved that the amount of pills he had managed to 'encourage' his wife into swallowing hadn't been enough to result in her death. However the amount of glyphosate (weed killer) he'd been giving her in drinks over the previous several weeks had directly caused her death.

The detective's on-going investigation also turned up a long standing mistress who seemed very happy to inform McCusker that the doctor had boasted to her that they'd, "be rid of my wife shortly, for once and all, but certainly in time for us to get to Wimbledon for the semis and finals." The doctor was so confident he was going to get away with it he hadn't even bothered to take the trouble to stage a believable suicide.

McCusker took no pleasure from solving the case so quickly. No, instead he dwelled more on the fact of what might have been if only he'd listened to the words of the wife rather than being influenced by the arrogant, sociopathic prat she'd chosen as a husband.

Luckily enough for McCusker his boss Superintendent Larkin was not aware of this case, and neither was he the type of policeman to interfere in his team's work. According to DI Lily O'Carroll, though, he was a big fan of McCusker's approach to detective work. Mind you, at the time O'Carroll imparted this information to McCusker, she was trying to blag him into covering for her so that she could nip off early and scoot down to Dublin with her sister to check out the quality of the single men down there. O'Carroll had never discussed the success or failure of the trip and McCusker hadn't asked, but he supposed the fact that he heard no more about it pointed to an unsatisfactory journey.

They had an unsatisfactory journey of their own that Thursday morning as they travelled to Willowfield Street to the Ross Wallace household. Someone cut them up badly on Great Victoria Street. O'Carroll grew very mad and slightly reckless in an attempt to try and get her own back. She was as upset as McCusker had ever seen her. Feeling at least one of them had to remain cool, McCusker said: "Who's the worst, the man who cut us up back there, or us if we had retaliated?"

"Sorry?"

"Okay, let's put it another way: If someone beats the crap out of your brother and then you go over and beat the crap out of him, tell me which of the two of you is the worst?"

"He is of course," she said. "I only beat the crap out of him because he beat the crap out of my brother."

"So what you're suggesting is that you were justified in dishing out your hiding?"

"You bet your life I was justified."

"But what if he'd been justified?"

"Like how?"

"What if your brother got his attacker's sixteen-year-old sister pregnant?"

"But did he?"

"Well that's kind of the point, we don't know and surely we should first take the trouble to find out before we rush in all guns blazing and beat the crap out of him. Don't you see? Before we retaliate we need to find out if our actions are justified."

"So you're saying that if it's justified I can beat the crap out of him?"

"Well what I'm saying to you is this: if you're justified then you just might have a reason to *consider* beating the crap out of him."

"But surely even if I am justified and I beat the crap out of him then I'm the same as he is?"

"Well that was kinda my starting point, don't you see?"

"Yeah, you're absolutely right," she conceded, but with a smile of devilment creeping across her face. "So tell me this McCusker: If we ever see that berk in the Merc again, is it okay if I cut him up and then say 'Sorry!'?"

McCusker didn't have to answer because just then they pulled up in Willowfield Street, home to Ross and Samantha Wallace.

The former Portrush detective was surprised when the door to the household opened to reveal a well-dressed and groomed Mrs Wallace, since he'd been half expecting a house-and-child-tied wife. Samantha was 5' 10" (McCusker chastised himself for still not thinking in metric), and a big-boned woman.

"Augh, sure why don't you come on in," she gushed from her doorstep. "Ross told me all about the chat you had with him. He told me I should expect you at some point."

O'Carroll followed Samantha Wallace down the narrow but spotlessly clean hall as McCusker brought up the rear after closing the front door quietly behind him.

"It was a shame about Adam, wasn't it?" the lady of the house said as she invited them to sit at the child-free breakfast table. "I've just got the house tidied up again after the daily morning hurricane of getting the kids off to school. I was about to put my feet up and have a wee cup of coffee and an elevenses or three; will you both join me?"

She seemed totally intent on ignoring their answer – not to mention, good intentions – as she busied herself about her kitchen brewing up a strong-smelling coffee and removing eight freshly baked scones from her Aga. If the smell now wafting its way around the kitchen was anything to go by, McCusker knew his resolve would melt away just as quickly as the butter would melt into the delicious hot scones.

"Were you at Queen's at the same time as Adam and Ross?" McCusker asked, as Samantha poured three cups of coffee.

"Oh my goodness, no – I never went anywhere near as grand a place of education as QUB proper. I attended Stranmillis University College – for teacher training – and my best friend's brother knew Ross. That's how we hooked up."

"Right," McCusker replied, enjoying the scone but not the coffee. "How long had you known Ross before you met Adam?" he asked, heading off in the easiest, if not the shortest, direction on his line of questioning.

"Possibly as much as a month, not very much more," she began, verbally chastising herself for opting for a chocolate Penguin rather than the scone. "Mine and Ross' relationship took quite a time to get into gear. For my part I admitted to liking him – liking him a lot in fact – but I kept thinking that it was much, much too early a point on my life path…actually, it wasn't just that…yes, I remember now…Before I came down to Belfast an adorable boy had just broken up with me and I'd been hurt. We all very quickly forget exactly just how big a gunk it is to be told by someone you love – and whom you thought loved you – that they feel it's just not going to work out. The vastness of the emptiness you feel is totally devastating," she paused to shudder. "Just to think that once he was the most important person in my life and now I can't even remember his face. So when I met Ross and we started to get on well I thought 'Here I am starting the circle all over again.' But augh, sure anyway, I ignored all my natural instincts and over one particular weekend I fell completely and utterly in love with Ross and he with me, to the degree we started to make plans."

"Wow!" O'Carroll said. "What age would you have been at that point?"

"Oh, let me think...I'd have been 24 and Ross is two years older than me."

"And you knew by then?"

"Yes we knew then," she replied smiling largely. "I'd always figured that I'd have a great teaching job by the time I was twenty-eight, then I'd meet someone, get married and start a family before I passed the big three-oh barrier."

O'Carroll was about to say something when McCusker said: "But you didn't get married first did you?"

Mrs Wallace looked a little shocked, but only slightly shaken. "Yes, actually you're correct it didn't happen the traditional way with us. First I fell pregnant with Tom, our firstborn. Strange term that isn't it? 'I fell pregnant '– sounds like I caught a disease, doesn't it? As it happened, he's turned out to be a wee dote. Mind you he wouldn't want me referring to him in that way now; he's twelve years of age, taller than me and has reached the point where all parents are uncool."

Again she'd gone off track, the McCusker track, and why wouldn't she? Why would she admit her secret to two complete strangers?

"Would you and Ross and Adam have spent a lot of time in each other's company?" McCusker asked, heading back towards his goal.

"Well I may be wrong, although something deep in my heart tells me I'm right, but I would have known Adam quite well, yes I would, if that's what you're asking?"

McCusker couldn't be sure, but he thought he noticed the first signs of concern appear in her brown eyes.

"We're very anxious to get some kind of idea of Adam as a man," McCusker started, trying to get her to loosen up a bit about the deceased. "I'm just trying to get a sense of him; anything at all, any background would be extremely helpful to us."

"He…I suppose the best way I could describe Adam is that he was always very funny in company, very friendly but…beyond a certain point he never really allowed himself to be engaged. Now that of course could have been for lots of reasons: perhaps, deep down, he was just too shy, perhaps he was really a sad person, but he seemed to enjoy his sadness, if you know what I mean?" She stopped talking and her eyes glazed over as though she was returning to an incident in her past. "I do remember a few occasions when Adam was around at ours for dinner and ah…as usual I'd more than a few wines, well more than Ross was happy with, and I remember trying to take it to the next level with Adam, conversation-wise, you know? I wanted to peel some of the layers of his boyish protection away to see what made him tick."

"And?" O'Carroll asked, following a few seconds of embarrassing silence.

"Well, he'd always resort to his favourite trick of turning everything around and into a joke."

"Did you ever get anything out of him?" O'Carroll asked.

"You know, maybe I did, maybe it was me and not him who was at fault. Maybe I was just a wee bit too drunk to understand what he might have been trying to tell me. Strangely, the only thing I remember him telling me that stopped me in my tracks, and don't be getting your hopes up because I really don't think it shows a great insight, but I just found for the first time that maybe there was something else going on there – that he did have a heart."

"And what was it he said?" McCusker prompted, when it looked and sounded like she'd reached the end of her line of thought.

"Oh yes, sorry. Well, on one famous occasion, just out of the blue, he said, 'Do horses not really feel pain when the blacksmith hammers nails into their hooves?' I mean, now when I repeat it to you here in the cold light of day it made me think we might all have been stoned or something."

"Did he ever open up to Ross?" McCusker asked, thinking "stoned" sounded like a very apt word under the circumstances.

"I don't believe so," she admitted. "But Ross reckons that Adam was at his happiest when he was hanging out with his sister, Julia. Ross' theory is that Julia might have been the only person in Adam's circle who accepted him for who he was. Ross was clearly fascinated by their relationship and he told me he once asked Julia why she and her brother got on so well together. She replied that she was the only one who fitted in with all of his moods. She said they were both totally content just to be in each other's company. She said they spent entire days together without saying a single word."

"Someone told us that Ross and Adam were best friends?" McCusker said.

"I think at one time early in the Queen's days they probably were. Although I never felt it was that intense. I think when Adam first came to Belfast he was a stranger, in a strange city, in a strange land. He'd probably never, ever been so exposed in his life before. So my guess is that he was very vulnerable and having someone – not just anybody, for instance Ross – fulfilling the role of best friend probably brought him the comfort he mistook for friendship."

"What was their relationship like more recently?" McCusker asked, glad of Samantha's third small insight into Adam Whitlock.

"Sorry, look – can we just backtrack a wee bit here?"

"Sure, of course," O'Carroll said quickly.

"You know, I'd just hate to be coming across as someone sitting here spouting off and claiming to be the oracle on a poor man that had just died. And to insinuate that he and I had a deep and meaningful relationship when that was certainly not the case. Adam, like the rest of us, worked on whatever level succeeded best for him at the time. For myself I love to get down to it and try to see what makes people tick. I'll admit to you that this has, on a few occasions, destroyed potential relationships. Ross, on the other hand, is very happy with leaving everything at face value; and of course I'm not suggesting that's bad. Adam, now Adam came from a totally different culture to ours. He was far away from home and the older my Tom grows, the more I realise how much I feel for Adam and all he went through when he left all of his family behind to come to a foreign land. But then that's another thing about him; Adam would never discuss his feelings for his mother with me."

"That's interesting," O'Carroll said, making yet another note.

"And…" McCusker promoted.

"Oh yes, sorry," Samantha said, looking genuinely apologetic. "You asked me about Ross and Adam's relationship of late?"

"Yeah," McCusker nodded.

"Well, you know, we've two children together and one of the things I love about Ross is that he's a hands-on father. I respect him so much as a father of my children. He's such a good dad; I really couldn't have chosen a better father for my children. Now I suppose from Adam's point of view the downside of that was that Ross had less time to be running down to the student's union bar every night to get pissed. The bottom line is that they grew up and I suppose to some degree you'd have to say they also grew apart. I always think of how all of us have changed since our formative years when I hear that Crosby, Stills & Nash lyric: 'Don't let the past remind us of what we are not now.'"

"Did you and Adam ever spend any time together?" McCusker asked so awkwardly, O'Carroll looked like she wanted to poke his eyes out with her pen.

"Sorry?" Samantha replied, appearing less upset than she might have done, maybe because of disbelief or a delayed reaction, McCusker thought.

"I just wondered there…when you said that you wanted to peel away his layers and see what made him tick, you know, if you and Adam had ever…?" McCusker asked, hoping the natural momentum of his words would finish his question for him.

"Good God man! I mean, I am talking symbolically, not physically," she protested. "I can't believe you just suggested that! No McCusker. Never ever like that."

"Look Mrs Wallace, there is really no easy way for us to talk about this…" O'Carroll began, taking up the baton McCusker knew he had just dropped rather clumsily. "It has been suggested to us that Adam was Tom's father."

Now it was McCusker's turn to grimace, but no matter how much butt-clenching he did, he still wasn't prepared for Mrs Wallace's answer.

"And my daughter's as well."

CHAPTER TWENTY-SIX

When the dust settled, as it inevitably did, a very composed Samantha Wallace continued: "Ross and I discussed this shortly after Adam was found dead and we agreed if this came up, we would be very candid with you in the hope that you'd be equally discreet about it."

Not surprisingly both O'Carroll and McCusker nodded, differently, but both in a non-committal manner.

"I'll take that as you'll do the best you can," she said sweetly. "I always wanted children, so did Ross, and we both agreed that we wouldn't be one of those career couples who would only breed when their career paths decreed they could. Even before we thought of marriage we thought of children. Sadly we discovered that Ross suffered from an immune disorder called hypothyroidism which resulted in him being infertile. We discussed adopting and spent quite a bit of time looking into that – again, this was way before we discussed marriage. Ross eventually came up with one of his classic lines: 'Look, if we're going to become parents, we're going to have to be adult about it.' He'd obviously thought a lot about it and figured it all out in advance and then he came and presented me with his solution: to find a sperm donor. This way, he argued, it would be less painful, physically and emotionally, and the most successful way, although compromised given the circumstances, for us to continue our line.

"Ross hadn't stopped there with his research; he didn't want us to take pot luck with our sperm donor, no – he wanted us to find someone, someone of good stock."

"Someone like Adam Whitlock?" O'Carroll responded.

"Exactly," Samantha replied, appearing somewhat relieved. "We went to Adam with our idea and he was receptive. So we set up the procedure by the book – it was all very clinical in fact. Adam was equally receptive two years later when we had a conversation about our wish to complete our family and we repeated the process which produced my daughter, Macy. His only condition was that nobody should know about our arrangement. He claimed it would be much better for the children that way."

"How did anyone find out about it?" McCusker asked, realising that of course she had known but she maybe hadn't intended to let slip how the information had gotten out.

"We just don't know – if anyone did the information certainly did not come from Ross or myself. Our clinic is above reproach so Adam must have let it slip. Then an ex of mine picked up the gossip and ran with it. We – Ross, Adam, and myself – all agreed to just laugh about it. Then my ex moved to California and the storm in the teacup settled."

"Did you ever get the sense that Adam had any emotional attachment to the children?" McCusker asked.

"Well, all I can tell you is that he was a piss poor example of a godfather to Tom."

"Do you think there is any chance that Adam and Ross grew apart over this?" McCusker asked.

"Being the godfather or being the sperm donor?"

"The sperm donor...?"

"The continual presence of the elephant in the room you mean?"

"Well, yes."

"Ross and I eventually figured out that Adam had forgotten all about the procedures, either that or he had intentionally wiped the entire episode from his memory."

CHAPTER TWENTY-SEVEN

Samantha Wallace furnished the detectives with the details of the clinic she'd attended. In light of this openness and willingness to co-operate they decided that they would not bother contacting her husband for another chat, at least not for the time being. But McCusker was still reluctant to remove them entirely from his slim suspect list.

"Next stop the BBC please!" he announced as they climbed into O'Carroll's distinctive yellow Mégane.

"Mrs Robinson, here we…" O'Carroll declared, and then her voice tailed off by some distraction or other. Most likely she was considering her next date, McCusker guessed.

Instead of being annoyed at seeing them again so soon after her last, rather liquid, interview, Angela Robinson, senior BBC Radio producer, grew animated at their arrival: "Perfect, perfect timing in fact. I need a hit of nicotine badly!" and she led them through to the smoker's shelter out in the Broadcasting House's courtyard.

Angela lit her ciggie quickly, very quickly, a wee bit of desperation noticeable. She took a long slow drag, creating fierce lines around the bridge of her nose. She furiously waved away the exhaled smoke from her face. The resultant movement created a new cloud in the wake of the first. "You probably weren't getting much sense out of me at the end of our last chat."

"Well, we had taken up a lot of your time," McCusker offered graciously.

"I can tell you I'd a splitten' head this morning," she continued, as another fifth of her death stick disappeared straight into her lungs. "How can I help you today?"

"At the end of our last chat I was trying to find out from you if, when Adam Whitlock gave you some money, whether or not there would be a paper trail, you know, did he pay you with a cheque, make payments on your behalf or give you cash to make the payments with?"

"Yes, yes I might have been tipsy but I realised you were trying to find out if there was any way at all that Richard had discovered my special relationship with Adam."

"Yes," McCusker affirmed. "And do you remember how Adam would have covered some of your bills, like for instance, you'd told us that he paid for the hotel where you held your wedding, the Culloden I believe?"

"Yes, yes of course," she said. "Well in that instance Adam paid them direct and I believe Richard thought my family took care of it, as would be the norm."

"And other payments?"

"Do you really think that Richard is the kind of man who would spend all day going through my things looking for stuff and then find out something to link me to Adam? Something which would make him so jealous as to go and murder Adam? Is that not too big a stretch of the imagination?" But before McCusker had a chance to even think of a response she added: "Well, I suppose he does sit around the house all day doing nothing."

"Also, you said that you and he were together at the time Richard claims he went by himself to the Errigle Inn," McCusker admitted.

"Richard...out in public...by himself," she repeated the words and stage-laughed. "Don't you realise one of the reasons Richard will never ever leave me is that he is socially dependant on me? When I first met him he'd tell me tales of his horrors of being in public by himself. Richard's biggest nightmare is to be at a wedding and be stuck beside a stranger and have to make conversation with them over the duration of an entire meal. He left his last three places of employment because he just couldn't stand to be with other people. I'm not making fun of him here because it's really a very serious phobia. He is petrified about having to make social contact and conversation with people; he'll literally be thinking to himself 'okay, now it's my turn to say something and I can't think of anything to say.' Then he'll break out in a cold sweat and mentally fight with himself over what he should say and what he'll be capable of saying."

"He seemed fine with us?" McCusker said.

"He's fine in situations where he doesn't have to make conversation. You ask him a direct question, it relaxes him and he can answer. He just can't do small talk, but it's more than that – he's actually petrified about having to try."

"So you don't think he was at the Errigle Inn on Saturday night then?" McCusker asked.

"No, he just wouldn't have been able to," Angela offered, sounding genuinely sorry for her husband's plight.

"But he wasn't with you as you informed us during our last chat?" McCusker said quietly.

"How did you know that?"

"Because when I asked you about Richard being at the Errigle Inn on Saturday you didn't say that he was with you, you said 'No, he wouldn't have been able to'."

As Angela was left pondering that thought, McCusker instructed O'Carroll to go and pick up his "person of interest" and bring him into the Custom House for questioning.

"Holy shit, I've just felt a shiver go the whole way up my spine," Angela said, her entire body still shuddering as O'Carroll quickly walked back into Broadcasting House. "This is serious, isn't it?"

McCusker could only grimace.

After a moment's consideration she continued "Is this a good or bad thing for me? Look, should I be tipping our news team off on this or not?"

"I'd ask you to please keep it under your hat," McCusker said. He stayed in the courtyard with her while they waited for DS Barr to ring. When he did, he confirmed that Angela's husband was in custody.

"I'd recommend a strong cup of tea with an extra sugar or two to help you get over your shock," McCusker offered, as he left her lighting her third ciggie with the butt of the second.

"I think a Bushmills will do the same trick, but much quicker," she added.

CHAPTER TWENTY-EIGHT

"Okay, Willie John," McCusker began, "you nip in there and try and start up a conversation with our grey man – don't worry about asking him questions, just talk to him and leave gaps in the conversation."

The grey man, aka Mr Richard Robinson, was visible to all of them – McCusker, O'Carroll, Cage, and DS WJ Barr – through the one-way window adjoining the interview room in the permanently cold and damp basement of the Custom House. As well as four sets of eyes, three video cameras monitored Robinson's every move as per regulations. Inside the room Robinson sat at the table, his eyes focused on a point on the opposite side of it. He didn't look nervous, fidgety or guilty. He merely resembled a still life caught forever in one of Roland Davidson's fine studies.

Barr eventually joined the still life and introduced himself, adding he was there to keep him company until the solicitor arrived. Robinson's eyes followed the detective sergeant until he took a seat on the same side of the table. It looked to McCusker like Robinson was wearing the exact same clothes as he'd been wearing the day before; either that or he had an identical change of clothing.

"What are you in here for?" Barr asked and then before Robinson had a chance to reply he continued, "I find it weird sitting here with a stranger, don't you?"

Robinson muttered something completely inaudible and then made a quick scribble in his ever-present notebook.

"Do you have a team you support?" Barr asked.

Okay, McCusker thought, a direct question, which should be an easy one for Robinson.

"McLaren," Robinson replied after a painful thirty seconds.

"Oh, so you support Formula 1?"

"Well, I don't visit the races, but I do watch it on TV."

"Why McLaren?" Barr asked. "Isn't Red Bull the best?"

"Actually that was last year; Mercedes is by far the quickest this year. Red Bull do have the best car designer in the history of the sport though, but they're having engine problems this year. In Red Bull, Daniel Ricciardo is a fellow Australian. Flying the flag well for us by outpacing Sebastian Vettel most weekends."

Barr appeared to be considering this point when, in fact, he was doing exactly what McCusker had directed: he was leaving a space in the conversation.

"I think Button is one of the best drivers on the circuit," Robinson, growing ever so twitchy, eventually said. "Give him a Newey-designed car and he'd win every race."

Another gap, this time Barr ended it: "Actually, I meant football."

"Can't stand all those spoilt over-paid brats," was Robinson's immediate response, delivered in a pure Australian drawl.

"I hear what you're saying, but when you think about it, it's the talent of the players that draws the fans to the grounds and I think I'd rather the ones with the talent took home the large pay cheques than the owners."

Robinson had no response to this so after a long pause of silence Barr eventually continued: "My team is Manchester United and as we're proving at the minute, it really is the manager who counts."

"Do you know how long I'm going to have to wait here before someone comes and talks to me?" Robinson countered, confirming his lack of interest in football.

McCusker conceded that his idea wasn't working – Robinson wasn't growing unsettled the way his wife said he would. Maybe Barr was just too nice a man.

"I believe the minute your solicitor arrives we'll start the questioning."

As the conversation with Richard Robinson was taking place in one of McCusker's ears, with the other he was listening to DI Jarvis Cage, still badly bruised from his run-in with the bollards, imparting his newly gathered information on the suspect.

"He seems to be a loner. He walks around his neighbourhood a lot. There've been a few reports of him around playgrounds or sports fields over the years but none of them ever came to anything. It would appear that they were from overprotective mothers who'd been watching too much TV. He's never been in trouble, not even as much as receiving a traffic ticket in his time in Belfast. It looks like he is truly a grey man in danger of slipping off the page altogether."

"So what would make him so mad that he would do that to Adam Whitlock?" McCusker asked, addressing the question to himself as much as Cage and O'Carroll.

"McCusker if someone is serially bonking your wife, eventually it must get to you," O'Carroll offered. "Don't forget we're talking here about a period that ran over several years. On the other hand, maybe he was okay about it because when she was going out with Adam it spared him from any social duties."

"I wish his solicitor would get here so that we can find out why he lied to us about where he was on Saturday night," McCusker said, barely blinking for fear he would miss something in Robinson's demeanour. He was concerned that Barr had struck too sympathetic a chord with Robinson with his line about finding it weird sitting in there with a stranger. At which point Station Duty Sergeant Matt Devine was seen entering the interview room with a local solicitor O'Carroll identified as "David Lewis, from Lewis & Co. Lewis & Co is a one-man organisation," she explained, "namely the aforementioned David Lewis– his '& Co' consists entirely of a telephone answering machine. But he's honest and fair."

On the other side of the one-way mirror Lewis was introduced to his client. McCusker closed the shutter and switched off the audio link, giving solicitor and client their privacy. Cage raised his eyebrows in surprise, but didn't say anything. McCusker figured if he wasn't going to avail Lewis and his client of one of the Custom House's solicitor/client rooms then the very least he could do was to give them complete privacy.

***

Ten minutes later McCusker entered the interview room, switched on the tape recorder and announced: "Thursday, 17.03, interview with

Richard Robinson. Those present DI O'Carroll, Mr McCusker, solicitor David Lewis and his client Richard Robinson." By the time McCusker had finished his announcement, his, 'you do not have to say anything but anything you do say will be…' caution and sat down, DS WJ Barr had left the room.

"Okay Richard, thank you for coming in," McCusker said, despite Robinson having no say in the matter although, technically speaking, O'Carroll had invited him to accompany her to the Custom House.

"Does that mean I can leave if I wish to?" Robinson asked innocently, writing another few words in his book – his social blanket.

"Let's just see the nature of the questions they want to ask you first, hey Richard?" the soberly dressed Lewis offered.

"We wanted to discuss with you your whereabouts on Saturday evening last," McCusker said, crossing his fingers in hope that the solicitor's co-operation would continue.

"Yes – asked and answered," Robinson replied, using a prompt he'd obviously picked up from a TV cop show – shows which were becoming the bane of McCusker and public prosecutor's lives.

"Just for the record, Richard, humour us and tell us again," McCusker said, looking at Lewis.

"I told you that I went down to the Errigle Inn to see 57 Joe, a musical entertainment group I write lyrics for."

"Right," McCusker said forcing a smile, "you see, I've a wee problem with that."

"How so?" Robinson said.

"Well, I went down to the Errigle Inn myself and spoke to both the drummer and the manager and they said as far as they were concerned you weren't down at the concert on Saturday Night…"

"Gig, it was a gig on Saturday night," Robinson interrupted, knowingly.

"Sorry?" McCusker said.

"If the performance is in a seated hall it's called a concert but if it's in a stand-up club it's called a gig."

"Right," McCusker said. "Okay...the manager and the drummer of 57 Joe said that you were not at the *gig* on Saturday night."

"No," Robinson cut in again, "I'd bet what they said was that they didn't *see* me at the gig on Saturday. The venue was crowded and, yes, I didn't bump into any of the group."

"But surely if you work with them," O'Carroll said, "you'd have gone backstage at some point to chat with them and wish them well?"

"Oh, I can't abide dressing-room scenes," Robinson replied. "Never have...it's all so false. You're forced to say nice things about the gig because it gets heavy if you tell them the truth about the show."

"Did you ever used to go backstage Richard?" McCusker asked.

"Yes of course."

"But you didn't like not being able to tell the truth, so you stopped?"

"Correct."

"But I bet that when you did go backstage, you would have played the game, you know, telling them it was a great show, when in fact you didn't believe it was a great show?"

"Correct."

"So," McCusker shrugged his shoulders, "in fact you would have been lying to them about their show?"

"Well, yes."

"Like lying to them to spare their feelings?"

"Of course."

"So sometimes it's necessary to lie, you know, to spare people's feelings?"

"Correct."

"So, Richard, were you lying to us when you told us you were down at the Errigle Inn on Saturday night in order to spare someone's feelings?"

"You patronising smug bastard!" Robinson spat back, his Australian drawl causing a mini explosion in the process. He then turned full on to Lewis with a get-me-out-of-here glare.

"Richard, you're still claiming that you were down at the Errigle Inn on Saturday night?"

"Yes."

"Okay," McCusker said, deciding to change tack. He removed a folded A4 sheet of paper from his inside pocket. "I have here 57 Joe's actual set list from the conce...sorry, from the *gig* on Saturday night. Can you tell me the title of their first song?"

"I didn't get there in time for that."

"Okay, they did two Van Morrison songs on Saturday evening – can you give me the titles?"

"Sorry. I can't remember."

"Okay, someone joined the band onstage for one song...can you give me their name?"

"Shit, not Van the Man," Robinson replied. "I must have been in the bog when that happened."

"Ah no, not Mr Morrison," McCusker continued patiently. "Can you tell me what Beatles song 57 Joe performed on Saturday night?"

" 'Help!' " Robinson offered and then laughed heartily at his attempt at humour.

"Can you tell me the title of one song that 57 Joe performed on Saturday night?" McCusker asked, setting up his trap. "Just one song title please?"

"Of course, they did 'What Shall We Give Back', their Belfast City anthem."

"And whereabouts would that have been in the set?" McCusker said, trying to draw him in even further.

"The end of the set of course, it's always the end of the set," Robinson boasted, smugly.

"Yes you're correct," McCusker started. "'What Shall We Give Back' *is* usually the final song of the set..." McCusker paused again noting Robinson's muscles relaxing. "However, on Saturday night, due to a malfunction on their laptop, they were unable to trigger the necessary sample required to perform that particular song, so they finished with their second Van Morrison song of the evening – a rousing version of 'Gloria'."

McCusker's perseverance with 57 Joe's drummer had paid off and securing the set list for that night had been the crowning glory. At this stage in the "cop show," the suspect would usually collapse and confess everything.

"You know," Robinson started, about to prove he wasn't really that fanatical a follower of that type of show himself. "I do believe you're correct in this instance, yeah, you're spot on in fact – they did do an extended version of 'Gloria' on Saturday."

"Were the three Js all on the door on Saturday, you know, Jerry, Jerry, and Jimmy?

"Augh yeah," a relieved Robinson said, sensing another trick question coming up and this time being prepared for it. "They were *all* there, and don't forget Kitt, hitting people on the head and knocking them out," he laughed.

McCusker nodded his head slowly from side to side, "Sorry Richard, caught out again – Johnny was missing from the door because he was down in Galway for the weekend to attend his sister's wedding."

"So? Two Js, three Js – who gives a shit?" Robinson moaned, and again looked to his solicitor to save him.

"Okay Richard, here's the thing," McCusker said, as Robinson gathered himself up again in preparation for another searching question. "Either you were at the Errigle Inn and my DS WJ Barr will verify that when he's had a chance to go all through the discs from the front-door cameras, or you were where your wife said you were on Saturday night."

"Where did Angela say I was?" Robinson asked, looking totally thrown.

"First, will you concede that you were not in fact at the Errigle Inn on Saturday night?" McCusker asked. This was not going as well as he had hoped. He'd always been mindful that, should Robinson turn out to be the murderer, this very interview would be analysed in great detail for years to come, and he'd done little to be proud of so far. Maybe, just maybe, he hoped, they'd reached a crucial point in the proceedings.

McCusker wondered what was going through Robinson's head at this point. There were two scenarios. One, Richard Robinson was the murderer, he was in the process of being caught out for lying and he was about to try and mend that damage. Or, he wasn't the murderer and, at this point in the investigation, he was the only one in the world who knew he wasn't. If that was the case, he'd probably be wondering why his wife had given him an alibi for the time of the murder. Maybe she wasn't so much giving *him* an alibi as herself?

If Robinson wasn't the murderer, why had he said he was somewhere he wasn't? Yes, the Errigle Inn on a Saturday night would have been crowded and he perhaps believed that to be useful to him.

If he wasn't at the Errigle Inn, and he wasn't with his wife as now became apparent, where had he been? What had he been doing? The thing about lying is that people lie for a reason – usually *have to*. What was his reason? Why would his wife have initially given an alibi and not confirmed the alibi with her husband? Were they both worried that the other had carried out the murder?

Of all the permutations of scenarios running through McCusker's head, he was still taken back by Robinson's next statement:

"Do you think there is a chance my wife murdered this Adam Whitlock fellow?"

***

The interview wound down quickly after that with Robinson, on his solicitor's advice, admitting that he had not been at the Errigle Inn the previous Saturday night. He still would not admit where he had been and refused to answer any more question until he had talked to his wife. McCusker felt he'd no option other than to remand Richard Robinson in Police detention and let the clock start running. He didn't want to allow his chief suspect out so that he and his wife could compare notes and tie up their alibis. At the same time, with her husband in custody, Angela might feel more secure in whatever it was she had been up to with feeling the need to create a false alibi, murder or not.

CHAPTER TWENTY-NINE

"Let's go back and see Angela again?" McCusker said, as much to himself as O'Carroll, as they exited the ever-cold basement of the Custom House.

O'Carroll checked her watch.

"Look, I'm okay to do it myself," McCusker offered.

"It's cool – I'm good, I've got a big date tonight but I'm good on time."

A few minutes later they were on the steps of BBC Broadcasting House having a brief chat with the brothers O'Neill, both dressed very cool and on their way in to do yet another TV interview to raise the profile of Larry's List. As they chatted, they met Angela Robinson, exiting the building.

In spite of everything she still had a big smile for McCusker and O'Carroll, only this time it looked more of a nervous smile than one of friendship. On his walks around the city, McCusker was surprised how often strangers smiled at each other. Smiling seemed to be a precursor to saying hello.

"Oh," she said, continuing down the ramp to the left of the front door. "Do you need to speak to me again? How did you get on with Richard? Is he at home yet?"

"He's still helping us with our enquiries," McCusker replied.

"Is that really a euphemism for someone who has been arrested but has yet to be charged?"

"Not at all," McCusker replied, hoping he was sounding sincere, "and we would like to have another chat with you, please?"

"In that case I need a drink. Do you mind if we nip into Deanes?"

She brushed off all the heads turning in her direction, at her million dollar hairstyle with "What can I tell you? I've discovered the secret of staying young...lie about your age."

They found a quiet corner in the busy bar and McCusker said: "Bushmills for you, Mrs Robinson?"

"No, actually I'll have a vodka, please."

"Really?" McCusker repeated, genuinely surprised.

"Yes, vodka is much cheaper than botox and paralyses more muscles," Robinson deadpanned, flashing her trademark Princess Diana tilted-head.

McCusker returned with the drinks just in time to hear Angela saying, "...Macca, he looks just like Ken Dodd these days, but without the sense of humour."

"Here's to you Mrs Robinson," McCusker toasted, when finally seated and drinks distributed.

Robinson smiled. McCusker didn't know why, perhaps about something she and O'Carroll had been discussing in his absence.

"So, I think we have now ascertained that your husband was not where he claimed he was on Saturday night," McCusker began, after the first sip of his white wine, which turned out to be a very pleasant little nail varnish remover. He would concede that the fault was all his because, unless he was having a meal, he had a taste for little else but Guinness.

"So where was he?" Angela replied, showing she was having no such worries about her own drink.

"Well, we haven't discovered that yet, we now know two places he wasn't, so by process of elimination and deduction..."

"...you still have Belfast's 125 bars, 127 churches and 112 restaurants to check and just over 260,000 people – at last count – to ask whether they'll give him a proper alibi for the time in question."

"Of course, that would be just 259,999 people to check," McCusker offered with a smile. "You must have been concerned that he was involved when you gave him a false alibi?"

"Or were you worried about where you'd been yourself?" O'Carroll pushed.

Angela Robinson took another large sip of her vodka.

"Where exactly were you on Saturday night between the hours of midnight and 3 a.m. on Sunday morning?" McCusker asked patiently.

"As I said to you, I was at home," she eventually countered. "But, as you now know, Richard was not at home with me."

"Where do you think Richard might have been?" O'Carroll asked.

"I honestly don't know," she admitted.

"Does he go out often without you?" O'Carroll continued.

"Of course, he goes out a lot at night."

"And you've never wondered what he gets up to?" McCusker asked.

"You mean…am I worried that he's getting up to no good?"

"Or he's seeing another woman?" O'Carroll suggested.

Angela laughed. She just laughed. "Look," she eventually said, "it took Richard years and years to get it together with me and he was so keen, not to mention patient, he hung around while I was going with other boys, so, no – I don't think he was getting it together with some-one else. Besides, as I mentioned to you the other night – because I was feeling guilty about my relationship with Adam – I always made sure I never resisted Richard's infrequent advances, so please believe me: I would have known. Men can lie but they can never hide their carnal attraction."

"And you're convinced Richard was totally unaware about your relationship with Adam?" O'Carroll asked, revisiting this line once again.

"Totally," she said coldly. "Look, if I'd been in love with Adam maybe I'd have been more careless. I believe that the reason most women who are cheating on their husbands get found out is because deep down…they really just don't care. Don't you see? They have the insurance of the love they have for the other man. Maybe even a good percentage of them want to be found out, you know, just to bring it to a head. But with Adam, well as I said, he certainly wasn't in love with me and I was in lust with him."

"But surely…" O'Carroll started.

"But surely nothing," Angela quickly interrupted. "Look, sadly – very sadly – Adam is dead and I'll admit to you I really don't miss him – I'm as surprised about that as you are, by the look on both your faces. But I'll also admit to you that I most definitely do miss having sex with him. It's like…it's like I'm being forced to go through some cold turkey kind of thing to get over missing my regular fix."

O'Carroll visibly grimaced.

"What?" Angela asked gently.

"It's just you're missing out on the whole…"

"The whole meeting someone, falling in love, and living happily after thing...is that what you're referring to?"

"Well yes," O'Carroll admitted.

"Let me tell you what comes after living happily ever after, shall I?" Angela said, and proceeded without waiting to see if any resistance would be offered. "What comes after happy ever after is *nothing*. You still need to eat, to sleep, to work in order that you can continue to eat, sleep, and work. The only thing we have that is bigger than that – and that is not chemically induced – is the joy we take from pleasuring each other's bodies. It's not making love, it is just pure unadulterated animalistic sex. Adam and I had that part of our lives off perfectly – it might have been the only thing that either of us did do perfectly."

McCusker wondered if this was the reason behind Adam's spending so much time with Julia, with Angela spending the same amount of time with her husband. In Adam's case, could Cindy's untimely death have been a major factor in how his apparent loveless life had turned out? Was Angela in a marriage merely to facilitate her relationship with Adam?

McCusker studied Angela as they sat in the wine bar. Yes, her hair was absolutely amazing, but he found none of her boyish features alluring. She wore black trousers that were very baggy around the bum, but tight around her ankles, and he couldn't stand the look of them. She had some shapeless wrap-around jumper, also black and equally disagreeable, to his mind. Still, she probably felt exactly the same way about him and the suits he loved to wear.

The biggest turn-off was her over-sexualised nature. But now that Adam was out of her life, would she find another man to obsess over? And if that man was prepared to give back just a little bit more than Adam, how quickly would her marriage disintegrate? Then again, if her husband *was* involved in Adam's murder, he'd be out of her life for good anyway.

And with that looking more and more likely, could Angela Robinson ever bring herself to play the role of the perfect jailbird wife, traipsing out to Maghaberry, the big and ugly modern prison near Aghalee in County Antrim, on monthly visits?

For some strange reason a vision of Anna Stringer flashed into McCusker's mind (he still always thought of his ex-wife by her maiden name.)

McCusker wondered why he'd never considered divorcing Anna Stringer. Mind you it wasn't as if there had ever been a queue of women looking to replace her. Not even one in fact. Name wise though he didn't need to, they'd never really shared 'McCusker' as a name. At first it was as much his fault as hers, as he always, but always, referred to her as Anna Stringer. But then after a few years even she started to refer to herself again by her maiden name; she even went as far as changing the name on her passport from McCusker back to Stringer. He hadn't questioned her over it. McCusker often wondered what it really meant to share a name, to share a life. He puzzled for ages over how you would/could actually physically share a life. How could people be there for each other; what did that even mean? Be where for them? He wasn't hers and she wasn't his. He didn't own her and she didn't own him. But McCusker also knew that wasn't really the full story. On the other hand they hadn't bickered, they hadn't fought. In fact all things considered, they had coexisted quite successfully. But there was no chemistry, no magic and there was no love. Now Mc-Cusker certainly knew from his work how sometimes (but not all of the times) the existence of magic or chemistry could bring a relationship to a very sad end. This was the result when the magic was cast aside while one partner in the marriage or relationship mistook the novelty of newness of another lover for chemistry or magic. That's when there was a distinct possibility of jealously coming into play from the discarded partner.

McCusker wondered how would he have felt if he'd discovered Anna Stringer had been having an affair; would he have considered killing the other man, and in a way that would have been a clear sign for his wife. Or would he have just sought out the other man and asked him if he'd managed to solve the mystery of this woman, because he certainly hadn't.

"So you said that Richard goes out, late at night..." McCusker said, "are we talking about one or two nights a week?"

"No, more like five or six nights a week," Angela guessed.

"And you never wondered where he was going?" O'Carroll asked.

"Look, Richard is a writer..."

McCusker grimaced, remembering what the member and manager of 57 Joe had said about Richard's lyrics. He thought he was being inconspicuous but Angela picked up on his indiscretion immediately.

"No, no, that's unfair McCusker!" she immediately protested. "I've read a lot of Richard's writing and, believe me, it is very good, and I'd be more critical than most. But his writing is very...visual. I'd also admit that it's stylised, which I guess could also mean it can be very difficult to read, if you're not in the right frame of mind. But Richard definitely has a unique voice."

"You were about to tell us what you thought Richard went out for late at night?" O'Carroll asked, looking impressed that Angela had stood up for her husband. McCusker was equally impressed; Angela and Richard Robinson enjoyed one of the strangest relationships the Portrush detective had ever known, but there was something very heartening about her show of loyalty, especially in the current circumstances.

"Oh yes, I was about to say that Richard is a writer, he loves to be alone with his thoughts and I assumed walking the streets late at night was where he found his muse."

"What time would he get back home?" McCusker asked.

"Some nights he was so late he wouldn't bother me when he came in – he'd go straight to the spare room and I wouldn't see him 'til teatime the next evening."

The detectives' run of questions simultaneously came to an end, although McCusker now had a fair few more for Richard Robinson.

As they were saying their goodbyes Angela asked: "When can I see him?"

Neglecting the fact that the only visits Richard Robinson would be permitted would be those for either legal or medical reasons O'Carroll replied with, "It's best you liaise with David Lewis, he'll get you in quicker than we could."

***

"Fancy a quick pint at McHugh's?" McCusker asked when they were back out on the busy Bedford Street. "I need something to get the terrible taste of fermented juice of the grape from me mouth."

"Go on then," O'Carroll agreed, checking her watch again.

Ten minutes later they were nursing their pints of Guinness. "Oh jeez!" O'Carroll said. Her eyes were glued to a spot just over the top of McCusker's left shoulder.

"What? What O'Carroll?"

"I've just lost you."

"Sorry?"

"Don't look now but the woman of your dreams, the one with the French bob, has just walked in by herself."

A few minutes later, after the woman with the French bob had found a seat and been served a glass of chilled white wine, McCusker plucked up the courage to steal a few glances.

"You're staring McCusker," O'Carroll warned. "I told you about that last time."

"But she's just so naturally beautiful."

"Hold that thought McCusker, it's a healthy one."

"Would you just look at her..." he whispered, now powerless to avert his eyes, even if he'd wanted to. "She is perfect really, such an attractive and beautiful face, and her body...I've never seen anyone so alluring in real life. She looks like...she looks like an angel."

"If that's the body and looks of an angel McCusker, it's no wonder God is having so much trouble up in heaven at the moment."

They both sipped at their pints, happy to also drink in the vision before them, both lost in their thoughts, or maybe even fantasies, for a while.

"Look McCusker," O'Carroll began, breaking their silence, "a bit of advice for you: if you're ever lucky enough to go to bed with an angel, say for instance *that* one, just listen to me now for this is very important, okay?"

"Okay."

"You must be very careful and ensure you always, but always, allow her to go on top..."

McCusker winced – too much information, he thought.

"I'll tell you, no matter how great the man you think you are, she still won't want you to go crushing her wings," O'Carroll said, laughing heartily at her own joke. She dragged her eyes off the French-bob woman and studied McCusker in detail for the first time since they'd come into the bar. "You really have never slept with a woman other than your wife have you?" she eventually said, spoiling his daydream.

"You're so sharp you could advertise Elastoplasts."

"Actually they're known as Band Aids in this century, McCusker. Anyway, as you have a habit of saying, 'tell me this...'" she continued, revealing that the Guinness was kicking in, "have you ever tried making love any other way, you know, other than the missionary position?"

McCusker's eyebrows declared what was going through his mind at that precise moment but he said, "Oh yes, sometimes I partook in my wife's personal preference."

"And that was?" O'Carroll pushed, her eyes lit up like a Christmas tree.

"WSS."

"WSS?" she repeated, appearing confused.

"Yes, WSS," he replied as though everyone in the world would know what he was talking about.

"What the feck is WSS McCusker?"

"While she slept, of course."

"McCusker, you brute!" she shouted, clearly genuinely shocked and drawing the attention of even the beautiful angel. "You can forget all about me ever introducing you to our Grace!" she hissed before downing her pint and leaving McHugh's without another word.

Sadly for McCusker, after a few minutes the blonde-haired woman with the French bob and red lips also left the bar.

He sat contently on his own nursing the remainder of his Guinness. At one stage, even just a few months ago, he could never have imagined sitting alone, drinking in a public house in Belfast. He admitted to himself that he actually felt happy being in Belfast. He realised - as if someone had just turned on a big light - that Belfast people are committed to being in Belfast. To McCusker people in places like Portrush were in the town mainly simply because that was where they grew up and the vast majority didn't even think about their hometown anymore. But Belfast was a completely different kettle of seahorses altogether. Belfast city folk were in Belfast because they wanted to be there; because they had to be there. There was a willingness and energy (but not desperation) for the city to succeed. McCusker still wasn't quite sure what it was about the city that made people feel so, although he was experiencing glimpses of it. There was still a large residual undercurrent from days gone by, but now people had an energy to just get on with things and to be a part of whatever exciting and positive thing that was happening next; happy to be part of this movement to make things better. Just like Paul McCartney had happily sung,

"It's getting better all the time." Before McCusker allowed himself to get too excited or content, he accepted that John Lennon's counter-balance of, "It can't get much worse," had also been spot on, if now (hopefully) in the past tense. He downed the remaining quarter pint and chastised himself for being too reflective. He vowed once more to keep the promise he'd made himself as he left Portrush; forget the past, ignore the future, and get lost in the present.

CHAPTER THIRTY

The following morning McCusker went straight to the Europa Hotel. He was keeping his promise of updating Wesley Whitlock III on the progress of the investigation into the death of his son. McCusker had arranged to meet O'Carroll in the lobby at 8.20 a.m. for their 8.30 appointment. At 8.31, as he boarded one of the lifts to the eleventh floor, he thought he recognised the person exiting the other.

Whitlock's surviving son Jaime answered the suite door to McCusker's knocking.

"Lord have mercy, I think that it's the cops," Jaime said, in apparent good humour.

"Ah McCusker!" Wesley shouted from the other end of the suite, "I've taken the liberty to order you your usual breakfast, or at least the breakfast you had on Tuesday morning. It'll be with us in a few minutes."

"Sounds good to me," McCusker replied, noting from the dirty dishes that a couple of the Whitlock clan must have eaten breakfast already. "Unfortunately Detective Inspector O'Carroll was unavoidably detained."

"I understand completely," Wesley said, walking into the living room of the suite, and drying his hands energetically before shaking McCusker's hand furiously. As Mr Whitlock III walked across this plush carpet, the detective noted he walked with his right hipbone cocked out; perhaps it was how he supported that rucksack of his.

Whitlock went straight from shaking McCusker's hand to lifting his iPad from the counter underneath the television. He focused on that for a few minutes before saying, "Ah right, yes...we now know for a fact that Bing Scott was witnessed at a family do last Saturday afternoon in Boston, so we can also remove him from our list."

"Good to know," McCusker said.

"Talking of lists, McCusker – how are you getting on with yours?" Whitlock Senior asked as the breakfast arrived.

"Well..." McCusker hesitantly replied, worried about how his development would go down, "we do have someone in custody."

"Wait a minute, wait a minute..." Wesley Whitlock said, looking every one of his seventy-seven years on this planet and needing the support of a chair. "You've got him?" His finger froze mid-flick on the iPad screen and his eyes started to well up. He bit his bottom lip for a few seconds to compose himself before he could continue, "You've got the man who murdered my son?"

"Well sir," McCusker said, "I would caution you that it's still very early in our investigation and we've by no means solved the case yet but, as I say, we have someone in custody with whom we're continuing to question."

"For heaven's sake man, who is it?"

"Of course you know I can't tell you that, but as we promised each other on Wednesday, I do want to keep you up to speed on developments."

"Is it someone who knew Adam? What's the motive? Personal? Business? Political?" On and on Whitlock Senior bombarded McCusker with his questions.

"I'll be happy to update you as soon as we conclude our enquiries," McCusker said as they settled down to breakfast.

"I'll be a victim of my own impunity of character and not push you any further on this matter," Whitlock eventually conceded, for the second time in two meetings, seemingly accepting that he wouldn't get any more information from McCusker. "And, as Warren Buffet once very famously said, 'It's only when the tide goes out that you learn who's been swimming naked.'"

McCusker laughed heartily, mostly in relief, adding, "In our case, I think we can substitute 'been swimming naked' for 'not got an alibi'."

Before he left the Europa Clinton Suite, McCusker did agree to telephone Whitlock after the interview for a progress report.

"That's all I ask for, McCusker – all you need to do for me is to keep me in the loop," Whitlock Senior said as he walked the detective out to the lift and pushed the button. When it arrived, he got into the lift with McCusker and put his foot up against the door to stop it departing. "But let me just add this McCusker – and this might be very important – if, when you are convinced you've caught this man and you receive any static from seniors or politicians or whomever, come straight to me and I'll deal with all of that nonsense. I don't care if this creep works for the army, the government, or even Baskin Robbins, I still want his short and curlies on a plate."

He pressed the lobby button and stepped out of the lift. As the doors were closing with McCusker on the inside the American whispered as he winked, "You'll find I'm a very appreciative man, if you get my drift."

***

"Don't mention my name when I tell you who I am," an unknown female announced to McCusker by way of greeting in a phone call to the Custom House later that Friday morning.

"I'm listening," he replied, equal parts intrigued, amused, and wary.

"I'm Lily's sister."

"Oh, right, of course Gr…"

"Don't say my name, don't say it!"

"No problem, sir," McCusker tried.

"Okay, now that was good, that was very good," Grace said. "Keep that up. Now, what do I call you? I know all about you not being a proper policeman, but I don't feel comfortable calling you by your last name. My father always taught me that was just plain bad manners."

"Brendy is good."

"So you do have a first name – Brendan, then."

"Brendy *is* good," McCusker repeated, indicating he was happier that most people used his surname.

"Okay Brendy," she said. "Yeah, I see what you mean – McCusker is probably better. Right look, have you seen Lily this morning?"

"Yes," McCusker replied.

"How does she seem?"

"Hard to say…she's kept her sunglasses on all morning and she keeps nipping out to the toilet…she's there now I think," McCusker replied. "I imagined she'd a late night last light."

"Yeah," Grace O'Carroll replied half-heartedly.

"Look, is everything okay?" McCusker asked.

"Not really," she said quietly.

"What can I do to help?"

"She was on a date last night," Grace started, her voice becoming emotional.

"Yes?"

"And he beat her up."

"Oh my…"

"For heaven's sake McCusker, don't overreact, just in case she comes back in again! She must never know I told you."

"Do you know who it is?" McCusker asked.

"Yes…it was the guy she went on a bad date with earlier in the week," Grace said calmly.

"The man with the odd socks?"

"Jeez, that's him…she really must tell you everything," Grace continued, sounding encouraged.

"Who is he?"

"All I know is that he is called Terry, he runs a marketing company – Rall and Bain – and his office is just across from 'The Black Man' statue above a sandwich shop."

"You really mean 'The Green Man,' don't you?" McCusker said, scribbling away furiously in his notebook and clocking DI O'Carroll returning to her desk. "Okay, leave it with me, sir."

"She's back in the office then?"

"Oh yes," McCusker replied, folding the notebook and putting it in the inside pocket of his crease-free blue suit jacket.

"Don't forget: Mum's the word," Grace O'Carroll added before disconnecting simultaneously to saying "Toodaloo."

CHAPTER THIRTY-ONE

"Toodaloo," McCusker thought as he gently replaced the receiver, hoping that by setting the phone down quietly, O'Carroll wouldn't clock that he'd just been talking to her elusive sister.

Even though she'd been troubled in the call, Grace had sounded friendly, familiar even. In a way he'd already gotten to know her a little through Lily. Perhaps she'd been so familiar with *him* for the very same reason.

"You haven't mentioned my pair of Roy Orbison's so far," O'Carroll said, interrupting his thoughts.

"You have an altercation with a door?" he offered, trying to be helpful.

"Yeah, something as thick as that," she replied half-heartedly. "I just hope the sun stays up."

"Be difficult in the basement," McCusker whispered, their chairs so close they were almost touching, and then in a normal level voice he said, "Look, I can interview Richard Robinson with WJ Barr; hopefully we'll get this tied up by lunchtime. You can get stuck into those files on your desk."

"I wouldn't miss our big interview for anything," she said. "What time is David Lewis due?"

McCusker checked the office clock, crowned with Larkin's sign "This clock will never be stolen; our employees are too busy watching it!" The sign was seriously faded with age but still proud. It was 9.53 a.m. on the last day of the first week of his investigation into the death of Adam Whitlock.

"About five minutes," McCusker replied. "WJ is bringing Robinson to the interview room any minute now. Hopefully his overnight in custody will have sharpened his sense of truth. Are you ready?"

"For anything bar life," she replied. "Do you think we've really got our man?"

McCusker thought about her question for a few moments. His mind fast-tracked through everything he'd learned so far on the Adam Whitlock case. He mentally checked off the names on his suspect list. Once again he ended up with the one name he always ended up with: Richard Robinson. He eventually answered O'Carroll's question: "It can't be anyone else.

***

Once again, McCusker announced for the benefit of the tape recorder those present at the interview.

Local solicitor David Lewis started off the proceedings. "Okay, my client would like to make a statement as to where he was on Saturday night."

"Okay," McCusker replied, obviously relieved. He couldn't determine what O'Carroll was thinking because she hadn't removed her sunglasses.

"Richard," Lewis continued, "could you please tell Detective Inspector O'Carroll and Mr McCusker where you were on Saturday evening?"

"I was at work."

"Sorry, I thought you were unemployed...were you concentrating on writing your lyrics?" McCusker offered, completely taken aback by the claim.

"Mr Lewis says I need to apologise to you for wasting your time and I do, I apologise, but don't you see? I didn't want Angela to know...didn't want her to know that I'd taken a menial job because I wanted to have some money of my own," Richard elaborated. "I didn't want to have to keep humiliating myself by going to her and asking for money."

"So what is your job?" McCusker asked, as O'Carroll sat motionless, asleep, for all McCusker knew.

"Here's a photocopy I obtained last night," David Lewis said as he removed a folded piece of paper from inside jacket and passed it to the detective.

McCusker unfolded it and discovered a photocopy of a clocking-in card at the Royal Victoria Hospital. The solicitor got up from his chair and came around from his side of the table. "Here," he said, pointing to a line on the page. "This shows that Richard clocked in at 11 p.m. on Saturday last and clocked off at 6 a.m. on the Sunday morning. The signature across the photocopy is the signature of Richard's boss, Mr Henman Cooper, confirming the photocopy is authentic and that he personally saw Richard several times on the evening in question. I have made him aware that you will need to contact him to verify this information in the very near future."

"How long have you been working there?" McCusker asked, now jotting down his own notes.

"Since last September."

So this was where he'd been on his late-night excursions, McCusker thought. "They're undertaking a £95 million refurbishment and needed night staff to guard the site. It really was the ideal job for me – not too many people around, which also meant no one would report it back to Angela."

"Why Richard?"

"With all of Angela's rich friends and her job at the BBC I could never tell her. She'd be *so* embarrassed. And, as I said, I do have my pride and I didn't want to keep hitting her for subs."

"But would she not have grown suspicious when you no longer needed money from her?" McCusker asked, perceiving that O'Carroll was understandably off her game.

"I told her I sold some articles, essays and lyrics," Richard said, and shrugged. "Also, all I do is sit around all night, trying to work out how much has changed since the night before, so really it's the perfect time for me to get a bit of writing done as well. I've started to write this book, it's called *Too Close To The Flame*, and it's all about…" Robinson looked at his solicitor, obviously thought better about what he was going to say and continued, "I don't need to bother you with that; I've wasted enough of your time."

David Lewis nodded agreement.

"No Richard, what is your book about?" McCusker asked, gaining the first stirring from O'Carroll since the interview started.

Robinson visually jumped up in his chair. "Well, it's about these two people who live together. They don't really know each other. If they ever did get to know each other, what they'd find out about each other would mean they'd never ever be able to stay together," he gushed as if he was being interviewed on the *Graham Norton Show*.

"How much of it have you written?" McCusker asked.

"About three-quarters of it?"

"How long has it taken you?" McCusker asked, figuring where he wanted to go with this, but noticing that Lewis was looking a little restless.

"Just over a year," Robinson said, "but I haven't been working on it all the time, not all the time. You see, I ran into a problem with the plot and didn't make any progress for about two or three months."

"So the two people in this story; how old are they?" McCusker asked.

"Oh, they're students."

"At Queen's University?" McCusker suggested.

"Well yes, but not really, if you see what I mean."

"Sorry?"

"Well, in my mind, when I'm thinking of the characters I'm thinking of Queen's University, but on the page it's meant to be in London," Robinson explained.

"Right...and the main two characters; what is it they're hiding from each other?" McCusker asked. O'Carroll sat up in her chair seemingly impressed with McCusker's line of questioning.

"Well, the boy wants to be a professional golfer but the girl can't abide golf, but she is secretly in love with one of her lecturers, who happens to be a female," Robinson offered, unwittingly shooting McCusker's theory down in a large heap of smoke.

"Look," McCusker started, putting away his notebook and starting to tidy up the table, "I think it's very important that you tell Angela what you have been doing. I'm speaking from experience here, Richard, and I can tell you that you really do need to keep your wife involved in your life on a day-to-day basis."

"Does this mean I can go?" Richard Robinson asked, looking from McCusker then quickly to Lewis.

"It'll take us a few minutes to double check this on the phone, Richard." McCusker said. "Then we'll advise Angela to come and collect. Even then don't be leaving the city without telling us."

***

"Well, I'm shocked McCusker," O'Carroll admitted across their chair-backs ten minutes later.

"Yeah, me too."

"No, not about that, not about Robinson's night job and his alibi."

"Well, about what then?" McCusker asked, as he helped himself to half of the house to house reports Barr had left on O'Carroll's side of the desk.

"About the fact that you're not totally gutted that the main suspect in our case has just walked scot-free."

"Well, I'm always happy when an innocent man goes free; that would always be my preference."

"Do you fancy a bit of a lunch on me this time, I've got a few white fivers?" she asked.

"White fivers?" McCusker asked, once again caught on the hop with her turn of phrase.

"Augh you know, luncheon vouchers, we call luncheon vouchers white fivers," she said, appearing happy to continue his education.

"Oh right, good to know," he said, hoping he didn't sound quite as sheepish to her as he did to himself. "But no thanks, I'll take a rain check on lunch. I already have a PB appointment for this lunchtime."

Her eyebrows did a great impression of wondering what his personal business was.

***

McCusker was about to start into the files when O'Carroll returned to the office just after lunchtime. She'd removed the sunglasses and, McCusker assumed, had accomplished quite a bit of repair work with her make-up, because she looked okay.

"McCusker, I just wanted to tell you that a few minutes ago while you were at lunch I got a call on my mobile from Mr Odd Socks...you remember him?"

"Yeah, I think so, but it's difficult O'Carroll...so many, you know?"

"Anyway he wanted to apologise for last night and he said he would never ever bother me again."

"That's good," McCusker said, nonchalantly. "Maybe you misjudged him."

"Not so quick McCusker, I hadn't finished," she persisted. "He sounded like he was in a lot of pain but he went to great trouble to plead with me to tell you that he'd rang up to apologise?"

"He probably knew that as we're partners, you'd have told me about the incident."

"But McCusker, I'd never told you about the incident?"

"What incident are we talking about here?" McCusker said, trying to pull off a nonchalant lack of interest.

"McCusker...what's going on here?"

After some prodding, he eventually admitted paying Mr Odd Socks a visit, which descended into challenging him to a fight. "But it was a fair fight with witnesses," McCusker claimed.

"Nonetheless, you still beat the crap out of him."

"Technically no," McCusker replied, knowing he could still be in trouble with her.

"'Technically no'?" she repeated. "Really?"

"Well, I don't believe he needed to send for his brown trousers."

"Augh McCusker!" she moaned. "But then what was all that rubbish you were on about the other day when I said I'd go and beat the crap out of someone and you said 'no, you can't do that – you're just stopping to the same level'?"

"Well, I never claimed to be perfect," McCusker replied and then mumbled something.

"What did you just say?"

"I never claimed to be perfect."

"No, the bit after that...the bit you mumbled?"

"Besides you're family," McCusker mumbled again, but this time clear enough, barely, for her to understand.

"I still need to discover how you found out about this, but let's leave it for now, we've a real case to solve," she said and wandered the very short distance to his desk on the pretence of collecting some of the files he'd removed from her desk. Instead, she playfully punched him on his arm and returned to her chair.

Then, as last time, she quickly grew self-conscious. So much so, in fact, that McCusker felt that if it weren't for her heavily applied make-up, her blushing would have betrayed her.

CHAPTER THIRTY-TWO

McCusker, Barr, Cage, O'Carroll, and Superintendent Larkin – who seemed as relaxed as McCusker about losing their main suspect – gathered to study the names on the Perspex board by the large ancient windows at the opposite end of the office to O'Carroll and McCusker's desks.

Bing Scott
Craig Husbands
Angela Robinson
Richard Robinson
Julia Whitlock
Ross Wallace
Samantha Wallace
POPU

McCusker took a cloth and rubbed until only three names remained:

Angela Robinson
Julia Whitlock
POPU

"You're leaving Angela Robinson and Julia Whitlock on the list?" O'Carroll asked.

"Well we need *some* names up there," Larkin offered, only half joking.

"And POPU is looking more and more the favourite," McCusker said, offering up what everyone was likely to be thinking, everyone, that is, apart from DI Cage.

"The more I think about this the more I'm favouring MWM."

Cage – out there, standing in his field, as opposed to outstanding in his field, McCusker uncharitably thought.

"So, you've upgraded it from CWM?" Larkin, the memory man, asked.

"Well, the victim of this particular crime was most definitely murdered."

"Okay DI Cage," Larkin said. "If that is the case and this is murder without motive, what did you learn from this conference of yours that will help us solve this particular MWM?"

"The secret, sir, is not to look for any logic, motive, or connection between the victim and the murderer."

"Yes...I think I get that bit DI Cage," Larkin said a little short. "But how do we solve it?"

McCusker tuned out. He'd become preoccupied by a small germ of an idea, an idea so tiny that he knew if he didn't focus on it exclusively, he would lose it and lose it for good. It hadn't as much sprung from Cage's MWM line of investigation, no, it had rather budded shyly from it. He excused himself and returned to his desk, followed a few seconds later by O'Carroll.

"You got something McCusker?"

McCusker continued to write furiously in his notebook.

"You want to share it with me?" O'Carroll continued, oblivious to McCusker's thought process. "Okay McCusker, I'll just start into these files and you can continue to just ignore me," she said, lifting a file and pretending to read.

McCusker stopped writing and studied his notes.

"McCusker...you'll never guess who's just walked through the door..."

Still no acknowledgement whatsoever from the agency detective.

"It's Miss French bob," O'Carroll quipped, christening McCusker's object of desire with the moniker in the process. He continued to ignore her, so she continued, "She's walking over to you McCusker. Oh my goodness, you'll never guess, she's started to take off her clothes. You know, McCusker, I think you were correct – I think she might well be an angel."

McCusker was happy that he'd managed to get his idea formulated on paper and – under his breath of course – he thanked DI Cage for the springboard. "Great to see you're back on form again O'Carroll," he announced, as he returned his notebook to the inside pocket of his jacket.

"McCusker you totally blanked me out," she said, glaring at him, "as in *totally*. I've never seen you behave like that before. Did you used to do that to your wife?"

"As in, now you know why she left me?"

"Well, now you come to mention it."

"I heard everything you said and it was all rubbish and so I didn't feel a need to deal with it," McCusker said. "On top of which I'm not due to see French Bob until 7.30 tonight."

"Sorry?"

"Yeah – I bumped into her at lunchtime and I invited her out to dinner and she accepted."

"Oh my goodness, that's brilliant!" O'Carroll gushed with a certain degree of pride, tempered with concern, in her voice. "You jammy barsteward, you. And you're actually going to go out with her?"

"No, of course not," McCusker said. "But at least I got you going! Now can we get back to our investigation? We need to have another chat with both Wesley Whitlock III and his daughter."

CHAPTER THIRTY-THREE

Needless to say Wesley Whitlock III, as he'd had embroidered on his rucksack, and his shirts, and even his iPad cover, was very surprised, yet admittedly happy, to entertain McCusker in his hotel suite for the second time that day. On this occasion he was accompanied by DI Lily O'Carroll who felt a need to detain McCusker in the lobby for a few extra minutes while she touched up her make-up again.

"Good or bad news, Mr McCusker?" Wesley Whitlock offered by way of greeting.

"Well, that depends," McCusker started.

"Depends on what?" Whitlock demanded, the smile fading from his red-flushed face.

"Well, let's just say we've had to set an innocent man free, which must be a good thing right?"

"Always," Whitlock replied. "If you're sure of course?"

"We're sure," O'Carroll offered.

"Now we need your help, sir," McCusker continued.

"Name it," Wesley offered immediately, and invited them to sit in his lounge.

"Okay," McCusker said taking a large gulp of air and deciding to bite the bullet. "We're still checking a few leads out, but I keep on hitting the same brick wall – I can't seem to find anyone with a grudge against Adam."

"Right," Whitlock Senior said, absent-mindedly flicking his index finger across the screen of his IPad every few seconds.

"So, it came to mind that perhaps your son was targeted not because of his enemies…"

"Yes, and?"

"Well, it would seem that Adam actually had no enemies so…"

"…so now you're thinking it might have something to do with one of *my* enemies?" Whitlock said enthusiastically, setting his iPad to the side for the first time in their meeting.

"Well, perhaps," McCusker continued tentatively, "I remember hearing somewhere that you worked in the city for a few years and…"

"I like your line of thought, McCusker," Whitlock said, seeming very happy to go with the detective's logic.

"You see, if we take Belfast as being the common denominator, perhaps someone with a grudge against you discovered that Adam was now living here in Belfast and he sought his revenge through your son?"

"I'm still with you."

"Okay, so the most obvious question then would have to be were you ever involved in a legal case where a father, or even a mother for that fact, lost a son?"

"Wheeew," Whitlock blew a long breath through a nearly closed mouth. "You know, I can't think of anything off the top of my head. But I still believe you might be on to something."

"Would you have taken your case files or notes back to Boston or are they still in the Belfast office?" McCusker asked, as O'Carroll fulfilled the note-taking part of the partnership, being as she was totally in the dark, although she did appear to be committed to his new approach.

"They'd all still be here, in Mason, Burr & Co's vaults."

"Okay, let's get around there now and get stuck into them?"

"They're just about to close for the weekend…" Whitlock announced, as he'd checked his watch. "Let's get in there first thing Monday morning."

"Look, sir, all we'll need is the files, a large room, a continuous supply of coffee, doughnuts, and Paris buns and we'll get our forensic team around there immediately."

Whitlock seemed to waver.

"We can't afford to waste any more time sir," McCusker pleaded.

"Okay, I'll tell you what," Whitlock offered. "You go back to the Customs House and organise your team and I'll meet you at the firm's office and have everything organised for you. Let's meet in forty minutes, say 6.30, and I'll have everything set up for you by then – and I promise I'll also have the coffee, Paris buns, and a box of mixed Krispy Kremes ready for you as well."

McCusker was going to argue but then the more he followed the line of this new approach the more he liked it. He decided against discussing it further with Whitlock Senior. He was feeling so good about it he didn't even bother to correct the American's common mistake of referring to the PSNI base as Customs House and not Custom House. "Okay, that's good sir. I really appreciate it. We'll see you there at 6.30."

CHAPTER THIRTY-FOUR

Things didn't quite go according to plan. That is, they didn't quite go according to Wesley Whitlock III's plan. By the time he arrived at the offices of Mason, Burr & Co at 5.59, thirty-one minutes early for his meeting with McCusker, he discovered that McCusker and DI O'Carroll were already there waiting for him. Even his best-feigned smile failed miserably.

Whitlock's gung-ho attitude visibly faded, only confirming that it had been the old lawyer's intention to furnish them with an edited version of his case files, perhaps with certain files missing altogether. McCusker had known that if this idea was to work, his team were going to need access to *all* of Whitlock's files – particularly those the young-toothed, thick-skinned American clearly didn't want them to see – and if he and O'Carroll couldn't get access to all of these files, they'd be wasting valuable time going google-eyed through the remainder. It was imperative they did this properly, so they'd decided to contact the more reliable DS WJ Barr rather than following protocol and summoning DI Cage. They'd had Barr quickly organise a team, as many as he could muster, at the offices of Mason, Burr & Co. on Royal Avenue.

Upon their arrival, the detectives had immediately sought out the firm's senior partner, Kurt Wolf, to brief him on their visit: they were here to search all of Whitlock's case files from his years of employment at the firm. Herr Wolf took the detectives to the attic storage space himself and located the files, which were proudly marked "WWIII."

McCusker had had one final favour to ask the senior partner. "Could you please have one of your secretaries come up immediately and log all of Mr Whitlock Senior's files?"

"Why of course."

"I'm sorry for the rush," McCusker had explained. "It's just that we're keen to get started and for obvious reasons I need to keep it 100 per cent official and ensure we leave you with the same number of files you gave us."

"That's easy," Wolf had explained, as he'd opened the first of the seven boxes of files. "You see here, inside the lid? There is a list of all the files contained therein. We have a photocopier on this floor so it won't take long."

By the time Wesley Whitlock III arrived at 5.59 McCusker had completed all of his housekeeping, even to the extent that he'd had the friendly secretary make up an additional two copies of the officially signed list of files: one for the firm and one for Wesley Whitlock III.

Whitlock himself looked like a spare rooster at a hen's wedding. "Maybe if we divide them up, we'll get through them a lot quicker," he offered.

"No, it's absolutely fine, sir," McCusker responded, trying to sound as friendly as possible. "Our team have their own perfectly tuned system. There are only seven boxes and hopefully we'll get through them all tonight."

"I'm afraid you're not going to be able to do that," Whitlock said. "The offices need to be totally vacated by 9 p.m. at the latest."

"Yes, we were notified of that rule," McCusker started, sounding hesitant. "Then Herr Wolf explained to us that the rule could be broken should one of the senior partners be present, and he kindly volunteered to stay with us until we are finished. He was very keen to assist in any way he could with the investigation into what happened to your son."

WWIII strolled off, muttering something that sounded like he was suggesting an alternate use for Belfast's famous Paris buns.

***

McCusker and O'Carroll remained behind to guard the seven boxes of case files as though their lives depended on it.

"Just think; you could have been out with the hottie with the hair by now," O'Carroll said, looking for a wee bit of entertainment at McCusker's expense to fill the time.

"I told you that was a joke, didn't I?"

"Yes, you did McCusker, but the fact that you were prepared to make such a joke, even at your own expense, shows you're getting your confidence up. Don't get too confident McCusker; it wouldn't suit you."

"Aren't you mistaking me for DI Cage?"

"And don't get all fussy on me McCusker," O'Carroll said, totally ignoring him.

"Sorry?" McCusker replied, now confused.

"You know, with French Bob – don't go chasing perfect. Just remember, you're not exactly God's gift yourself."

"Well, thank you very much," he replied. "Actually, I believe that imperfections are known to add to a man's character."

"While imperfections in women make men turn their noses up," she countered.

McCusker sighed. O'Carroll obviously had a lecture to give and there was clearly a reason for it, so he thought he'd better let her get on with it now rather than waiting until she'd absorbed the fact that tonight was going to be an all-nighter, a fact she seemed very much in denial of.

"I see the look in men's eyes," she continued. "They note a wee bit of a tyre appearing round the middle, not enough make-up, just one day overdue at the hairdressers, bum and breasts refusing to continue to defy the laws of gravity, ankles filling out…and on and on McCusker. Then they start to turn their nose up, or they start to need a few pints before…"

"Oh no, no, no, O'Carroll, much too much information – please, at all times feel free to spare me those kind of details."

"But at the same time," she continued, still totally ignoring him. "If men are unshaven, have bad breath, wear scuffed shoes – that's always a bad sign McCusker, men wearing scuffed shoes, that's a bad one – oh...where was I?"

"You were giving me a list of what I shouldn't do as a man."

"Oh yes: scuffed shoes, dirty fingernails, soiled collars, unshaven."

"You've mentioned unshaven twice O'Carroll, land the plane for heaven's sake."

"Well, there was good reason for mentioning it twice McCusker, you see there are two different kinds of unshaven – the first is where a man shaves quite regularly but has left it a day or two over his comfort zone, and the second – more irritating, physically and mentally – when a man just gets lazy and lets it grow for a few weeks and it gets to looking all scraggy and unkempt and cuts the face off you. But anyway…oh where was I?"

"Scuffed shoes, dirty fingernails, bad breath, soiled collars, unshaven – example a) for a few days, and example b) for a few weeks," McCusker replied, immediately proving that at least he'd been paying attention.

"Yes, all of the above…if a man inflicts a woman with all of the above he's deemed to be a bit of a character, but if a woman is less than perfect she's classed as an auld dog. So, you listen to me Mr McCusker: if you have any designs on French Bob make sure you get your act together before you ask her out."

"You think I should ask her out?" McCusker asked, knowing that he too was guilty of hearing only what he wanted to hear.

"Nagh, I wouldn't bother if I was you."

"Sorry, give me that again?"

"Don't bother."

"What…she's married?" McCusker said, sounding and feeling devastated. "Or you know she's going out with someone? Is that it?"

"None of the above but I'd suggest to you that you are now enjoying a perfect relationship with her."

"Sorry?"

"Well at this stage, it's all in your head, in your imagination, and of course she's perfect. But once you make the next step you risk ruining it."

"How so?"

"Well, what if it's all window dressing? It'll be good for a few nights," and here she paused and looked over at him. "Well, maybe in your case – you know, obviously it's been a long time, so let's extend your period of interest to a few months. You see, my point is that at this time and from this distance there is nothing to dilute your attraction to her, but…when you eventually get to hear her accent, well maybe she's from the bog, or she likes football and you don't, or she's not very deep, or she leaves her clothes lying around, or your normally tidy bathroom is always a mess because of all of her must-have, can't-do-without lotions and potions, and on and on. You get the picture, don't you? Yes, she looks good, I'll even give you she looks great, but that's a cultivated look and it's all about snaring a man. You know she'll probably go to seed very, very quickly McCusker, so do yourself a favour, don't bother – your dreams will be so much better."

"Right," McCusker replied, quietly holding that thought.

"Okay," she said changing the tone of her voice. "I'd predict that if the noise on the stairs is anything to go by, they're just about to start rehearsals for this year's Opera House pantomime. Either that or DS Barr and the gang have arrived."

CHAPTER THIRTY-FIVE

By the time the team had left Mason, Burr & Co the following morning at 8.13, both McCusker and O'Carroll had problems keeping their eyes open. The files had so far produced no leads. McCusker reckoned if they'd managed to turn up one suspect with even the vaguest of grudges against Whitlock Senior, they might have been able to hit a second wind and keep going. Whitlock, it turned out, was no caped crusader, having never been responsible for putting anyone away.

When McCusker offered to treat them all to a breakfast before going home, all opted for going straight to their beds. All, that was, except DS WJ Barr who, claiming it reminded him of his cramming days, insisted he remain alone and keep working his way through the files. Herr Kurt Wolf graciously offered to remain behind with Barr.

McCusker walked home slowly, shaved and showered – always in that order – and went to bed, only to wake up twenty-eight minutes later thinking he'd been asleep for at least twenty-four hours. He'd hopped out of bed and followed his Saturday morning ritual of changing his sheets and making his bed before he realised his mistake.

Deciding to make the most of his error, he dandered over to Stranmillis Road – enjoying the walk while still missing the big sky of Portrush – nipped into Café Conor and ordered up the full heart-attack Ulster Fry. While he waited for his food, he reflected on his first full week in charge of a case at the Custom House.

He didn't really have a lot to show for a week's work. No, he thought, scrap that, he didn't have *anything* to show for a week's work. The phone in his dark-blue suit jacket pulsed gently against his chest and he answered it immediately.

"So you couldn't sleep either?" Lily O'Carroll said. "Shall I pick you up?"

"Yes and yes," he replied, "I'm in Café Conor."

"Order me up an omelette please and I'll be there in five."

"A shells only omelette?"

"Sorry?" she said.

"No, I mean I was just wondering if you were one of these modern people who eat whites of eggs only, or yolks only, or even shells only omelettes?" McCusker offered, rueing the golden rule of jokes; when you have to explain them, they aren't.

"Oh right," Lily signed loudly. "You need a bit of work on the auld sense of humour side of things McCusker."

"I'll add it to the list."

"Better," she conceded. "Could you just order me a Spanish omelette and a strong double shot decaf cappuccino – tell them to sprinkle the chocolate in the bottom of the cup before they start, keep the cappuccino very dry with the cup not filled to the top and with a tad of chocolate on the top, but only on the left side of the cup with semi-skimmed milk in the mix but frothed up with full fat and make sure they do it in a takeaway cup."

McCusker laughed in spite of himself.

"Now *that* was funny, McCusker," she boasted, as she disconnected.

As fate would have it, and it sometimes does, just as her Spanish omelette was arriving so was O'Carroll.

"How sad are we?" she began, as she positively tore into her food.

"Count me out of your group please, I'm happy enough."

She made short work of her omelette and then pushed her empty and extremely clean plate away from her as she delicately dabbed the corners of her mouth.

"I wish I hadn't eaten that," she said, after the efficient waitress removed her plate.

"Sorry, why on earth not?"

"Oh you know, eggs, cholesterol, clogging up the auld arteries," she began, the worry lines playing havoc with her forehead.

McCusker tutted.

"Come on McCusker, I need to make sure I've got some steam left in my engine for if and when I should ever meet up with my Jenson

Button," she replied, shooting his half-finished breakfast a blatant judgemental stare.

"You worry too much about stuff," McCusker replied.

"People need to worry, McCusker," O'Carroll started, out of nowhere, following a few minutes' silence when McCusker happily tucked into finishing off his breakfast.

"Nagh," he replied, not really interested in picking up her bait.

"People do worry about stuff all the time," she said, continuing unperturbed with her own train of thought. "Stuff like their jobs, their mortgage, their families, financial stability, their love…"

"Their love?" McCusker interrupted.

"Yes McCusker – everyone needs someone to love."

McCusker raised his eyebrows but decided to leave it there.

"Their cars," O'Carroll continued unperturbed. "Their house, their kid's schooling, their kids leaving home and starting their own families…"

"Phew," McCusker wheezed, sounding exhausted. "And what do they do with their time when they've resolved all those issues?"

"Oh, if they are happy and have resolved all of the above," she said, sounding like she'd never considered that possibility, "they probably worry about getting hit by a double-decker bus."

***

Half an hour later they were being buzzed back into the Mason, Burr & Co. office by a revitalised DS WJ Barr.

"Any success?" McCusker asked.

"Well maybe," he said, leading them back up to the loft storage space, and nodding at eleven files he'd separated from the seven boxes. He'd spread out the contents on the makeshift desk he had created out of a window seat and empty upturned box files.

O'Carroll was still coffee-hyper and looked like she was ready to beat the information out of Barr.

"Okay," he eventually started, looking a little frustrated since he'd not quite had time to go over his theory. "I started to think maybe we were coming at this from the wrong angle, you know, looking for someone who had reason to believe that they'd suffered an injustice because of Mr Whitlock Senior – someone he'd helped to put away or someone he'd uncovered who'd been embezzling or even someone he'd caught cheating red-handed."

"You mean someone who was actually guilty of a crime and was aggrieved to be caught out by Whitlock?" McCusker asked, if only to slow proceedings down so that Barr could properly collect his thoughts.

"Yes," Barr nodded visibly relaxing. "Then I thought: what if there was someone out there who Mr Wesley Whitlock III had wronged for some other reason?"

"Good thought Barr," O'Carroll said, as Barr searched diligently through his files. "Picture me impressed."

"I'm not so sure envy is such a good colour on you," McCusker whispered to O'Carroll just out of Barr's range.

"So I ploughed through the files again," Barr offered, and then on noticing McCusker's pity, he continued. "Oh, it was so much easier second time around, it really was. Anyway I dug out these eleven files and in my mind I've pretty much narrowed it down to three, these three in fact. I thought I'd have a bit more time to go through them again in greater detail before you came back. Maybe the three of us could do that together now and see how we get on."

"And they are?" McCusker said, hoping he might recognise one of the names.

"In no particular order," Barr started nervously, "Dan Kidd, Maud Stephens, and Natalie Gilmour."

CHAPTER THIRTY-SIX

"Okay, let's do them chronologically," McCusker suggested.

"In that case..." Barr began, shuffling his files, "during 1987 and 1988 shortly after Whitlock Senior first moved to Belfast one of his first clients was a widower called Daniel Kidd, known as Dan. His wife, Jean, had died a very painful cancer-related death in 1985 and by 1987 he had decided to sell up his wine-importing business, which was based on Lisburn Road. Dan and Jean had no children, so he'd no heirs to pass his business on to. But it was still a thriving business and he owned his premises. Turns out that Wesley Whitlock persuaded him to sell both the building and the business as a going concern. It would appear that the American, as a result of a bidding war, secured an over-the-top-offer of just over half a million quid which Dan felt, along with his savings and pension, would enable him to see out his days nicely. Dan Kidd and Whitlock became friends and apparently, as is common with all of these cases, they had dinner together once a week."

"Whitlock was cultivating the friendships?" McCusker suggested.

"It would seem so," Barr replied, appearing surprised at the interruption. "Early in 1988 Whitlock came to Dan Kidd with a property that one of his other clients owned and needed to sell quickly. Kidd had all his money on deposit and Whitlock convinced him it would be a great investment. In fact, this proved to be the case and Kidd sold the property within three months making just over £95,000 clear profit.

"Whitlock found three other investments for Kidd before the end of that year. The first one made a profit of £48,000, the second one made a loss of £19,500 and the third one made a profit of £67,000."

"Seems like a great kind of friend to have as a lawyer," O'Carroll offered.

"Seems so...just under £100,000 in a year," McCusker added. "What age of a man was Dan Kidd?"

"Seventy-four when he died early in 1989," Barr said, checking his summary notes at the top of the file.

"Oh," McCusker said, sounding genuinely sad.

"And guess who he left all his money and his house to?" Barr asked them both.

"Whitlock," McCusker and O'Carroll replied in unison.

"Yes, and the only reason there is a file on the case is due to the fact that some of Dan Kidd's money was still in his Mason, Burr & Co's client account at the time of the death and the partners felt they needed to conduct a thorough investigation into the dealings to protect their reputation."

"And their findings?" McCusker asked.

"Everything done totally above board and by the letter of the law."

"So there doesn't appear to be anything suspicious there?" O'Carroll said, her disappointment written all over her face.

"Seems so, and if you hadn't asked me to go through the three cases chronologically I wouldn't have started with that one. Personally, I think it appears to be harmless enough..."

"Well, still highly beneficial to Whitlock even if it is harmless," McCusker offered.

"Look this old man," O'Carroll started, "he didn't have any living relations, right?"

"Well, none came forward to contest the will," Barr offered, by way of agreement.

"So he'd lost his wife...have we any idea how long they'd been married?" O'Carroll asked, interrupting herself.

Barr checked his notes, didn't find what he was looking for and hoaked through the file until he came up with an answer. "Forty-six years. As I say, he lost his wife, who was most likely also his best friend, to cancer. It appeared that he put all his energies into his business to fill the void she'd left. Once he'd sold that business, his life probably felt very empty, and then this magnetic American comes along and not only does he befriend him, he also presents opportunities for the widower to greatly increase his nest egg. So, when the time came to start thinking about his will, he most likely didn't have a lot of options."

O'Carroll twitched her mouth from side to side, appearing to consider something; McCusker encouraged her with his eyes.

"You know," she said after a few more moments silence. "My older brother, he made a few right moves, has…well, let's just say he's done very well for himself. Last year his solicitor persuaded him it was about time he made a will. He said the first part was easy, you know – if anything happened to him everything would go to his wife and their two kids. But he said the next part was more difficult where he had to decide what would happen to his estate if they all died together or neither his wife nor their kids survived him. He said he went around for a few days thinking 'Okay, I've taken care of my family and my friends and I've still got a shit load of money unallocated, what am I going to do with it?'"

"And what did he decide?" Barr asked.

"He never said," O'Carroll replied. "But the point was that he'd worked really hard all of his life to make a bunch of money and he was quite literally having trouble giving it away."

"I bet he didn't have any trouble taking holidays after that," McCusker offered O'Carroll and then addressed Barr. "Tell me this: Who drew up Dan Kidd's will?"

"Oh, it wasn't Wesley Whitlock III, in fact it wasn't even Mason, Burr & Co. – it was a totally different company," Barr said as his eyes scanned his notes. "It was Henry's Ltd."

McCusker scratched beneath his left ear with his right hand, merely to find something to stop him voicing his disappointment.

"As I say, I included this case merely to show what I think is a pattern: Whitlock appears to go out of his way to befriend his clients, particularly his older clients. This all leads me nicely to the next case, which is not as clear-cut as Dan Kidd's. This next one," Barr said, exchanging one file for the next, "concerns Miss Maud Stephens. Miss Stephens was a spinster."

"Oh please don't call her that," O'Carroll interrupted immediately, suffering minor convulsions. "That's such an offensive word…let's just say…"

"Miss Maud Stephens never married," Barr suggested.

"Yes, WJ, that's much better."

"Miss Maud Stephens never married, she was an academic, she came from good stock, a wealthy family who provided well for her, but apparently not as well as they would have had she produced heirs. She worked her way around several senior partners in Mason, Burr & Co. She never fell out with any of them, she just always needed new blood, new intellectual stimulation...that was, of course, until she met Wesley Whitlock III.

"It would appear that the time she met up with the American in 1989 was right around the time that she realised that the funds she'd once felt would be fabulously sufficient for her years, were, in fact, no longer capable of seeing her through 'til the end of her days. She had, on the surface, a humble lifestyle for one so wealthy; she lived in a beautiful late-Victorian house overlooking Wallace Park in Lisburn and for the winter months she'd relocate to her small rustic cottage near Carcassonne in the south of France, to benefit from the milder climate. She owned both properties outright."

"What age would she have been then?" McCusker asked.

This time Barr knew the answer. "In her file Whitlock describes her as a 'young seventy-six'."

"So she felt she needed to increase her bank balance?" O'Carroll prompted, checking her watch and no doubt thinking they'd still one more case to get through.

"Yes, indeed," Barr said, "she and Whitlock enjoyed a weekly dinner, always in her home. Apparently the subject came up several times about how she could increase her financial resources without investing in the property market. Whitlock described a hedge fund he'd created and recommended she speak directly to a couple of people already involved with it. The references checked out sufficiently for Miss Stephens to invest £750,000 in Whitlock's fund."

"Wow..." O'Carroll gasped. "Was that all of her inheritance?"

"Apparently, according to Whitlock's notes, it was 30 per cent of her net worth at that point."

"How long did she think she was going to live for?" O'Carroll said, to no one in particular. When no one in general replied she added, "I could retire easily on that even today."

"In her letters to friends, Maud Stephens wrote that Wesley Whitlock III frequently reported to her that 'her nest egg was doing well.' When Miss Stephens died later that year Wesley Whitlock reported to the partners in Mason, Burr & Co. that his hedge fund had suffered badly through overseas investments, including one very big loss on a Hong Kong tower block, which had never even got off the ground. The net result was that Miss Stephen's estate received a cheque for only £23,763 from Wesley Whitlock III.

"Whitlock was investigated by the partners. No action was taken, save he was to refrain from any future potential conflicts of interest and no longer involve any of his personal clients in the investment funds that he was directly or indirectly involved in. It should also be noted that by this point he was the second most senior partner in the firm."

"Wow," O'Carroll said.

"It doesn't end there," Barr continued. "Unlike Dan Kidd, Miss Stephens had several friends who were up to speed with her financial situation. None had a vested interest because all of them were aware that she had left her entire estate to set up a charity fund, in her family name, to help secure further education for Lisburn's under-privileged. Led by the executor of her trust, Mr Joseph Harris, they vigorously went after Mason, Burr & Co. and Wesley Whitlock III, both together and separately, for the full £750,000 plus interest."

"And?" McCusker asked impatiently. "Did they win?"

"Four years later they eventually gave up, resigned to the fact that much of the money meant for the charity's under-privileged was being spent on legal fees, without any apparent hope of success."

"This Joseph Harris...is he still alive?" McCusker asked.

"I still need to find that out," Barr admitted.

"And your third case WJ?" O'Carroll asked, checking her watch once again.

"Natalie Gilmour, this one is more complicated and a lot sadder than any of the above. Natalie Gilmour was in her early eighties when she met Whitlock. Whitlock was assigned to her husband's account when he first started working with Mason, Burr & Co. in 1987. Samuel, the husband, had retired from a career in banking a few years previously. He didn't really have a lot of need for a lawyer but for some reason or other Whitlock struck up a friendship with him and they dined together frequently, if not weekly. Samuel Gilmour had always kept himself in good shape, ate well, never smoked, drank little and so everyone was in total shock when he, quite literally, just dropped dead of a cerebral aneurysm.

"Natalie never really recovered from the shock of losing her soul-mate and within six months she was bed ridden, more from a broken heart than a physical ailment.

"Again, Whitlock was in attendance and frequently visited the widow – and all above and beyond the call of duty, you understand. He befriended both her nurse, Sally Magill, and her doctor, Jack Rowley, and would regularly check in with them for progress reports.

"The file shows that on the 16 March 1989 Wesley Whitlock III made yet another of his frequent visits to see the widow Gilmour. The main difference on this visit was that a very weak Natalie Gilmour changed her will, making Whitlock the sole beneficiary. The will was witnessed by both Dr Jack Rowley and Sally Magill, both of whom admitted to being paid for their witnessing services."

"How much was her estate worth?" O'Carroll asked.

"Including the Belfast house and a wee cottage up at Rathmullan in Donegal – and after all death duties – it was worth just over £1.7 million."

"Serious change for Whitlock Senior," McCusker said. "If he'd been drilling for oil he couldn't have done much better."

"If he'd been drilling for oil at least he'd have gotten his hands dirty," O'Carroll added.

"But this one doesn't end there either," Barr said. "It all looked to have been done and dusted when out of the woodwork stepped a son of Samuel Gilmour's first marriage who'd emigrated to Canada in the seventies and apparently had been mentioned in Natalie's first will."

"Okay," O'Carroll said, through a smirk, "*now* he needs to get his hands dirty."

"Well, not really," Barr continued. "Whitlock Senior made a song and dance about not wanting to deprive anyone of their heritage. At the same time he made it very clear that as Natalie's estate was her gift to him, he wasn't going to be disrespectful by not accepting it. So, what he did was dig out the original will and make a grand show of generosity by paying Samuel Gilmour's son what he'd been left in the original will, which was exactly £60,000."

"And the son from the first marriage bit his hand off?" McCusker said.

"Only until he found out later how much Whitlock Senior pocketed," Barr said. "By which time he'd already accepted the £60,000 as a full and final settlement."

"So you think this is a motive for the first son…what's his name by the way?" O'Carroll asked.

"Tim Gilmour."

"So you think Tim Gilmour had enough of a motive to murder Wesley Whitlock's son?"

"Well…there's not much else," Barr suggested.

"But 'there's not much else' can never be the reason we accuse someone of murder, Willie John," McCusker said, reflecting on his slim pickings. "Most certainly, let's check out Tim Gilmour, but I'm not convinced. Mind you, this is all great work. You've shown us a side of Wesley Whitlock we never knew existed."

"Aye, a tinker in a gentleman's suit," O'Carroll said. "Of course, I've also realised for the first time that I've been pronouncing his name incorrectly all of this time."

"Really?" McCusker asked, not having noticed her doing so.

"Yes," O'Carroll started flamboyantly. "From what DS Barr has just told us I now realise his correct name is: Wesley Whitlock the Turd."

Chapter Thirty-Seven

McCusker headed off to thank Kurt Wolf for his kind hospitality and to make one final request. "Could you possibly do me up a list of all of Wesley Whitlock's holding and investments?"

"Yes, that'll be easy," Herr Wolf claimed. "It'll all be in the partner's minutes. Shall I drop it around to the Custom House, perhaps after lunchtime?"

"Perfect," McCusker said, and thanked him again.

"Have you anything you need to be doing?" McCusker asked O'Carroll, after they'd tidied all the files back into their seven boxes, but only once they'd helped Barr to complete his summaries on the eleven files he'd selected for closer examination.

O'Carroll checked her watch and appeared shocked to discover it was 12.38 p.m.

"I'm okay for a while," she announced. "I'm meeting up with our Grace at three and I'll need an hour's kip before that, so I can give you a good hour."

"What adventure are you off on tonight then?"

"Well, we're off the see an amazing Belfast band called The Sea Horses," she announced proudly.

"Oh yes – I've heard of them," McCusker replied, visibly surprising her. "I've seen their logo all around the city on lampposts and parking bollards."

"You eejit – the wee golden sea horse is the city emblem!" O'Carroll laughed and added, "Anyway, what do you have in mind?"

"I would like to go and interview Julia Whitlock again," McCusker said.

"You have a lead?" O'Carroll asked, her interest certainly perking up.

"No, but I'd like one," McCusker admitted.

"I'll head back to the Custom House, write up my notes on these files and try and track down Tim Gilmour," Barr volunteered. "If you need anyone after your Miss Whitlock interview I'll be available."

"I might just take you up on that WJ," McCusker replied.

The blues (and the agency's McCusker) came rolling down Royal Avenue, buzzy and building up to its peak of Saturday shoppers.

McCusker wanted to walk, while O'Carroll wanted to drive, so they compromised: they'd drive over and McCusker could walk himself back home or to the Custom House.

Spring was around the corner but, still for all of that, it was a glorious day, the sun shining, the sky blue, very blue. "The perfect day for walking," McCusker reminded O'Carroll.

"Why do you not want to talk to Wesley Whitlock?" O'Carroll asked, as they entered the Arc, which was an oasis of peace and quiet following the vibrant Royal Avenue.

"Oh I do," McCusker replied immediately, "it's just that I don't feel I've got enough information yet to be able to question him properly."

"Do you think there is a chance he knows who murdered his son?"

McCusker looked at O'Carroll. Her concession to the fact that it was a Saturday was that she had forsaken one of her normal trouser suits for a black maxi skirt, which covered the majority of her brown leather boots. She finished the look with a white polo-neck jumper and a brown, waist-length leather jacket. Normally her dark brown hair was parked up in a complicated arrangement secured with numerous hair clips and clasps and such like, but today she'd allowed it to flow freely and she looked much, much younger with it worn down. Her green eyes were glued to the pavement, but were betraying the fact that she was picking her way through the case more than navigating the vast courtyard of The Arc. He knew she was right there with him in more ways than one.

"Yeah, you're right, we'd be fools not to think so," he conceded. "But if he isn't aware of the actual person at this juncture, he'll be aware of whoever it turns out to be."

As luck would have it Julia Whitlock was not in her twelfth-floor corner apartment in block twelve of The Arc, or if she was, she wasn't answering the members of the PSNI ringing her doorbell. As better luck would have it they met Miss Whitlock down at street level on their way out.

"Ah McCusker!" she exclaimed, appearing pleased to see him. "Are you here to see me?"

McCusker nodded and smiled, saying, "And this is my colleague Detective Inspector Lily O'Carroll."

Julia Whitlock barely gave O'Carroll the time of day, focusing all of her attention on McCusker. "And guess what," she said, "I've just been down to buy some of those Eiffel Towers you were telling me about."

"Paris buns, actually," McCusker offered, now acknowledging for the first time the bakery smells his nostrils had recently been tuning into.

"Whatever," Julia replied. "Let's pop back up to my crib, have some coffee and these delicious fresh buns. We can chat up there while I defrost my fridge."

***

The views from her living room were no less spectacular the second time around –even O'Carroll was mightily impressed and they both gravitated towards the big window with the magic view. McCusker had discovered since his last visit that the weird silver building, which would have looked more at home on the film set of a Krypton movie, in the foreground to the side of the lazy Lagan was in fact the six-storey Titanic Centre, part of the new Titanic enterprise. McCusker resisted the obvious thought, but by doing so he'd clearly entertained it.

Julia Whitlock removed her flimsy and flaccid raincoat-cum-wind-resistor affair, revealing a sleeveless wine-coloured polo neck under a white buttoned-up waistcoat and a pair of thick tights, which left absolutely nothing to the imagination. Her brown wild mane was in full flow and today she was make-up free and, to McCusker's less than discerning eye, all the better for it.

She had started to flutter around in the kitchen area, getting cups and plates, knives and spoons out of various discreet cupboards, filling the electric kettle, putting milk in the jug, slicing the two Paris buns into thirds and generally ignoring the detectives.

Coffee ready, she invited them to join her at the high counter which separated the kitchen from the living room area. O'Carroll chit-chatted away about how amazing the view was and Julia thanked her, but in a tone that implied she was prepared to take full credit for nature's stoic work.

McCusker's two-thirds of the local bun were gone before either of the ladies had time to pick the bits of icing sugar from the pinnacle of their first.

Julia made it clear that she was upset: her father has gotten over her brother way too quickly by concentrating his energy into trying to track down the murderer. "But it's most likely his way of getting over Adam – by getting lost in helping to solve the crime," she offered.

"We all have our own ways of grieving" O'Carroll offered.

Julia Whitlock didn't look like she was suffering from grief so much as existing on it. "So how is the investigation going into the murder of my brother?" she asked, as she went over to the worktop and removed the largest knife from her set, secured safely in a block of wood. She then crossed to her fridge, opened the top freezer section and started to expertly stab away at the overgrowth of ice, in an effort to defrost the freezer.

She was creating quite a racket, and since McCusker wished to remove the temptation of nicking another third of the buns, he got up to fill the kettle, plugging it in.

In the meantime O'Carroll was giving her an extended version of the standard "we're in the middle of an on-going investigation" line.

All the time McCusker had been filling the kettle, Julia hadn't even batted an eyelid in his direction. It was as though they were a lifelong couple going about their much-rehearsed domestic chores.

"Tell me this Julia: Do you have a hot water bottle?" McCusker asked as the kettle peaked.

"No…I mean yes, I do…" Julia replied, clearly flummoxed. "But aren't you meant to romance me a bit first?"

"Augh these Ulster lads!" O'Carroll said through her giggles. "Believe you me, they don't let the grass grow under their feet."

"Well, I suppose it is our second date after all," Julia laughed, as she removed a fuzzy Kermit the Frog hot water bottle from a cupboard underneath the sink. All the time she still retained the knife in her hand and was laughing, with a bit of occasional loud baying, at her and O'Carroll's attempts at humour.

"Let me show you a wee trick," McCusker said, taking the laughter at his expense in good humour. He filled the hot water bottle, returned the cap and placed Kermit carefully in the freezer, closing the door after him. "We'll let Kermit do all the hard graft for you while we have a chat, eh?"

"Delightful!" the American declared as her laughter subsided and she took a seat alongside them.

"The last time we spoke," McCusker started carefully, "you were just about to tell me what you were doing on the night Adam was killed."

"Oh yes, of course I was, and then I realised the time you asked me about, midnight on Saturday until 3 a.m. on Sunday was the time poor Adam lost his life and I'm afraid, as you're well aware, I just lost it."

"Yes," McCusker replied.

She chose that exact moment to put the entire last third of her bun in her mouth.

McCusker remained quiet, playing with his empty plate and toying with his coffee. It wasn't great.

Julia Whitlock enthusiastically washed down the remains of her Paris bun, but she still hadn't said anything.

"So what were you doing on Saturday night and Sunday morning?" McCusker eventually felt compelled to ask.

Julia gave him a large nervous smile.

For a moment O'Carroll thought Julia was on the verge of admitting that it had been her who had murdered her brother. It had something to do with how well the American had bashed the knife around inside the freezer, making short work of difficult chunks of ice.

Julia remained in her silence: either she was trying to make something up or considering whether or not to tell them the truth. "It's difficult," she began.

"You are having an affair?" McCusker suggested.

"How on earth did you find out?"

"We know that Adam had a long-standing relationship with Angela Robinson," McCusker offered, "so we have to assume that some, if not all, of your dinners with Adam, Angela, Craig Husbands, and yourself must have been a sham?"

"So you were just guessing?"

"Well yes," he admitted, "but I figured if Angela and Adam were involved with each other most of the time that must mean that you and Craig..."

"Oh," she screeched. "Me and Craig, give...me...a ...break!"

"Sorry, so who is it you're trying to protect then?" McCusker asked.

"I can't say."

"Don't you realise that you might just be helping Adam's murderer get away?" O'Carroll weighed in, hitting her where it should hurt.

"I don't understand..."

"Okay," O'Carroll continued, "if we can't rule you out we have to spend time investigating you and that's time that would be much better spent chasing the real killer."

"So you don't think it was me then?"

"No, I don't as a matter of fact," O'Carroll admitted.

"Well is that not enough then?" Julia pleaded. "If you know it wasn't me then why do you need to know who I was with?"

"Because we *think* it wasn't you Julia," McCusker said. "But we don't *know* for a fact that it wasn't you and we really do need to rule you out."

"Even Adam didn't know who he was," Julia eventually said. "Can you promise me you'll keep it 100 per cent quiet?"

"Miss Whitlock, we just can't make such a promise," O'Carroll offered. "But we can tell you that we'll be as discreet as possible."

"I was with Ross Wallace," she eventually confessed.

"Sorry...Ross...but surely he's married with two children? Adam was the best man and Ross' son's godfather?" McCusker said, admitting to himself immediately he was sometimes too naïve for his own good.

"Oh, it wasn't anything serious," Julia said dismissively. "I met up with him one night by accident at the Merchant Hotel. Adam, Angela, Craig, and I had been out for dinner, a real dinner in fact." She paused and glared at McCusker for a split second. "I'd had a few drinks and fancied another one before going home alone. Ross was already in the very masculine wood-lined bar, and he was quite a few sheets to the wind, as you would say. He admitted his wife was no longer interested in sex but he couldn't find a way to allow himself to cheat on her. He felt it was all too sordid. I told him what he needed was to find a woman who wanted nothing more from him than sex. He said he wasn't interested in hookers. I said 'That's good to know, let's get a room.'"

"That must be the American equivalent to the local chat-up line 'get your coat, you've pulled,'" O'Carroll offered, looking visibly shocked.

"Oh he's a nice man, he loves his family, he wasn't looking for any emotional involvement, which suited me perfectly and…most importantly he's clean!"

"There's something else you want to tell us, isn't there?" McCusker asked.

"Yes, I suppose so," she said quietly, not even bothering to ask him how he knew. "The really sad thing is that I blew Adam out on Saturday night, just so I could see Ross. I keep thinking if I had seen Adam on Saturday this would never have happened."

"Tell me this Julia: What would you and Adam have done if you had met up on Saturday?"

"Oh a pizza and a movie," she said immediately, without thinking.

"And what time would you have gotten home at?" McCusker continued with his line.

"Oh 10.30, 10.45 at the latest…we like to get off the streets before the drinkers come out," she said and then thought about it. "Okay, okay, I realise where you're going with this, you're suggesting I wouldn't have been with him anyway…and it's really very nice of you and the next time you ask me to get my hot water bottle I promise I won't…" her voice trailing off into incoherence.

McCusker strode across to the freezer and opened the door. There was good news and bad news. The good news was that Kermit had worked hard and performed as McCusker had predicted, and the freezer was de-iced. The bad news was that the green frog had taken a severe drenching in the process and was looking to be in a very sorry state.

***

After leaving The Arc, O'Carroll walked McCusker over to the water's edge. "You admitted to Julia that you didn't think she murdered her brother; how did you come to that conclusion?" she said as they looked to the opposite bank.

"They were good friends, they hung out together, they dined regularly together, she followed him over from Boston for heaven's sake just to be close to him, so she's not going to murder him. But why do *you* think she didn't do it?"

"When I keep returning to the thought of her murdering her brother I start to think about my brother and about my sister and I know there's no way it's possible," she said, staring deep into his eyes, making him feel very uncomfortable.

"But sisters have murdered brothers before and sisters have murdered parents and brothers have murdered sisters and parents."

"Yes, but she's clearly not unbalanced," O'Carroll said, pausing for a moment before saying, "well, maybe that's not strictly true."

"Sorry?" McCusker asked, thinking he might have missed out on something.

"Well it appears she might fancy you, so I'd worry if I was her."

"Very funny," McCusker said.

"I'm not kidding, McCusker – I know about these things; I study them closely," O'Carroll protested earnestly. "Your wee hot water bottle line worked a treat for you. Our American friend, Miss Julia Whitlock the first, is yours for the taking."

McCusker was basking in his newfound glory for all of, what...two seconds at most, when his partner screamed at the top of her lungs, "Oh shit, oh shit, look at the time, I'm outta here! Toodaloo!"

CHAPTER THIRTY-EIGHT

McCusker strolled around the open space of The Arc trying to get a grasp of his case. Nothing revolutionary struck him, so he slowly walked back to the Custom House. He enjoyed the walk so much he resolved to get up early the following morning, Sunday, and go for a long walk along the Lagan side.

Custom House Square, what used to be the local equivalent of Hyde Park Corner, was quite busy when he arrived, and so he headed to the opposite side of the square and took one of the seats overlooking it. He was watching the tourists or thrill-seeking locals – he could never work out which – dodge the water fountains, which shot up like sharp lasers of light and traced the original path of the River Farset, which had long since been culverted to help create the square.

From the outside, the 155-year-old Italianate Custom House was such a magnificent building. On the inside with mostly non-descript box-style offices you really had no hint whatsoever either of the perfection of such architecture, nor such historic significance. The ever-cold basement, the splendid staircase, the glorious conference room, and the long room which housed Larkin's team all still bore Charles Lanyon's distinctive proud signature.

Still he couldn't get his mind into gear, so he walked across the square to the Custom House and nodded to a spot in the roof space to his left, as he always did, in the direction of the house's legendary ghost, who supposedly hung out two floors above where the novelist Anthony Trollope had once diligently gone about his work. On this fine March morning, McCusker wondered if perhaps there was a connection between the house's two most famous inhabitants.

From the reception he buzzed up to Barr on the second floor of the north wing. The conscientious Detective Sergeant was still there and McCusker invited him to lunch, adding that he would meet him over at McHugh's in a few minutes.

McCusker admitted to himself that perhaps he'd chosen McHugh's on the off chance he might run into French Bob again. He resolved the next time he saw her to definitely initiate a conversation with her. He was wondering exactly how one should go about such an endeavour when Barr entered the restaurant.

Barr, as ever, had no time for pleasantries and got right into it. "How did you get on with Julia Whitlock?"

McCusker brought his DS up to speed on the interview he and O'Carroll had recently concluded with Miss Whitlock. Needless to say, he omitted the bits about the hot water bottle and O'Carroll's thoughts on how favourably she felt Julia Whitlock was disposed to McCusker should he ever come calling. All the time, Barr made notes in his wee book.

"So how do you think this changes things?" Barr asked, just as their food arrived. "Do you think it puts Julia or Ross Wallace, or even his wife Samantha Wallace, in the frame?"

McCusker looked like he hadn't considered this, even if it was in fact the first thing he'd considered.

"I doubt it," he admitted, tucking into his well-done steak.

"Yes, I interviewed Mr Wallace," Barr said, ignoring his appetising piece of salmon as he flicked back through the pages of his book quickly. "And he said he and his wife were at home that evening with his in-laws having dinner. He claimed the in-laws had stayed until 1.00 am and then Mr and Mrs Wallace retired to bed at 1.30. We checked with the in-laws and they reported that it was more likely to have been 1.20 by the time they left the Wallace's home. Had you been hoping for more from Miss Whitlock?"

"Not really," McCusker admitted. "I just wanted to tie up the loose ends from my previous visit when she'd omitted to give me her alibi."

"Where does that leave us?" Barr asked, carefully finding a safe spot for his book and pen on the table.

"Good question, WJ – you tell me."

"Well I think the line of investigation into Wesley Whitlock III's enemies is by far our best bet."

"That's what we'll do then, WJ, and, thanks to your diligent work on the files, we're off to a great start on that front."

Barr stopped eating, freezing knife and fork mid-frame. He stared at McCusker for a few moments before offering, "I must say, sir, you don't appear to be all that worried over the investigation."

"Well, WJ, it's a puzzle, and you know when it's hardest to solve a puzzle?"

"When you're drunk?" Barr offered confidently.

"Well, yes," McCusker said smiling gently. "But that wasn't the one I was thinking of. I always think it's hard to solve puzzles when you're stressed. When you're stressed you never allow yourself the luxury of putting the full capacity of your brain to your task. So I always think I can best serve the innocent – and the guilty, for that matter – if I can just think of this as nothing more than a big puzzle. You know the best method of solving a puzzle?" McCusker asked. Then feeling perhaps he was coming across a little bit patronising, added immediately, "But of course you do; it is to first assemble as many of the pieces of the puzzle as possible. Of course we can solve the puzzle without actually having all of the pieces, but the more pieces we have the better a chance we have of solving the case properly."

Barr seemed to consider this for a time before offering, "Okay, so what do we do next?"

"Well, I just nipped into the bar on my way here and noticed that Man United are due to kick off against Man City at 3 p.m. and I know you've a vested interest in that so if you leave now…"

"I can always watch it on *Match of the Day* if you need me."

"No WJ – by my reckoning you've now put in a thirty-hour shift and all I'm going to be doing is reviewing the files for the rest of the afternoon, so enjoy the match and the rest of the weekend and I'll see you first thing Monday, when we'll get stuck into this again."

Chapter Thirty-Nine

Mccusker returned to his office in the Custom House where he found on his tidy desk a foolscap manila envelope proudly bearing the Mason, Burr & Co. logo, front centre. He quickly but carefully opened the envelope which contained two pages of the minutes, listing Wesley Whitlock III's assets while a partner at the firm. Paper clipped to the two-page memo was a comp slip from the desk of Kurt Wolf and a note saying:

Please find info as promised. If you should require any additional background info you can get me on my mobile number (below) over the weekend.

sincerely

It was signed flamboyantly in blue ink by Mr Wolf himself.

McCusker couldn't be sure, but maybe Wolf wanted to appear to be going beyond the call of duty in his efforts to help the investigation. He brewed himself a cup of tea, photocopied the two pages, removed his Magic Marker from his desk, and got to work.

Helped, no doubt, by Barr's diligent investigative work into the seven boxes of files, he honed in on familiar names.

Samuel and Natalie Gilmour had bequeathed a staggering £1.7 million to Whitlock Senior and Dan Kidd had bequeathed £530,000 to the American, while Maud Stephens had invested £750,000 into WWIII's hedge fund. McCusker spent about twenty minutes going through the remainder of the list but Barr's trio were by far Whitlock's biggest benefactors. The remaining twelve names had left him a minimum of £5000 and a maximum of £10,000 with a collective total of £91,500.

Whitlock was a full partner in the Mason, Burr & Co. although it didn't mention his shareholding. He also had local investments in UTV, Harland and Wolff, O'Electronics, and DMC–the DeLorean Motor Company. It was this in particular that caught McCusker's attention. Had John DeLorean, a fellow American, been an acquaintance of Whitlock? He checked Whitlock's client list and found no sign of DeLorean. Perhaps he'd been a client of one of the other partner's in the firm? McCusker made a mental note to check this with Kurt Wolf.

DeLorean had been a charismatic American who'd persuaded Maggie Thatcher to invest taxpayer's hard-earned money into his company in return for his promise to base the company in employment-deprived Ulster in general and Dunmurry in particular. All seemed to be going well until DeLorean himself was caught on camera trying to pull off a rather large drugs deal. His plan was to smuggle $24 million worth of cocaine into the USA. Supposedly, he'd earmarked the proceeds of this particular venture for his ailing company. DeLorean was duly convicted, but got off due to his lawyers successfully arguing that he'd been entrapped.

Perhaps, McCusker thought, DeLorean had spent most of his time in legal boondocks wishing that if only Stephen Spielberg's hit movie trilogy *Back To The Future* had appeared even just three years earlier – DeLorean's stainless steel-panelled car with its iconic wing doors being one of the stars of the series – it would have meant a very different and somewhat more successful end to his story.

All of Whitlock's other investments were in the international blue chip league. Frustratingly, the partner's minutes didn't mention whether or not Whitlock had actual shares in the company and if so, whether or not he had subsequently retained them upon leaving the company. McCusker reckoned his mental list of questions for Wolf was now hitting ten, and he found himself dialling the mobile telephone number written on the comp slip.

"Ah Inspector, I've been expecting your call," Wolf offered, in his perfectly spoken English.

"I've got a few questions – could we meet?"

"Yes, when would suit?"

"Immediately?" McCusker said, chancing his arm.

"That would be fabulous," Wolf replied.

McCusker wasn't sure that fabulous was exactly the right word, but he wrote down Wolf's address and hurried downstairs.

Herr Kurt Wolf lived in a beautiful hundred-year-old house on Sandhurst Drive overlooking the spectacular Botanic Gardens. McCusker hopped in a cab resolving to walk home the long way round once he'd completed the interview.

McCusker admitted that he'd somewhat overlooked Wolf up to this point. The German was in his mid to late fifties, wiry framed, and 5' 10". He wore his black curly hair short and was fresh faced with a few wrinkles around the eyes. Today Wolf was dressed expensively in his comfortable brown cord trousers, green V-neck-but-collared jumper and with a reddish cravat tucked into his jumper. He wore what looked like genuine Native American moccasins.

As Wolf showed McCusker through to his study, he had the feeling that the house was a lot like the lawyer, in that there were several rooms he was never going to see.

Wolf left McCusker explaining that he wasn't a detective but a free-lance policeman employed by the PSNI, to go over and turn his very professional and hi-tech-looking stereo system off. McCusker liked the music – it sounded so melodic he thought it must be Mozart.

"Will you join me in a drink?" Wolf offered, as he showed McCusker to one of the grand leather chairs guarding either side of the generously stoked fireplace.

"Will there be enough room for both of us?" McCusker asked, repeating one of his father's favourite lines but immediately regretting doing so, feeling it was perhaps a tad inappropriate.

Wolf had a fit of laughter which nearly caused a seizure – tears literally ran down his cheeks.

"That was so funny," Wolf said, as he offered McCusker a couple of fingers of brandy.

They settled in the extremely comfortable leather fireside seats. The large book-lined study had clearly originally been two separate rooms.

"You have some questions for me?" Wolf asked, immediately setting the tone of the proceedings.

"Yes, firstly, I wanted to thank you for your assistance yesterday evening, last night, for staying with us the entire night, and then getting me the partner's minutes so quickly."

"It really was not a problem and I was happy to help you."

"Okay," McCusker continued, enjoying the aftertaste of the brandy. "I know that Wesley Whitlock was a partner in Mason, Burr & Co., and he worked here in Belfast with you for five years. Did he also have shares in the company?"

"Yes, he was, in fact, an equity partner. The Whitlock family have been on our board since before the Second World War. When Wesley Whitlock joined us the family holdings were 15 per cent. They had always intended to become more involved but first the war and then the Troubles postponed their efforts, until Wesley joined us in 1987. He remained with us until 1991. It had been his intention to double the family holding in his tenure. When he left, the family owned 27 per cent of Mason, Burr & Co."

"So he nearly succeeded in his efforts?"

"Yes, but not quite," Wolf replied wryly, helping himself to a generous finger of brandy and shivering visibly as it successfully worked its way into his bloodstream.

"I see that Mr Whitlock III had some shares in the DeLorean Motor Company, but I also note that he wasn't their lawyer," McCusker said. "Tell me this: Was someone else in your firm their lawyer?"

"No."

"Did Whitlock lose his investment entirely?"

"All £50,000," Wolf said, slightly smugly. "But you know he also had two of the DeLorean cars, in perfect factory condition, shipped back to Boston and they have become collector's items. I notice that one of the cars used in the film was sold recently for a staggering $300,000, so maybe he fell on his feet on that one as well."

Wolf finished off his brandy and then refreshed both their glasses. He studied McCusker the way one would while considering whether or not they were going to share some information. "You know, I am permitted to only answer the questions you ask."

"Okay, okay," McCusker asked, his brain clicking into gear. "Let's back up a wee bit here. Do you think Wesley Whitlock, while involved in his DeLorean dealings, did something that would have resulted in someone wishing to take revenge on his son?"

"No, I don't think you need to look any further into the DeLorean affair."

"When Whitlock left Mason, Burr & Co. did he retain his shares?"

"That is a good question, McCusker," Wolf said, breaking into a wry smile. "No, he did not."

"Did he sell them to you...to someone else?"

"That is two questions – which one would you prefer I answer?" Wolf asked earnestly.

"Did Wesley Whitlock do something that meant you forced him to sell the shares back to you?"

"My partners permit me to give you the following explanation to Whitlock's departure," Wolf began. "During our investigation we uncovered no actual infringements of any known laws, however, we did feel that some of his moral judgements called into question the integrity of this firm and, by association, the integrity of the partners. Because of this, we invited him to tender his resignation. Part of the settlement deal we concluded was that the firm would buy back his family shares at the then current market value."

"But surely..." McCusker began, "surely his son worked there?"

"That was also part of the agreement, as was not volunteering any information about the settlement, which is why I have to tread so carefully."

"Your staff treated Whitlock Senior like royalty when I came in to hear the reading of his will?"

"Most of the current staff would not have been around in 1991 when he departed – they would know him only as the father of Adam who was always very popular in our office."

"So Kurt...what exactly did he do that made the partners eventually invite him to resign?" McCusker asked.

"I am not permitted to answer that question," the German replied plainly. "If I answered such a general question it could be argued I was volunteering information."

"Okay," McCusker said, trying to retrace his steps to safe ground and taking out the two pages Wolf had delivered to him earlier that day.

"Is there anything in his dealings with the UTV shares which could have compromised his son's life?"

"No."

"Harland and Wolff?"

"That is not a question."

"Is there anything in Wesley Whitlock III's dealings with his Harland and Wolff shares which could have compromised his son's life?"

"No."

"Okay Kurt, let's try this: is there anything in Wesley Whitlock III's dealings with his O'Electronics investment that could have compromised his son's health?"

"I am permitted to tell you that Wesley Whitlock III was James O'Neill's lawyer before Mr O'Neill became a director of O'Electronics."

Suddenly a very bright light switched on in McCusker's brain. That morning in the Europa Hotel, as he was entering the lift to go up to Whitlock's eleventh floor suite, McCusker couldn't be sure but he spotted a man he thought he recognised exiting the other lift. When McCusker had finally entered the suite it was clear that Whitlock had already entertained someone for breakfast. McCusker now realised the man exiting the lift was none other than James O'Neill.

But why would James O'Neill want to murder his lawyer's son?

CHAPTER FORTY

As McCusker was leaving Herr Wolf's study he made a slight detour via the German's stereo system to check the title of the music that had been playing when he entered. He was shocked to find it was not Mozart or even Beethoven, which would have been his second wild guess. No, in fact he had been totally off base. The music which had impressed him so was none other than the original soundtrack for the movie *Jonathan Livingstone Seagull* and the composer and performer was none other than Neil Diamond.

Late that Saturday he hoofed it around town until he found a copy of the CD in Head Records, at the Victoria Square shopping centre, just as it was closing. He spent all of Sunday lazing around enjoying the soundtrack and reading the papers. He was still listening to it at 7.20 a.m. on Monday morning when DI Lily O'Carroll called around to pick him up.

"Ah Neil Diamond," she said as she entered his tidy flat. "I didn't know you liked him. Grace and a few of us went to see him in Dublin in some football stadium last year – he was mega."

"How was your weekend? You seem in fine spirits?"

"Sorry, oh yes, The Sea Horses were incredible," she enthused. "Not a big crowd, but that's probably because no one knows them yet, although I did overhear someone at the door ask for his money back because John Squire wasn't with them. The wee girl in the box office told the annoyed patron that was the English group and they spelt their name as one word and no longer existed."

"Right," McCusker muttered conceding that she'd lost him after, 'not a big crowd.'

"But Grace and I enjoyed ourselves...even though there was not one eligible man in sight." She paused for a sip of her coffee. "Also I made a decision, a major decision, but I'll talk to you about that later. In the meantime, how did you get on Saturday afternoon after I left?"

McCusker spent a few minutes bringing her up to speed on his interview with Kurt Wolf.

"And here we are wasting time talking about Neil Diamond and The Sea Horses! We should nip around now to O'Neill's house and pick him up."

"Nagh," McCusker sighed, checking his watch, "I'd prefer to speak to Polly O'Neill first and it's best we wait for James O'Neill to get out of the house or she won't say a word to us."

"Yes, I remember now," O'Carroll said. "When she was trying to get her husband to cough up the ransom she told me she'd had to threaten him with revealing their affair behind her first husband's back. When that didn't work she'd threatened to tell anyone who would listen that O'Neill had cheated her first husband out of his shares of the company."

"This should be interesting," McCusker said, as he turned off his stereo. "But first we've time for a breakfast."

***

By 8.40 a.m. they were parked up a discreet distance from the O'Neill's grand residence in the Malone Park, which was so expensive you felt you should wear new shoes just to go in there. At 8.53 James O'Neill was chauffeured in his racing green Jaguar S-Type out of his drive and off into the distance. McCusker and O'Carroll waited another three minutes before walking up to the front door and ringing the doorbell.

A startled Polly O'Neill, still wearing the same Barbour uniform, gingerly opened the door a minute or so later, but only after O'Carroll had rang the bell an additional three times.

McCusker studied the woman as O'Carroll re-introduced herself and her colleague. Polly O'Neill looked like she might be a shadow of her former self. The thing about looks, McCusker thought, is that he and O'Carroll had just recently met Polly O'Neill and so as far as they were concerned this is what she looked like. But if they'd known her ten or even twenty years ago, how would they feel about her looks now? Would they think that she'd gone off? Or would they think she'd gotten better with age? At what point in our lives do we look like we're meant to look? Is there that perfect time when we're finally at our best, while up to that point we're a work in progress and from that point onwards we start to disintegrate?

For all of that Polly O'Neill, when she eventually remembered them both, flashed them a smile so large it lit up her entire person. She was very gracious and enthusiastic as she invited them into her kitchen in the back of the antiquated house, saying she'd never had a chance to thank them both for bringing her sons back to her safe and sound.

"How are they both doing?" O'Carroll asked, as they took seats in the small add-on conservatory overlooking the perfectly manicured garden.

Again Polly O'Neill's face lit up like a Christmas tree as she discussed her favourite subject: her sons. "Oh, since they've got back Larry's List has been going from strength to strength. They're never off the television – they've been on the local news three times now and even made the national news once."

"That's brilliant," O'Carroll offered.

"Yes, Ryan says their solicitor has been working hard getting all the funding they need in place to give their site the profile it needs."

"Do you know if they managed to pay off the loan shark?" McCusker asked.

"Terrible people, terrible people," Polly shuddered violently as if just thinking of them could contaminate her. "I forced my husband to pay them off. That's the reason the boys got into trouble in the first place and as I explained to James, he's already got more money than Harrods. I'll let you into a little secret, shall I? I had to throw another wobbly and threaten to air some of the skeletons in our cupboards unless he coughed up. He really couldn't believe the interest rates *those* people were charging. I took great pleasure in reminding him that it would have been a lot less money if he'd just given it to the boys in the first place.

"Anyway," she continued, rubbing her hands in obvious glee. "If Larry's List is one-tenth as successful as everyone is predicting it won't be long before the boys are independent. I do believe they are both mature enough to take more pleasure from it than James ever seemed capable of doing. Now listen to me, nattering on like you've come to visit me in an old people's home; I'm being a terrible hostess...tea, coffee, or shall we have a celebratory sherry?"

"We're on duty, we'll stick to tea but you should enjoy a sherry," McCusker replied.

She seemed to hesitate in her tracks for a few moments. "You know what," she said, "I think I will. You put the kettle on and I'll raid James' stash in his study."

Five minutes later they were sitting down in the conservatory again, the police with their tea and incredible Ditty's Bakery Fruit Cake and Polly with the smallest serving of sherry McCusker had ever seen.

"We actually wanted to talk to you with reference to another case we're working on," McCusker said, taking the lead in getting down to business.

"Please continue."

"It involves Wesley Whitlock III..."

At first Polly rolled her eyes but then added, "It's really so sad about his poor son isn't it?"

"Yes," O'Carroll said. "Have you known the father a long time?"

"I'll say..." she offered tentatively, "he was also involved with my first husband."

"What was your first husband's name?"

"Ray O'Sullivan," she said and stopped talking as her eyes focused out into the garden and even beyond. "You know he's the real father of Ryan and Lawrence? Now *he* was a good man...I just didn't realise it at the time."

"How so?"

"Well when I first met Ray he was a very exciting young man. He was a bit of a boffin and even while we were out on dates I'd frequently lose his attention and his mind would be off in invention land, jotting notes down on napkins..." Polly started, her eyes going all misty. "I feel this is going to be a long conversation, excuse me while I just nip into James' study for a refill."

McCusker and O'Carroll were still staring at each other in disbelief when Mrs O'Neill returned with another micro helping of sherry, which barely covered the bottom of the petite glass.

"Where was I?" she asked herself, "oh yes, anyway, Ray and I were getting on great, we were married in 1981 the same year he invented..."

Here she paused and chuckled to herself before continuing, "You know, to this day I still don't know exactly what it was he invented or developed, or even if there is a difference between the two, but anyway it was something that went into the back of televisions or stereo systems which gave the signal a more natural sound rather than the usual electronic sound, if you know what I mean. I believe it was a filter of some kind. I seem to remember they called it a gate; yes, that's it, the O'Sullivan Gate.

"Anyway," she said, raising her glass to the heavens. "This invention caused quite a furore and absolutely everyone wanted to buy it from Ray. Now if Ray ever made a good decision in his life it was to refuse to sell his invention. He chose instead to manufacture it himself and sell the finished product on to the various big companies. So he set up O'Electronics. It was originally going to be O'Sullivan Electronics but Ray wasn't comfortable with having his name plastered around everywhere and so he shortened it to O'Electronics. Pretty soon they literally could not keep up with demand and that's where and when Wesley Whitlock entered the picture.

"He was a partner at the firm and represented Ray. He persuaded my husband that he could raise enough finance to expand in order to keep up with demand.

"Now lately I've come to realise that my poor husband was an amazing boffin but a terrible business man. And, yes, he most certainly developed other projects, but he was forced to spend the majority of his time trying to run the business side of O'Electronics. And he just, pure and simply, didn't enjoy that side of things. He became another person altogether; permanently at his wits end. He was always off to the doctor and taking some prescribed medication for one ailment or another. In the middle of all of this Lawrence was born in 1983 and then Ryan came along shortly thereafter in 1985, and so I was preoccupied with my boys and I will admit that I wasn't paying proper attention to my husband and his business affairs.

"In hindsight I now realise that if only I had been tuned in to him and found someone for him, someone he could trust to run the business side of things, leaving Ray to be the inventor he so desperately wanted to be, he as a business and we as a family probably would have been perfectly fine. But, as I say, I was preoccupied with the boys.

"Anyway, water under the bridge, spilt milk, cracked eggs or whatever you want to call it. I didn't and that's that and I spend so much time these days talking to my sons about it and regretting it.

"However, Wesley Whitlock had his finger in the pie and he wasn't about to see his investment go down the drain, so he came to us one night for dinner and he brought a magnificent bottle of wine, flowers and chocolates, as was his style. Everything was very social and he was as entertaining as ever, and then over coffee and chocolates he got to his point. He said he felt that Ray was just not up to running the company by himself. He said he felt they needed to bring in a business biased director to run O'Electronics and organise their expansion plans, leaving Ray to put his white coat back on and go and invent some more gizmos to feed the machine for their future years...sorry, I'm out of sherry again...won't be a mo."

Once more she positively sped out of the conservatory and returned a few seconds later, but this time her glass was not only filled to the top, but it was so full that she spilt some as she sat down. She carried the half full bottle in her other hand.

"Right that's better," she said helping herself to a genteel, yet generous, sip. "While Ray and I were both feeling warm from the alcohol, our American benefactor got straight to the point and said he had the perfect man to come in and run the company for us. He was a man already wealthy in his own right and experienced, having successfully run his family cattle feed business. Enter stage left a certain James O'Neill, overweight even in those days. Wesley made the point that James was also prepared to put some of his own money into O'Electronics.

"Now, here's the clever bit of the story: If Wesley had made this pitch direct to Ray, he, as usual, would have run a million miles from these straight business people. Mr Whitlock knew that I was already worried about my husband, so by presenting his plan to both of us together, he most likely knew I would support him.

"Wesley insisted that James meet both Ray and I together and he took the three of us out for a grand dinner and we all – James, Wesley, and myself, I'm sorry to admit – successfully persuaded Ray this was the way forward for O'Electronics.

"James came to run the company, and also to flirt his socks off with me. Ray put his white coat back on and seemed much happier for it, on the surface.

"But behind the scenes what I've subsequently learnt was that, between them, James and Wesley owned 45 per cent of the company. Ray and I owned 55 per cent and we'd given 10 of that to various members of both of our families. James diligently worked away behind the scenes and eventually bought 6 per cent for an over-the-top price from shareholders on both sides of our family.

"Wesley Whitlock called an extraordinary meeting. He said O'Electronics needed to shape up, join the big boys on the world platform, and to do that we needed to raise more funds. Ray was in shock and said in his current situation there was no way he wanted to invest more money. He felt that by agreeing to bring James O'Neill on board they'd all start to take some money out of the company for the first time. But Wesley and James overruled him; said it was a done deal and if he couldn't or wouldn't invest, they'd have to 'reluctantly' replace him. Ray reminded them both that he was the major shareholder and nothing could be instigated without his approval. And then Wesley smugly waved three leaves of paper at Ray and announced that he and James had now successfully secured enough shares to make them the majority shareholders. If you'd had a camera on Ray's face at that moment, you would have been able to see all the life physically drain out of his eyes. It never returned.

"James O'Neill took over as managing director of O'Electronics in 1986. My husband Ray was like a zombie. He ignored the boys. He ignored me. Most importantly he ignored himself.

"I'm not proud of myself but I'd been ignored for too long and I'll admit to you that eventually I succumbed to James' advances. On my boys' lives I do not believe that Ray was aware of my affair, but the following year he took an overdose of his medication and ended his life. The year after that I married James O'Neill and the longer I live with him the more I wish I had paid proper attention to poor Ray."

"The ten shares you and your first husband gave to your family: Do you remember how they were broken down?" McCusker asked.

"Yes, we gave our parents four-a-piece, that's two each, and my sister and her husband got the remaining two."

"Do you know which of those shares Whitlock and his partner, your second husband, managed to buy?" McCusker continued.

"Yes, as a matter of a fact I do..." she admitted. "My parents were going through a very bad time financially and needed the money.

My sister never liked Ray and would have been happy to give away her shares. As it turned out, Whitlock and James did not take advantage of this fact."

"So Ray's parent's kept their four shares?" McCusker asked, knowing he might be heading for troubled waters but feeling there might be some mileage with this line of questioning. "Have they still got them?"

"Sadly they passed away within a year of each other in the mid-nineties."

"Do you know what they did with their shares?" McCusker said.

"Yes, they willed them, and not much else, to Lawrence and Ryan," she said quietly.

"I suppose Lawrence and Ryan needed to sell their shares to support Larry's List?" McCusker asked quickly.

"You've got to be kidding!" she laughed. "I'm happy to say my boys have been more loyal to Ray than I was – you couldn't prize those shares away from the boys if their lives depended on it."

"Did Ray have any brothers or sisters?" O'Carroll chipped in.

"No, he was an only child," Polly replied wistfully. "You know, that just might have been part of his problem. If he'd spent more time with siblings, maybe he'd have been better prepared for the rough and tumble of life."

"Did Ray have any good friends, best mates?" McCusker asked.

"Just me, I'm sorry to say. It's my biggest regret that I didn't look after him properly."

Silence ruled the room.

"Are you married Inspector?" Polly eventually asked, looking at O'Carroll and draining the remainder of her fresh glass of sherry.

"No, not yet."

"Well, when you do, you promise me you will remember to always support your husband, take very good care of him. The one thing I have discovered in my life is that the male species don't do very well left to their own devices."

CHAPTER FORTY-ONE

Either Wesley Whitlock III was aware of what they'd uncovered through searching his old case files at Mason, Burr & Co., or he'd spent the weekend soul-searching, but either way he was a changed man when they dropped into his suite in the Europa later that Monday morning. To McCusker it seemed like he'd made a conscious decision that he no longer needed to preoccupy himself with the murder of his son. If only the Portrush detective could have found a way of getting the senior American citizen to pass the information on.

He wondered if there had been something more obvious in the files that they had missed. But then it had seemed to McCusker that Herr Wolf had gone to great trouble to steer him down this particular road.

McCusker and O'Carroll could immediately tell how far they'd dropped down Wesley Whitlock III's priority list in that not only did he not offer them breakfast, he didn't even offer them a cup of tea.

"Oh come in, I have been expecting you," was his greeting from inside the room as one of his Amazonian girls answered O'Carroll's knocking on the door. "So?"

"So," McCusker started, "we've…"

"I know where you've been, I know what you've found out," Whitlock admitted through his perfectly white gritted teeth. It appeared to McCusker that the older Whitlock looked more ridiculous as his teeth appeared. Polly O'Neill clearly still felt enough of a wife to James to have told him of her conversation with the officers. James O'Neill had equally felt duty bound to relay the same information to Whitlock.

"I'd like to tell you a story," Wesley said, surveying the suite to ensure he had their undivided attention. "You know, Monty gave each of

his infantry seven Woodbines a day? Well, by doing so he most likely
was responsible – long term of course – for more of their deaths than
Hitler ever was. My point is that he clearly felt that he was being a
good commander; he was looking after his men as best he knew how
with the information he had access to at that time. That is to say, nicotine relaxes you, relieves your stress."

"So you're actually suggesting to us," O'Carroll snarled, "that you
felt you were doing Ray O'Sullivan a favour; that you were looking
after your client properly?"

"It certainly started out that way," Whitlock explained, "and the
company most certainly grew and grew and eventually the company
became the important issue. The decision we were all faced with was
what was best for the company? Ray was just a casualty of those strate-
gic moves, there was nothing personal."

"So," McCusker started, feeling his blood boil, "to continue your
war-time analogy, Ray O'Sullivan was just collateral damage...an acceptable loss?"

"Exactly!" Whitlock enthused, his confidence appearing to grow
now he believed he had someone on his side.

"You piece of..." McCusker started as O'Carroll glared him into
silence.

"Sorry?" Whitlock said, in a bring-it-on tone.

"What I was about to say..." McCusker started again. This time
O'Carroll looked like she was about to get up and bop him one, "is
that all you needed to do, all the O'Sullivan family, all Ray, Polly,
Larry, and Ryan needed you to do was to put someone in to run the
business side of O'Electronics, leaving Ray to continue to do what he
loved: invent and develop. All you had to do was pay someone to run
his business. You did not need to give them a share of the business. You
did not need to eventually side with your chosen Lieutenant against
your client in a coup to take over the business."

"Listen to me now," Whitlock barked. "I did nothing illegal. I never
broke a law. I did nothing that is not being repeated in boardrooms up
and down your country and my country every day of the week, every
week of the year."

"Sir, not actually breaking the law is nothing to boast about," Mc-
Cusker said quietly, having gained control of himself again. "Laws are

nothing more than manmade rules that your profession has created to allow you to line your pockets and to create your 'acceptable losses' for mankind. What your criteria should have been is this: Would I have wanted my father to have been treated this way? Would I have wanted my mother to have been treated this way? For heaven's sake, man, even on a more selfish level, would I want to be treated this way? There are moral rules which we should follow. We should follow them not because we'll get sued or thrown in prison if we don't, but just because it is simply not our right to break them."

"Oh don't be so fucking naïve," Wesley Whitlock III hissed.

"That's as may be Mr Whitlock, but we're here today investigating the death of your son and it appears to us that your actions were most likely the motive behind someone murdering your son. It is becoming apparent to us that if you hadn't acted the way you acted then your son Adam would still be alive today."

O'Carroll's comment was lethal. It hit the mark with such precision that its impact was immediate. An animal when shot will still try to continue moving. Animals have no comprehension that they have been fatally wounded, they don't understand that they should fall to the ground to prolong their lives – they will do their utmost to maintain their momentum, to keep on going, to stumble onwards. Whitlock, mentally speaking, behaved like a mortally wounded animal.

"So you're here to tell me you're about to make an arrest?"

"We're here hoping that this time you really will help us with our enquiries," O'Carroll offered.

"But who are the victims here?" Whitlock asked in reply. "Who are the real victims?"

"It's always the innocent sir," McCusker quietly offered.

"I just don't know what else to say," Whitlock muttered, as much to himself as O'Carroll and McCusker. "I just don't know what else to say," he repeated, proving the error of his first statement.

Wesley Whitlock did not say another word that morning. One of his Amazonian girls went off down the corridor to fetch his surviving son and the police left him tending to his father.

As McCusker left the suite, he realised for the first time that the less charitable reason for Whitlock being pedantically courteous to all of his staff was because, behind the scenes, he really was such a shit.

***

"So you've turned the case around McCusker," O'Carroll offered, as they sped back to the Custom House.

"Yes but I'm not exactly sure where we've turned it around to," McCusker replied, checking his safety belt. "We've turned away from a few slim pickings of suspects only now to be facing absolutely no suspects whatsoever."

O'Carroll pondered on this for a while. "Well, I suppose I could argue that perhaps Polly O'Neill could be a suspect?"

"Nagh, that doesn't work for me," he sighed regretfully. "She wouldn't be capable and because of the way she fusses over her boys, I couldn't in a million years see her murdering someone else's son. Now if it was her husband who was currently lying in the morgue, well that would be a different matter altogether and she'd be at the very top of my list of suspects."

"Then the boys themselves?" O'Carroll suggested.

"That was my first thought," he admitted, "but we already know they've got an unbreakable alibi."

"Of course they have," she replied as the penny dropped, "I hadn't put it together before you said that just now, but of course – they were conveniently kidnapped at the time Adam Whitlock was murdered."

CHAPTER FORTY-TWO

McCusker returned to his desk and spread out the scene of crime photographs. He thought he spotted something. He summoned Barr. "Watch this," he said to O'Carroll.

When Barr arrived the agency detective stood up and put his hand on the DS's shoulder. Then, out of the blue, he quickly traced an arc towards Barr's solar plexus with his other hand. Barr instinctively threw his hands up to protect his abdomen.

"Sorry WJ," McCusker announced as he sat down. "I was just trying to demonstrate how one unconsciously reacts when one is about to be stabbed."

"Okay, I get it, both hands were immediately deployed in a self-defence mode," O'Carroll said. "So your point is?"

"Please take a look at these photographs of the victim," McCusker replied.

"Oh, right I've got you now..." O'Carroll said, rising out of her slumped position in her swivel seat. "There are no knife marks around Adam Whitlock's hands, wrists, or even arms."

"Which means?" McCusker asked.

"Whitlock was drugged or unconscious when he was stabbed?" Barr offered, clearly enjoying himself.

"Not according to the autopsy report," McCusker said, nodding at O'Carroll for her suggestion.

"He was stabbed by someone who knew him?" O'Carroll said audibly grabbing at the straws McCusker was clearly hanging on to.

"Possibly, or?" McCusker continued.

"Or he stabbed himself," DI Jarvis Cage offered from the opposite side of the office.

"Not this much," McCusker replied tapping on the photograph. "Or...it could imply that someone held him while someone else stabbed him."

"He was murdered by two people?" O'Carroll said, appearing to repeat the words for her own benefit.

***

They spent the remainder of the morning going through the files they had amassed thus far. DS WJ Barr eventually traced Tim Gilmour and ruled him out because he'd been in the Antrim hospital for a kidney procedure over the weekend in question. Consequently another potential suspect bit the dust.

McCusker started to wade through the piles of files from the house-to-house visits down on Cyprus Avenue. Some of the interviews had produced bizarre replies, which had been duly noted by the coppers on the beat, if only to prove that they had knocked on the doors. The reports ranged from the downright strange:

"Sorry I can't help you with your enquiries just now; I'm watching *Crimewatch*."

"I gave it at the office."

"Have you come about me reporting that Hitler is alive and well and living in the house just across the road, the one with the grey door? Yes, of course, he's shaved off his moustache, but he's not fooling anyone; I'd recognise that haircut anywhere."

"The only thing I remember about that night was a big-headed alien with a red motor bike. I know it was an alien because it was pushing the bike, not riding it."

"No, I don't want to make another donation to the Policeman's Ball, they're already big enough."

"Are youse still searching for Belfast's Manchester City fan?"

"The fancy dress party is three doors up."

To the more traditional:

"We were up in Donegal that weekend."

"It was Saturday night, there are always lots of noises on a Saturday night; the secret is to learn to ignore them."

"I've seen all the cop cars and wondered what was going on; is it true it was a ritual killing?"

"I think he was an American – he was always very polite when I met him on the street."

"My father who works…well, I can't actually tell you where he works…but he said it was all the work of an Iraqi hit squad."

And on and on McCusker ploughed through the 38/36s. When he eventually reached the bottom of the pile, he returned it to the file, slapped the file down on his desk and felt sad that the only statements that stuck in his mind were the alien pushing his motor bike and Hitler taking up residence across the road. The sadder fact was that there hadn't even been a full moon on the Saturday night in question.

About 4 p.m. on the following afternoon O'Carroll took a phone call. After hanging up she said: "Oh jeez."

"What?" McCusker asked.

"I messed up big time."

"What, what did you do?"

"Remember this morning I said I'd made a decision and I would tell you about it later?"

"Yeah, and?"

"Well the decision I made," she said, wheeling herself closer to McCusker's chair and whispering, "was that you and Grace should go on a blind date."

McCusker wasn't as fazed by the prospect as he thought he might have been. "Okay, well yeah, harmless enough," he offered, "but I can't work out how you messed up?"

"Well, the big blind date is for tonight," she admitted, "which was fine when I set it up with Grace yesterday afternoon but I forgot all about it until now."

"Probably best," McCusker said, still feeling nonchalant about it, "that way I didn't have to worry about it for days. So...where am I taking Grace for our big date?"

"You can figure that part out all for yourself, but you're meeting her in the Fitzwilliam Hotel tonight at 7.30 sharp."

McCusker spent the remainder of his day toying with an idea he'd had regarding the Adam Whitlock case. He borrowed O'Carroll and Barr's notebooks for a good chunk of time. There was a germ of a theory floating around in the back of his head, but he had a major problem with a certain aspect of it. A major aspect of it in fact, but he was not allowing himself to completely dismiss this new approach.

Before he knew it, the day had flown by and it was time to go home, and shower and change for his big date.

CHAPTER FORTY-THREE

McCusker checked himself out in the large mirror in the public restrooms of the Fitzwilliam Hotel. As he did so, he realised he'd barely looked in a mirror since his wife had left him. He'd changed his clothes three times – that's one, two, three times – before he'd left his mews accommodation.

He hadn't actually been on a date for going on twenty-five years. Yes, it would be exactly twenty-five years the following January since he'd been on his first date with his then wife-to-be, Anna Stringer. He had been twenty-six years old and she claimed she was twenty-seven. In fact, it turned out that she was actually thirty-one, a point McCusker didn't pick up on until they had to produce their birth certificates for their wedding. McCusker was furious, not at the deception itself but by the fact she was prepared to tell him such a blatant lie. He got over it and the wedding went ahead, although she had confessed to a mutual friend of theirs that she thought she'd blown it. Hard as he tried, he could not invoke a mental picture of her, probably because those particular cogs were busy conjuring up an image of his first date in a quarter of a century. The last time, a dozen or so kisses later, he'd gone on to get married. This time, however, he was even more excited about just meeting his date, a certain Grace O'Carroll.

Detective Inspector Lily O'Carroll had gone, she said, against all her natural instincts in setting her sister up with McCusker. He hadn't even suggested or pushed for it, although he admitted to being more than slightly intrigued about the sassy character who, like her sister, stumbled from one romantic disaster to another. He'd only ever spoken to her once before, and after McCusker had "resolved" that matter with Mr Odd Socks there had been no further contact.

McCusker washed his hands, dried them with the paper towels provided, smelled his breath by putting the palm of his left hand up to his mouth and nose, looked in the mirror one final time and then checked his watch. It was 7.22 – only eight minutes to go. He looked into the mirror again. "Well old son, what do you think of what you see? The auld hair is still a bit of a problem," he replied, "but you know what? From what I've heard, she's been out with a lot worse."

He exited the restroom and made his way to their rendezvous point by the big fire in the lobby. DI O'Carroll had been very particular about this. "She's not going to want to be seen out on a blind date. So no carnations or meeting under the leaning clock or by 'the Black Man' or whatever. No, you have to make it look like you already know her."

McCusker's eyebrows had obviously conveyed the large question mark in his mind because she continued, "I'll make it easier for you, McCusker, I'll have her wear her high-collar electric blue dress. It's absolutely amazing and she has to pour herself into…anyway, that's what she'll be wearing."

As McCusker made a mental note of this fact, O'Carroll mistook the look in his eyes. "Okay McCusker, I would like to remind you that she's my sister, so no ogling, okay?" she paused and waited for his compliance. "I'm serious McCusker. I'll hear absolutely everything, chapter and verse. So if you even think about doing anything naughty, I'll get Larkin to put *you*, not Cage, on duty monitoring the sinkage of the Custom House…but the only difference between you and DI Cage is that you'll be doing it for the rest of your career."

McCusker took the seat nearest to the fire, which gave him a view of the front revolving door. He wondered what DI O'Carroll thought might happen between her sister and her partner. More importantly, he wondered what Grace O'Carroll thought might happen between herself and her sister's partner.

His mind flitted nervously. Dates were hard enough, but blind dates? Would he tick the right boxes? Would she want to see him again? Or maybe kiss him? Or perhaps even go to his house, join him for a late-night coffee...perhaps go all the way? He certainly looked pretty good: his trousers were pressed, his shoes bulled to a grade 'A' shine - thanks to his training days at the Depot in Enniskillen and Kiwi polish and spit. McCusker had recently showered, shaved and was a hundred per cent certain of passing any show parade. He was well mannered, polite and genuinely enthusiastic about meeting Grace. But how far did he really want it to go?

At 7.26 p.m. McCusker experienced a flash that Grace O'Carroll was not going to show up. Then he comforted himself with the thought that, where she might be prepared to let him down, she wouldn't do the same to her sister. However, as she'd been let down herself by so many men in the past, how would she respond to him?

At 7.28 McCusker started to feel hot, so hot in fact he started to regret sitting so close to the faux fire. He could feel his cheeks were flushed and he started to worry about being red-faced. His confidence began to wane as he waited; what would be the acceptable time to make an exit if Grace didn't show?

His nerves started to get the better of him. "I really don't need to do this," he thought. "Look where it got me last time; working all my life for a retirement, the luxury of that only to be stolen by my wife." Well, he would have to admit that she'd really only stolen half of it; the other half you could say was legally and morally hers anyway. But taking only what had rightfully been hers hadn't been enough, had it? McCusker had long ago come to the conclusion that the wronged rarely seek to redress the balance in the name of fairness – no, they crave only vengeance. His wife had been no exception.

As the big 7.30 arrived in town - well at least in the airy lobby of the Fitzwilliam Hotel, minus its star attraction, Grace O'Carroll - McCusker tried to set his mind at rest. She'd probably got stuck in traffic, which was notoriously bad on a Friday night. Then he remembered it wasn't a Friday night but in fact a Monday night, when the roads were usually at their most clear. Perhaps Grace was up to speed on the details of his life and the messy break up with his wife – maybe she'd had second thoughts. Surely he ought to have been on her to-be-avoided list?

As 7.35 came and went he began to get fearful – not that the evening would go badly, but that everything would work out. What if he did tick all of Grace's boxes and coffee back at his place *was* on the agenda? And what then?

It had been a long time, and he wasn't used to the modern woman. Several minutes later he started to wonder, should the situation be reversed, just how much leeway would his date have given him before she upped and left and he'd blown the whole thing? But he'd have called up the hotel reception, asked them to pass a message on, let her know he was running late. After all, it was simple common courtesy. But there was no message forthcoming and Miss Grace O'Carroll was now officially ten minutes late. No wonder she was having trouble finding a man if she treated them all like this. "Come on," he chastised himself under his breath, "things happen, and sometimes we can lose control." Besides, he thought, perhaps she'd give him more of a chance now she'd kept him waiting – well, wouldn't she?

Finally, at 7.42 all of his worries washed away when a woman dressed in blue strode purposely through the revolving door, the click-clacking of her high-heel shoes drawing everyone's attention. The dress wasn't quite how Lily had described it – most noticeably a different collar – but she had a great figure, perhaps not as stunning as her sister had let on but then they were sisters after all. She had a very nice smile though.

McCusker stood up as she slowly, maybe even hesitantly, walked towards him. He noticed that she was checking the rest of the lobby as she made her way across it; perhaps he wasn't quite what she'd expected either and she was lining up a fall-back option? The former Portrush detective scanned the room and saw little better than what he'd seen earlier in the mirror.

Just then, as though reading his mind, the woman in blue broke into a larger smile. She body-swerved McCusker at the last possible moment and he heard her saying "Darling, how wonderful you look." He turned to see her planting a kiss on the cheek of the elderly man sitting to his left.

McCusker felt a wave of embarrassment rush over him. Now he was on his feet, he couldn't just sit back down – he had to move. Should he just give up and go home or maybe even cross the road to the popular Crown Bar and enjoy a solitary Guinness? But then what would happen if Grace O'Carroll showed up five minutes later and he wasn't there? Lily would give him major static. Instead, to save his embarrassment, he dandered over to the bookshelf and helped himself to the late edition of the *Belfast Telegraph*. Luckily for the brothers O'Neill the Larry's List story still had legs. Luckily for McCusker, the majority of the people waiting in the lounge were either completely ignoring him or too busy texting to have clocked his near-major faux pas.

At 7.55 McCusker experienced a vast emptiness in the pit of his stomach. He started to accept that Grace wasn't going to show. He'd wait in the lobby for at least another ten or fifteen minutes, but it was now clear he'd been stood up. Devastated, he struggled to put a positive spin on the situation. He was totally shocked at how worthless life felt, and all because a blind date had failed to appear. There was one positive, though: he resolved to never put himself through another bout of such public humiliation. He could do without ever feeling that bad again.

At 8.05 he walked out of the lobby, feeling extremely sorry for himself, and he slowly set off for home. The usual ten-minute journey took him twenty-five minutes, which he accepted as a side-effect of wallowing in his own self-pity.

At 8. 20 a.m. the following morning his intercom buzzed and his wallowing was finally broken by DI O'Carroll shouting "Where the feck were you last night?"

It turned out that McCusker, or Grace O'Carroll, or maybe even both had misunderstood DI Lily O'Carroll's instructions for the meet, and so while he had waited in torment in the Fitzwilliam lobby, Grace had turned up at the Europa Hotel and spent a similarly tormented time waiting for McCusker by an even warmer fire.

Had Lily sabotaged their relationship on purpose? For her part, she'd take no part in accepting responsibility, claiming that she'd clearly told McCusker that the rendezvous point was the fireplace in the lobby of the *Europa* Hotel.

Either way, McCusker felt his chances of a re-match had been well and truly scuppered.

CHAPTER FORTY-FOUR

McCusker was quietly surprised, not to mention relieved that he had barely thought of Grace's no-show the following morning. Already, his brain was locked into the Whitlock case, which left little room for anything else. He felt as though he had shed the skin of the previous piteous evening. He reckoned that was the advantage of putting on a fresh shirt, snazzy pair of socks, a tie and a new suit from his rotation; today felt as new and invigorating as the new chapter of an exciting book. Not that he had much chance for reading anything other than case-related material these days.

He re-examined the statements from the House to House enquires and read through Barr and O'Carroll's notebooks, while furiously scribbling away into his own. Meanwhile, Barr was beavering away, his head buried in Wesley Whitlock III's finances while O'Carroll made a fuss over making a fuss over her paperwork.

McCusker didn't want to get into a discussion with any of the team about the case. He couldn't allow himself to voice his germinating theory for fear it would all disappear before his thoughts were fully formed. He was worried that Superintendent Larkin would come calling for an update. It would be a request he couldn't refuse and a request that might just end the case, or at least his participation in it.

Just after midday he came up for air. He hadn't quite reached a conclusion yet – he still had two important facts to uncover – but he was much happier than when he'd left the Custom House the previous evening. Well, that wasn't strictly true, but still he managed to veer his thoughts away from the bungled blind date.

As he and O'Carroll left the office she looked at her watch and said, "I knew that your appetite would eventually bring you around."

"Sorry? I see...no, no, I really needed to go through something," he protested as the climbed into her Mégane. "I'd like to make one quick call down on Cyprus Avenue then we can think about lunch if you want."

Fifteen minutes later they pulled up on Cyprus Avenue outside the house just opposite the one in which Adam Whitlock had lost his life ten days earlier.

"Who lives here?" O'Carroll asked, when she realised they weren't in fact visiting Whitlock's former residence.

McCusker checked the name and address at the top of the statement. "A Mr Ivan George," he said, handing it over to O'Carroll.

"McCusker, have you completely lost your marbles?" she said, making to get back in the car. "Look, it's okay – really, it was nothing, a genuine mistake."

"What on earth are you on about," he said to her over the bonnet of her car.

"Grace. This is all about Grace isn't it?"

"It's not," he hissed.

"Yeah, right!" she sneered. "Look, for the tenth time, it was nothing personal, she didn't stand you up, it was a genuine mistake and I admit it was probably mine."

"That's good to know," McCusker replied. "Now, let's go and see what Ivan has to say."

She was still pleading with McCusker through gritted teeth when the door was opened by a rosy-cheeked wee boy of about eight.

"Is your father Ivan in?" McCusker asked.

"Da! It's that girl from *Strictly Come Dancing* with her geezer for you!" he shouted at the top of his voice.

"This is going to be so embarrassing..." O'Carroll whispered. "We've still got time to apologise and leave McCusker."

"Sorry about that," Ivan George said through a large smile. "Our wee Gary is at the age where he is convinced that absolutely everyone he sees is from the television."

McCusker was picking up O'Carroll's "I told you so" loud and clear. The two of them flashed their ID cards. "I wanted to talk to you about a statement you made to one of our officers the morning after..." McCusker struggled to finish his sentence.

"Oh, you mean Sunday week past –the morning after poor Mr Whitlock was found murdered?" Ivan said, pulling the door behind him but not shutting it entirely, clearly to spare wee Gary's ears from what could potentially be a disturbing conversation.

"Yes that's it," McCusker replied. "You told our colleague that you saw something in the early hours of the morning?"

"Yes, actually I did," Ivan George continued, dropping his voice to a much lower volume.

"Do you remember what it was that you saw exactly?" McCusker asked, as O'Carroll took out her notebook. He reckoned that was her way of distracting herself from a fit of the giggles.

"As I told the other copper, I wake up a couple of times a night every night, so I find if I get up, go to the toilet, come back, turn my pillow case over, it's easier to get back to sleep again. I don't wake up to go to the toilet, don't you see...I go to the toilet *because* I wake up."

"Right," O'Carroll smirked, as she scribbled furiously away.

"So," Ivan George continued, "I got up, it was just after the 2 a.m. news – I'm pretty much like clockwork. I look out the window, as you do, and I see this geezer pushing something..."

McCusker checked his statement. "Did you say it was a motorbike?"

"Ah, that would be a no," Ivan claimed. "The conversation actually went along the lines of, I said he was pushing something, the copper said, 'you mean like a bike?' I said, 'no, it looked like it would have had a motor,' so that's obviously where that confusion came from."

"Okay," McCusker said, "and then what?"

"Well, that was it really; I saw a man silhouetted by the street light," he continued, "I remembered it, because the image was very weird. The man obviously had a crash helmet on, so I believe I said to the policeman that in the street light with this big head – an illusion of course – he looked like an alien who'd landed here, stolen a scooter, didn't know how to work it so he was pushing it away."

"Just now you used the word scooter...that word wasn't in your statement...did you think afterwards that's what it was?"

"No, I remember the distinctive circular shape around the back wheel. I would definitely have told him it was a scooter."

"Do you remember what colour the scooter was, sir?" McCusker asked.

"Yes, as I mentioned it was illuminated by the street light, it was red."

"Do you remember anything else about the man pushing the scooter and wearing the crash helmet?" McCusker asked, as O'Carroll's note taking grew a little more serious.

"Sorry, he'd his back to me, he was wearing a crash helmet, darkish clothes...I can't really tell you any more about him to be honest."

"Well look, thank you Mr George, you've been very helpful," McCusker said, as O'Carroll put away her notebook.

Ivan George stood on his doorstep and he was still smiling at them when O'Carroll drove off.

"So," McCusker started up again as they pulled out of Cyprus Avenue and he checked and then read aloud quoting original statement. "The only thing I remember about that night was a big headed alien with a red motor bike. I know it was an alien because it was pushing the bike, not riding it."

"Unbelievable," was all O'Carroll could find to say.

"The 'big headed alien with a red motor bike' was in fact the person who had murdered Adam Whitlock and didn't want to draw attention to himself by causing a racket while starting up the scooter in the early hours of the morning. So, he pushed the scooter, most likely around the corner to Beersbridge Road, before he kick-started it and drove off into the night."

CHAPTER FORTY-FIVE

"You know who it was, don't you?" O'Carroll asked, as they both sat down to a delicious smoked haddock and leek gratin in Deanes on Howard Street.

McCusker continued eating.

"And here I was thinking you were fretting about our poor Grace. Who is it McCusker?"

"If I tell you who our big headed alien is you'd definitely think it was much more bizarre than the alien was in the first place."

"Ah come on McCusker...try me?"

"Nagh, I've a lot more work to do before I get to that stage," he admitted, as much to himself, as he returned to the serious business of eating.

Just after lunchtime, and before McCusker had a chance to fully formulate his thoughts, Superintendent Larkin made a visit for an update on the case.

"Okay," McCusker said, walking over to the board, flipping it 180 degrees and beginning to write on the clean side. "Thanks to some very diligent work from the team and some serious co-operation from Herr Kurt Wolf at Mason, Burr and Co…"

"Stop the flannelling and get on with it McCusker," Larkin ordered, immediately seeing through McCusker's stalling.

"Right," McCusker said, writing "Adam Whitlock" with a blue magic marker in the centre of the board. He circled it and drew a line out to another containing the name Wesley Whitlock III. From there he drew lines to Ray O'Sullivan, Polly O'Neil (née O'Sullivan), and then on to James O'Neill, then to the brothers O'Neill (Ryan and Lawrence). From the Brothers O'Neill circle he drew one single solid line back to Ray O'Sullivan, whereupon he changed his marker to a red one to draw a new and final circle around Ryan O'Neill's name. This he joined to the central circle and Adam Whitlock. He turned around to survey the room: everyone was staring at his handy work and waiting, he presumed, for the inevitable explanation.

"Okay, long story short," McCusker said taking a large breath. "Wesley Whitlock III invests money in Ray O'Sullivan's O'Electronics. Whitlock, while exploiting O'Sullivan's obvious inadequacies as a businessman, piggy-backed one of his other clients, a Mr James O'Neill, into O'Electronics. Eventually Whitlock III and James O'Neill gang up on O'Sullivan and in a boardroom coup they steal the company from under his feet. O'Sullivan, a broken man, commits suicide a few months later. James O'Neill then proceeds to take O'Sullivan's wife, Polly, as well and becomes stepfather to O'Sullivan's two boys, Ryan and Lawrence.

"Ryan discovers this series of betrayals and it festers over the years until ten nights ago he takes his revenge. Ryan holds Whitlock Senior responsible for the loss of his dear father, and so his revenge would have more impact if Whitlock had to live the rest of his life without his son, especially knowing he was in some way responsible for his death."

"Works perfect for me," Larkin announced, as McCusker blew a sigh of relief.

Too soon.

"Except for the fecking great big green elephant in the room," Larkin barked at the top of his voice. "Which is: at the time Adam Whitlock was being murdered, Ryan O'Neill – not to mention his brother, just in case you get any other smart ideas – was being held by kidnappers – a very convenient alibi."

"Fair point," McCusker conceded, "fair point. That's really the point I'd reached when you came in."

"Okay McCusker, keep at it, let me know how you get on," Larkin said and got up from McCusker's desk where he'd been sitting for the duration the presentation.

"I can't believe that," O'Carroll pitched a little too high, the minute McCusker sat down again.

"What can't you believe now?" McCusker asked.

"Well, I'm trying to work out whether I can't believe that you really think Ryan O'Neill murdered Adam Whitlock or that you actually told Superintendent Larkin that Ryan O'Neill murdered Adam Whitlock."

"Yeah, he caught me on the hop a bit..." McCusker admitted, "I still hadn't worked out the finer details of my theory. When was the last time you heard from either of the O'Neill brothers?"

"Funny you should say that," O'Carroll replied, searching through the mess of files and paperwork which was her desk, "yes, here it is. Lawrence rang in last Thursday evening at 8.50. He had just gone into the Duke of York."

"Where's that exactly?"

"It's just around the corner from their offices, and not too far from their apartment. On one of the oldest streets in Belfast – Commercial Court; actually it's more of an entry than a street," she said and then looked spaced. "You made me lose my thread McCusker...where was I?"

"Lawrence had just entered the Duke of York."

"Right, right, yes, and he immediately spotted one of the kidnappers. He said he panicked and ran outside and rang here. We sent a car down, they met Lawrence freezing on the cobbled entry outside the Duke of York and they went into the pub but the kidnapper had clearly done a runner by then."

"Why don't we pop around and have a wee chat with Lawrence and Ryan and see how the auld Larry's List is progressing?" McCusker started. "And you know what? I've also got an interesting wee question for them that will test just how resourceful their list is."

Larry's List had relocated from the boy's apartment in St Anne's Square to just around the corner in an open-plan, warehouse loft unit in Hector Street, under the shadow of St Anne's Cathedral.

The O'Neill's prime-time TV coverage looked like it had paid off: some serious cash had been sprayed over their web enterprise, both in terms of equipment and staff. Ryan and Larry had added four members to their workforce; one male, looking like he could be no more than fifteen years of age, a female, dressed in Gothic black, and two receptionists, both older and both very keen to fuss over "their first visitors," McCusker and O'Carroll.

"Do you need me?" Ryan said, warmly shaking O'Carroll's hand, "I'm just on the way to see the bank manager." Indeed, in his shiny suit, new white shirt and sober tie, he looked like he couldn't be heading anywhere else.

"No," McCusker replied slightly surprised at the lack of a hand-shake. "You're fine, sir, we actually came to see Lawrence on this occasion – we can catch you later." Lawrence barely looked up from his computer in the far corner of the loft.

"Lawrence!" Ryan called out, as he exited the large swinging doors, which bore, on both sides, full-length pop-art style blue and pink Larry's List logos. "Detective Inspector Lilly O'Carroll and her oppo are here to see you."

Lawrence O'Neill was tall where tall was still strange to him. He looked more comfortable arched over his computer, in that the elec-tronic coupling completed him. But when he rose up from his seat and walked over to them, McCusker feared they might witness a Bambi moment. However, rather than topple over he politely air-kissed both of O'Carroll's cheeks and, like his younger brother Ryan, he virtually ignored McCusker altogether.

"We've come to check up with you on your sighting on Thursday night of one of your kidnappers?" McCusker offered as way of expla-nation for their intrusion into the IT sanctuary.

"Oh right," Lawrence said, as though it had all come flooding back to him. He absentmindedly played with the small tuft of white hair, which fell from beneath his hairline and over his forehead.

McCusker wondered if the object of the exercise was in fact to make the white tuft less noticeable by separating it from the upper black mass and curtaining it over his forehead, which itself was snow white from a lifetime of avoiding the sun. "We wondered if perhaps you could give us a fuller description of the kidnapper?" he asked.

"You see," O'Carroll chipped in, "I thought you and Ryan had told me that you never actually got to see your captors with their masks off."

"Yes, that's the weird thing," Larry replied, sitting on the corner of his untidy desk to minimise his height. "The minute I walked into the pub on Thursday night the first thing I saw were these two eyes star-ing at me and it totally freaked me out because I immediately recog-nised them as one of the people who'd held us captive."

"O-kay," McCusker said very slowly, "I see now."

"And you're sure it was the same man?" O'Carroll asked.

"Oh, please believe me – you never forget the eyes of the man who you thought was going to kill you."

"Who were you with when you went into the pub?" McCusker asked.

"I was just by myself. I was meant to be meeting Ryan there."

"It was very cold that night wasn't it?" McCusker continued, shifting to casually conversational tone.

"You better believe it was," Lawrence laughed. "I froze my wotsits off waiting outside in the entry for your squad car to show up."

"And there's no chance you'd been in the pub for awhile, you know, before you spotted this man, the man with the eyes?"

"They'd all eyes," Lawrence wise-cracked, although now warily studying McCusker's face.

McCusker faked a laugh. "Of course, yes good one...but the kidnapper, I meant the kidnapper, with the distinctive eyes..." the Portrush detective explained, knowing that Larry knew full well what he'd meant. "Are you sure you weren't in the pub for awhile before you recognised the eyes of your captor?"

"No, I'm sure about that," Larry confirmed instantly. "The minute I walked into The Duke and the door swung shut behind me, those beady evil eyes locked into mine. It was really freaky, I can tell you. I don't think I'll ever be able to go back into The Duke again."

"Tell me this," McCusker asked, scratching his head, "I keep feeling I'm going to sneeze. Would you have a Kleenex on you?"

"Sorry, no I don't," Larry replied, not even bothering to check his pockets.

One of the receptionists rushed to his rescue, "I'm never without them," she smiled sweetly.

McCusker took the tissue and looked back to Lawrence. "Do you ever go and see the bank manager as well?"

"Nagh, Ryan gets to do that for both of us; he gets to wear the tie," Larry replied.

"Yeah, that's what I thought," McCusker said.

"Is there anything else you can remember about the kidnapper that you can tell us, having now seen him in the pub?" O'Carroll asked, trying to help McCusker through an awkward patch in the interview.

"Well let's see...as I told your uniformed officer on Thursday, he was either totally bald or he'd shaved his head, he was very tall – he stood out from all the people around him, which is probably why I focused on him immediately. He was wearing a rugby shirt."

"Which team?" O'Carroll asked.

"I wouldn't have a clue."

"Tell me this Lawrence," McCusker started slowly, "when you entered the Duke of York was it crowded?"

"Yeah, packed as usual with Belfast's young and hip set," Lawrence replied. "You'll recognise them immediately if they ever bump into you because their shoes are so pointed they could poke your eyes out...and I'm just talking about the boys by the way."

McCusker acknowledged the attempt at humour with a more successful attempt at a laugh. "So it would have been hot then?" he continued.

"You better believe it."

"Have you been wearing glasses for long?" McCusker asked.

"Ah, actually I've been wearing them since I was three," Larry replied, again looking slightly confused by McCusker's shift in the line of questioning. "My mother told me that in the early days I was so annoyed at being forced to wear the hideous things that I used to break my glasses and hide the pieces under the carpet."

"My dad used to wear glasses," McCusker started, while still smiling at Lawrence's recollection. "And you know what bugged him the most about having to wear them?"

"Ah no," Larry replied, openly surprised by the question.

"Yeah, I only remember this because it *really* bugged him," McCusker recalled warmly. "But on a cold night when he would go into his local up in Portrush, no sooner would he have walked through the door of the pub when the hot air of the pub would hit the cold of his glasses and the lenses would instantly steam up on him. He wouldn't be able to see anyone or anything for at least a few minutes until his glasses heated up naturally or he rubbed them with a handkerchief to heat up the lenses."

Larry O'Neill looked at McCusker. The detective could actually see the young man's brain working overtime. He looked like he'd just Googled something on his mental computer, hit the return key and he was waiting to see the search results. "Well lucky enough," Larry replied, just a heartbeat too late, "unlike in the good old days, we now have air conditioning as a standard in all pubs."

McCusker didn't bother to continue to argue the point that this didn't make an ounce of difference. No, for McCusker, the main object of the exercise was to make it known to Larry that he knew he'd been lying. That he'd know that the detective knew he'd never seen his kidnapper in The Duke of York. And, more importantly for Mc-Cusker, Larry would pass this information on to his brother the moment he returned to headquarters. "Look, I know you're busy here, and thanks a million for your time, but would you mind just before I go if I asked one of your team a question for Larry's List?" McCusker asked.

"Sure," Larry said, air-kissing O'Carroll goodbye. "Sean's your man – he'll do you one question for free, then he'll have to charge you."

Larry seemed to be the only person to find his remark funny, and he turned away to resume his work.

"Okay," the teenage Sean said, rubbing his hands at the obvious glee of putting his skills to the test. "How can I help you?"

"Right Sean," McCusker started talking just loud enough to ensure that Larry could still hear him. "What I'm after – what I'd really like to source – is who in the city here deals in vintage Vespa 125 scooters?"

Following a spat of Sean's ultra-fast typing and a few prompts from the cursor and the return key, the slick-looking Larry's List produced a new list: this time of three Vespa dealerships in Belfast.

CHAPTER FORTY-SIX

As they walked back to O'Carroll's canary-coloured Mégane, Mc-Cusker had her ring DI Jarvis Cage and order him to take a constable in a battenburg to Mr and Mrs O'Neill's house. He was to park right outside, where everyone would see them. McCusker hoped that should Ryan or Lawrence O'Neill come calling, they'd spot the police car and drive away immediately. However, should they try to gain access to the house, then DI Cage should detain them and bring them in to the office for questioning.

"So, going back to our wee scene back there in the office; you wanted Larry to know that you knew he was lying about the sightings, right?" O'Carroll said as she started up the car.

"Right."

"But if they were going to go to the trouble of creating such a sham, would it not have made more sense for Ryan to have reported the sighting?" O'Carroll asked.

"No, because by…"

"By having Larry make the call," she interrupted, as she opened the car door, "they made it all the more believable."

"Exactly!" McCusker replied, fastening his seatbelt.

"And you dropped the Vespa dealership in there because you also wanted Larry to tell Ryan that you're onto the fact they used the scooter to pick up the ransom money and that they also used it as the getaway vehicle after the Adam Whitlock murder…so…do you think they were both involved in the murder?"

"No, just Ryan," McCusker replied. "Ivan George reported only one big headed alien leaving the scene of the crime.

"And you think it was Ryan because…"

"Because he is definitely the leader, he's closest to his mum and he was the one who was battered and bruised after the fake kidnapping."

"The allegedly fake kidnapping?" O'Carroll said, correcting him.

"Agreed."

"And Ryan was also the one who couldn't get out of the office quick enough when we arrived."

"Yes," McCusker agreed. "You're right; but we still have a lot to work out."

"And because of your play-acting in there, the clock has started running."

"I find that if I have something in my life that annoys me," McCusker said, changing subjects and staring out of the window. "Something like...oh, you know, replacing a fuse in a plug, or a bulb in an awkward location, or fixing a wobbly leg on a coffee table, or sorting your CDs into their proper sleeves – I'm talking about things that just need to be done...some time...but mostly in the future. But don't you see these chores are never a major concern, I can get through life without them and *choose* when to sort them out. I find that those little problems, niggling away at the back of my mind, actually help to distract me from the big problems."

"And Ryan O'Neill is one of your current problems?"

"Yes. It's just that I'm still not 100 per cent sure which of the two categories he fits into."

***

It was a rainy day in Belfast and as they walked up the front steps, originally the rear entrance to the Custom House, McCusker pondered whether Ryan had genuinely had a meeting with his bank manager or it had been an elaborate avoidance tactic.

McCusker decided to give Larry's List HQ a cold-call; he was "Doing a credit rating on the company and needed their bank details to complete it." The girl receptionist happily obliged, reading the details from the chequebook she claimed she had right beside her.

McCusker then put a call through to the bank in question and asked to speak to the manager's secretary. Once through to her, he read out the account details and asked his questions. "What's your number? I'll call you once I've checked these out," she said, helpfully. A minute later, she was back on the line, confirming that the details were indeed those registered to Larry's List, but that no one from that company was scheduled meet with the manager today, or even that week for that matter.

McCusker spent a long hour going through the various potential scenarios that might emerge after that morning's developments. Surely Ryan and his brother wouldn't do a runner: no, that would be a direct admission of their guilt. Whatever the eventual outcome, just as he was sitting in his office plotting how best to trap the brothers, he was certain that they in turn would be frantically calculating their next step.

The detectives entered Superintendent Larkin's office to fill him in on recent developments. They requested permission to seek three search warrants, the first for the O'Neill brother's apartment, the second for the Larry's List offices and the third for the parents' house in Malone Park.

"I'm sure we will get them," Larkin offered, "but I'm not so sure that, with what you've got so far, you should."

O'Carroll and Barr were left to fill in the necessary paperwork and, forty minutes later, departed together to seek a friendly Justice of the Peace whose signature they'd depend on.

Upon their return, warrants duly signed, McCusker felt that he'd delayed picking the brothers up for as long as possible. He had Barr take a search team to the O'Neill's apartment on St Anne's Square. Top of the search list was a bloody knife, blood-stained clothes, the remainder of the ransom, a false black beard, the holdall and any signs of a ransom note having been created.

DI O'Carroll was ordered to search Larry's List HQ, where she would invite Ryan O'Neill and Lawrence O'Neill to return with her to the Custom House to help the PSNI with their investigations into their reported kidnapping and the death of Adam Whitlock. O'Carroll would leave the remainder of her team behind at the office to conduct a similar search to that being undertaken at Saint Anne's Square.

McCusker took the remaining warrant – the one reserved for Polly and James O'Neill's residence – and placed it into his inside jacket pocket.

Now all McCusker could do was wait – wait, and decide whether to interview the brothers together or separately.

CHAPTER FORTY-SEVEN

"Right lads," McCusker started, "thanks a million for volunteering to come in…"

"We didn't know we'd a choice," Ryan O'Neill grumbled.

"I never like to arrest someone unless I really have to," McCusker offered, trying to keep some degree of civility in the proceedings. "But I just wanted to have a wee chat with you both about this auld kidnapping lark."

"It wasn't the most pleasant weekend we've ever had," Ryan admitted, as Lawrence stared at the interview room table as though it were a computer screen.

McCusker has once heard that great musicians can hear notes and melodies without needing to play their instruments. He wondered if the same thing was happening here, and Lawrence was imagining himself back at his computer screen. Whatever he was thinking, he clearly was not mentally with the other people in the room: McCusker, O'Carroll, Ryan, and their mild-mannered solicitor Pat Tepper, whom Superintendent Larkin insisted be present.

"Now before we start lads I have to say I think that as a scam it was just brilliant, pure genius…which one of you dreamed it up?" McCusker said, staring at Lawrence.

"Dreamed what up?" Ryan said, twitching a bit on his seat. "What are you on about?"

"Very good Ryan," McCusker said, taking a large breath before he jumped off the edge, and even as he was, he couldn't be sure from what exactly he was jumping. "Of course, I'm referring to your kidnapping scam."

"Look Inspector…" Ryan started.

"McCusker will do."

"Oh yes, I forgot, of course you're not a proper detective," Ryan continued, trying to gather up a head of steam. "What I was about to say is this: the reason we're here is because Detective Inspector Lily O'Carroll was the one responsible for rescuing us and so I felt we owed it to her to accompany her here – unless you've something better to talk to us about, we're outta here," Ryan looked at Pat Tepper, McCusker imagined, for support.

"We might as well hear what he's got to say, Ryan," Tepper offered. "Otherwise next time they want to bring you in they'll arrest you and even though it might all be a wild goose chase, it'll still hurt your mother."

Lawrence's eyes flickered in awareness for the first time during the proceedings. "And Larry's List," he muttered.

"And Larry's List," Tepper confirmed.

Ryan made a big fuss about slumping back into his black plastic bucket chair.

"Can you make your point, please?" Tepper said, directing his plea to O'Carroll.

"Well, look lads...I just wanted to say that your kidnapping is perhaps one of the best scams that I've ever seen," McCusker continued, in his friendly quiet voice. "Right from the beginning you didn't put a foot wrong; it was truly a master plan. You sent two untraceable notes; that was your only communication. You used letters cut out from newspapers and magazines and you were careful to wear gloves as you prepared them. We didn't find any trace of you on or about the notes. There was no way you could be linked to them. More importantly, most kidnappers are caught out through their dealings with the person paying the ransom, the one part they have no control over – the weakest link, as it were. How will that person react? Perhaps they'd be drawn into a deal with the police, with the promise of a pay-off, to entrap the kidnappers themselves. Whatever the outcome, you cleverly avoided this pitfall by avoiding direct contact with the paymaster by leaving your ransom notes on your mother's doorstep. And this is where your plan was extremely well thought out because you picked an amount that you knew your target, your stepfather, could comfortably pay off. You knew he wouldn't have to make a fuss about raising the money.

"Then the scene of your incarceration; you'd no food or purchases lying about that could be later traced to yourselves."

"But if we were so clever," Ryan impatiently interrupted, "in this make-believe scenario of yours, how come you figured it all out?"

"Good question Ryan, very good question," McCusker replied, happy for this turn in events. "The first thing that caught my attention when DI O'Carroll here rescued you out at Ballycultra in the Folk Park was the fact that, although Lawrence was tied up and lying on a bed, his glasses were neatly folded and carefully placed on the little table beside that bed. If he'd truly been bound by kidnappers, he wouldn't have had a chance to remove his own glasses. If, and this is most unlikely, a kidnapper was kind and considerate enough to remove the glasses for him, he would have yanked them off and thrown them on the table. I personally thought the sight of those neatly folded glasses was strange, in that it didn't appear natural to that situation. But in the euphoria of finding you both safe and sound, I put the thought to one side…at first."

"And that's it?" Ryan pushed.

"No," McCusker eagerly admitted. "Later, due to another investigation myself and O'Carroll were working on, I had reason to re-examine your kidnapping and I discovered quite a few other things that pointed in your direction. But let's leave the other investigation to one side for now and just deal with the kidnapping, shall we?

"When you, Lawrence, were untied and released, not once did you ask about the well-being of your brother, despite you being separately detained and your 'captors' having threatened certain death if your stepfather didn't pay up. While, you Lawrence, you only asked about your mother. Of course, the explanation is that you already knew that Ryan was okay, but you wouldn't have known how your mother was coping.

"When you, Ryan, were untied in the room you said you were amused that you'd been detained in the Folk Park – but how would you have known that Ryan? You previously said you'd been shoved in a van, a bag placed over your head, and you were taken straight to the house. My point being that you wouldn't have realised you were in the Folk Park.

"On the camera you and Lawrence sent to your parents – you know the disposable one you pretended was from your 'kidnappers?'

There was not a single photo with you both in the same shot, which leads me to believe one of you was behind the camera in each photo.

"The other thing that gave you away was the fact that only you two would have known about your mother's early morning routine, the fact that she took the dog out for a walk early every morning. You knew if you left your ransom notes and camera with the milk bottles, your mother, and not your father, would find the notes. You also knew that your mother would be the one to 'persuade' your father to pay the ransom, but more about that later.

"Finally, Lawrence, it was you who ultimately confirmed that I was on the right track when you rang in and made that ludicrous claim that you'd recognised one of your kidnappers in the Duke of York. With your eyesight and steamed-up glasses, we both know that would have been totally impossible. But you were so keen to continue the kidnap sham, maybe even get a bit more press for Larry's List, that you…"

"I told you that was a stupid idea," Ryan spat across the table at his brother, silencing McCusker.

"Shut up you idiot!" Lawrence barked. "The only thing we're guilty of is playing a trick on our stepfather to get some of *our* money out of him."

McCusker was confident about his conclusion, 100 per cent confident, but he was still shocked by Ryan's remark in particular – he obviously believed the flaw in the scam to be Lawrence's fault. For his part, Lawrence had already come up with a new spin: they'd simply played a trick on their stepfather; clearly he felt they hadn't broken any law.

"Okay," McCusker announced for the benefit of the recorder, "I'd like to leave it there for now. We'll charge you both with wasting police time and blackmail. We'll process you both and I imagine, with Mr Tepper making the right noises, we'll be releasing Lawrence under his own recognisance. However, Ryan, I should advise you and your solicitor that I will want to question you shortly with regards to your involvement in the murder of Adam Whitlock."

This time it was Lawrence's turn to explode; he shot out of his chair and, effing and blinding, his lawyer had to hold him back as he flailed towards the detective.

It was Ryan who immediately took charge. He calmly told his brother to shut up and leave immediately with their solicitor. Reluctantly, Lawrence did as he was bid. The most telling part of the exchange was to confirm McCusker's suspicions: that Ryan, and not the older brother, was the boss in this relationship.

CHAPTER FORTY-EIGHT

McCusker took a break to check in with his team of Crime Scene Investigators. He wanted to know if they'd found anything incriminating at either the Saint Anne's Square apartment or Larry's List HQ. Both locations reported there'd been nothing so far.

The detective watched as Lawrence said goodbye to his solicitor on the steps of the Custom House and walked across the square as a free man. He tipped DI Jarvis Cage, who was still in position outside Polly and James O'Neill's residence in Malone Park, that there was a chance Larry might come calling. McCusker ordered him, under no circumstances, to allow Lawrence onto any part of his parents' property.

Twenty minutes later, McCusker, O'Carroll, Ryan O'Neill, and Pat Tepper returned to the interview room.

Ryan, no doubt encouraged along by the sheer weight of McCusker's evidence – albeit mostly circumstantial – had fairly readily admitted responsibility for the ransom subterfuge. McCusker thought a similar approach with the murder case might bring about the same result.

"So Ryan...part of the thing DI O'Carroll and myself have to do when we're working on a murder investigation is to discover three things: who committed the crime, why they committed the crime and how they committed the crime. Admittedly we don't always discover the answers in that particular order. In fact, if anything it usually works out in reverse.

"So...*how* the crime was committed..." McCusker said, pausing for a brief swig of tea. "That's usually relatively easy. Someone discovers the body, they report it to us, we visit the scene of crime with our team of experts and begin trying to figure out what happened.

"Once we've identified the deceased and how they were murdered, we're off to investigate their lives. Who were they? What did they do for a living? Who were their friends and family? Who were their loved ones? Did they have any enemies? And so on and so forth. And eventually somewhere in the heap of information we amass we discover a motive and the motive hopefully leads us directly to the murderer.

"Two Saturday evenings ago an American gentleman by the name of Adam Whitlock lost his life and DI O'Carroll, myself, and the team here at the Custom House went off to find out everything we could possibly find out about the deceased. Now, the problem is that everyone, all of us, have some things we like or need to hide, something we would never own up to or want anyone to know about. Usually these things are not even illegal, but by virtue of the fact that we want them to remain hidden, these things do tend to confuse and prolong any investigation.

"Take this particular investigation into Adam Whitlock's life. As is usual, we had lots of leads, which lead us to lots of theories, which lead us to lots of suspects. Eventually, one by one, these suspects all fell by the wayside...until, that is, we started to focus in on Adam Whitlock's father, Wesley Whitlock III," and here McCusker paused again and stared deep into Ryan O'Neill's eyes, but the youngest brother was giving nothing away. If anything, he seemed somewhat intrigued by McCusker's narrative.

"Initially we treated Whitlock III as the grieving father, but as we lost our suspects one by one, we started to look a bit deeper. Perhaps Wesley Whitlock III was guilty of having done something to someone that could have resulted in them seeking revenge in the most painful way.

"Turns out that Wesley Whitlock knew your real father, Ray O'Sullivan, and he was also very familiar with your stepfather, James O'Neill. Then we discovered that Wesley Whitlock and your stepfather were guilty of defrauding your father out of his business and his revolutionary invention, some kind of a sound filter if I'm not mistaken. If one wanted to, one could also argue that perhaps your stepfather was indirectly responsible for your father committing suicide. In any case, he certainly had an affair with your mother while your father was still alive and eventually, as we know, after your father died, your mother married James O'Neill."

The previous indifference in Ryan's eyes had been replaced by pain. McCusker wondered if perhaps he might have been guilty of being a bit too direct, but he was dealing with a murderer here, and if he was to have the success of gaining a full confession, he needed to reopen all the old wounds, no matter how painful.

"The first problem, well actually I'm being a little flippant – the major and only problem – I had with you as a suspect was the obvious one. At the time Adam Whitlock was losing his life you were incarcerated by your kidnappers. So my theory was quickly flushed down the toilet. That is to say that you clearly couldn't have been murdering someone when you yourself were being detained against your wishes.

"Then, as I mentioned earlier, I suddenly remembered the scene of Lawrence's glasses neatly folded by the side of his bed in the Ballycultra village in the Folk Park and, inspired by that one minuscule nugget of doubt, I was able to prove the entire kidnap was a sham.

"Of course, I neglected to mention in our earlier interview with your brother a second connection – the one that led me straight to you, Ryan. That day at the station, up in the King's Hall area, the day your mother brought the ransom money to that platform: you were the man who picked up the rucksack and scarpered off down the road. That was very clever. We were convinced you were going to hop on the train to make your escape and had prepared for such an event. But your obvious knowledge of the area – your parent's house being close to the station – stood you in good stead. We chased you down the Lisburn Road and lost you at the gate to Malone Lane. You'd conveniently parked your trusted red Vespa 125 scooter on the other side of the bollards, where you hopped on it and scootered off into the distance.

"We have a witness who has testified that he saw that exact same scooter being wheeled away from Adam Whitlock's home and down Cyprus Avenue on the night of the murder. You clearly didn't want to draw attention to yourself by starting the scooter up outside Adam's house."

Ryan O'Neill looked like this last point had made some connection with him. But he made no such acknowledgement of his responsibility, as he had during the earlier interview regarding the kidnapping cover-up. In fact, he refused to say anything.

When McCusker felt he'd gone as far as he could go he announced the end of the session and switched off the tape recorder. He'd obviously taken the wrong approach. He was still convinced he'd got his man, but maybe he'd made a tactical error. He would now need more hard evidence to take the case further. Larkin could authorise for Ryan O'Neill to be detained for another 48 hours. He had only two days to prove his theory correct.

Just as he was getting up to leave Ryan O'Neill, as if reading McCusker's thoughts, muttered "It wasn't me."

Chapter Forty-Nine

O'Carroll and McCusker immediately sped around to the O'Neill residence at Malone Park. Jarvis Cage reported no sighting of either of the brothers.

Polly O'Neill was surprised to see them back again so soon. Nonetheless, she was very hospitable and they small chatted for a while, McCusker retaining the search warrant in his pocket. "Tell me this," he said, "I suppose since the boys got their swish apartment in Saint Anne's Square they've had to park up the scooter around here...?"

"Yes, of course," she replied, "they have one of the garages out the back where they left a pile of their stuff – computers and what have you – and the scooter is also parked up in there."

"I suppose Ryan would also keep his crash helmet out there as well?" McCusker asked, crossing his fingers deep in the trousers pockets of his pinstripe suit.

She glared at him with a look of confusion. McCusker thought she was annoyed at him because she'd twigged what he'd been up to. He waited for her to explode.

But she didn't, instead she said, very matter of a fact, "You're obviously confused Mr McCusker – Ryan can't ride the scooter, never could. He even tried to take the test and failed, twice, and then he gave up. Lawrence is the one who's the Vespa fanatic."

CHAPTER FIFTY

An all-ports warning was put out on Lawrence O'Neill immediately.

McCusker appreciated the fact his partner had said nothing about him happily releasing the murderer less than an hour before.

The CSI team took over the Polly O'Neill premises, but only after McCusker had presented her with the search warrant.

In the garage, and not even hidden, was the infamous vintage red Vespa 125 scooter with its iconic pregnant back wheel guards. Suspended from the handlebars was the crash helmet, which – with the wide red flash from front to back over the crown – had given Lawrence his alien-like appearance as he had departed Adam's house down on Cyprus Avenue on that fateful Saturday night. The chin-strap looked like it had been chewed continuously over the years and McCusker was sure they would find Lawrence's DNA on it.

McCusker asked that the helmet first be taken to the pathologist, Anthony Robertson; he wanted the canny Scot to check out whether the crown of the helmet could have been responsible for the bruising on Adam Whitlock's chest. Perhaps this could account for the lack of self-defence marks on the victim's hands, wrists and arms. If Lawrence had rammed his helmet-adorned head straight into Adam's chest as he opened the door, then Whitlock would have, at the very least, been severely winded and unable to defend himself as he was repeatedly and savagely stabbed to death. (McCusker felt it was vitally important to keep reminding himself that a young man had lost his life as a result of Lawrence's actions.)

McCusker joined the search in the garage; there was something else he was keen to find, which would enable him to wrap up the first part of the case. He searched high and low, emptying box after box in growing frustration. He had never in his life seen such a collection of telephone directories – Lawrence's obsession with them had obviously started way back in his youth. He flipped through the ancient directories in the hope of discovering a scooped-out hiding place within their pages.

The Grafton Recruitment's agency detective even went as far as having one of the CSI team fetch him a ladder so that he could inspect the eaves of the garage. Once again, he enjoyed no success.

McCusker had more than enough evidence to prove the brothers were responsible for the fraudulent kidnapping. But even with Ryan's vague admission, it was based on circumstantial evidence at best, and once it was turned over to lawyers, they'd be all over it, just like the cheap suits they wore. No, he always wanted to put his cases beyond the arguments of clever lawyers.

In fact, uncovering the remainder of the ransom was pivotal to proving both his cases. If it was found on one of the properties associated with Lawrence, they could conclusively prove that there was no kidnapping, thereby immediately throwing Lawrence's alibi for the night of the murder out of the window. But the balance of £999,950 had not been found at the Saint Anne's Square apartment or at their offices, and so far not a note had been discovered in their parents' home.

McCusker wondered how much of the original amount remained. Just how much of it could they have pumped into the hungry-for-cash Larry's List operation in one week? Had they paid the deposit and advance rent for their new HQ in cash, filling it with new office furniture and equipment by the same method? It wouldn't be too difficult to find out. Yes, just as when McCusker was growing up, some people still preferred good old cash to a plastic transaction. But just as much as they loved their cash in hand, they reviled a knock on the door from the Inland Revenue, the PSNI's neighbours back at the Custom House. He made a mental note to set the diligent DS Barr onto it when his workload permitted.

An hour and twenty minutes passed. There was still no sign of the dosh and no sign of Lawrence. His solicitor claimed he'd neither seen nor heard from him since he'd bid him goodbye on the steps of the Custom House upon his release on bail. McCusker believed Pat Tepper.

Ryan O'Neill claimed he hadn't a clue where his brother would have gone. McCusker wasn't so sure but Ryan, now back in his mother's house, looked extremely relieved to be no longer detained on a murder charge.

Each time McCusker had an inspired idea as to where the cash might be hidden and it turned out to be fruitless, he'd return to the Vespa 125 and dander around it, hoping for new inspiration. McCusker had seen Lawrence, although he didn't know that it was him at the time, running down Lisburn Road, carrying the holdall, nearly getting knocked over by "undercover" DI Jarvis Cage, hopping on to his Vespa and driving away. He was sure the holdall was a black canvas one and that's what he'd been looking for, as well as the cash. What if Lawrence was clever enough to get rid of the incriminating holdall...then where would he have transferred the funds to?

He walked around the Vespa, examining it in a desperate attempt to eke out further inspiration. The famous 125 CC engine was housed on the left-hand side of the rear wheel guard, but on the right he suddenly spotted an area where the paintwork had been scratched. The damage was around a small panel which had a wee latch protruding. McCusker, still legit in his blue disposable gloves, pushed the latch down. The panel flicked open and McCusker stood in sheer disbelief as he faced several wads of £50 notes, which had been carelessly stuffed inside the hollow wheel guard. Once all the money had been removed they discovered a fake black beard on the floor of the compartment.

He found it incredulous that Lawrence was so cavalier is his approach to hiding the evidence of his crime right under his father's nose. He was happy for what he and his team had just been gifted; disbelieving but happy.

But before he allowed himself to get excited about his discovery, he once reminded himself that young Mr Adam Whitlock had lost his life.

CHAPTER FIFTY-ONE

McCusker and O'Carroll headed back down the Lisburn Road to the Custom House. As they entered the building – knowing it had descended at least a gnat-hair's depth deeper into the Lagan-side earth than it had been when they left – they were greeted by an effervescent Station Duty Sergeant Matt Devine, who advised McCusker that someone, possibly Lawrence O'Neill, had just been spotted behaving suspiciously by the owner of one of the boats at the back of the Odyssey entertainment complex.

The Grafton Recruitment Agency detective, McCusker, and an officer of the Police Service of Northern Ireland, DI Lily O'Carroll, pulled up just outside the Premier Inn five minutes later. As they ran past the cheap and cheerful hotel on their right, and the rear of the Odyssey on their left towards the Lagan-side, McCusker worried that if the mystery person, assuming it was indeed Larry O'Neill, had paid a visit to another of Wesley Whitlock's children; this time his daughter Miss Julia Whitlock? Did the computer whiz kid think that murdering one of Wesley Whitlock III's children just wasn't enough? Maybe revenge had not proved sweet enough and, now that McCusker was onto him, he'd decided to go for broke and target Julia as well. But had he been spotted on his way to her apartment, or running away from it?

When they arrived at the scene they were greeted by DS WJ Barr, who had contained a growing number of gawkers in the far right of The Arc, coincidentally just below the balcony of Julia Whitlock's apartment in block twelve. McCusker had one of the uniformed officers present run up to Julia's apartment to determine whether or not she was safe.

Barr took McCusker across the forecourt of The Arc. He pointed out the character of interest who was sitting on a small boat at the far end of the floating jetty, which ran alongside the rear of the Odyssey. McCusker wondered if perhaps the big stars who came to perform at the venue preferred this solitary route in order to avoid the screaming fans. He did not need Barr's offer of binoculars to positively identify Larry O'Neill – his flyaway white tuft of hair betrayed him.

McCusker and O'Carroll decided to keep their distance for the time being. Barr ran back to the crowd and spoke to a man who followed him back towards McCusker and O'Carroll's vantage point. "This is Gary Mills," Barr said, by way of introducing the well-dressed gentleman with the smiling eyes, "Mr Mills made the call to us about…"

"What raised your suspicions?" McCusker asked.

"Well, when I arrived down here to do some maintenance work on my boat he was sitting on the back of it as cheekily as Louis Walsh sits on *The X Factor* panel."

"Is that your boat he's on now?" McCusker asked.

"No, no, that's my one there, the *Cry For Home*," he said, pointing to the boat at the closer end of the jetty. "To tell you the truth, it shouldn't really be there, but I know the production manager in the venue and he lets me leave my boat there sometimes during the week. At the weekends I usually take it up to Newry."

"Did you speak to the lad when you arrived?"

"Aye, I asked him what he was doing on my boat! He said to leave him in peace and if I didn't scoot off he'd pour petrol over himself and the boat and torch both. I said 'to hell you will,' and I hopped on the boat immediately, caught him by the scruff of the neck and tossed him off my boat, but not before I'd given the wee bollix a good clip on the ear."

"Then what did he do?" O'Carroll asked.

"He ran on down to the end of the jetty and hopped on that boat and took out three large bottles and doused himself with something – I couldn't tell you if it was petrol or not," Gary Mills volunteered and concluded with, "but I thought I better ring it in just in case.

"Lucky you did, sir, thank you very much," McCusker said to the have-a-go hero.

In part inspired by Gary Mills' actions, but also because he could-
n't think of any other way of ending this without another person getting hurt, McCusker took off his jacket and handed it to O'Carroll
before setting off down the jetty.

He was surprised by just how unstable it felt beneath his feet. He
was also a little shocked at how cold he was without his jacket, but
he'd had to remove it to show Lawrence O'Neill that he wasn't armed.

The closer he got to O'Neill the more he realised just how
drenched the murderer was. He wasn't completely sure, but he didn't
think he could detect the smell of petroleum.

Again, following Mills' lead, he didn't pussy-foot around when he
reached the boat. He hopped on board and sat down on the deck opposite Lawrence O'Neill, who was shivering fiercely.

"What are you doing?" O'Neill barked.

"I've just come for a little chat with you," McCusker said, in a very
quiet and friendly tone, as his nostrils started to pick up the distinctive
scent of petrol for the first time.

"You should get off," O'Neill warned, "I'm going to torch myself
and the boat."

"Look Lawrence; it's not your fault," McCusker continued.

"Don't patronise me for fuck's sake."

"I wasn't going to," McCusker said, rubbing his hands to try and
get a bit of heat into them. "All I was going to say was that there are
some things that happen to us which we think we have no control over.
Your father Ray…"

"How do you know about my dad?" Larry asked, appearing very
shocked.

"Part of my job is to try and work out why things happen and we
discovered how your father was treated by your stepfather and Wesley Whitlock."

"He took everything; *every fucking thing* away from my dad,"
Lawrence said, his chin starting to wobble involuntarily, betraying the
fact that tears were on the way. "He took his company, his invention
and then as if that wasn't enough he took my dad's wife, my mother,
then he took Ryan and me and then eventually he even took my father's life."

"I know he did," McCusker admitted, as honestly as he knew how.

"But you know I never really blamed my stepdad – I always felt he was just another pawn in Whitlock's game."

McCusker felt sure the smell of petrol was growing stronger, particularly when he looked away from Lawrence.

"You know, I lived with it through all my youth and then it all kicked off again a few years ago when I saw how my stepfather treated my mum. He didn't love her. My mum had become a ghost in her own house, and that just wasn't fair...my mum deserved more. She began to think fondly of my real dad again and she would reminisce to Ryan and me for hours about him. After one of these sessions Ryan said 'You know, killing would be too good for Whitlock.' That's really what set me off. I thought he was right and I started to figure out what could I do that would hurt Whitlock as much as he had hurt my mum and Ryan and me and then...well, you know the rest."

"Most of it," McCusker offered, trying to encourage Lawrence to continue.

"Well, Ryan and I had two main problems: one, we needed money to get Larry's List off the ground. My stepfather wouldn't give us a penny. That really drove me mad because I knew that everything he had, he had stolen, with Whitlock's help, from my real dad. The second problem I had was that I'd become obsessed about getting my revenge on Whitlock.

"Then I came up with the idea of faking our kidnapping so that we could get some of my dad's money back from our stepfather. And then I thought while we were being detained by our kidnappers I would have the perfect alibi, which would allow me to creep out while I was supposedly kidnapped and take my revenge."

McCusker noted that O'Neill avoided using the word "murder" and also mentioning Adam Whitlock by name.

"Did Ryan even know what you were doing?"

"He knew about the kidnapping, but not about the rest. He hadn't a clue. I tell you, he hadn't a clue. I slipped out of my cottage in Ballycultra at the Folk Park and went around to Cyprus Avenue. I'd hidden my scooter in the bushes down by the old mill in the Folk Park. Whitlock's son opened the door. I'd kept my helmet on. Maybe he thought I was the pizza man come back again. I rammed my head straight into his chest, knocked him over, maybe even unconscious and..."

"Why was it that Ryan was a bit battered and bruised when you and he were discovered at the Folk Park?"

"We drew cards for that one," Larry started back up again, clearly happier with this line of conversation. "We had decided in order to make the kidnapping realistic it would have to look like one of us had been beaten up. Ryan won the draw and he decided he'd be the one to take the beating. I would have done the same thing, had I won the draw. Anyway, we kept delaying it and eventually we had to do it and it grew into a farce because I didn't really want to hurt him and I obviously didn't want to bruise my own hands when I was doing so. In the end I tried to surprise him by shoving him against the wall a few times. But we were in stitches of laugher at the time."

Larry's mood had seemed to lighten up a bit over the last part of his story.

"Don't you think we should maybe go in and get you out of those soaking clothes?" McCusker suggested. "I don't know about you but I'm bleeding freezing out here."

"Weren't you scared that I was going to set myself and the boat alight?" Larry asked, as he stood up and shook himself furiously to try and get his circulation going again.

"Not really," McCusker admitted.

"Not really?"

"Well, I figured that, what with all the water you poured over yourself, you would have ruined your matches or lighter."

Lawrence sniggered.

"Although I was worried as I walked up to the boat, because there was quite a small strong smell of petrol, but, as I sat closer to you I realised it was the smell of the boat and not the liquid you'd thrown over yourself."

"Well, it's lucky you came to rescue me," the murderer said, "because as I was sitting out here I'd worked out that I'll probably be out of prison in about eight to ten years, by which point Larry's List, captained by reliable Ryan, will be mega, and that's before we even think of the book and movie deals. Also, with me out of the way for awhile, Ryan should finally get it together with Susanne."

"I wouldn't count on the eight to ten if I were you," McCusker cautioned. "I'm sure with all the fugitive stuff and what with you endangering people and property we'll easily get you up to the late teens."

***

McCusker handed Lawrence O'Neill over to the safe custody of DS Barr. After he watched them drive off he and O'Carroll nipped up to Julia Whitlock's apartment in the left-hand tower of the triad of towers that was The Arc. En route, McCusker popped into the bakery and bought four Paris buns, which he dangled in front of him as she opened the door.

"Goodness is that fuss all over?" she asked, stepping aside to allow them in.

"Yes Julia," O'Carroll replied. "We've apprehended the person responsible for your brother's death."

Julia didn't know whether to laugh or cry and in fact made a good attempt at both before O'Carroll, rescuing the bag of buns from McCusker, continued, "I'll tell you what, I'll start the brew up, get our buns ready, and McCusker here can tell you all about it."

Once inside, McCusker started to recount the developments. Julia insisted he tell her the truth in full, and she refused to settle for McCusker's attempts at softening the blow of her father's morally deficient past. She wanted to know exactly what her father had done all those years ago that could cause her brother to lose his life in such a terrible way.

As their conversation came to an end, she went over to the window and stared out at the spectacular backdrop of the edge of the city framed in her large window and slowly shook her head from side to side. O'Carroll arrived with the tea and buns. "Those poor boys," Julia Whitlock eventually said as she turned back into her living room and dried her eyes.

Of all the things McCusker had been expecting her to say this most definitely would have been the last.

"At the appropriate time I'd like to go to Polly and Ryan O'Neill and apologise on behalf of my family," she continued. "I can't help Adam anymore and I certainly can't bring him back, but I do know it's what he would have wanted me to do."

She sat down beside McCusker and O'Carroll and played mother, by pouring out the tea and smiling as she offered out the sliced buns.

They chatted for a few minutes and then, quite close to tears, she said, "I won't allow the actions of my father to hurt this family any more.

Our Adam would have been very disappointed in me if I let this ruin my life as well. I remember being very upset at his decision to come over here to study and I asked him why he wanted to do that and he went very quiet and just said 'I need to get as far away from him,' meaning our father, 'as possible.' He must have known a lot more than he admitted." She stopped talking again; her pride not allowing her to falter like she had on previous occasions in the company of the detectives, and instead hid her real feelings behind expressing enjoyment at the baked goods. "These wee buns really are a marvellous invention. It really was so kind of you to bring them for me McCusker. But look, there's one thing I'm having trouble working out. I would have thought you would be happy now you'd solved this case, but if anything you seem very down?"

McCusker thought long and hard about how to answer her question. He too used a mouthful of Paris bun to buy himself some time.

Eventually O'Carroll filled in the gap for him. "In the short time I've known him," she started, avoiding all eye contact with McCusker, "I've come to realise he's more preoccupied in protecting the innocent than he is in punishing the guilty."

CHAPTER FIFTY-TWO

The detectives left Julia, who invited McCusker, and then, clearly as an afterthought, O'Carroll, to come back and pay her a visit any time they were in the area.

About ten minutes later, as the fuss down below at The Arc subsided, O'Carroll took a call on her mobile. She bent her head and started speaking in quieter tones, the way McCusker felt one only did with a lover. Perhaps at long last she was enjoying some success in the romantic part of her life. But, unusually for O'Carroll, she hadn't mentioned anything about her recent nocturnal activities for a few days now. Perhaps the blind date had something to do with it, and that now she was fixed up with someone, she was keen for her sister to make a connection as well. He quickly chastised himself for returning the blind date to his consciousness.

He walked across to the water's edge and sat down to think – about Adam Whitlock and how his father, motivated by greed, made a silly error of judgement that would later cause Adam to lose his life. The fact that he'd been living in a strange land and the incident in question had happened thirty odd years ago hadn't altered the eventual outcome.

Lily walked across to him, head still firmly down and talking quietly and smiling a lot. She sat down beside him and said into her mobile, "Okay, okay, I'll put him on."

She passed to phone to McCusker.

"Is she still there beside you?"

It was O'Carroll's sister, Grace, and McCusker recognised her sensual voice immediately from their one previous conversation.

"Aye."

"The wee skitter..." Grace said. "Tell her toodableedin'loo from me and tell her to scoot off and give us a bit of privacy."

"Tell her I heard that," Lily said, laughing and starting to walk away. "The wee skitter herself – tell her some of us still have work to do anyways."

"I feel like a referee at a John McEnroe tennis match," McCusker said, addressing both of them.

"I've told you before, McCusker, don't show your age!" Lily said, wagging her finger back at him.

"So," Grace began, as McCusker stared out over the lazy Lagan in the direction of the Black Mountains, "I believe congratulations are in order. I hear from our Lily you've turned out to be a bit of a Sherlock Holmes?"

"Oh, I was just lucky enough to have been assigned to run the case on behalf of the Super – really, the whole team worked hard on solving it."

"Modest as well," Grace continued on the other end of her sister's mobile. "Listen, I never got a chance to thank you for helping Lily out with Terry – the man with the odd socks. You know, I should have thanked you at the time but I just didn't want our Lily to find out I was involved."

"It's totally fine Grace," McCusker said, feeling there was something intimate in addressing her by her first name for the first time, especially after having been involved with Lily in so many conversations about her. "I was real happy you did tell me because your sister certainly wouldn't have."

"The thing I remember most from that telephone conversation was talking to you for the first time, of course I was very nervous, I'd heard so much about you from our Lily, and you asked if everything was okay, and I said 'Not really.' And you immediately, without even a moment's hesitation, said 'What can I do to help?' There was no pussyfooting around to see if it was something you'd be bothered to get involved in. No, you just said it, straight out, and I was so moved that our Lily would have such a great friend that I very nearly had to set the phone down."

"Listen, your sister has been very good to me, at a time when I..." McCusker started confidently, but Grace had to come to his rescue.

"So what's all this about standing me up on our big date then?"

McCusker laughed, but didn't say anything.

"Do you think our Lily sabotaged it?"

"I think she was so concerned about the outcome she made a genuine mistake over the locations."

"It wasn't a nice feeling, I can tell you," Grace admitted. "The last time I was stood up was by a wee boy...oh, best forgotten...So?"

McCusker filled in the silence. "Look, would you like to try again – perhaps go out to dinner one night?"

"Phew, that was close – I was starting to think you'd never ask and I was going to have to ask *you* out," she laughed. McCusker just loved her sensual laugh. "Yes, Brendy, that would be very nice – I'd like that."

"How about the weekend?" McCusker asked.

"A whole weekend?" she chuckled. "Goodness, that's very adventurous, not to mention forward for a first date!"

"No sorry, I just meant..." McCusker gushed.

"It's okay Brendy, I know exactly what you meant," she replied in a more sympathetic tone. "Look, what about tonight?"

McCusker was relieved – as he'd offered to take her out on the weekend, he suddenly worried she'd meet someone else before then. "That's perfect," he said, "I'll see you tonight."

"Right. Look, you're not very good at this are you," she said and then quickly added, "and that's a quality by the way. But, ahm...we're meant to pick somewhere to meet?"

"Oh yes...of course."

"Look, shall we just keep this simple and meet in the usual place and go somewhere from there?"

"Yes, right," McCusker replied, now very confused and hoping he wasn't sounding too flummoxed. "Er, the usual place?"

"Right...okay, sorry," she said, "our Lily obviously hasn't told you then?"

"Told me what?"

"Well, we haven't exactly met before," Grace started hesitantly, "but we've both seen each other, you know, a few times in fact, always in McHugh's. Yes, I believe you refer to me as 'French Bob'."

And with that, McCusker realised that the girl of his dreams was also the girl on the other end of the phone and he started to babble ever so slightly.

"Stop drooling McCusker," she said, "I mean, it's extremely flattering and all, but it could be considered unhealthy when you're by yourself. I look forward to seeing you tonight in McHugh's at 7.30 sharp; you can book somewhere else for dinner for 8 p.m. Toodaloo!"

***

McCusker sat looking at O'Carroll's phone for a few seconds trying to figure out how to turn it off. But he was still lost in his thoughts: French Bob was Lily's sister? And not only that, but he was also going out on a date with her that very night.

"Don't!" O'Carroll said, walking over to McCusker and retrieving her mobile.

"Don't what?"

"Don't look like the cat that's just got the milk."

"Sorry?"

"It's not becoming of a man your age," she continued, "and besides – you know what they say..."

"Pride comes before a fall?" he offered.

"No," she said thoughtfully, "I was thinking more that unless you're very careful there is a good chance that in all the excitement, the milk might get spilt."

McCusker noted her caution but still couldn't resist doing a wee jump and attempting a heel click as he set off after her.

The End